A Good Clean Fight
HARVILL PRESS
TARGET FOR TONIGHT

D0897718

DAMNED
GOOD SHOW

To Flight Lieutenant Frank Lowe, DFM,
and to his comrades of RAF Bomber Command
in the Second World War.

Derek Robinson

DAMNED GOOD SHOW

CASSELL

Cassell & Co
Wellington House
125 Strand
London WC2R 0BB

British Library Cataloguing-in-Publication Data
A catalogue record for this book is available from the
British Library

ISBN 0-304-36310-3

Designed by Goldust Design

Printed and bound in Great Britain

PART ONE
High Alert

FINE FETTLE

1

The group captain aimed his pipe at the wireless set. A Mess waiter hurried to switch it off.

'Never trust a man who carries an umbrella wherever he goes,' Rafferty said. 'He thinks it will protect him. He deludes himself.'

'I know it's a big job, being Prime Minister,' Hunt said. 'I just wish he wouldn't sound like an undertaker who's lost the body.'

They were in the Mess ante-room of RAF Kindrick, a bomber base in Lincolnshire. From here, 409 Squadron flew twin-engined Hampdens.

Only a handful of officers had joined them to hear the Prime Minister's broadcast. 409 Squadron had been on alert for a week, and all flying personnel were in their crew rooms, listening to their own wireless sets. Rafferty was station commander: a big, broad, hook-nosed group captain with medal ribbons and faded wings from the First World War. Wing Commander Hunt led the squadron. He was thirty and looked younger, except for his eyes. Peacetime flying in the RAF had always been a risky business. Before they got Hampdens, 409 had flown canvas-skinned, fixed-wheel, open-cockpit biplanes that were not far removed from the machines of the Royal Flying Corps. Hunt liked a degree of danger; he believed the RAF thrived on it, and ultra-cautious pilots annoyed him. But he also resented pointless waste, including time wasted writing letters to next of kin. His feelings showed in his eyes. He had angry eyes.

'Chamberlain backed the wrong nag,' the Intelligence Officer said. 'He's lost his shirt.'

'Got rotten odds, anyway,' the adjutant remarked. 'I said so at the time.'

'We can't put all the blame on Chamberlain,' the Medical Officer said. 'Let's face it: everyone cheered when he flew back from Munich. 'Peace in our time,' he told them, and that's exactly what they wanted to hear. Even the *Daily Express* –'

'Gibberish!' Rafferty said. 'Pure gibberish. He waved that bloody silly piece of paper as if Hitler had very kindly given him the last bit of bog-roll in Europe.'

'In a sense, he had,' the Intelligence Officer said.

'That speech ...' The adjutant pointed at the wireless. 'I wonder if he wrote it. 'Consequently this country is at war with Germany' ... Not the most thrilling call to arms I've heard.'

'And all in aid of Poland,' the Intelligence Officer said. 'That's a clever trick, considering Poland's beyond the range of any of our bombers.'

'Cheer up!' Rafferty heaved himself out of his armchair, and everyone stood. 'The good news is we're in business! The balloon's gone up. The gloves are off, the fat's in the fire. Cry havoc and something something something.'

'Let slip the dogs of war, sir,' the MO said.

'Too damn true,' Hunt said. He looked at his watch. 'Briefing in twenty minutes.'

2

It was the wrong kind of day to go to war: mild, sunny, not much breeze. That sort of weather, in early September, was meant for watching a decisive match in the county cricket championship, with a pint of beer and a popsy who couldn't tell a square cut from a ham sandwich, and didn't care either. Rafferty was forty-three, a bit old for popsies. As he strolled with Hunt to the briefing room, he was thinking about that line, *Let slip the dogs of war*. Did it do justice to the boys of 409 Squadron? Dogs of war? Decent, cheery, honourable chaps? Then he remembered some of the pilots he'd known in the RFC. Not what you'd call nice men. Ruthless killers, more like. Fellows who didn't enjoy their breakfast unless they'd crept up behind some foolish Hun, put twenty rounds in his petrol tank and made a flamer of him. Dogs of war, all right. About as chivalrous as jackals. Still, this war would be different. The bomber boys weren't looking for blood, their job was to knock out precise military targets, every bomb a coconut, until one day *Der Fuehrer* would discover that he had no more toys to play with. With pluck and skill, 409 could become the crack squadron of Bomber Command. With a bit of luck, Rafferty could become an air vice-marshal. Press forward hard enough, and you find yourself leading. Quite right, too.

Hunt wasn't thinking about promotion. He was wondering what it would be like to lead a squadron in action. He had a small face and a slim build. His nickname was Pixie, not very flattering but he didn't mind because it meant that careless pilots who were called to his office got a shock from the blast he delivered. Some came out looking whipped. In the Mess, Pixie Hunt was relaxed, sometimes funny, and he enjoyed argument. In the air, he demanded high standards of flying and a fiercely competitive spirit. When one of his pilots began running around the airfield every day, in training for the marathon in the next Olympic Games, Hunt got rid of him. He had nothing against the Olympics, but there was room for only one obsession in this squadron.

That was in peacetime. Hunt wasn't so blinkered as to think that 409 was trained to the peak of perfection. For a start, fuel and ammunition had been rationed – the Air Ministry was always on a tight budget – so there was very little night-flying, and usually none at weekends. For the same reason, his crews had no permanent air gunners or wireless operators. Those jobs were done by volunteers from the groundcrew, fitters or electricians or armament mechanics, as and when they could be spared from their duties. An AC2 – the lowest rank in the RAF – got paid an extra sixpence a day for manning a gun in a Hampden. An AC1 or LAC got a shilling for manning a gun *and* a radio. Brave men and keen, and Hunt knew they'd do their best against the enemy, but he'd seen their scores at the annual gunnery exercises: dismal.

At least the gun positions were enclosed, so gunners weren't exposed to the freezing, battering gale as they had been in the bombers that the Hampden replaced. Too bad it didn't have powered turrets. Swinging a machine gun was hard on the arms. It took a lot of practice for a gunner to track his target, especially when it was a fighter that was diving and skidding and rolling at two or three hundred miles an hour and looking thinner than a pencil when it was only two hundred yards away. Hunt knew that his part-time gunners never got enough practice.

Too late to worry about that now.

He followed Rafferty into the briefing room. All the aircrew officers were there. They stood. *One direct hit from a Hun bomb and 409 would be finished*, Hunt thought; and was immediately ashamed of such alarm and despondency.

Rafferty told everyone to sit.

'They've started it,' he said. 'Again. Some people never learn. Now it's up to us to finish it. Well, I know the Hun, and I'll tell you this: when you kill him he's dead. We killed great quantities of Huns in the last show. We duffed up the Hun then, and we'll duff up the Hun again now. Wing commander?'

Hunt stepped forward.

'War is full of surprises,' he announced. That got their full attention. 'Here's the first. The United States of America is involved. President Roosevelt has asked all the nations at war not to bomb civilians.' He let the words sink in. 'Mr Roosevelt doesn't want us to bomb undefended towns. That's not a problem, we weren't intending to bomb them anyway. He also doesn't want us to attack any target if there's any risk of hitting civilians living nearby. Britain has agreed. So has France. It comes to this, gentlemen: we must not bomb the German mainland.'

A rumble of disbelief turned into loud laughter. This was anticlimax in spades. 'Bags me two weeks' leave!' someone called.

'That's not all,' Hunt said, and they were silent again. 'Poland's out of range, of course, but the enemy has a coastline. He has warships which threaten our shipping. They might even bombard our towns.'

'Tried it last time,' Rafferty said. 'Shelled Scarborough, Bridlington, Whitby Abbey. Sorry, wing commander.'

'We can bomb German warships at sea or at anchor without upsetting Mr Roosevelt,' Hunt said, 'because a ship at anchor is not part of the mainland.'

'Bloody clever,' someone muttered.

'The Intelligence Officer will give you the details.'

This was a heavy-set flight lieutenant, very bald, with a moustache thick enough to hide his expression. Above the medal ribbons, his half-wing of an observer had weathered to pearl grey. He was the only man in the squadron to wear spectacles. Everyone called him Bins, short for binoculars.

He unrolled a map of northern Europe. 'To refresh your memory: Germany has two stretches of coastline,' he said. 'One on each side of Denmark. Obviously, the more important, for us, is the North Sea coastline. It's nearer, and it has important naval bases at Wilhelmshaven and Emden, plus the inland ports of Bremen and Hamburg. Beyond Denmark, on the Baltic, the German navy also uses Brunsbüttel, here at the mouth of the Kiel Canal. All those warships are available for attack under the Roosevelt Rules. Provided ...'

He hooked another roll of paper over the map and let it fall open.

'This is Wilhelmshaven. You see the town *here*, and the docks *here*. The area in blue is the bay. Now, if a German cruiser, for instance, is tied up to the dockside, you must not bomb it.' He surveyed them over his horn rims. They looked unhappy. Good. That meant they were listening. 'Civilians live nearby. Some may be dockers. Your bombs might harm them.'

'Hard cheese,' someone growled.

'Any German vessel, warship or otherwise, attached to the dockside is part of the mainland and therefore immune. But ...' Bins indulged himself in a short pause, '... if the ship is out *here*, offshore, maybe anchored, maybe not, it's considered to be at sea. You can sink it with a clear conscience.'

'Are the Huns playing by the same rules?' a pilot asked.

'The German government has not yet responded.'

'Too busy bombing Poland.'

'Possibly. A few words about Denmark, Holland and Belgium. They are neutral and anxious to remain so. Fly over them and you may get shot at by their anti-aircraft guns, perhaps even attacked by their fighters ...'

Bins answered a few questions and removed his maps. Rafferty stepped forward. The briefing had disappointed him: too flat, not enough gusto. 'One last thing,' he said briskly. 'Don't believe anything an air marshal tells you.' That made them stare. 'When he's called Hermann Goering.' They laughed, which was what he wanted. 'Half of it's lies and the other half's tosh. That's not our style. The Royal Air Force might not get everything absolutely right but at least we don't appoint an air marshal who's too fat to get in a cockpit.' They laughed more freely. 'And remember this. You're lucky, damned lucky. This war isn't going to be all mud and blood, like last time. This will be the war of the knockout blow, and you're the boys with the big punch. Good luck!'

Walking back to the Mess for lunch, Rafferty said: 'The chaps are in fine fettle, aren't they? Itching for a scrap.'

'It's quite crazy, sir,' Hunt said.

'Of course it is, old boy. Totally lunatic.'

'We're not trained to bomb ships. Nobody in the Command is.'

'Of course not. You counted on mainland targets. We all did. You're damn good at hitting them, given a spot of decent weather.'

'Warships dodge about so much.'

'Yes. They carry a lot of guns, too.'

'That's another thing, sir. What's the best way to hit a ship? Should we go in low?'

'If it was me, I'd be up at eight or ten thousand feet, where the guns can't reach. Not the light guns, anyway.'

'From ten thousand, the target's as thin as a pin and the bombs drift with the wind.'

'Well, in that case the whole thing's absurd.'

'Crazy.' Hunt kicked the head off a dandelion. 'But I suppose we'll go ahead and do it anyway.'

'Certainly. Lunatic orders are in the finest tradition of the Service. Don't think too much. Just do it.'

3

At about that time, an RAF Blenheim took off and headed across the North Sea. The weather was calm. A couple of hours later, the pilot was pleased to discover that he was bang on course, high above the approaches to Wilhelmshaven. That was good flying, plus a slice of luck.

Soon the crew looked down on a perfect view of fourteen German warships in formation: three battleships, four cruisers and seven destroyers. That was a really thick slice of luck. Immediately the Blenheim's wireless operator reported the sighting. His radio wasn't powerful enough to send a signal nearly four hundred miles. Bomber

Command HQ received tattered fragments of the message and made no sense of them. Nobody's luck lasts for ever.

The Blenheim turned for home and flew into a storm. For the rest of the afternoon the pilot struggled against a thumping headwind. He landed shortly before five p.m. and made his report.

When the order to attack reached 409 Squadron, every crew wanted to go. All week they had been at various stages of alert; all day they had been on standby, sitting in their crew rooms, playing cards, reading stale news in newspapers, dozing, waiting, thinking. The sudden promise of action blew away boredom, but not for everyone. 'Five aircraft,' Hunt announced. 'That's all they want. Five. I'm leading.' He quickly picked four experienced crews. They took off at six-fifteen.

Already the light was poor. To the east it was worse: black with thunderstorms. They crossed the coast at Lowestoft. It was their last sight of land for almost six hours. Before long the wind was gusting so badly that Hunt opened out the formation, to avoid collision. They flew with their navigation lights on. Hunt knew that his five were only part of a large force of bombers – eighteen Hampdens and nine Wellingtons – all aiming for the same spot on the map. The longer they flew, the greater the risk that two machines might try to occupy exactly the same spot at the same time. Each with a full load of bombs. He put it out of his mind.

Once, in the fading light, he thought he saw aircraft far to the north. Then cloud blotted out the dots.

The rest of the trip was a matter of increasing misery and fatigue. The Hampdens bucketed through a succession of storms. The rain made a racing skin on the windscreens and the pilots flew by instrument. Always the wind was violent, and without doubt it was changing direction. The observers were navigating by dead reckoning: we are flying on *this* compass bearing at *that* speed so, allowing for such and such a wind, we must be *here*. The storms made fools of the compass and blew the predicted winds to buggery. The Hampdens slogged on. With luck they ought to strike Germany somewhere in the hundred-mile gap between Denmark and Holland.

Perhaps they did. The light was so poor and the weather was so thick that none of the bombers made a landfall. Nobody found Germany, let alone Wilhelmshaven, let alone a pin-thin, blacked-out warship.

Hunt gave up the search after three hours. His arms and legs ached from the endless struggle to keep the Hampden on track. He had long since lost contact with the others. He got a course for home from his observer and steeled himself for another three hours of this wretched, bruising flight.

The last of his Hampdens touched down at ten minutes to midnight. Some of the gunners were so stiff with cold that they had to be lifted out of the aircraft.

The crews went to interrogation, then to supper, then to bed. Rafferty and Bins strolled to the Mess for a nightcap.

'At least we didn't lose anyone,' Rafferty said.

'Hell of a long way to go for nothing, sir. Suppose that German fleet was making twenty knots when it was spotted. Could be two hundred miles from Wilhelmshaven by now.'

'You won't mention that to the chaps.'

'Of course not. The brighter ones know it anyway. They had plenty of time to work it out for themselves, didn't they?'

4

After a late breakfast, Hunt called a meeting of the crews who had taken part in the operation. He wanted to pool their information. It made a small pool.

Nobody had seen anything. Even if they'd seen a ship, in that lousy weather nobody could have told the difference between a German cruiser and a Swedish freighter. The Bristol Pegasus engines had performed well, thank God. But on such a long flight, navigation had been a mix of faith, hope and guesswork. And the Hampden was an icebox, especially for the gunners. Two hours made them stiff as wood, three hours turned them numb, after four they were in pain, after five … They couldn't remember how they felt after five frozen hours. They couldn't remember much of anything.

'None of the other squadrons made contact,' Hunt said. 'Not a wasted evening, however. Valuable training, jolly valuable.' He saw that they were not convinced of this. 'We got thrown in at the deep end. A night op in stinking weather with orders to hammer the Hun in his backyard, and the war not a day old! You chaps came through with flying colours. All right, that's all. Carry on, except Pilot Officers Silk and Langham.'

The others left. Hunt picked up two buff files and flicked through their contents. 'Luck,' he said. 'Do you have any views on luck? You should. It's lucky for you two this war came along when it did, isn't it?'

'Sir?' Langham said.

'You're what, twenty-two? Not many jobs out there for a pair of sacked bomber pilots with no ability except farting about.'

Silk blinked, twice. Otherwise he showed no emotion. He was taller than average and strong in the shoulders, as a good bomber pilot should be. He had dark hair and a clean-cut, open face, the kind that old ladies looked for when they wanted to be helped across a road. Hunt had seen many fools or liars or both with clean-cut, open faces; he disliked Silk and distrusted him. Silk was too well-tailored, his collars were a little too crisp, the thrust of his tie a fraction too dashing. His hair was wavy, which was no crime, but it had a rich, burnished glow that made Hunt suspect excessive brushing. Long ago he had written in Silk's file: *Is this man a bloody fop? Where's his handbag?*

'If you get kicked out, you'll vanish,' Hunt said. 'Into the army, probably. Lose your commissions, of course. Infantrymen. Brown jobs, that's what you'll be. Because why? Because we don't need clowns in the Royal Air Force.'

'Certainly not, sir.'

'Shut up, Silk. Last June, on a navigation exercise, you flew a Hampden under the Tamar railway bridge in Plymouth.'

'Chaps in Fighter Command do it all the time, sir.'

'Don't bring my squadron down to the level of those playboys, Silk.'

'No, sir.'

'In May, a Hampden beat up a point-to-point in Northamptonshire. Some clown flew around the course and jumped half the jumps. That was you, Langham.'

'Sir, I explained –'

'You invented a bunch of lies. One reason the RAF has always been short of funds for fuel and armaments is clowns like you make idiots of themselves in front of MPs at point-to-points.'

'Yes, sir.'

'And there's more. Look here: tedious complaints of aircraft playing silly buggers. No proof, but I know it's you two. And horse-play on the ground, too. God knows that Guest Nights can get a bit wild, but you, Silk, had to pick a fight *with an air commodore.*'

'He challenged me, sir.'

'He was *drunk*, Silk. Pie-eyed. Why didn't you run away?'

'Matter of honour, sir.'

'Matter of a broken arm.' Hunt's left foot kept kicking his desk. 'That man couldn't play bridge for six weeks. *Six weeks.* Didn't stop him signing snotty reports on this squadron. And as for your record of alcoholic excess, Langham ...' Hunt glanced at him. Peculiar pair. Silk looked too young, Langham too old. He reminded Hunt of the jack of spades. Black hair, dark eyes, an obvious shadow where he'd shaved. Pity he didn't act his age. 'I haven't forgotten your obscene behaviour with the barmaid and the snake.'

'Allegedly obscene, sir. Case never came to court.'

'Only because Group Captain Rafferty plays golf with the Chief Constable.'

'She was an exotic dancer with a python, sir. They got into diffi-culties and I tried ...'

'Bunkum. Now listen. If this squadron hadn't had such bad luck with accidents, I'd have kicked you out months ago. And I'd dump you now if it wasn't for Adolf bloody Hitler. What gripes me is you've both got ability. Silk, you should have made flying officer long ago.'

'I'm satisfied with my rank, sir.'

'I'm not. War is good for promotion. Pull your fingers out. You could be flight lieutenants in a year. But for Christ's sake keep your snotty little noses clean. Now buzz off.'

Another pilot who had taken part in the operation, Tubby Heckter, was hanging about outside the building, playing with the adjutant's dog. 'Cosy chat?' he said.

'Pixie offered me fifty quid to marry his ugly sister,' Langham said.

'He tore you both off a strip. Thought so.' They headed for the Mess, booting an old tennis ball for the dog to chase.

'The Wingco's trouble is he doesn't understand us,' Langham said.

'What a shame,' Heckter said. 'What doesn't he understand?'

'Oh, our modesty. Our humility.'

'Not his fault,' Silk said. 'He's thicker than us, that's all.'

'He can't be,' Heckter said 'You're one of the thickest blokes on the squadron.'

'I'm not thick. I may be dense, but I'm not thick.'

'Yes, you are, Silko. You're as thick as fog. Pug Duff said so.'

'Pug Duff? Dear little Pug, who trained with us? If I hadn't let him sit on my lap he'd never have got his wings. Pug is my biggest fan.'

'You pinched his girl,' Langham said. 'He tried to kill you with a hockey stick.'

'Well, my smallest fan, then.'

'You can tell him how much he loves you,' Heckter said. 'He's been posted here. He's in the Mess now.'

Pug was a nickname. He got it when he was five, on his first day at school, in the playground. He started a fight with a larger boy. Briefly he had the better of it, using fists, knees and feet with a rare ferocity, but he soon exhausted himself. His lip was split and his nose was streaming when a master arrived, grabbed each boy by the ear and dragged them apart. 'Enough!' he roared. Duff kicked him on the shins. The master released the bigger boy, who was in tears, and cuffed Duff so hard that his nose sent a splatter of red across the asphalt. Duff tried to punch him in the stomach but his reach was a good twelve inches short. 'What a pugnacious child,' the master said. After that, Duff was called Pug.

He was always short for his age, and always getting into fights; perhaps he tried to compensate for size by anger. Usually this kind of behaviour gets worn smooth by the friction of the family. Pug Duff had no immediate family. His father had died ingloriously one night in 1917, sitting in a cinema in Amiens when it got hit by a bomb from a German aeroplane whose pilot was lost, and tired, and decided to jettison his bomb and go home. Captain Duff was in the cavalry, so his death made no difference to the war. It made a huge difference to his widow. She lost her will to live, and the influenza epidemic did the rest. By 1919, young Duff was an orphan at the age of five.

Aunts, older cousins, grandparents all took their turns at raising him, shunting him around England like a small, scruffy, wrongly addressed parcel with too much unpaid postage. He was a foul-tempered little brat. Why not? Wherever he went, nobody wanted him and nobody loved him.

But there was enough money in his mother's will to send him to boarding school, and that was a great relief to everyone.

He went to Wellington. It was a muscular school where they prepared boys for the Army, and Pug found plenty of fights without looking for them. Being small, he usually lost. After a year or so he calmed down. Sheer physical strength, he realised, proved nothing. The way to dominate was through success. He worked hard and put his rivals in their stupid place. He didn't have a great brain but he got the most out of it. His short body expanded through ruthless exercise; when he was fifteen his chest was so wide that his shirt-sleeves reached his knuckles. Then, abruptly, the money came to an end and with it, school.

He was standing on a railway platform, waiting for a slow train to a dull job with a reluctant uncle, when he saw a poster advertising the RAF School of Apprentices at Halton.

Duff found a home in the Royal Air Force. For the first time he knew the solid reassurance of total security. He stopped worrying about his career, clothes, food, health, pay, religion, sport. Halton organized all that. In return it demanded that Duff learn what made aeroplanes fly.

'Forget your air commodores,' a sergeant instructor said to Duff's class of apprentices. 'Forget your group captains, your wing commanders, your squadron leaders.' No light shone in their eyes. They had been in uniform only a few weeks, and anyone with rings around his sleeves was god. 'Forget your drill corporals,' he said. That was different. Drill bloody corporals had been marching them up and down and across and around the parade bloody ground, cursing them, hating them, drilling all the individuality out of them. Forget drill corporals? The apprentices cheered up. 'And for why?' the instructor said. 'Because none of them can do what this little beauty can do.' He was standing beside an aero engine, a Rolls-Royce Kestrel, cut away to expose its workings. 'Nobody, from drill corporal to air marshal, can get an aeroplane off the ground. Only an engine can make it fly.' He turned the propeller and they watched the slow march of the pistons. 'Suck-squash-bang-shove. Make that happen a thousand times a minute, and your aeroplane will climb to ten thousand feet while the drill corporal's still polishing his buttons.

What is the purpose of the Royal Air Force?' he shouted. '*Why does it exist?*'

'To fly aeroplanes,' they chanted.

'Never forget it! If you're not helping get an aeroplane off the ground, you're not earning your pay. The Royal Air Force exists to fly. No other reason.'

Pug Duff did well at Halton. Later, he applied for pilot training and did well at that, too. Eventually he got his commission. The public-school background helped: the RAF liked a chap who knew how to speak and which knife and fork to use. He had strong arms and legs. The RAF made him a bomber pilot. By the time he reached 409 at RAF Kindrick he was already a flying officer: one rank ahead of Silk and Langham.

They found Pug Duff eating peanuts in the Mess ante-room.

'There must be some mistake. You can't have been posted here, Pug,' Silk said. '409 is a top squadron.'

'Clerical error, I expect,' Langham said.

'Silko owes me ten bob from two years ago,' Duff said, 'and I got tired of waiting. Also, Air Ministry wants to improve the standard of flying on this squadron.'

'Oh dear.' Langham signalled for drinks. 'Poor Pug has lost his mind. How sad.'

'Look under the bed,' Silk suggested. 'Offer a reward.'

'Talking of losing things,' Duff said. 'I hear you two were out for hours and hours last night but you still couldn't find Germany. Or was it Europe?'

'No, it was Germany we couldn't find,' Langham said. 'We probably shan't find Norway tonight, and tomorrow night we're not going to find Luxembourg. Or is it Spain?'

'I think it's Ireland,' Silk said. 'But it doesn't matter.'

'Good God,' Duff said. 'You're a pretty useless lot, aren't you?'

'We share the work. I'm pretty, and Tony's useless.'

That ended the usual courtesies. They moved on to the eternal topics of pilots: the peculiarities of aircraft and aerodromes, the styles of leadership of COs and station commanders, the ups and downs of men they had trained with. Eventually Duff went away to freshen up before lunch.

'Pug looks awfully keen, doesn't he?' Langham said.

'To tell the truth, I could scarcely see him,' Silk said. 'I think he must have shrunk in the wash.'

5

This was the second day of the war. The storms had cleared the North Sea and moved on to soak Scandinavia. The same Blenheim crew that had spotted a battlefleet near Wilhelmshaven was sent on another reconnaissance and, amazingly, found yet more German warships, this time at anchor in Wilhelmshaven harbour. Once again, Bomber Command went into action. 409 Squadron was not required to take part.

The attack was made in daylight. It was briefly reported by the BBC.

A couple of days later, Pixie Hunt heard all about it from a visiting wing commander called Faraday, an old pal, now on the staff at Group HQ.

'Command sent fourteen Wellingtons and fifteen Blenheims,' Faraday said. 'Quite a strong force.'

'Twenty-nine bombers should make a mess of something,' Hunt said.

'The Wellington packs a punch. The Blenheim's too lightweight for this sort of job. Anyway, five Blenheims cocked up their navigation and never found the target. Low cloud.'

'Still leaves ten Blenheims.'

'True. Those ten actually found a couple of battleships and a cruiser. Cloud was so low they had to attack from five hundred feet. No good. Bombs bounced off the decks like ping-pong balls. Meanwhile, heavy flak. *Very* heavy flak. Flak knocked down five Blenheims.'

'Five out of ten,' Hunt said. 'I see. And the Wellingtons?'

'Most never saw a damn thing and came home. But six Wimpys ploughed on, found a battleship at Brunsbüttel, bombed it, missed it. Two kites didn't return.'

'So we sent twenty-nine and lost ... seven?'

'That's one way of looking at it. Another way is to calculate our losses as a proportion of aircraft that actually attacked.' Faraday got a pencil and did the arithmetic. 'Seven out of sixteen is 43.7 per cent.'

Hunt could only stare.

'Don't expect to read about it in the papers,' Faraday said. 'And don't be surprised if operations are a bit quiet for a while. If my guess is right, Command is having a good think.'

'Yes. Very likely.'

Faraday got up to leave. 'Oh! I nearly forgot,' he said. 'The Danish government has complained that a Wellington bombed the town of Esbjerg. Killed two civilians. Esbjerg is one hundred and ten miles north of Brunsbüttel.'

'Poor show.'

'Quite. And the next bomber to stray over Denmark can expect several large Danish shells up its arse.'

THE FIRST WHIFF
OF GUNSHOT

1

Faraday was right: Bomber Command had a good think about North Sea operations and losses, and whether one was worth the other.

Meanwhile 409 Squadron did nothing but train, and fly the occasional shipping-search patrol. The only ships they met were British destroyers, which fired at them. Apart from that, the crews saw no action. They soon grew bored. When war was declared everyone had been tense, eager, nervous, expecting massive air attacks and quick retaliation. All this hanging around made a mockery of courage, skill, the aggressive spirit. In mid-September, when Poland was obviously finished, Hitler agreed to the Roosevelt Rules. So now nobody was going to bomb anybody's mainland. The war was a flop.

Yet 409 was kept on stand-by. Nobody was fighting, everybody was getting cheesed off. Something had to be done. The Wingco made Pilot Officer Silk the squadron entertainments officer.

'I don't care what you do as long as you brighten them up,' Hunt said. 'Give 'em something to look forward to, something to talk about except bloody Poland.'

'Yes, sir. Is money available?'

'Within reason.' The Wingco hunched his shoulders. 'What's that stuffed up your left sleeve?'

'My handkerchief, sir.'

'Silk, isn't it? Some sort of clever-clever trademark, I suppose. I don't like it. Makes you look like a ponce. I don't suppose I can stop you poncing around the station, but at least you'll do it properly dressed, without bits of haberdashery hanging off you. And listen, Silk.'

'Sir?'

'Entertainment does not include pornographic cabaret acts with naked dancers and reptiles. Understand?'

'That was Langham, sir, not me.'

'Don't argue. Get cracking. If I see you standing still I'll know you haven't got enough to do.'

Silk went in search of Tony Langham and found him soaking in a bath so hot the steam rushed out of the door. Langham had just landed after a four-hour patrol over the North Sea. 'Fucking ice all over the kite,' he said. 'Fucking squall line. Bounced about like a rubber fucking ball. Took her up to fifteen thousand. Fucking heating system failed. Instrument panel froze fucking solid. Icicles in the fucking oxygen tubes. Turned for home, got shot at by the Royal fucking Navy, so naturally my observer gave me the wrong fucking course, we made landfall at Berwick-upon-fucking-Tweed, and now I think I've got frostbite in the goolies.'

'Just another day in the office, then.' Silk sat on the bath stool. 'What colour are they?'

Langham submerged his head and blew bubbles, and came up. 'One's green and one's blue,' he said.

'That's pleurisy. My aunt died of it. Look here, the Wingco's made me Entertainments Officer. What shall we do?'

'Hold a dance, of course. Best way to keep the troops happy is let them get their hands on female flesh.'

'We haven't got a band.'

'You're bloody useless, Silko. Get me a phone, I'll get you a dozen dance bands, all assorted colours. Where's your initiative?'

'My wicked stepfather cut it off when I was seven.'

'Chuck me a towel.' Langham stood up. 'The trouble with your family was the wrong father got shot.'

Silk nodded. He admired Langham for his candour, his readiness to think the unthinkable and speak the unspeakable. Very UnEnglish. Very refreshing. Langham was right, of course; Silk had often wished his stepfather dead and his real father alive instead. Completely irrational, he knew that. Especially when the stepfather was rich.

'If he hadn't paid my fees at Clifton,' Silk pointed out, 'you and I would never have met.'

19

'Yeah. The old bastard's done his good deed, it's time he went.'

'A bit hard on my mother.'

'No, it's not. What do you care, anyway?'

Right again.

Silk's real father had been shot dead in an ambush in County Cork. This was back in the Twenties, after the Irish Free State was set up. There was a civil war of a peculiarly Irish kind, tangled and merciless. What in God's name was ex-Captain Silk, previously of the 2nd Royal Dublin Fusiliers, doing down there? Making money, somehow. That was all his wife knew. She was in England with a four-year-old boy and, after the funeral, precious little money.

She remarried fast. The market was alive with young war widows; it was no time to be seeking Prince Charming. She accepted a widower, Beresford Cronin QC, fifty-one, specializing in patent law. Later he became a judge. At the age of ten, young Silk got taken to watch his stepfather in court. Counsel spoke at a slow dictation speed and Judge Cronin wrote down every word, using an ordinary steel-nib pen, which scratched and scratched. Silk thought the law was worse than school.

On the other hand, school was better than the grey, passionless respectability of home, especially when the boy was old enough to be sent away to Clifton College.

At first the place scared him. It was too big, too hearty, and he didn't understand the unwritten rules, so he hung back, took no risks, and was ignored. He wasn't unpopular; just ignored. Tony Langham was in the same year, and Silk envied him because he was good-looking, athletic, free-spending and popular; but Silk was too nervous to speak to him. Most of the time, Silk felt both ravenous for friendship and incapable of it. One day, halfway through his second year, he was sprawled on the grass in a gloomy corner of the school grounds, chewing a thumb, brooding, his eyes damp with tears, when Tony Langham walked up and said: 'Can you give me five shillings?'

Silk shook his head.

Langham poked him with his boot. 'Why not?'

Silk shook his head again. Langham poked him harder. 'Speak up, dummy.' Silk turned away. Langham said, 'If you won't speak up, you can cough up. Five bob.' Another prod.

A rush of rage overcame self-pity. Silk jumped up and punched Langham just below the breast-bone. Langham crumpled and sat,

too badly winded to speak. Silk was astonished, then afraid, then –
as Langham slowly revived – proud of his strength.

Langham wheezed and spat. 'Bloody hell,' he whispered. Threads
of saliva fell from his lips.

'You started it.' Silk was beginning to regret that punch. It would
have been nice to have had Langham as a friend. Now he was an enemy.

'Half a crown would do,' Langham said, still wheezing.

'What's it for?'

'Buy an aeroplane.'

Silk laughed. The more he looked at Langham, the funnier he was.
Langham couldn't laugh but he grinned a bit. In the end they went
off together and contrived a letter to Silk's mother, all about a broken
fountain-pen and imminent exams. A postal order for ten shillings
came back. They bought a model kit of an SE5a and spent the change
on ice-cream sundaes.

Building the plane took three weeks. The SE5a was one of the best
fighters flown by the Royal Flying Corps, a single-seat biplane with
a machine gun fitted on the upper wing so that its fire would clear
the propeller arc. The kit was ambitious. The frames and stringers
for the fuselage, the ribs and spars for the wings, every part of the tail
unit, had to be cut from sheets of balsa. Bits broke. Silk and
Langham argued over the meaning of the plans. They cut their
fingers; ran out of glue; assembled items wrongly and had to start
again. But when the fighter was finished – doped, painted, gleaming
– its making had built a bond between them. For the first time in his
life, Silk felt worthwhile.

On a day when the rest of the school was watching a cricket
match, they sneaked out with the SE5a. There was a perfect place to
fly it nearby: the Downs, a mile or more of parkland. 'Here?' Silk
said, but Langham was carrying the model and he kept saying there
was a better place further on.

After fifteen minutes he stopped at the edge of the Downs, where
the Avon Gorge fell sheer for a couple of hundred feet. 'This is a fat
lot of good,' Silk said. He had to look over the wall, it was irresistible, and his guts clenched at the depth of this huge, airy canyon,
with seabirds wheeling far below. 'Watch!' Langham called. As Silk
turned, Langham launched the plane into space.

The image stayed with Silk for the rest of his life: that splendid
little fighter, bright in the sunlight, whirring away into the terrible

void, sometimes bucking as the breeze caught it but always sailing the air, as balanced as a bird. He watched every dip and turn the SE5a made until it crashed into an old quarry face a quarter of a mile away. When he looked around, Langham was watching him with a small, crooked smile.

Silk chased him until his lungs burned and he stumbled and fell. Langham sat on his heels a safe distance away and made a daisy chain.

Eventually Silk said. 'You can't do things like that.'

'Yes you can. Anyone can do anything. You can do something about your rotten haircut, for instance.'

'Three weeks' work. And you deliberately crashed it.'

'Didn't it look marvellous? A mile high, it looked. I'm going to learn to fly.'

'You're potty. You're cuckoo.'

'Well, cuckoos fly.'

'Mine's a perfectly good haircut.'

'It looks like a perfectly good lavatory brush. And your shirts don't fit and you can't tell jokes and whenever a girl comes in sight you go cross-eyed. I bet you can't dance.'

'Go to hell.' It was a word Silk had never used aloud before.

'You can't swear properly, either. Look: come and stay with me in the holidays and my sisters will teach you the foxtrot.'

This was all too much and too fast for Silk. 'Why?' he asked.

'Oh ... because. I'm thirsty. Let's get some ice cream.'

Langham, and Langham's sisters, showed Silk how to live. He discovered a taste for good clothes. He discovered a sense of humour. He discovered that girls were no threat, which doubled the pleasures of life at a stroke. And above all, he discovered that almost nothing was worth taking very seriously because he was intelligent enough and handsome enough to stroll through life with little effort.

After Clifton, he had strolled into the Royal Air Force, into a commission, into Bomber Command, and now into a war. No doubt it would be risky but it would also be fun. And there was always Tony Langham for good company.

Perfect.

Langham got on the phone and found a dance band: Joe Buck and his Buckaneers. 'Can't do this week,' the bandleader said.

'Are you all booked up?'

'All cancelled, is more like it. Bloody government's gone and shut down the dance halls because of the emergency. That'll teach Hitler a lesson, won't it?'

'But if you're cancelled, why aren't you available?'

'Sax, trumpet and bass are working night shift in the munitions factory. Clarinet's gone to Sheffield for his medical. Trombone's on ARP duty. I can do you piano and drums.'

'No, I want the lot. How about next week?'

'Maybe. I'll need some petrol for my van. This rationing's bloody murder.'

Langham went to tell Silk and found him very chipper. 'Sergeant Collins has a brother-in-law who's a theatrical agent,' Silk said. 'I've booked a troupe of Russian jugglers and a comedian and a hypnotist. What have you got?' Langham told him. 'Bugger,' Silk said. 'No dances, by order? We'd better go and see the group captain.'

Rafferty let them talk while he signed letters.

'Where is your band coming from?' he asked.

'Bury St Edmunds, sir,' Langham said.

'And who will the men dance with?'

'We thought nurses from the hospital –'

'Definitely not. The country is in a state of national emergency. This airfield is at a state of high alert. Security is paramount. The last thing I need is hordes of civilians wandering around here.'

'Suppose we find a hotel, sir,' Silk suggested. 'Book the ballroom.'

'And suppose the Hun attacks while half my personnel are elsewhere, doing the Gay Gordons. What then?'

'How about a variety show here, on the station?' Silk said. 'With performing artistes?'

'Such as?'

Silk checked his notes. 'Um ... well, Boris Blatsky, sir. He's a hypnotist.'

'He's a Russian.'

'Oh. Is he?'

'No Bolshevik in going to infiltrate this base.'

'Correct me if I'm wrong, sir,' Langham said, 'but it appears that you won't allow outsiders in, and vice versa.'

'You got that right,' Rafferty said. 'Goodbye.'

Silk reported this development to the Wingco. Someone had just

barrage of cheering. 'To fight a war against tyranny and fascism, this government has given itself all the powers of a tyrant and a fascist. Therefore I urge you to vote for the motion: that Nazi tendencies at home are more dangerous than Nazi aggression abroad.'

LAC Barber sat down to thunderous applause.

Someone tugged at Silk's arm. It was the Wingco. 'Come with me,' Hunt said. They went outside. 'Is this your idea of entertainment?' It wasn't a question; it was a charge.

'They seemed to be enjoying it, sir.'

'That display is probably treasonable. It's certainly contrary to good order and discipline. You're not an Entertainment Officer, Silk, you're a disaster. You're sacked.'

'Yes, sir.'

'And where the hell have you been all day?'

'Yorkshire, sir. We had a flat tyre.' There was a pause. In the darkness, Silk realised the Wingco suspected he was being facetious. 'Honestly, sir. You see –'

'I don't care. There was a time, Silk, when I thought you were a prat. I see now that I flattered you.' The Wingco strode away.

Silk had a quick bath and got dressed and went to the Mess. Tony Langham was drinking with a bunch of pilots and observers. 'The motion was carried,' he told Silk, 'by a hundred and seventeen votes to three.'

'Good God. Well, Pixie's taken the job away from me. Was all that stuff true? What LAC Barber said?'

'Every word. Where've you been all day?'

'Oh, *bollocks*,' Silk said.

Langham shrugged. 'You always were a bad loser, Silko. Remember the maiden flight of the SE5a? You behaved very badly then, I thought.'

2

The Wingco appointed another Entertainments Officer. The government grudgingly allowed cinemas, theatres and dance halls to reopen. Bomber Command discovered the reasons for its heavy losses in ops on the second day of the war. The pilots were at fault. Their attacks had been too low and too near the flak batteries on the docks at Wilhelmshaven and Brunsbüttel. Therefore crews should fly higher and concentrate their attacks on ships at sea. It was noticeable that no aircraft had been lost to German fighters. If all crews kept a close formation so as to coordinate their gunnery, British bombers would be more than a match for any fighters.

LAC Barber was posted to an RAF weather station in Orkney.

For the next few weeks, Bomber Command attempted no raids on German warships. 409 Squadron could relax a little. 'We're obviously keeping our powder dry,' Rafferty said. 'Keeping Hitler guessing.' But on 29 September, two other squadrons sent eleven Hampdens to search the Heligoland area, about fifty miles north of Wilhelmshaven. The bombers were in two formations. One group of six Hampdens found a couple of destroyers, bombed them, missed them, went home. The other group of five Hampdens was swamped by enemy fighters, probably Messerschmitt 109s. That's what German radio said in its English-language broadcast, and the crews at Kindrick (who were regular listeners) thought it was probably true, because there was no denying the fact that all five Hampdens had been shot down.

Silk, Langham and Duff visited the Intelligence Officer. 'Five out of eleven, Bins,' Silk said. 'Not a funny joke, is it?'

'Rotten luck.'

'Luck? You reckon it's just luck?'

'In the absence of hard fact, Command isn't about to leap to any conclusion. It could have been a freak loss. Maybe some of the guns jammed. Perhaps a collision. Or a Hampden lost an engine and fell out of formation.' Bins shrugged.

'Or they all got struck by lightning,' Langham said. 'All five.'

'Stranger things have happened.' Bins sharpened a pencil; he found the chore soothing. 'This episode has jogged my memory. Something I haven't thought of in an age. France, 1917, my squadron got given half a dozen brand new Bristol Fighters. Splendid bus, two-seater. The gunner had a tremendous field of fire. We were ordered to fly these machines in tight formation and use our crossfire to hack down any Hun who came near.'

'Sounds familiar,' Duff said.

'And we lost five Bristol Fighters out of six on the first patrol.'

'Sounds very familiar,' Duff said.

'Still, we won in the end, didn't we? Despite everything.'

'Hoo bloody ray,' Silk said. They went out and left him still sharpening.

WIDE BLUE YONDER

1

Adolf Hitler was not the only enemy. German measles struck RAF Kindrick.

Not surprisingly, the disease spread rapidly in the ground staff who serviced the bombers: men who worked closely together, messed together, shared the same billets. It spread so fast that the MO stopped sending its victims to the sick bay and instead isolated entire barrack blocks. By then nearly half the ground crew had a fever, swollen lymph glands and a rash that itched like nettle-sting.

Group Captain Rafferty took a dim view of such failings until he began sweating and scratching. He telephoned the Wingco. 'I've got the fascist pox, don't come near me, you're in command,' he said. 'Keep the flying personnel healthy, that's crucial. Use your initiative, I'll back your decisions, it's bed for me.'

Hunt telephoned Group HQ and got approval for his plan. He gave 'A' Flight three days' leave. With luck they would escape infection; then 'B' Flight – if they were healthy – could disappear for three days. Having only half the squadron available was better than losing everyone to German measles; and in six days the worst might be over.

'London,' Tony Langham said to Silk.

'Can't. Broke.'

'Use your overdraft.'

'Spent it. Lost it. Blew it on a pair of kings.' When Langham rolled his eyes, Silk said, 'I was bluffing. I nearly won the pot, it was a hell of a good bluff, everyone said so. They gave me a standing ovation. What have you got?'

'Couple of quid. Not enough for return tickets to London.'

'Train's too slow, anyway. Why don't we drive? Borrow Black Mac's Bentley, scrounge some petrol, hit the road.'

Black Mac was Flight Lieutenant McHarg, the Armaments Officer, a big man with a dark complexion who had boxed for the RAF at heavyweight. He rarely smiled. 'Mac's a miserable sod. He'll never lend us his car,' Langham said. 'It's always locked up.'

'I know where he hides his spare key. He's not going anywhere, he's got the measles. He resembles a large helping of spotted dick.'

'What about petrol? That Bentley must drink the stuff.'

'I have friends in the MT Section. Sergeant Trimbull will fill her up if I promise him a flip in a Hampden.'

'That's scandalous,' Langham said. 'Has the man no morals?'

The Bentley was open-top, so they wore their fleece-lined flying jackets. McHarg kept his car in excellent condition. The engine had a deep and throaty roar, the gear changes were slick and sure, the big, wide wheels had a love affair with the road. They raced across the flatlands of Lincoln, picked up the Great North Road, stormed down through the shires of Huntingdon and Bedford and Hertford, and were in London too soon. 'Damn. The pubs aren't open,' Silk said.

Langham was driving. He crossed Marble Arch, cruised down Park Lane, turned into Piccadilly. 'I'm hungry,' he said. 'You're navigating, Silko. Where can we get food and drink at half-past three?'

'Well, there's the Ritz hotel on the starboard beam.'

It was a joke. Langham's couple of quid wouldn't buy tea and crumpets at the Ritz. He made a U-turn and stopped outside its entrance. A doorman in top hat and tails stepped forward.

'Unbelievably silly mistake,' Langham said to him. 'I was sure my friend here had the invitations, and he thought I had. My cousin's wedding reception.' He gestured helplessly with his wallet, the one without the invitations. 'Have you got a large wedding reception in progress? We're frightfully late, but ...'

'Would it be on the occasion of the Honourable Richard and Patricia Byng-Shadwell's marriage, sir?'

Langham slapped the steering wheel. 'Told you it was the Ritz,' he said to Silk. They got out and he gave the doorman the Bentley's keys and a pound note. 'Put her somewhere safe, would you? Thanks awfully. Chocks away, Silko! Cousin Richard awaits.'

They went inside. 'You gave him a whole quid,' Silk said.

'He seemed to like it. Now then: half the guests at a wedding reception don't know the other half. Fact.'

'Besides, we're war heroes,' Silk said. 'They wouldn't dare throw us out.'

'Damn right.'

They strolled into the reception, smiling modestly and discussing the weather. Nobody paid them any attention. The happy couple had ceased receiving guests; now everyone was drinking and talking. The average age looked to be over forty. 'This is more like a wake than a wedding,' Langham said. But there were waiters with champagne. They each drank three glasses while they wandered through the crowd. 'Bloody good fizz,' Silk said. 'I can hear music.'

A small band was in the next room, playing a foxtrot. 'Ah! Popsies,' Langham said. 'Bags me the long-legged blonde.' But the girl he was soon dancing with was a trim brunette with a fragile face that would bust a bishop's gaiters.

'I don't remember seeing you at the church,' she said.

'I was thinking the same about you. How could I have possibly overlooked this stunning creature, I thought.'

'Not very easily. After all, I was a bridesmaid.'

'Of course you were. And I was at thirty thousand feet, so I missed the whole show. My loss.'

'You mean you were flying?' Her look of admiration made his journey worthwhile. 'What do you fly?'

'Spitfire. Nice little bus. Climbs like a lift.'

'Ah.' For an instant she was breathless. In 1939 a Spitfire pilot was the most exciting and romantic partner a girl could want. Here was a man in charge of the deadliest yet the most beautiful fighter in the world. Every day he soared into the blue at speeds beyond imagination, and did it in defence of his country. She had danced with film stars, Olympic athletes, the sons of dukes. None was touched with the glory of a Spitfire pilot. What's more, this man was good-looking. And modest. And funny.

'How fast can you fly?' she said.

'Can't tell you that, I'm afraid. Official secret.'

'Oh.'

'Fast enough to catch any Hun who's foolish enough to show his ugly face.'

The music stopped and they did not release each other. 'I won't let go till it thunders,' she said, which made him laugh. The band began again. 'I know this one,' he said. 'It's called "Embraceable You".' He hummed a few bars. They were dancing more closely now, so closely that she could gaze at the wings on his tunic without betraying her fascination. 'You have a wonderfully masculine fragrance,' she said. 'Is that from your Spitfire?'

'It's more likely to be from my Bentley.' He felt good about owning a Bentley. 'With perhaps just a hint of spaniel.' What was a Spitfire pilot without a spaniel at his heels?

The dance ended. 'I hear thunder,' she said, and let go of his hand. 'Look ... I've seen too much of these people and not nearly enough of you. That's a shocking thing to say, and it isn't at all the way I was brought up to behave, but I don't care. So will you walk me home? I simply must get out of this dress. Damn. That's not what I meant.'

'My arm is yours.'

He walked her to the top of Piccadilly. She had an airy apartment in Albany, furnished in rich, soft, countryside colours. Her name was Zoë Herrick. 'A cross between a haddock and a herring,' she said. 'James the First is said to have invented it for one of his favourites because the boy was neither one thing nor the other, so the king said. Later on the lad got a knighthood, so he can't have been a complete failure. Actually I'm Zoë Herrick Herrick. No hyphen. Sounds like a hiccup. There's some absurd family reason behind it.'

'I knew a boy at Clifton whose uncle is General Gore Gore Gore Plantaganet Finbar-Gore,' Langham said.

'Poor chap.'

'Known as Gore-Blimey, for short.'

'Make yourself a drink, while I get changed.'

'What I really need is a ham sandwich. I missed lunch.' Langham sucked in his cheeks and crossed his eyes.

'*Don't* do that. *Please.*' She was upset; he stopped at once. 'I can't stand it when ...' She never completed the sentence; instead she embraced him and kissed him on the lips several times.

'Perhaps the ham sandwich is unimportant,' he said; but his gastric juices spoke softly and contradicted him.

'No, no, obviously you must have food, you poor thing, we'll go to the Savoy, they always have everything ...'

'I'm sure they do, my sweet embraceable you,' he said gently.

'Unfortunately I don't. Especially money. The banks were closed by the time we –'

'Oh … *cobblers*,' she said. 'Whatever that means.' She went to a desk and came back with a bundle of notes. 'Here.'

'Fifty quid.' Two month's pay. 'You scarcely know me.'

'Well, *you* scarcely know *me*.' She stood, hands on hips, bright-eyed, more delicious than a plate of ham sandwiches. 'So now we're quits.'

That night they went to several parties. Compared with RAF Kindrick, this was Shangri-la with knobs on. Zoë seemed to be plugged into an endless network of pleasure; they began in a penthouse in Soho, moved to a Chelsea studio, to a townhouse in Belgravia, to a huge cellar in Notting Hill where a roulette wheel was doing big business. After that he stopped asking where they were going. Who cared? As long as Zoë knew, and the taxi-drivers knew, and the drinks were big, and she was welcomed everywhere (which made him instantly popular too) and the young and beautiful of London were having a bloody good time, many of them in uniform, damn good types, damn good music, damn fine party, then who gave a damn? He liked music. Never realized how much. They were in the cellar, dancing, when he told her: 'I would say you're like thistledown, but I can't pronounce thistledown.' The music stopped. He went over to the band and asked them to play "Embraceable You", and turned and saw Silko with his arms around two redheads.

'These are my twins,' Silk said, speaking carefully. 'I'm in love with one. She's the one who hasn't got a mole on her bottom, but she won't show me, so I don't know where I stand.'

'You can't stand,' one redhead said. 'If we let go,' she told Langham, 'he falls down.'

'Have you got somewhere to stay tonight?' Langham asked him.

'Can't tell you, because … I don't know where I stand.' Suddenly he cackled with laughter. His knees folded.

'We'll look after him,' the other redhead said.

'I'll meet you at the Ritz,' Langham said. 'Day after tomorrow.'

'Bloody good joke, that,' Silk said.

Then the band was playing, and Langham was dancing again. 'Apologies,' he said. 'Should have introduced. That was Silko.'

'Silko was blotto,' Zoë said. Not criticising. Just observing.

'Bravo Silko!' he said, and she smiled; so he said, 'Bravo Silko blotto pronto Groucho Harpo Brasso Blanco!' and she laughed, so he quit while he was ahead.

Next morning he woke up in her apartment. He was on the couch. Luckily it was a big couch. The royal aroma of freshly brewed coffee promised to wash all his sins away. He sat up, the blanket fell off, he was in his underwear. He never slept in his underwear. NCOs and Other Ranks slept in their underwear. Also convicts in American films. He saw his legs. Covered in ugly black hair. Except the feet. Why no hair on the feet? Nasty-looking things, feet. And kneecaps. Both bald as an egg. Not things of beauty. So God created trousers.

Zoë came in with coffee on a tray. 'I couldn't get you into bed,' she said. 'Too heavy. But at least I got your uniform off.'

'Trousers come in pairs,' he said. 'Nobody has ever seen one trouser all on its own. Odd, isn't it?'

'I've sent everything to be cleaned. It smelled dreadfully of rum. You can wear this.' A tweed suit hung over a chair. Also a shirt and tie.

'Curiouser and curiouser.'

She poured coffee. 'Drink. This stuff is black magic.'

The suit was a reasonably good fit. He dressed and went out and bought a pair of brown brogues and a tweed hat to go with the suit, and retrieved the Bentley from the Ritz. The doorman got two pounds, and Langham got a salute worthy of a Wingco. It seemed appropriate. He felt meritorious.

They drove to Oxford. He parked in the High.

'I want to see all these lovely colleges before Hitler bombs them to bits,' she said. Langham asked why he would do that. 'Look what he's done to Warsaw,' she said. 'And the *Daily Telegraph* reckons that if his bombers come here they'll kill six hundred thousand people in two months.'

'Let 'em try. We'll make mincemeat of them.' But he remembered the RAF's annual exercises, only that summer, when 409's Hampdens had played the part of an enemy force arriving from the North Sea. They had flown deep into England, cruised around for hours, never seen a fighter. On the other hand they never found their tar̶g̶e̶t a factory near Reading. Never found Reading, come to that. ̶m̶u̶c̶h low cloud.

̶ a friend in the Home Office,' she said. 'Toby Stone-Pelham. ̶ ̶m̶ass graves have been dug in the suburbs. All his family ̶ ̶m̶ost tremendous liars. Perhaps we should go and look, except I'm not exactly sure where the suburbs are.'

'And you don't seem hugely upset about it.'

'No, I'm not. Are you? Yesterday morning I might have cared if six hundred thousand Londoners got killed, but since I met you nothing else matters.' She was calm and content. They were walking arm-in-arm. He really didn't want to talk about bomb damage; he'd driven all the way from Kindrick to escape the war. 'You'll feel better after lunch,' he said, and wasn't sure what he meant.

'I don't want to feel better. Were you listening to me?'

Langham had a chilled and fluttering sensation in his stomach, a feeling he sometimes got at take-off, when he was convinced that both engines were going to fail just as the Hampden got airborne. 'Yes, I was listening,' he said. 'It seems that we're in love with each other. Rather an amazing coincidence.'

'Quite stunning. You look slightly stunned.'

'That's hunger.'

They lunched at the Randolph. Watercress soup, braised pheasant and bottled Guinness, lemon syllabub.

'Now that we know each other rather better,' he said, 'and since this suit obviously wasn't made for you ...'

'It's my brother's. Spencer Herrick Herrick. At Eton they called him Herrick Squared, very suitable, he's got a brain like a brick. He's in Rhodesia now, thank God. When father died –'

'Slow down. Who was father?'

'Who cares? He'd dead. He despised me, and I detested him.' She ate the last of the lemon syllabub, and licked the spoon. 'Should I have another? Probably not.'

'For a piece of thistledown, you're a hearty eater.'

'I do my best. Father did his worst, smoked in bed, the whole manor house went up, nothing left to bury, not even bones. I got an obscene amount of money. Spencer got the title and fifty thousand acres of beef ranch in Africa and the apartment in Albany, rather a long way from Africa so he lets me use it, and unless you know some reason why not, such as bigamy or insanity or – God forbid – impotence, I suggest we marry. Fast.'

He took a deep breath, held it while he counted to five, let it go. 'This time yesterday we hadn't met. How can we be sure that ...'

'Oh, tosh. We knew after ten seconds. Ten weeks' thinking about it won't change anything, will it?'

'No.'

'Good, that's settled. I can call you darling now. I've been itching to do it all morning. Get the bill, darling. We must order you some more suits, darling. You look ravishing in tweed, darling.'

'Well, ravishing is what I do best.' *Oops*, he thought. *Bit premature, that.* 'Or so my horoscope says.'

'I expect we could get a room here,' she said, 'if your lust is overflowing.'

'No, no. Not necessary.' As he paid the bill he wondered why he had said that. Why be so coy? So cautious? Of course his bloody lust was bloody overflowing. She looked like a nymph and dressed like a dream and called him darling. How was he supposed to feel? He over-tipped hugely, and felt slightly better.

They strolled through a few colleges. She said enough to prevent awkward silences and no more. Her mind was busy making and unmaking thoughts which she was afraid to put into words in case they spoiled the happiness of the moment. She was twenty-six, utterly determined never to marry a man who was merely suitable. London was littered with suitable men. She had told so many of them they were wasting their time, that her friends had decided her standards were impossibly high. But all she wanted was someone to give her what she didn't know she wanted until she got it.

Not just sex. Sex might be essential but it wasn't crucial. Or perhaps the other way around, she didn't care, sex happened, it was glorious but it was predictable. Life wasn't all sex. She wanted to be surprised from time to time. Maybe shocked, even frightened. That's what made Langham a perfect match for her. She was looking for trouble and he was a trouble-maker. He thought he could hide it. She knew better.

On the way back to London she saw a lone Spitfire doing aerobatics. Langham stopped the car and they watched it. Wing-over, plunge, soar, loop, roll, level out, steep bank, circle. 'Probably doing an air-test,' he said. 'Making sure none of the screws are loose.'

'Thrilling. Doesn't it thrill you?'

'It interests me. *You* thrill me.'

She was silent, which made him look. Blood had rushed to her cheeks. He was impressed by his own powers.

That night he did not sleep on the couch. Again, he was impressed by his own powers until she said: 'There's no hurry. We've got hours and hours.'

He felt the light sweat drying on his body, and listened to his heartbeat dropping to normal. 'Yes,' he said. 'Of course.'

'We'll call that an air-test.'

'Agreed.'

'Now we know that none of the screws are loose.'

'Exactly. We can explore the wide blue yonder.'

'Infinity for eternity,' she said. 'Yummy.'

Langham had never known a popsy who talked like that.

Next morning they walked to Savile Row and ordered some suits from Latham & Nunnerley. Zoë charged them to her brother's account. Then they drove to Richmond and lunched at a riverside hotel. The air was easy, and there was just enough haze in the sky to soften the heat of the sun. An anti-aircraft gun had been set up on the other side of the Thames. The soldiers were playing cricket with a tennis ball. 'This war is a swiz,' Langham said. 'I want my money back.' It had been a busy night and now he felt very idle.

'Where do you want to get married?' He had no quick answer, so she said: 'Not in a church. Ever since the Hitler-Stalin Pact I've gone off God. I don't think God's playing the game, do you?'

'Probably not.' He didn't care, one way or the other. 'I rather think I've got to get permission from my CO.'

'Oh. Shall I come with you?'

'Good heavens, no.' He had an image of her surrounded by hungry Hampden pilots while she searched for Spitfires.

'I don't see how he can approve unless he meets the bride-to-be.' But food arrived, and she forgot the CO. She skipped from subject to subject; nothing obsessed her. He liked that. Flying was his life, and people who interfered with flying annoyed him. She made him proud to be a pilot, maybe not a Spitfire pilot and something would have to be done about that, but still there was plenty of time ...

They drove back to Albany and suddenly she was almost in tears. 'Go now,' she said. 'Don't wait. It's too painful. Go, go.' He packed his bag and kissed her. For a second she responded, but then she could barely stand to look at him. He thought he knew her. Obviously he didn't. He felt as if he had been poked in the stomach with a walking-stick. He left as silently as a burglar.

2

The Bentley coasted onto the forecourt of a petrol station near Stevenage. A long way from Lincolnshire.

'I was in the last lot,' the owner said. He was middle-aged, gaunt and gloomy. 'Durham Light Infantry. *Very* light, by the time the Armistice came.' He raised his left arm; the sleeve was pinned up at the elbow. 'So don't think I'm not patriotic.' He looked enviously at the wings on their tunics. 'Can't you get filled up at an aerodrome?'

'Never make it. We're running on fumes,' Silk said.

'We got recalled from leave,' Langham said. 'Urgent telegram, top priority. The whole squadron's on operations.'

'Dawn patrol,' Silk said.

'Everything's coupons, coupons,' the owner said. 'Bleeding inspectors ...'

'Rules are made to be broken,' Silk said. 'We thought you might have a few pre-war gallons still in the pumps. At the going price, of course.'

'You'll get me shot, you will.' He sold them two gallons of petrol for three pounds. 'Nice motor,' he said. 'Lucky sods. We marched every bloody where, we did.'

They drove north, in the gathering dusk. 'Look,' Silk said, and tapped the petrol gauge. 'You can actually see the needle going down. She's drinking like a fish.'

'I'll drive fast,' Langham said. 'That way, we'll get there before we run out.'

Near Peterborough it was obvious that the plan wasn't working. They stopped at a coaching inn and had dinner. 'You look terrible,' Langham said. 'Eyes like poached eggs. What happened to you?'

'Two redheads,' Silk explained. 'It's one too many for a mere boy like me. I was keeping the second-best for you, but you disappeared.'

'I was otherwise engaged. In fact, I don't know how, but I actually *got* engaged. You know: to be married.'

'Ah.' Silk frowned, and nodded. 'Well, now.'

'She thinks I'm a Spitfire pilot.'

'Explains a lot. Bloody glory boys, they are.' Silk drank beer and watched Langham over the rim of the glass. 'I hear no cheers.'

'She's a wonderful, beautiful girl. I'm very lucky.' He made it sound like a death in the family. Silk changed the subject.

Somewhere near the edge of Lincolnshire, with the fuel gauge nudging zero, Langham switched off the engine and let the Bentley coast down a long and gentle slope. He saw a small farmhouse, all dark except for a slight gleam of moonlight on its windows. Parked on the grass verge was a Ford shooting brake. He stopped alongside it. 'What's up?' Silk asked.

'Not a word,' Langham whispered. 'Take the wheel. Be ready to depart with all speed.' He held up a coil of rubber tube. 'I pinched it from that garage.'

One end went into the Ford's petrol tank. Langham sucked on the other end; pinched it shut and breathed hard; sucked again; repeated the routine; finally tasted petrol. One last suck and he had a mouthful; stuffed the splashing tube into the Bentley's tank and spat vigorously, again and again.

'Dog,' Silk said quietly.

It was on a chain, in front of the farmhouse. When it howled, the sound was so raw that Langham almost dropped the tube. 'Nice doggie,' he muttered. 'Back to sleep.' It kept howling, and the chain rattled as it lunged. A bedroom window was flung open, an angry threat was shouted. Still the dog howled. 'How much longer?' Silk asked. 'Nearly there,' Langham said. Now the angry man saw them, and cursed, and vanished. 'I bet he's got a gun,' Silk said. 'Farmers always have guns.' The dog was becoming hysterical. 'Another twenty seconds,' Langham said. 'I'm not doing this twice.' Silk turned the key in the ignition: no success. 'Please, please,' he said. 'Please with pink icing on.' A door slammed. He tried again: nothing. 'Could that stuff be diesel?' he asked. More windows, lights, voices. 'Eighteen, nineteen, twenty,' Langham said. 'Now go!' He vaulted into the back seat. The engine fired and the Bentley accelerated in a spray of gravel and black exhaust just as the farmer skidded out of his gateway and tripped on his nightshirt. The shotgun blew a hole in a hedge. By the time he got up, the Bentley was fifty yards away and backfiring like a cowboy movie. 'I don't think she likes your petrol,' Silk said.

When they put the car back in Flight Lieutenant McHarg's lock-up, they noticed the dirt on the wings and the windscreen and the petrol splashes around the filler cap. 'We'll worry about that tomorrow,' Langham said.

3

'B' Flight went off to enjoy its three-day leave.

The threat of German measles faded. Many groundcrew recovered, enough to ensure that at least half of 409's Hampdens were available for action. Three of these bombers and their crews were kept on stand-by. It was a tedious duty: Command could find no German naval targets for them to bomb. The stand-by crews argued about this. According to the newspapers, the Luftwaffe had not bombed anything in the West, so maybe some neutral statesman was brokering a settlement. Mussolini was the popular choice. But when Hitler made a speech and told Britain and France that the war could stop at once, they turned him down flat. Any ceasefire would condemn the world to slavery, they said. So the war wasn't off. But it wasn't altogether on, either. Except in Poland.

Germany had agreed to the Roosevelt Rules against bombing targets where civilians might be hit. By then the Luftwaffe had energetically bombed any number of Polish towns and villages. Civilian targets could (and would) be bombed, so the German High Command announced, because Polish civilians were involving themselves in the fighting. A week later, Germany declared that all organized fighting in Poland had ended. Warsaw was now defenceless. The Luftwaffe sent an armada of Heinkels and Dorniers to bomb the city. Ten thousand civilians died. Hitler made another speech, saying he was willing to make peace. Nobody believed him except the German people, and they had no choice in the matter.

Meanwhile, 409 Squadron's Hampdens waited on the tarmac hardstandings. Their crews hung about, listening to the wind-up gramophone grinding out the hit songs of 1939, 'Red Sails in the Sunset', 'This Can't Be Love', 'South of the Border Down Mexico Way', 'Two Sleepy People'. The morning papers were eagerly seized but they had little to report except stuff about Poland, and everyone knew that the Poles were total goners. Hitler and Stalin had carved up the country between them. Was that part of a deal to make Hitler's eastern border safe? Probably. Cunning bugger, Hitler. Sweden announced it was neutral. Was that news? Probably not. Belgium, Holland, Denmark, Norway, Finland and Iceland were neutral. Rumania, Bulgaria, Greece and Turkey were neutral. Italy and Spain were neutral. Ireland was neutral. Someone bought a record of 'I Get Along Without You Very Well', and the crews played it and sang it until the joke wore thin. This was turning into a very unsatisfactory war.

4

Silk was not on standby duty the day that Flight Lieutenant McHarg was declared fit and came into the Mess.

German measles had not been kind to him. He looked gaunt and grim. Also angry. He hated waste, and that included waste of time. He had joined the RAF as a boy apprentice in 1922. In the years between the wars the Treasury kept the Armed Forces on a very tight budget. McHarg learned that the road to promotion demanded a mean and miserly grip on stores; ideally, nothing should be used. He was good at that. Even so, it was twelve years before he got commissioned: a pilot officer at the age of twenty-eight. Now he was thirty-three, and dealing with aircrew who were pilot officers at nineteen. They knew nothing of tradition. They treated his bombs as cheaply as boiled sweets. If they met a strong headwind on their way home, or if an engine began coughing, they cheerfully jettisoned their load in the sea. McHarg and generations of armaments officers had carefully guarded those bombs ever since they were stockpiled at the end of what McHarg called the Great War. The aircrew thought him an old man. That amused him. With his bare hand he could unscrew the most corroded fuse on a bomb faster than they could open a bottle of lemonade. They were children.

Silk observed McHarg from the opposite side of the Mess and decided that he didn't look happy. It could mean anything. Silk went off to find Sergeant Trimbull in the Motor Transport Section.

Trimbull said he was fairly sure that Flight Lieutenant McHarg had not been near his Bentley since he got over the measles. Of course he couldn't be positive.

'The car may be a bit muddy,' Silk said. 'A wash and a polish would be nice.' Trimbull sucked his teeth. 'My Hampden needs an air test this afternoon,' Silk said. 'Can you get away for an hour or two?'

'Easily, sir. Wash and polish. As good as done.'

'Splendid.' The sun was shining. 'Perfect day for stooging around England. Um ... You might find the odd footprint on the back of the Bentley.'

'Don't worry about it, sir. Will we be doing any practice gunnery?' Silk was about to say *Probably not* when Trimbull added, 'Only I've always had an ambition to fire one of those machine guns.'

Silk thought of what the Bentley had been through. 'This is your lucky day, Sergeant.' Neither man smiled: conspiracy was a serious business. 'Not a word to McHarg, of course.'

'Of course, sir.'

The bombers were dispersed around the edge of the airfield as a safeguard against enemy attack; nobody noticed Trimbull, in borrowed flying overalls, climb into the Hampden. He had never flown before. The take-off, twice as bumpy and ten times as loud as he expected, made his heart race with excitement. The climb was alarmingly steep; his ears popped; the countryside was shrinking into a toytown world. Trimbull was fascinated. The bomber was so narrow that when he stood behind Silk, his elbows brushed the fuselage. He began to count all the gauges and switches and indicators crammed onto the instrument panel and overflowing down the sides, reached twenty-five, saw a dozen more and gave up.

Silk found a field of cloud and made fun of it, skimming the surface, rushing down slopes, charging up hills. Then they were over the sea. It looked as if it had been spray-painted a deep metallic blue. Silk found a fluffy cloud and flew slowly around it while Trimbull, installed in the upper gunner's position, raked it savagely with bursts of fire while the real gunner guided his arm. Trimbull enjoyed watching the tracer bullets most of all. They streaked like red devils. Silk flew home at a hundred feet, hurdling the power lines, while Trimbull gripped the pilot's seatback and flexed his knees and silently cheered. Altogether, a successful trip.

5

At Clifton College, Langham had won prizes for his English essays. His sentences grew like ivy. They were rich with subordinate clauses and parentheses; his handling of the semi-colon was masterly. Often his sentences ran until they made complete paragraphs. He could qualify a statement five different ways without breaking sweat. But he couldn't write a letter to Zoë Herrick. He tried, and immediately felt swamped by a flood of remembered lust. If he put this hunger into words, his writing became a scribble and then an exhausted scrawl. He gave up. He telephoned her. Easier. Also more dangerous.

'Darling!' she said. 'How sweet of you. By the way, you forgot to take your underpants.'

'Damn ... Look, chuck them out.'

'Never. I'm wearing them. Not as nice as you next to the skin, but I suppose a girl has to make sacrifices. There's a war on. Have you been looping the loop in your sexy Spitfire?'

'Actually, there's been a bit of a change. I'm off Spitfires. We're flying Hampdens now. Twice as many engines, and a ton of bombs. Plus a crew to boss about. So I'm frightfully high-powered.'

'What fun. I had a dog called Harrington when I was small.'

'Not Harrington. Hampden.'

Brief pause. 'Harrington. King Charles spaniel. I should know, darling, he was my bloody dog.'

He let her win. 'What are you up to? Apart from my underwear.'

'If I were apart from your underwear, darling, I'd be stark naked.'

'Ah.' His loins gave a small leap. 'I know a few pilots who wear their girl-friends' silk stockings on a long flight. Keeps the legs warm.'

'Precious, you may have the pick of my lingerie the instant we're married. Are you free a week on Wednesday? Lincoln cathedral, two o'clock. The bishop got a special licence for us. He's my godfather, he swore to protect me from the flesh and the devil but nobody said anything about Spitfire pilots.'

'That's because we're unspeakable.' Let her think he flew a Spitfire. What harm could it do?

43

6

Silk lay stretched on a sofa in the Mess ante-room, engrossed in a paperback called *A Bullet for Your Pains*. He was within a page or two of discovering whodunit when a servant presented Flight Lieutenant McHarg's compliments and requested Mr Silk's presence in his office on a matter of some importance.

This had never happened before.

McHarg was at his desk. He pointed to a straightback chair without looking up. He was reading a typewritten report and following every word with his forefinger. Silk looked around the room, and saw framed photographs of McHarg and his Bentley everywhere, so he looked at the floor instead. McHarg finished reading and stapled the pages with a crash of his fist that made Silk jump. 'What doesn't grow on trees?' he demanded. His voice was still grounded in Glasgow.

'Fish,' Silk said. 'Footballs. Fountain-pens. I give up.'

But McHarg had lost interest. He plucked at a hair in his left nostril until he detached it and rubbed his fingers together to dispose of it. 'You carried out an air test, Mr Silk,' he said, and sneezed so violently that his torso convulsed. 'During the flight, your upper gunner expended two drums of ammunition.'

'That's right.'

'An air test is not a gunnery exercise.'

'True.'

'So this was a case of negligent discharge of ammunition.'

'On the contrary. I authorized it, for the defence of the aeroplane.'

'Against which enemy machine? None has been reported over England.'

Silk relaxed. 'That's where we differ. Any fighter that comes sniffing around me is hostile, in my eyes. That's what happened. A Spitfire pilot came too close and I told my gunner to scare him off.'

'You attacked a Spitfire.'

'Damn right I did. Didn't you hear of the Battle of Barking Creek? Three days after the war began, a bunch of Spits went up to intercept raiders in the Thames estuary. The Huns were actually Hurricanes but that didn't stop the Spits shooting down two of them, did it? Well, my Hampden looks a lot like a Dornier 17. I don't trust fighter pilots.'

'Two drums.'

'Yeah. Very nosey, he was.'

'You didn't report this.'

'What's the point? I couldn't identify the bastard.'

McHarg spent a long time staring at him, before he said: 'I don't like negligent discharge. The man who squanders bullets can't be trusted. Ammunition doesn't grow on trees.'

'That's a relief,' Silk said. 'I was beginning to think it might be footballs after all.'

He walked back to the Mess, where a noisy party had developed, with Langham at its centre. 'The wedding's definitely on, Silko! Lincoln cathedral, Wednesday week, fourteen hundred hours. My popsy fixed it. Isn't she clever? You're best man.'

Silk took him aside. 'I think Black Mac knows something. I could tell from the way he looked at me. He's got eyes like corkscrews.'

'Blast his eyes! We've got *real* corkscrews. Have a drink.'

'That bloody Bentley.' Silk took a glass. 'How does a sweaty armaments officer come to own a Bentley, anyway?'

'Won it in a raffle. Who cares? Drink up, Silko.'

In fact McHarg had bought it for a song when it was a wreck, and then spent ten years restoring it. He had never married. The Bentley responded sweetly and without argument, went where he steered it, and was admired by all. No woman could compete with that. The Bentley was his life's companion.

THIS HAPPY BREED

1

When half a dozen pilots were posted to 409 Squadron from an Operational Training Unit, the adjutant organized their rooms and their servants and then took them to the station commander's office.

Group Captain Rafferty always gave an introductory talk. He liked to impress on new officers that 409 was rather special, that it had a bit of swank. He had given the talk so often that it was well-polished.

'Shakespeare was right, as usual,' he told them. 'Here we are on this sceptered isle, as he put it. This fortress built by Nature for herself against infection and the hand of war. This precious stone set in a silver sea, which serves it as a moat defensive to a house, and so on and so forth. Rattling good stuff. Makes Hitler sound like a rag-and-bone man shouting in the street. Now, the current task of this squadron is to protect the moat, so let's take a closer look at Shakespeare's silver sea.'

Rafferty strolled over to a wall map of England and northern Europe.

'Between us and the Hun lies the North Sea. I'm sure you're familiar with it. It has some disadvantages. It's damned cold, damned windy, damned wet. It has one advantage: it's damned big. You can have as much of it as you like.' That got a brief laugh. 'At the moment, our job is to patrol a short beat – the German coastline between Holland and Denmark. A hundred-plus miles. But to get there you fly nearly four hundred miles. No landmarks in the sea, so good navigation is important. Get your sums wrong and you might overfly Holland or Germany. This will be indicated by anti-aircraft fire. If you observe shellbursts in your vicinity, make an excuse and leave. You are searching for ships, not shrapnel.'

He talked about the Roosevelt Rules, about neutrality, about the crucial importance of positively identifying warships as German before dropping any bombs. He talked of what to do if British anti-aircraft guns shot at them: fire off signal flares in the colours of the day. 'You never know,' he said. 'It might work.' But stay well away from the Royal Navy, he said. Sailors were notoriously quick on the trigger, and he had scars from the last war to prove it. As for German fighters: they never went to sea. But if you met a Hun, keep in close formation and your gunners' crossfire should make him think twice about attacking.

This was useful stuff, but not thrilling. So Rafferty ended on a note of brisk patriotism. 'I envy you chaps,' he said. 'You've got the best bomber in the world. Best crews. Fighting for the best country. I began with Shakespeare, so I'll end with him. Henry V, before Agincourt, sees his army. "This happy breed of men," he says. And Henry knew what they were fighting for: "This precious stone set in a silver sea." Of course we won! How could we lose? And with chaps like you, we'll win again.'

That seemed to go down well. A few men actually smiled.

'Any matters arising?' he said. Feet shuffled. Somebody coughed. 'Anything? Anything at all.' Silence. 'Well, then ...'

'One small thing, sir.' A tallish officer took a pace forward. Strong features. Thick hair. Deep, confident voice. 'Those lines from Shakespeare. They're not *Henry V*. They're *Richard II*. Act two, scene one.'

'Oh.' Rafferty was taken aback. 'Not Henry, you say. But still ... um ... relevant, surely?'

'Not relevant to Agincourt, sir. Wrong century.'

'I meant relevant to *patriotism*,' Rafferty said smoothly. 'To *England*.'

'Relevant to treachery,' the pilot said, 'if Shakespeare is to be believed. But of course the king doesn't speak those lines. He's not present. The speech comes from his uncle, John of Gaunt.'

The officers relaxed; they were enjoying this. Rafferty was out-gunned. He gestured: carry on.

'Well, sir, Gaunt makes such a fuss about "this sceptered isle" in order to contrast its past with its present, which he says is rotten and he leaves no doubt who's to blame: the King! Richard has pawned the country. England, Gaunt says, "is now bound in with shame, with inky blots, and rotten parchment bonds: that England, that was wont to conquer others, hath made a shameful conquest of itself".'

'Interesting,' Rafferty said.

'Smashing speech,' the pilot said. 'But I wouldn't describe it as a ringing endorsement of the Crown.'

'You were an actor, I take it.'

'Briefly, sir.'

'And your name is ...'

'Gilchrist, sir.'

'Are you as good a pilot as you were an actor?'

'I was a lousy actor, sir. That's why I became a pilot.' It made them laugh. Rafferty smiled, and dismissed them. He had recovered his poise, but he still blamed Gilchrist for spoiling his talk. He blamed Shakespeare, too. The Bard had let him down.

2

Rafferty told the Wingco that the new boys seemed a reasonable lot, although one, a chap called Gilchrist, was rather full of himself. A bit cocky.

'Good,' Hunt said. 'I'm laying on some cross-country flights and bombing practice for "A" Flight. This Gilchrist can navigate for Flying Officer Duff. That should keep him quiet.'

When he was listed as Duff's observer, Gilchrist went to see his flight commander, an Australian squadron leader called Tom Stuart. In his youth Stuart had fallen off several horses, which was why his nose was bent. His hair was silver-grey because everyone in his family had silver-grey hair. He was twenty-six. Gilchrist thought he was forty.

'Sir, I think you should know,' Gilchrist said. 'I'm not too hot at navigating.'

'It's bloody difficult. Last week my observer got lost in Lincoln. Said he'd meet me in the saloon bar of the Turk's Head. Never turned up. Doesn't know left from right. Raise your right arm.' Gilchrist did. 'You're halfway home already,' Stuart said. 'I'm very impressed.'

'This may be a silly question, sir, but … am I here as a pilot?'

'Maybe. You're certainly not going to be allowed to drive a Hampden, not yet. It's too valuable, you might scratch the paint.'

Gilchrist tracked down Duff and warned him that he wasn't a very good navigator. 'You can't be any worse than me,' Duff said. He was playing chess with Langham. 'I can never remember how to plot a course. To calculate distance, d'you divide time by speed? Or do you multiply?' He moved his bishop straight up the board. Langham put it back. 'Bishop moves *diagonally*,' he said. Duff made a face. 'See what I mean?' he said to Gilchrist. 'Nothing's easy.'

The cross-country exercise was a triangular flight: base to Carlisle, to the bombing range near Porthcawl in south Wales, back to base. Gilchrist worked out the routes with some help from a friendly observer called King.

'Avoid flying over towns,' King said. 'Leeds, York, Sheffield, Liverpool, they're liable to have a balloon barrage up.' Gilchrist made a note. 'Don't trust your compass,' King said. 'One degree out, and you're fifty miles off track. Get pinpoints if you can.' Gilchrist wrote that down, and asked: 'What are the best pinpoints to look for? Rivers? Bridges? Crossroads?' King shrugged. 'All rivers look alike to me,' he said. 'Towns are the best landmarks. You know where you are with a whacking great cathedral.' Gilchrist scratched his head with the blunt end of his pencil. 'Big enough for a cathedral,' he said, 'won't it be big enough for a balloon barrage?'

King nodded. 'It's a bastard, isn't it?'

At least the weather was good: bright and dry, with high white cloud. Gilchrist was not fooled. He had flown clapped-out Hampdens at his OTU, he knew how cold a leaky cockpit could be, he was well wrapped up beneath his Sidcot suit and fleece-lined boots, and already he was sweating as he followed Duff. They went up the narrow ladder that was hooked to the walkway on the port wing. The walkway led to the cockpit canopy, and the sliding hood on the canopy roof would be open, waiting. Duff turned and flapped his gloves, waving Gilchrist away. 'This entry is for the gentry,' he said. 'Tradesmen use the back door.'

'Sorry.' Gilchrist had to turn and shuffle back down. The ground crew and a corporal wireless operator watched, boot-faced. *Sprog pilot puts up a black.* That's what they'd be thinking. *Can't find his way to the nav position. Jesus wept.* The walkway was narrow. Suppose he slipped now and trod on the port flap. It was only canvas-covered, he'd put a boot through it, the kite would be unserviceable. What a colossal black ... He reached the end and the ladder was waiting. They'd known he'd be coming back.

He ducked below the wing and clambered in through a door at the side of the under gunner's compartment. There was no powered turret; just a cell where the fuselage ended and the tail-boom began. Fancy being alone in here for umpteen hours, sealed in by a bulkhead. Not a cheery prospect. He squeezed sideways through a door in the bulkhead and walked uphill, slowly and clumsily. At its maximum, the Hampden's interior was three feet wide. So was Gilchrist, carrying a parachute pack and a navigator's bag; and obstructions narrowed his path: oxygen bottles, fire extinguishers, cables, hydraulic pipes, parachute stowages and awkward-shaped chunks of unidentified equipment.

He struggled over the main spar, a massive alloy girder that linked the wings to the fuselage. Now he was standing behind the pilot's seat. Directly above it was the sliding hood. If he had followed Duff through that space, he would have ended up sitting in Duff's lap, with nowhere to go except back out through the hood. What an idiot he'd been, worrying so much about navigating that he forgot he wasn't the pilot. Failed before he began.

A crawl-space under the pilot's seat led down to the nose cockpit. Gilchrist slid through it feet-first. The nose was roomy; he had a swivel-seat, a folding table, plenty of light. He took out his maps and studied the route again. Almost immediately he knew something was wrong. Panic nibbled at his guts. Once, on stage during a first night, he'd forgotten his lines. Now he felt the same rebellion in his stomach: not butterflies but bats, bloody great bloodsucking bats. The port engine fired and grew to a thunder that made the bomber shake. Gilchrist put on his helmet. Then he remembered. He plugged in the intercom.

'Ah,' Duff said. 'So glad you could join us.'

'Sorry, skipper.'

'Sorry isn't the word. Pathetic is better.'

At take-off the navigator's position was behind the pilot. Gilchrist went up the crawl-space on his hands and knees and sat on the main spar. Take-off was exhilarating. Duff built the engine revs higher than Gilchrist would have dared, got the Hampden bounding across the grass faster and into the air sooner than he thought possible. At a thousand feet Gilchrist slid back to the nose cockpit. Plugged in the intercom. A dull roar filled his ears.

'Navigator to pilot. Steer three one zero degrees.'

No answer.

He said it again. No answer. His repeater compass showed they were flying on zero eight zero degrees: almost due east, instead of north-west. 'Navigator to pilot,' he said, and the Hampden dropped its left wing so steeply that he had to grab the table. Maps, pencils, papers, calculators were scattered. The left wing came up slowly. He relaxed his grip. At once the right wing dropped steeply and he fell out of his seat.

This went on for some minutes. Then the bomber stopped rolling and began pitching: diving and climbing, plunging and rearing. Gilchrist tasted the wretched memory of his last meal. The pitching ended. He was on the floor, collecting maps, when Duff asked: 'Where are we, navigator?' Gilchrist looked out and saw nothing but sea. 'Up the creek,' he said.

'The course we're on will take us to Norway, if that's any help.'

'Turn back,' Gilchrist said feebly. 'Fly west.'

'Too vague, old son. I need an exact course.'

'If it's any help,' the wireless operator said, 'we're twenty miles south-east of Spurn Head.'

Gilchrist found a map and made a wild guess. 'New course two eight zero, repeat *two eight zero*. Please confirm.'

'No need to shout,' Duff said. 'I heard you the first time.'

The Hampden turned and flew sedately for the next half-hour. Gilchrist recognized landmarks – the great gash of the Humber estuary, the four-square mass of York Minster – and he recalculated the route to Carlisle.

'I'm losing power in the starboard engine, navigator,' Duff said. 'I'm not going to risk crossing the Pennines. Give me a course to Newcastle and then I'll fly up the Tyne Valley.'

Gilchrist did it. Ten minutes later Duff said the engine had recovered and he'd decided to risk the Pennines after all. Gilchrist scrapped his calculations and began all over again. He gave Duff the new course. Duff said it would take them over an army gunnery range: not wise. Gilchrist worked out a large dog-leg to avoid this. Duff then became worried about a nearby Spitfire squadron, notoriously trigger-happy. Gilchrist worked out another big dog-leg to avoid *that*. His map was a mess.

They missed Carlisle by about forty miles. 'That's Lake Windermere down there, skipper,' the wireless operator said. 'I had a jigsaw puzzle of it when I was a kid. Know it anywhere.'

'Forget Carlisle, navigator,' Duff said. 'Give me a course for Porthcawl.'

He climbed to twelve thousand feet, above the cloud. Now they were breathing oxygen. Gilchrist could see no landmarks. After two hours of dead reckoning he decided they were four miles north of Porthcawl. 'Navigator to pilot,' he said. 'ETA Porthcawl two minutes from now.'

Duff dived through the cloud. To Gilchrist the land was a vast map of a foreign country. 'Any guesses?' Duff said. He kept diving. Gilchrist had lost all faith in himself. He saw water but it looked wrong so he stayed silent. Still Duff lost height.

'Cardiff,' the wireless operator said. 'There's the Arms Park, where the Welsh play the rugby internationals. By the river.'

Gilchrist stared at his map, at the thirty-mile gap between Porthcawl and Cardiff. 'I don't understand,' he said. 'I double-checked everything. Twice.'

'Forget Porthcawl. Forget the bombing range. Have a cup of coffee and a nice piece of cake. I know the way home. Watch out for factory chimneys.'

Gilchrist drank coffee and looked at factory chimneys. Their smoke was streaming towards Lincolnshire, so the wind was from the south-west. But the meteorological officer had told him the predicted winds were south-east. He had made his course-corrections on the assumption that the aeroplane was being blown west, when all the time it was being blown east. So his corrections had pushed it even further east.

That night, in the Mess, he bought Duff a beer. 'I made a pig's ear of that, didn't I?' he said.

'Things always go wrong. That's the first rule of flying.'

'*Everything* went wrong. You made sure of that.'

'I get bored easily,' Duff said. 'It's my fatal flaw.'

Word of Gilchrist's unhappy afternoon soon spread around the squadron. Pug Duff's flight commander, Tom Stuart, sent for him. 'That wasn't a very nice thing to do, Pug,' he said.

'I agree, sir. I'm not a very nice person.'

'You may well have destroyed Gilchrist's self-confidence.'

'Good. If he's so fragile, he deserves the chop.'

'No, I'm not going to recommend that.' Stuart cleaned his fingernails with a paperknife. 'When you came here, I took you to be a fairly decent sort. Now you're developing a thoroughly vicious streak. Keep it up, Pug, and you'll be a flight lieutenant in no time.'

'Good show,' Duff said.

3

Flight Lieutenant McHarg got into his Bentley and had a severe shock. The driver's seat had been adjusted to suit someone with shorter legs.

Of course that could have been done by Sergeant Trimbull, or one of his mechanics. No it couldn't. McHarg had a deal with Trimbull. From time to time the sergeant was allowed to fire a machine gun in the butts, which were in a distant corner of the airfield. In return he kept the Bentley clean and polished, its oil, radiator and battery topped up, its tyres properly inflated. None of that involved moving the driver's seat.

McHarg restored it to its correct position and began looking for other irregularities. He found bits of gravel trapped in the tyre treads, a couple of dead bugs on the headlamps. There was some unfamiliar mud on the underside of the rear springs. Now he was profoundly disturbed. He felt attacked, invaded, almost raped. Reaction set in at once. 'Calm down, calm down,' he said aloud. Maybe, while he had the measles, some idiot mechanic had driven the Bentley around the aerodrome, maybe the car itself had not suffered. But he had to be sure. His hand trembled slightly as he turned the key in the ignition.

He drove out by the Main Gate and nursed the old girl up to fifty, went back down through the gears to walking pace, then accelerated again, keeping a check on the revs and the juice and the temperature. All went well. He relaxed, cruised around the lanes, came back to the base, reversed his lovely lady into her garage, gave the throttle a final burst as a sort of nightcap, and switched her off. He was hugely re-assured, but not for long. The worst was saved for last.

McHarg always drove his Bentley sparingly. He kept a notebook in the car. After every trip, he recorded the distance covered. He took the notebook from the glove compartment and glanced at the mileometer reading. His heart lurched. Between his last listing in the book and the mileage on the dashboard, there was a difference of four hundred and seven miles. Deduct three miles for today's road test. Some stinking bastard had stolen his Bentley and driven it more than four hundred miles.

He'd been counting dead bugs on the headlights while this proof was shouting for attention. He thrust the notebook into the glove compartment and his fingers touched soft leather. He pulled out a pair of ladies' gloves. Very light. Very expensive. Very wrong.

Well, it had to be an officer. No NCO would dare. It had to be someone who'd gone on leave. That meant 'A' Flight. He rapidly considered them all but he knew it was Silk because Silk had been so shifty, so twitchy, when he'd questioned him about the negligent dis-charge. And if it was Silk, it had to be Langham too. After eighteen years in the RAF, McHarg could smell conduct prejudicial to good order and discipline several miles away.

Silk and Langham. Went together like blood and thunder.

4

The war was becoming a bore.

Group HQ now required 409 to have six Hampdens on standby at all times: fuelled, armed, bombed up, the crews kitted out and bored to tears by the sight of the inside of the crew room from dawn to dusk. 'Shipping strikes,' Bins told them when they asked what the flap was about. But Group found no targets for them to strike. The war seemed a long way from Lincolnshire.

The Royal Navy got a bloody nose when a U-boat sneaked into Scapa Flow and sank a battleship. Nothing 409 could do about that. Too far north. Anyway, the navy had their own aeroplanes. President Roosevelt officially denied rumours that Americans would fight in Europe, so there must be some truth in them. Did America have any bombers? Nobody knew. All of a sudden Russia wanted a chunk of Finland, in order to protect Leningrad. Protect it from what? Was Finland about to invade Russia? Nobody knew. Nothing 409 could do about it anyway. Too far east. The only war that mattered was to the south, and nothing was happening there. The Frogs had their Maginot Line. Jerry had his Siegfried Line. One Line couldn't attack another, so it was stalemate. Nothing 409 could do about that. The gramophone played "We're Gonna Hang Out The Washing On The Siegfried Line". Bloody silly song. Who was going to drive out the Hun? Not 409. With luck their two-hundred-and-fifty-pound General Purpose bombs might chip the concrete. Assuming they exploded. Someone dropped the gramophone record, smashed it, total obliteration, loud cheers. 409 had scored at last.

With half the squadron on standby, the other half did training exercises. They flew around England to improve their navigation. They flew to bombing ranges and aimed practice bombs at targets. They flew to gunnery ranges and fired at canvas drogues towed by obsolete aircraft. This was good for the crews but bad for the aeroplanes. After forty hours in the air, a Hampden needed a major service.

It worried the Wingco. The crews weren't sharp enough, some of them treated the war almost as a joke, they needed to be pushed harder, given a good stiff jolt. But the war might take fire at any moment. Suppose – when it did – the hangars were full of Hampdens with Pegasus engines getting overhauls? 409 would be caught with its pants down.

Wingco Hunt rationed the flying training. That, of course, meant less work for everyone. Yet Bomber Command was still on full alert, and no aircrew were allowed off camp until sundown, by which time it was too late to go further than the village pub. A great deal of hanging around the Officers' Mess took place. Nobody hung around more than Flight Lieutenant McHarg.

Maiming Silk and Langham had been his first impulse. For a day or two he lived in a hot reverie of revenge: he dreamed of beating them bloody with a coal-shovel; or smashing kitchen chairs over their heads, dozens of chairs, pounding the pair to their knees in a sea of splinters; or kicking them across the aerodrome until they rolled like logs and one final almighty boot sent them flying into a stinking ditch. Other fantasies involved whips. As a boy, in Glasgow, McHarg had often been whipped. His father whipped him, using the buckle end of his belt. Schoolteachers whipped him, using the tawse, which was the official instrument of punishment, forked like a snake's tongue to enhance suffering. He knew a lot about how and where to whip people. What infuriated him was the sheer patronising arrogance of these two. They had behaved as if they had a right to take anything they wanted. They had assumed he wouldn't notice. If he did notice, they didn't care. He was just the Armaments Officer. No better than the ghillie who carried the guns for the gentlemen stalking the deer.

With time, his rabid fantasies lost their grip. Grudgingly he thought of lesser forms of revenge. Report the pair to the Station Commander? Rafferty wouldn't welcome petty complaints about pilots, not when there was a war on. See the Wingco? Or the Flight Commander? They'd tell him to put a stronger padlock on his garage. Soon everyone would know, and it would be a sodding great joke against him. Serve him right for being so tight-arsed about his bloody Bentley: that's what they'd all think. Well, let 'em. It was his Bentley. He'd find a better way to make those bastards pay. And almost by accident, he found it. He befriended them. That frightened the daylights out of them.

The idea came to him in the Mess.

Where they went, he went. If Silk was reading a newspaper, McHarg pulled up a chair and read the back page until Silk became so nervous that he gave him the whole paper and moved away. If Langham was talking with some pilots, McHarg stood next to him, nodded when he spoke, brayed with laughter at his jokes, until Langham couldn't stand it and got out. If Silk and Langham played chess, he came over and watched. Sometimes he shook his head at a move. Sometimes he sucked air through his teeth. Sometimes he braced himself and made a soft, gentle fart. The game usually ended quickly. He always asked who won. He always seemed pleased. At meals he sat opposite them, and busied himself making sure they had enough toast, butter, salt, marmalade, sugar, potatoes, mustard, custard. Conversation was impossible. As soon as they began talking, he offered them the salt. The rest of the squadron watched and did not interfere. McHarg's crooked, kindly smile was enough to keep anyone at bay. Only Tubby Heckter asked Langham what the hell was going on. 'Brain damage,' Langham said, and walked away.

Later that day, McHarg met Silk and Langham as they were coming back from a routine inspection of the Hampdens. 'You'll not believe this,' he said. The grit of Glasgow had got back into his speech. 'Some streak o' piss of a pilot asked me could he borrow my Bentley! Would you credit it?' He was tittering as he strode away. The childish noise was grotesquely at odds with his heavyweight build.

'He knows,' Silk said. 'I told you so.'

'He wants us to know he knows,' Langham said. 'He's playing games. Why is he playing games?'

'He's pissed off because he can't fly. We have all the fun, he's just a bloody Armaments Officer. Counts his boxes of bullets all day. Dusts his silly bombs. Boring.'

They followed McHarg at a distance. His heels had left dents in the grass.

'He killed a wog in Egypt,' Langham said. 'The Adj told me. This Arab broke into some RAF stores. Black Mac clipped his ear, broke his neck.'

'Gin,' Silk said. 'I need a big gin.'

5

Rafferty was irritated by the sight of so many young men sprawling about the Mess, drinking, dozing, yawning. He called a meeting of the senior officers. 'I bet the Luftwaffe isn't permanently on its backside,' he said. 'I bet Goering's got them galloping around the airfields in gym kits, carrying large telephone poles.'

'We had bayonet-fencing in the last war,' the adjutant said. They waited for him to explain. 'Lousy weather. No flying. So everyone in the hangars. Rifles with fixed bayonets. One chap against another.'

He demonstrated an imaginary thrust and parry.

'Sounds dangerous,' the MO said.

'It was rather bloody. But it made the chaps jump. Good exercise.'

'No, no. Far too risky,' Pixie Hunt said.

'Put 'em in overalls,' the Engineer Officer suggested. 'Make 'em help service the kites.'

'God, no,' Hunt said. 'They'll break everything they touch.'

Other ideas failed, until Bins suddenly said: 'Escape exercise.' Rafferty grunted encouragement. 'If they come down in enemy territory,' Bins said, 'their duty is to escape. Why don't we drop them miles from here and –'

'You mean *parachute* them?' Rafferty asked. 'These chaps have never jumped in their lives.'

'Lincolnshire is just flat farmland, sir. Easy landing.'

'Half a dozen compound fractures,' the MO said confidently. 'Bet you.'

'Anyway, we're on full alert,' Hunt said. 'Dawn to dusk.'

'Do it at night, sir,' Bins said. 'Forget parachutes. Put the boys in sealed trucks. Empty their pockets. No equipment, no food, no money. Then dump them in twos and threes all over the county, just as if they'd baled out. Tell them to make their way here.'

'Without getting caught!' Rafferty cried. 'The army can play the enemy. They love manoeuvres.'

It was a splendid idea, made more splendid by the fact that others would do all the work. For the first and only time, Flight Lieutenant McHarg spoke. 'I know the land very well, sir,' he said. 'I'll guarantee to take the boys to places that will test their fighting spirit.' He got the job.

News of the exercise surprised the pilots and observers. Rafferty was pleased. 'Nobody knows when he may have to bale out,' he told them. The trucks were waiting. 'Your duty is to evade capture, and return to base,' he said. 'Enemy troops, in the uniform of the Black Watch, are out to hunt you down.' The night was heavily overcast. As they climbed into the trucks, rain began to fall. 'Your luck's in,' Rafferty said. 'This will lend you valuable cover.' Nobody spoke. 'Cheerie-bye,' he said. The canvas flaps were lashed shut. The trucks moved off, their hooded headlights intercepting streaks of rain. 'They seemed to get the hang of it,' he said. 'Now, who's for bridge?'

* * *

Silk, Langham and eight other officers were in one truck. No seats. No light. They sat on the floor, absorbing the merciless jolts of fast driving on bad roads. After an hour the truck stopped, the driver opened the back, and two men went into the night. This happened every ten minutes. Silk and Langham were the last pair. When the truck stopped, the man who opened the canvas flaps was not the driver but McHarg. 'Mind the puddle,' he said, but it was too deep and wide. They jumped, and water filled their shoes. 'Deary me,' he said. The truck drove away. The rain was a heavy drizzle. 'The farmers will be glad of this,' he said. There was just enough light to show that he was wearing an oilskin cape and gumboots.

'Don't tell me you're taking part in this farce,' Langham said.

'Och, no. I'm just out for a wee stroll.'

'A wee *stroll*?' Silk's voice cracked. 'Where are we? How far's the base?'

'Dear, dear. What a question. I'm not allowed to say.'

'Well, we intend to go the wrong way,' Langham said. 'So feel free to stroll in the opposite direction. Come on, Silko.'

McHarg followed them along the lane. It was not possible to see the liquid mud, the rain-filled potholes, the pools of cowshit. They slipped and stumbled. Muck splattered them to the knees. They walked a long way to reach a crossroads. It was no help: too dark, and in any case signposts everywhere had been removed in order to baffle German invaders. Silk chose the biggest road. They trudged along, feet squelching, icy hands in armpits, rain soaking steadily through to their underwear. McHarg trailed them. Sometimes he hummed a tune known only to him.

'Look,' Silk said. It was a shape in a field, a blur darker than the night. 'Wait,' he said. He climbed a gate and was gone. Langham thought the rain felt wetter when he was standing than when he was walking, but he said nothing. Silk appeared at the gate. 'Barn,' he said. 'Bloody big barn. Come on.'

It was dry inside, and even blacker than the night outside. 'Lots of hay over here,' Silk said. 'Stinks a bit.' Langham followed his voice. The hay was like a feather bed. Langham groaned as he sank into it and felt all his muscles relax. 'Genius,' he said.

McHarg had come into the barn. After a while he said: 'Your orders are to return to base as soon as possible.'

'Stuff the orders,' Silk mumbled.

'Someone should stand guard. Watch out for enemy troops.'

'You're up,' Langham said. 'You do it.'

'I'm not the one who's trying to escape. I'm just out for a wee stroll.'

'So stroll. Scarper. Go forth and multiply. Leave us in peace.'

Silk was actually asleep, and Langham was drifting out of consciousness, when a bang like a mid-air collision jerked them awake. Before their eyes could open, a brilliant blaze reached their eyeballs. They were half-dazzled as they struggled to their feet. McHarg roared, 'Escape!' Silk tripped over his own feet and went sprawling. 'Escape what?' Langham asked. The air stank of chemicals. 'Run, you fool!' McHarg shouted. 'Before you're surrounded!' A second bang seemed to rock the barn; its stab of light showed McHarg at the door, pointing. Silk and Langham ran into the night.

McHarg caught up with them a mile away, as they lay under a tree, resting their ruined lungs.

'You're all right now,' he said softly. 'I told them you went the other way.'

'Who?' Silk asked. 'And how the hell did they knew we were there?'

'Gordon Highlanders. Very clever wee soldiers.'

'Bastards.'

'Aye, probably. But cunning bastards.'

The rain was worse, and the tree gave little protection. Silk and Langham pressed on. Clay stuck to their shoes until they felt like oversized clogs. They found a lane and sat and peeled off the clay. 'Which way now?' McHarg asked. For answer, Langham hurled a ball of clay, and pointed. 'Wrong way,' McHarg said.

'We could kill him, Tony,' Silk said. 'Beat his head in with a rock. Blame it on the brown jobs.'

'Aye. Clever wee soldiers,' Langham said.

'Only trying to help,' McHarg said.

The lane went on, and on, and then Silk saw a farmhouse. 'Your turn,' he said.

A dog howled and lunged on its chain as they went up the path to the front door. 'I feel an unpleasant sense of *déjà vu*,' Langham murmured. He used the door-knocker. They waited. Apart from the bloody dog, now trying to choke itself, the place was dead. He knocked again. Light flared at an upstairs window. It opened with a crash and a woman with a double-barrelled shotgun looked out. 'Stop your noise!' she shouted. 'Get away from here!'

'Oh, Christ,' Silk muttered.

'Madam, we are RAF officers,' Langham called out. 'Pilots. We need help. Our aeroplane has crashed.'

'Serve you bloody right. Bloody RAF, bloody planes over my hen-houses so low I could touch the buggers, no wonder my hens don't bloody lay, now sod off fast.'

'There's a war on, madam. I'm sure a patriot like you –'

'You got a funny way of speakin'. You're one of they Sixth Columnists, aren't you?'

'You're thinking of *Fifth* Columnists. I assure you –'

She fired the shotgun at the sky. 'And I assure *you* the second barrel won't be wasted.' She swung the gun towards them.

They ran back to the lane. 'You're in breach of the blackout regulations, you miserable old hag!' Langham shouted; but by now the window was shut.

'No luck?' McHarg said. He was eating chocolate.

'I've been thinking,' Silk said. 'How did those explosives get into that barn?'

'Booby-trapped,' McHarg said.

'How did anyone know we'd use the barn?' Langham asked.

'Scots soldiers are clever wee bastards.'

They walked on, more slowly now because all their clothing was sodden and their wet socks were causing blisters. After half a mile they reached a railway bridge over the road, and sheltered under it. 'If a car comes we ambush it,' Silk said. No car came. The tunnel trapped a cold wind.

'How is your morale?' McHarg asked. No answer. Eventually Langham sneezed, twice. 'I'll take a wee stroll,' McHarg said.

Time passed. Five minutes, ten, twenty: nobody was counting. The same appalling *crack-bang*! deafened and dazzled them, worse this time because the explosion was in the tunnel. The noise sent them sprawling. 'Oh, sod it,' Silk said wretchedly. His brain seemed to ricochet around his skull. A second blinding blast struck them. They got up and staggered out and ran. Their lungs had been down this road before and they had no enthusiasm for it. Silk saw a gap in the hedge and he grabbed Langham's arm. The field was black and filthy and stretched for miles, like all bloody fields. They hid behind the hedge.

McHarg slow-marched up the lane, crooning "The Skye Boat Song" in his high-pitched, childlike singing voice. Headlights appeared; a Bren-gun carrier bustled towards him and stopped. A sergeant jumped out and saluted. 'Saw lights, sir. Looked like thunderflashes.'

'You mean like this?' McHarg tossed a couple of thunderflashes over the hedge. Briefly they demolished the night. 'Nobody here, is there? Ah, gunpowder has a braw peppery smell ... Look under the railway bridge, sergeant. That's where they're hiding.'

'No we're not,' Silk said. 'And we surrender.' They came out through the hole in the hedge and climbed into the Bren-gun carrier, 'Hello, Tubby. Fancy meeting you here.'

'I shall never bale out,' Tubby Heckter said. 'It's exhausting.'

Everyone got back to base, one way or another, by dawn. Eight members of 'B' Flight arrived first. They had seized the driver of their truck and his map-reading assistant, and spent the evening playing darts in a pub called the Goat and Compasses.

'We owe the landlord a fiver,' said the 'B' Flight commander, a squadron leader called Micky Byrd. 'His wife's nephew is a cook on a Wimpy squadron, so he trusted us. Who's winning, sir?'

Rafferty and Hunt were still playing bridge with Bins and the MO.

'Not exactly in the spirit of the exercise, was it?' Rafferty said.

'It was a democratic decision, sir. We all voted. And the two erks weren't hurt. In fact they each ended up as pissed as a fiddler's bitch, and I had to drive.'

'This situation was a simulated bale-out,' Hunt said. 'You escaped *before* you were dropped. It's not possible. It's nonsensical.'

'Nobody said anything about that at the briefing.'

'If you come down in Germany,' Bins said, 'do you think the enemy will let you capture his truck?'

'Well, at least we know how to set about it,' Byrd said defiantly.

'Three spades,' Rafferty said.

Apart from Micky Byrd's group, nobody escaped capture. Lincolnshire – flat, wet, and thoroughly blacked out – was too much for them. Most officers were caught, usually when walking in the wrong direction. Some surrendered. Pug Duff overpowered the soldier guarding him, escaped on a horse, but was finally surrounded. A wireless op fell off a farm gate and broke an arm. At breakfast next day, Wingco Hunt said, 'Well, that's given them a taste of the real thing, Uncle.'

'Oh,' the adjutant said. 'Do you really think so?'

A Mess waiter interrupted them. Hunt was wanted on the telephone. Urgently. He hurried off.

Bins said, 'It's not like you to sound sceptical.'

The adjutant chopped the head off his boiled egg. 'I think I'm the only man on this squadron who's actually baled out of an aeroplane. Flying display at Hendon, 1922. Fell into a tree. Cut my head. Couldn't see for blood.'

'Bad luck.'

'Yes. Fell out of the tree, broke an ankle.'

'Oh dear.'

'Chap gave me a swig of brandy and I was sick all over his shoes. Never give brandy to a man who's had a bash on the head, Bins. They do it all the time in films, don't they? Not a good idea. The tum doesn't like it. Up comes dinner. Now *that's* a taste of the real thing. Frightful taste, too. So you see, last night wasn't realistic. If those chaps had actually baled out, half of them would have ended up in trees, half in bogs, and half in hospital. Like me.'

'You can't have three halves, old chap.'

'Yes you can. Jump out of an aeroplane and anything's possible.'

BEATEN TO A FROTH

1

Hunt returned. Big flap on. Group wanted three Hampdens airborne now or sooner. German convoy reported off Friesian Islands. Breakfast ended instantly.

Hunt decided to lead the patrol. A Wingco's ops were strictly rationed by Group, so he liked to pick the tough jobs. It helped to remind the boys that he could be airborne as well as chairborne. He picked two crews from 'B' Flight, one captained by a Canadian, Stubby Gurnee, the other by a gloomy Welshman, Happy Hall. The Wingco knew them to be solid, competent pilots who listened to orders and worked hard at the job. This was no day for cowboys.

He briefed them in the crew room as they got dressed. 'Enemy convoy off the north German coast. Could be heading anywhere: Emden, Wilhelmshaven, Bremerhaven, up the Elbe to Hamburg, nobody knows. Certain to have an escort, destroyers probably. If so, we bomb the escort; if not, we bomb the convoy. We'll each carry four five-hundred-pounders. What are the winds?'

The Met man said, 'I'll spare you the technical analysis. It boils down to this: we expect strong easterly winds to cross the North Sea this morning. You might reach your search area before the gale gets there. Here are the predictions.' He handed out sheets of paper.

'So it'll blow us home,' Hunt said. 'Cloud? Rain? Fog?'

'Five-tenths cloud at first, thickening steadily. Intermittent rain, perhaps snow. Depends on your height.'

'We'll be low. Look at this.' The pilots and observers gathered round the map. Hunt's finger traced a broken necklace of oddly shaped islands off the shores of Holland and Germany. 'Remember, the German islands look like cocktail sausages, each smaller than the last. Our route leads to the last island, Wangeroog. If we overshoot it, we'll soon see the coastline where it turns north. We'll make a pinpoint and start the search. Bins?'

'Intelligence on the convoy is thin. It's either genuine or a decoy to test our response. We know that anti-aircraft defences on the Friesians are being strengthened.' Bins saw that Hunt was impatient. 'Avoid Holland and Denmark, which also have guns.'

They lumbered out, layered with flying kit, carrying parachutes, helmets, thermos flasks, sandwiches, chocolate, and piled into a truck. The Hampdens smelt cold and damp. A seagull had shat on Happy Hall's canopy and the groundcrew were cleaning it off and polishing the perspex. The engines were warm. The three bombers taxied out and formed a line abreast. The Wingco glanced left and right, and released his brakes. Even carrying nearly three tons of fuel and bombs, the Hampdens needed only half the runway. As they went over the perimeter, they panicked a flock of gulls on the ground. The gulls knew this was no day to go to sea.

2

'Darling!' Zoë Herrick said. 'Hullo,' Langham said. Then her arms were around his neck and she was kissing him, on the mouth, very warmly. He saw her reflection in a tall mirror. Right foot on the carpet, left leg bent, foot raised high behind her. Pure Hollywood. Damn nice legs. 'Come and meet Mummy,' she said. 'Delighted,' he said. Dissipated would have been more accurate, but he knew she wasn't interested in the night before.

The Scottish soldiers had been very hospitable. Silk and Langham had been taken to their Officers' Mess and revived with whisky. More captured escapees arrived; more whisky appeared. The soldiers were frankly disappointed that the exercise had ended so quickly. Some drunken fool of a pilot challenged them to Highland dancing. Then everything was a giddy whirl, powered by whisky. Langham couldn't remember going to bed. His batman woke him at eleven: a

Rolls-Royce was waiting. Lunch at Bardney Castle House. 'I can't,' he croaked. 'I'm on standby.'

'You can, sir. Your fiancée sent the car, and Mr Rafferty's released you.'

Langham scratched his head and found clots of mud. His mouth was so dry that it hurt. He summoned up a little saliva. It was worse. Tasted like a night in a glue factory. 'What happened?' he asked.

'Too much grog, sir, same as usual. I ran a bath.'

Bardney Castle House was five miles outside Lincoln. There hadn't been a castle for three hundred years; a Queen Anne mansion occupied the keep. It had enough fluted chimneys to keep a small colliery in business. Peacocks strutted in the park. When Langham got out of the Rolls he had a sinking sensation in his wallet. It quickly passed. Someone else was paying for this feed.

Zoë led him into a room lightly scattered with large pieces of furniture. 'Mummy, I'd like you to meet Tony,' she said. 'Tony, this is my mother, Lady Shapland.'

'How do you do.' As he came forward, Langham tried to hide the fact that he was both limping and hobbling. They shook hands. 'Call me Philly. Short for philistine or philanderer or some damn thing,' she said. 'I can never remember.' She was a deep redhead, exactly as tall as her daughter, and she was as American as Rita Hayworth. 'Not to be confused with the female pony of the same name. Which reminds me. I had a horse like you, but I shot him.'

'I say!' Langham's brain was still sluggish. 'Rather extreme, wasn't it?'

'Well, he couldn't run, so he wasn't worth a damn. What's wrong with your feet?'

'Ah. Yes. Training exercise last night. Got slightly wounded.' He smiled. 'Fortunes of war.'

'Take your shoes off. Let me see.' He began to protest but she said, 'Just do it. I own racehorses, I know about feet.'

'Mummy's horse won the big race at Newmarket last Saturday,' Zoë said.

'If you insist.' Taking off his shoes meant bending his legs. His right knee suddenly hurt and he grabbed it. 'Just a twinge.'

'Take your pants off too.'

'Oh, look here. Is this absolutely essential?'

'Nobody marries my daughter who's deformed, decrepit or defunct.'

He lay on a sofa. She pierced and drained his blisters, and coated them with a dark green cream. 'Snake oil,' she said. 'Comanche chief sold it me on his deathbed.' She manipulated his knee. 'Ice-cold compress tonight. Don't do the Charleston for a week.' She looked at the scratches and bruises on his legs. 'You got this way flying a Spitfire? Ever tried flying it *above* ground?'

Zoë had given him a big Scotch and soda. He felt strong enough to shrug.

'I'll take the rest of your equipment on trust,' Philly said. She handed him his trousers. 'This family needs a male heir. Husbands keep dying on me, and Zoë can't tell a dime from a dollar. I had an idea. You like this place?'

'Bardney Castle? I've only just seen it.'

'Take it. Wedding present. For you and her.'

'Frightfully decent of you.'

'Dump the staff. Or keep 'em, whichever you like. This is handy for your Spitfires, right? Your field's just up the road. Okay, let's have lunch.'

They went into another room. 'I was born in a shack in Kentucky you could fit in here and still have room to pitch horseshoes,' she said. 'This is the Bishop of Lincoln. Charlie, meet Tony. Mind you, the fried chicken was better in Kentucky.'

The bishop said grace. He was slim and brisk, with a full head of thick, silvery hair. Smoked salmon and wafer-thin brown bread were served, with a crisp white Bordeaux. 'You play the banjo, I'm told,' the bishop said, amiably.

'Do I?' Langham said. 'I don't think so.'

'That was the last chap,' Zoë told the bishop.

'Really?' He shot his cuffs, and read the pencilled notes on the left-hand cuff. 'Nobody told *me*. I'm only her godfather,' he said to Langham. 'Only the guardian of her morals. *Which* last chap?' he asked her.

'The stockbroker with the eyebrows.'

'You didn't like him, Charlie,' Philly said.

'Because he was obsessed with his banjo,' the bishop said. 'There is more to marriage than the banjo, which is perfectly useless for pro-creation, for instance.'

'We're going to procreate, aren't we, darling?'

'Morning, noon and night.' Langham was amazed at his own

candour; but nobody else seemed to notice. 'Here, there and every-where,' he added. Still no effect. Philly was asking the bishop if he had backed the horses she had tipped at Kempton Park.

A superb cheese soufflé was served, with a Provençal rosé.

'Have you noticed,' the bishop said, 'how we keep fighting our wars in *northern* France, where the wine is lethal, instead of, say, the Rhône valley, where it's at least robust?'

'Charlie was in the Trenches,' Philly said.

'Were you really?' Langham said. 'What did you think of the Royal Flying Corps?'

'We thought they made a jolly good target.'

'You mean you fired at them?'

'If they came close. Mistakes happen in war. We made our mistakes before they could make theirs.'

'Talking of mistakes,' Philly said. 'I had drinks at the American embassy yesterday. Joe Kennedy reckons this war is a poor joke. He says France hasn't got the guts to fight, and England hasn't got the money.'

'Kennedy's just an old bootlegger, mummy,' Zoë said. 'He's a dreadful thug. Everyone knows that. He doesn't understand Europe.'

'He's a successful thug. Bought and sold the Democrat vote in Massachusetts, didn't he? After Massachusetts, Europe is a kindergarten, believe me.'

'This is a silly question,' the bishop said to Langham, 'so feel free not to answer. Are we going to win?'

'At a canter,' Langham said; which at least made Philly laugh.

Pears in red wine. Coffee. Brandy.

Mother and daughter went off to discuss wedding plans. The men strolled in the grounds.

'Remarkable lady,' the bishop said. 'I can't imagine what it was like to be married to her. Good food but not much rest, probably.'

'Who gave her the title?'

'Lord Shapland. Second husband. Killed when his aeroplane crashed, poor devil.'

'It's a quick way to go.'

'Mm.' The bishop decided not to pursue that subject. 'Some say he was her third husband. Rumours of a liaison in Texas with an oil millionaire. The Church is awfully sticky about divorce. I prefer to turn a blind eye.'

'She's not at all what I expected. Very forceful. I must admit I'm glad Zoë isn't a bit like her mother.'

'No.' The bishop thought about it. 'I mean yes.' He cleared his throat. 'Shapland left Philly a vast amount of property. She's a major landowner, you know.'

'I do know. She's just given this place to me. Well, to us.'

They turned and looked at the building. From this angle, a separate chapel and a stable block were visible.

'You'll need a bicycle to get from the bathroom to the breakfast room,' the bishop said. 'I'd sell it, if I were you.'

Langham was shocked. 'But it's a wedding present.'

'Then buy a tandem. Put the butler on the front seat. You'll need all your energy, once you're married.'

3

When the Friesian Islands came into view they were the wrong size and shape. They were also twenty minutes late. Hunt couldn't believe it.

For nearly two hours his trio of Hampdens had cruised across the North Sea, seeing nothing but cloud above and water below. The cloud was grey tinged with black, the water was grey spiked with white. At first Hunt was able to let the automatic pilot do the flying. Then the cloud base came down to a thousand feet and the sea was more white than grey. The air should have got warmer as he flew lower, but it felt much colder. And much bumpier.

His observer was an experienced flight lieutenant called Paddy Mason, and he saw the island first. 'That's Terschelling on the starboard quarter, skipper,' he said.

'It can't be,' Hunt said. 'Terschelling's Dutch. We're miles past Holland by now. Aren't we?'

There was silence on the intercom while Hunt and Mason and the two gunners looked at the island. It was too distant to reveal anything except a thin, flat silhouette. 'It's Terschelling, all right,' Mason said. 'Look at the length of it. Twice as long as any German island.'

'Come up here, Paddy. Bring your maps.'

Mason crawled up the tunnel, plugged in his intercom, spread the maps. Hunt's finger traced the line of the Friesians from west to east. Texel, Vlieland, Terschelling, Ameland, Schiermonnikoog. 'Extraordinary language,' he murmured. Then some driblets of land before Holland ended and Germany began with the island of Borkum. Next came Juist, Norderney, Langeoog, somewhere unreadable in the crease of the map, finally Wangeroog where you turned right for Wilhelmshaven, which was where he had expected to be. 'If that's Terschelling,' he said, 'we're ten degrees off track, and your dead reckoning is completely duff.'

The Hampdens had no radio communication between them, but Stubby Gurnee had seen the island and guessed that Hunt was slightly lost. 'Try and get some bearings,' he told his wireless operator. 'See if you can cook up a rough fix.'

His wireless operator was Aircraftsman First Class York. His RAF trade was radio mechanic; flying was a bonus. He searched until he got a strong signal: a band playing 'Twelfth Street Rag'. He switched on his intercom. 'Skipper, I'm pretty sure I've got Radio Hilversum on a bearing of one eight two degrees.'

'That puts us off Terschelling,' the observer said.

'Let's hear it, Yorky,' Gurnee said. York connected the music to the intercom. The dash of jazz trumpet, witty and cheerful, was wasted in this grey alloy tube. 'Louis Armstrong,' Gurnee said. 'Never,' the under gunner said. 'More like Tommy Dorsey.' York blew a raspberry. The jazz ended, an announcer chattered happily. 'Is that Dutch?' Gurnee asked.

'Sounds kind of like Belgian,' his observer said.

Gurnee listened some more. 'What does Belgian sound like?' he asked. 'Never mind. Search east, Yorky. Maybe there's a Radio Hamburg.'

In the third bomber, Happy Hall was not surprised to see a Dutch island. 'I never trusted those bloody predicted winds, Kenny,' he told his observer. 'Silly sod of a Met man's got everything wrong again. What's our true ground-speed?'

'Pretty pathetic. I'll do some sums. Fuel consumption must be up.'

'Wireless op,' Hall said. 'Stop picking your nose and come up here and give me some coffee and a sandwich.' Buffeting made his voice shake. 'I don't intend to die hungry. This weather is turning into a real bitch. There goes Terschelling.' While he was speaking, rain blotted out the island.

The Wingco did what he must: he slogged on. At least he knew where he was. A course of seventy or eighty degrees should take the Hampdens parallel to the Friesians, provided they crabbed hard enough into the wind. Everything depended on its strength and direction. The North Sea was getting beaten to a froth. Wherever he looked, it resembled white corduroy.

In fact, the bombers never saw another island. Rain closed in until visibility was down to a few hundred yards. The silly sod of a Met man had got one thing right: the storm met them just as they reached their search area.

When Paddy Mason reckoned they were ten miles north of Wangeroog, Hunt began a square search for the convoy: ten miles north, west, south and then twenty miles east to set up the next ten-mile box. The cloud base kept dropping, pressing them down, seven hundred feet, six hundred. The wind hammered the bombers until it was impossible to keep formation. Hunt looked left and right and saw his wingmen dropping and climbing like horses on a fairground roundabout, only more so. Much more so. When they blundered into rain, which was often, it coated the Perspex and everyone was flying on instruments. Hail was worse.

He kept up the search for two hours. Maybe there was a convoy. Maybe it was in port by now. Paddy Mason got out the Aldis lamp and signalled to the other Hampdens: *Return to base*. At least the storm would blow them home.

Stubby Gurnee lost the other two in an especially black rain squall. It didn't matter; he couldn't miss England. After two and a half hours there was no sight of land; only the perpetually angry sea. The radio was playing up: York couldn't get a fix. At last Gurnee got a QDM from some station, but the signal was faint. When an aircraft asked for a QDM, the station responding gave a magnetic bearing. If the pilot flew along that bearing, then eventually, and making allowance for wind, he should reach that station. Gurnee got a QDM of zero three five degrees, which was almost north-east. But if England was north-east, Gurnee must be south-west. That would place him somewhere over the English Channel.

'D'you believe that?' he asked his observer.

'Only if the wind changed and blew us south.'

Gurnee tried to get another QDM. No luck.

The English Channel widens dramatically as you go west, so Gurnee was moving further and further away from the English coast. He heard nothing more. He didn't trust that faint QDM. If it was wrong, and he turned and headed north-east, he would simply fly deeper into the North Sea. An hour later – after more than eight hours' flying – he knew the QDM must have been right. Now he turned north; but now his tanks were down to the dregs, and soon the angry sea swallowed the Hampden like a titbit.

Langham found Silk in his room, lying on his bed, not reading a book. 'Guess what,' he said. 'My popsy's mother has just given us a house to live in.'

'Fancy that.'

'Big place. It's even got peacocks.'

'Well, that's nice.'

'Near Lincoln. Made me think, life's a bit like playing Monopoly, isn't it? Last night I was knee-deep in muck, running away from the army. Today I won a socking great country house.'

'More like snakes and ladders,' Silk said. 'Stubby Gurnee's overdue. In the drink, probably. Him and his crew.'

'Ah,' Langham said. 'Yes. I suppose that is different.'

For a few days, the MO discreetly observed the reaction of the aircrews, and saw their lack of reaction. Perhaps the Mess was slightly quieter the day after Gurnee was missing. It soon recovered. People were always coming and going on a bomber station: they got posted, sent on courses, developed tonsillitis, got lost and pranged the kite when they came down in Scotland and weren't seen again for a fortnight. Everybody moved, sooner or later. Nobody lost any sleep over it.

AWFUL RESTLESS STUFF

The Americans were beginning to call it the Phoney War. For the French it was *la drôle de guerre*: the joke war. In Germany they watched nothing happen on the Siegfried and Maginot Lines and christened it Sitzkrieg: sitting war. Churchill, who was in Chamberlain's Cabinet as First Lord of the Admiralty, called it the Twilight War, which was too poetic for the British. They preferred the Bore War. It was a pun on the Boer War. All but the thickest recognised that. And Britain had won the Boer War. Britain always won, in the long run. Everyone knew that.

Rafferty and Hunt were determined that 409 was not going to be allowed to be bored. The crews were kept busy. If they couldn't fly, they trained. They did PT, ran around the aerodrome, were drilled on the parade ground; and they went to lectures, endless lectures, on meteorology, bomb-aiming, optimum cruising speeds and fuel consumption, air-firing, aircraft recognition, the history of the RAF, military law, oxygen depletion, more meteorology, astro-navigation, first aid including resuscitation, aircraft recognition again. And then one afternoon, when 'B' flight was on standby, 'A' Flight went to a distant corner of the aerodrome for a lecture by Black Mac on Why Bombs Explode.

He stood beside an array of bombs, set up on the floor of a flatbed truck. The crews gathered in a half-circle. Silk and Langham hid at the back.

McHarg enjoyed lecturing aircrew. It allowed him to put them in their place. For a start, he adopted a bogus, over-educated Scottish accent: Edinburgh, not Glasgow: the kind of sing-song style he imagined a university don or a successful advocate might use.

'There are some folk,' he began, 'who regard the British bomber pilot and his friends as the cream of the Royal Air Force. Gallant knights in armour, sallying forth to fight His Majesty's foes. Nnn?' This tiny, nasal snort punctuated his lecture. 'A romantic view. Truth is, the bomb does the damage, so the bomb deserves the credit. Nnn? Rather like the butcher's boy on his bicycle, delivering the meat. Which matters more, the meat or the boy? Nnn? So now –'

'Don't agree,' said Tom Stuart, the flight commander. 'Your sausages are no good if your butcher's boy takes them to the wrong address.'

McHarg recoiled an inch. 'That thought never entered my mind, squadron leader. Totally miss the target, d'you mean? Is that a common occurrence, would you say?'

'No, but ...'

'That's a relief, then. We can ignore such a rare event. Nnn? Yes. All agree, the bomb is king.'

'He's taking the piss,' Silk whispered to Langham.

'Is there a question at the back?' McHarg asked, and stood on tiptoe. Silk and Langham ducked. 'No? Well now, let us meet the bomb family. Here we have the General Purpose two-hundred-and-fifty-pound and five-hundred-pound.' The bigger bomb was about five feet high and was painted olive green. He patted and stroked it like a pet dog. 'How many here think "General Purpose" means it's good for all jobs?' A few tentative hands went up. 'You're all buffoons,' McHarg said. 'GP simply means it will fit in the bay of any RAF bomber in service. We have three main types of this bomb: high explosive, armour-piercing, and fragmentation. HE overwhelms the enemy, armour-piercing underwhelms him, and fragmentation whelms what's left standing.' Nobody even smiled. He hid his disappointment. That had been his only joke, written down when he heard it told at an Advanced Armaments Course in 1937. Well, sod the lot of them.

'I could talk for hours about the ballistic properties of the GP bomb,' he said. 'Nnn? But what you want to know is precisely how the weapon is fused and armed. Nnn? Child's play. Take a detonator and a pistol. Not a handgun, you understand. Nnn? This pistol is a mechanical device inserted in the weapon. Upon release from the aircraft, the pistol is automatically armed. It contains a striker. On impact with the target, the striker is struck, and it impels by explosion an initiator cap into the detonator, which initiates a sequence ...'

It took him twenty minutes. A chill wind was whipping around the aerodrome. Hands were deep in pockets, tunic collars were turned up, legs were starting to stiffen. 'Turning to ballistics ...' he said.

'No. Forget ballistics,' Tom Stuart said. 'Just tell us what can go wrong with bombs. And what can be done about it.'

Everyone got interested.

'Well, of course, armourers never let anything go wrong, because that would be unthinkable. Nnn? But I've brought along two examples of what *could* theoretically go wrong if ...' He pointed to a two-hundred-and-fifty-pounder. 'Explosive is awful restless stuff. Awful *curious*. After a few years in a bomb dump it exudes. The word is from the Latin, meaning "sweat". It sweats through the pores of the casing and it crystallizes on the outside.' They edged forward to see. The bomb was coated with brown crystals like Demerara sugar. 'The exuded matter can be scraped off. The scrapings are what we call ... volatile.' He looked around until he found Silk. 'A wee experiment,' he said, and gave Silk a hammer. Everyone fell back. McHarg used a wooden spatula to scrape some crystals off the bomb. He walked away and placed the spatula on the ground. 'Give it a wee smack,' he said. Silk bent low, reached sideways, and gave the crystals a gentle tap. The bang sent him sprawling on his backside, and startled everyone except McHarg. He picked up the hammer. 'Awful restless wee things,' he said.

'So that's one problem,' Tom Stuart said.

'The other thing is very, very unlikely. We've been issued with what's called the Long Delay pistol.' He showed them one. 'For when your bomb does not immediately explode.' He stared at Langham. 'Now what would be the point of that?'

'To annoy Jerry's civil defence people,' Langham said. 'Bomb goes off hours later.'

'Or maybe sooner. There's a nose fuse that's very sensitive. The German bomb disposal laddies disturb it. Detonation occurs.'

'Tough on them,' Stuart said. 'Not us. Until the bomb gets armed, that fuse is harmless.'

'So it is, squadron leader.'

'Then what's the problem?'

'In theory, there's a very remote possibility that the arming device could be activated prematurely, while loading the bomb on the aircraft. Now, if its Long Delay pistol was set for, say, six hours …'

It was too late for Stuart to stop the discussion. 'You're saying it would explode six hours later. Perhaps during flight.'

'In theory. Not on this squadron, of course. My men take every precaution. No risk at all here.'

'Okay, that's enough,' Stuart said. 'This lecture's over.'

The crews walked briskly away, glad of the exercise.

'That was a bloody stupid thing to tell them,' Stuart said.

'You asked what could go wrong.'

'And what we could do about it. There's damn all my boys can do about Long Delay pistols except worry. Thank you very bloody much.'

'No mistake will happen here.'

'How d'you know? How d'you know Gurnee's bombs didn't blow him up two days ago, over the North Sea?'

'Gurnee was lost on a shipping strike. Long Delay pistols are never used for a shipping strike. You want detonation on impact.'

'In theory.' Stuart turned and strode away.

A hundred yards away, Silk said, 'He picked us out. Did you notice? First me, then you. He was sending a message.'

'What do Long Delay bombs look like?' Langham asked. 'Do they look any different?'

'Dunno. And for Christ's sake don't ask *him*. You might put ideas in his stupid head.'

STABILIZED BOLLOCKS

1

All over Britain the blackout was complete. No streetlights; all bus and train windows painted blue; vehicle headlamps masked so that only a gleam escaped. Shops rapidly sold out of torch batteries. Pedestrians walked blindly through the night, colliding with lampposts, telephone poles, trees, and each other. Also with moving vehicles. There was no change in speed limits, and so twice as many British people were killed on the roads in wartime than in peace. It got worse as the nights grew longer. The war might be phoney but the death toll was real.

Tucked away in the calm and quiet of Lincolnshire, where the biggest hazard on the roads was a rocketing pheasant or partridge, RAF Kindrick was relatively safe. Shame about Stubby Gurnee, but replacements soon arrived. Life went on.

Then the teleprinter clattered, and an order came down from Group HQ. With immediate effect, all Hampden aircraft carrying out training flights or air tests would do so with a full bombload, to duplicate operational conditions. It made sense; as Pug Duff pointed out, a crew should train the way it was going to have to fight. Even Langham agreed. He didn't trust Black Mac, he thought the man was capable of hiding delayed-action thunderflashes in the kite, timed to go off at ten thousand feet. That was ludicrous, of course; he wasn't so stupid as to play the fool with his own career. But Langham worried all the same. And he had one final air test to do. It was on the morning of his wedding.

His Hampden was D-Dog. He'd flown Dog for months; she was his, she had no vices, he was proud of her. So were his ground crew. A sergeant rigger had checked the control cables and noticed that two had stretched slightly. This worried him. Control cables linked the pilot's hands and feet to the control surfaces: to the ailerons in the wings, to the elevators and rudders in the tail. Slack cables took the edge off performance. The sergeant made adjustments.

Strictly speaking, Langham was off duty. Rafferty had given him four days' leave to get married. But Dog was his Hampden and he didn't trust anyone else to do the air test. So after breakfast he lowered himself into the cockpit, with his observer in front and two gunners behind, and slightly less than a ton of bombs beneath.

At once he felt comfortable and confident. He was at home in D-Dog, within easy reach of all the taps and switches. This was the office. It had an old familiar smell of oil and leather.

Earlier, he had walked around the bomber, counted the engines, kicked the tyres, manipulated the rudders. Now he went through the pre-flight test sequence, a routine as familiar as shaving. The ground crew were watching, waiting. He switched on the ignition and the starter magneto. He pressed the starter button for the port engine while the ground crew primed its induction system. The propeller kicked and jerked and suddenly spun as the Pegasus roared and belched black exhaust, and the aeroplane vibrated. The starboard engine started just as easily. He watched and waited for a few seconds. When he was sure they were both firing steadily he switched off the magneto. The ground crew screwed down the priming pump. Now the whole aircraft was pressed against its chocks, eager to go. He did the warm-up checks – hydraulic system, brake pressure – and then tested airscrews and superchargers and magnetos. He opened the throttles until the engines were howling for release, and he checked boost and oil pressure. All was well. He closed the throttles, waved the chocks away, eased the brakes off, and taxied slowly to the end of the runway. Over-eager pilots taxied too fast, got the tail wheel jammed in a rut, ripped holes in the rear end. Not wise.

Now he did the Final Drill. Hydraulic power control: on. Trim tabs: neutral. Mixture: normal. Pitch: fully forward. Fuel: cock settings and contents correct. Flaps: select down eighteen degrees. Superchargers: M ratio. Gills: both cowlings closed.

All okay. He looked again at the wings. The starboard flap often came down faster than the port flap, which made their angles unequal. But not today.

One last and definitely final check. He turned the control wheel from side to side and watched the ailerons respond. He called the upper gunner on the intercom, and played the rudder bar with his feet. The upper gunner confirmed that the twin rudders and the elevators were moving freely. 'Anything behind us?' Langham asked. Once, during Initial Training, he'd seen an aeroplane take off quite literally in the shadow of another machine that was trying to land. Unforgettable. 'Nothing in the sky, skipper,' the gunner said.

Now they could go. It was only an air test, up and down in half an hour, but Langham never took chances with cockpit drills. Killing yourself by bombing a battleship through flak as thick as soup was one thing. Falling out of the sky because you forgot to open or shut a tap was plain foolish.

Control shone a green light.

The brakes came off as the throttles were opened. A Hampden's body looked like a suitcase but it had wings like a buzzard, and at eighty-five miles an hour Langham gave the control column a firm backward pull and D-Dog stopped pounding the grass and rose as if gravity had suddenly quit. The raucous howl softened to a sweet and steady roar. He raised the undercarriage and let the speed build to one hundred and twenty before he began a serious climb. At a thousand feet he raised the flaps. Dog, perfectly balanced, responded to every touch.

Ahead stood Lincoln cathedral, the biggest thing in the county, so Langham flew there.

He knew it well from the outside, because its three soaring Gothic towers made such a splendid landmark, but he'd never been inside. 'I'm getting married there this afternoon,' he told his observer, a Rhodesian called Jonty Brown.

'I know. I'm invited.'

'Pity about the weather. I wanted sunshine.'

'Try upstairs.'

At five thousand feet a layer of thin, pearl-grey cloud covered the sky like paint. Langham climbed and burst through it. The sky was Mediterranean blue and the sun scattered its dazzle recklessly. 'Good idea, Jonty.'

'Like this every day in Rhodesia.'

'How bloody monotonous.'

He spent ten minutes putting the Hampden through her paces and everything worked until, for no apparent reason, the port engine began losing revs. Nothing else seemed wrong: temperature, oil pressure, boost were okay. Maybe the revs gauge was faulty. But Dog was swinging slightly to the left. He throttled back the starboard engine. Now Dog swung a little to the right. 'Behave yourself, you bitch,' he muttered. He was trimming the rudders, searching for a balance, and losing speed. Port engine revs kept falling.

'Give me a course for base,' he said.

'Dunno, skip,' Jonty said. 'It's just an air test, I thought you knew where we were.' Langham swore. Jonty said, 'Get below cloud and I'll soon find you a landmark.'

'Sorry to bother you, skipper,' the under gunner said. 'There's a Wimpy watching us. Seems very interested.'

Langham swore again. Within a few seconds the Wellington was a wing-length away on the starboard side. Too close. The thing was twice his size; it could eat a Hampden for breakfast. He banked left, a touch too sharply, and corrected the beginnings of a wallow. 'The Wimpy's signalling,' Jonty said. A lamp flashed from its astrodome. 'Tell them to go to hell,' Langham said. That was when his cockpit became bedlam.

The upper gunner appeared at his shoulder, holding a birdcage. 'The pigeons aren't very well, skip,' he said. Two carrier pigeons were, like the bombload, part of Dog's operational baggage. 'Look.' He opened the cage door, to give a better view. The birds fluttered and fell over each other. 'Get that bloody junk out of here!' Langham roared. The bomber hit a small air pocket and lurched. The gunner stumbled and dropped the cage. The birds escaped and in an instant the cockpit was full of panicking wings and claws and beaks. Langham beat them off with one hand and used the other to turn Dog away from the damn-fool Wellington. It was a lousy turn. He felt through the seat of his pants that Dog disliked it. She was not responding properly. He gave her full rudder. Now she was worse. His ears were full of gabble on the intercom. He searched the panel for the turn-and-slip indicator and couldn't see it for pigeons, wings flapping, feathers flying. One wild sweep of his right arm knocked them aside and they vanished. By now he knew what was wrong. Dog was skidding. Not turning, but skidding. And falling fast.

Well, Langham had got into a skid before, often, and got out of it. That's what controls were for. But not these controls. The ailerons had quit, the elevators were useless, the control column was as floppy as a broken leg. The rudder bar was locked hard to the right.

He got both feet on its left end, and thrust, and it wouldn't budge. Rock solid. Dog sliced through cloud and plunged into grey air, wingtip first, still trying to fly sideways.

Langham forced himself to think. The intercom was silent: they knew he was in trouble. What they didn't know was he had no idea how to get out of it. Dog had her teeth into this downhill skid. The altimeter kept unwinding briskly. He saw it race past three thousand feet. He heard creaks and groans. The aeroplane wasn't built for this cockeyed manoeuvre. Two thousand.

A desperate thought wandered into his mind like a lunatic on the run. Steer with the engines. No. With just one engine. His hand went to the starboard throttle, and hesitated. If this was wrong, cancel the wedding. One thousand feet. Against all instinct, he closed the starboard throttle, killed that engine dead, and opened the port throttle, banged it wide open, rammed it to emergency setting. Dog twisted as if kicked. The port engine's savage thrust forced her to straighten out. The rudders unlocked. All the controls came alive. Dog levelled out at two hundred feet, above a stampede of cattle.

Langham flew cautiously for a long minute. Nothing seemed broken. The starboard engine picked up. He climbed to a thousand feet. A sour taste of metal filled his mouth and would not go away.

'Course for base is two-three-zero, skipper,' Jonty said.

'Thank you, observer.'

'Distance fifteen miles, skipper.'

'Thank you, observer.'

Faintly, Langham heard one of the gunners mutter, 'Bleeding Christ on crutches.'

'Say nothing,' Langham ordered, 'unless you have something to say.' The intercom clicked off.

2

Twenty minutes later he was talking to the Engineer Officer, a brisk Londoner called Quinn who knew every nut and bolt in a Hampden. 'I'll have D-Dog checked at once,' Quinn said. 'Sounds like a duff revs gauge. When you asked for it, the port engine gave full power?'

'Saved my skin. All our skins. The kite's okay *now*, we flew home like a dream, all serene. But *before* ... She just wouldn't answer. No controls, not a damn thing. We fell five thousand feet. Long way. Didn't take long, I know that.'

Quinn looked at his notes. 'All this began when you banked to port.'

Langham's legs felt shaky. He sat down. 'To avoid the Wimpy,' he said.

'What sort of bank?'

Langham frowned. 'Not so much a bank. More of a skid.'

Quinn nodded. 'Stabilized yaw,' he said.

'Stabilized yaw?' Langham could barely say it, his mouth was so dry. He swallowed, and tasted bile. 'I thought that was just a joke.'

'It's in your Pilot's Notes. Para seventeen, sub-para six. From memory, it says, "At low speeds, large sideslips may cause the rudder to lock over. Flat turns should be avoided." Or you get stabilized yaw.'

'I nearly got the chop.'

Quinn gave him a copy of the Pilot's Notes. 'Para seventeen. I've marked it. You need a drink. I'll get someone to drive you to the Mess.'

Langham was drinking brandy and soda when his flight commander saw him. 'Thought you were on leave,' Stuart said. 'Christ, you look awful.'

'Took Dog up for an air test. Got buzzed by a Wimpy, banked to port, rudders locked solid, everything went to hell.'

'Ah, yes. Stabilized yaw.'

'That's all right, then.' Langham finished his drink in one long swallow. 'As long as it's got a name, there's nothing to worry about.'

'Your fault, Tony. You made a ham-fisted bank, didn't you? Put a Hampden in a skid, what happens is the front of the aeroplane blanks the airflow over the tail. You can't steer, so your skid gets worse. Now your rudders have got air blasting sideways at them. No wonder they locked. I thought everyone knew that.'

'Silly me. Fancy stabilizing my yaw.'

'Have another drink. You look bloody awful.'

Stuart left. Langham was finishing his second brandy and soda when the Wingco came in. 'Good grief,' he said. 'You look dreadful.'

'Air test, sir. Nasty skid. Nearly bought it.'

'Stabilized yaw,' Hunt said. 'You ought to know better. Still, no harm done. Have another drink.'

Langham did, and then dragged himself off to his room. He lay on his bed for five minutes and woke up two hours later when Silk pounded on the door and hurried in and shook him. 'The Rolls is here!' he said. 'Jesus, Tony, wake up! Get changed! What's the matter with you?'

'Stabilized yaw,' Langham said croakily. 'Thought I'd got the chop, Silko.'

'Stabilized bollocks. Come on, *move*. It's your big day. Stabilized marriage, that's what you've got lined up.'

'No, not that. Oh God, please save me.' His head was in his hands, his skin felt like rubber, he wanted to hide. 'Please, God ...'

By now Silk was in the corridor, shouting for Langham's batman.

3

When they got out of the Rolls, outside the cathedral, Silk said quietly, 'Anyone would think you're being tried for murder. Cheer up, for Pete's sake. *Smile*. Like this.' Langham watched him carefully, and copied him. 'Not so desperate,' Silk said. 'Never mind. Keep it.' He had got Langham to the church. Now all he had to do was get him down the aisle and deliver him to the bishop.

Langham went quietly. He was still in shock. He was in the third-largest cathedral in England, and its echoing gloom reminded him of a huge railway station. After a while, he was convinced of this. Individuals passed to and fro in the shadows: passengers waiting for a train, like him. He wondered where they were going, but when he looked for a destination board, he saw the glowing splendour of the east window. That explained everything. This was where you went when you got the chop. This was the terminus for the terminus. He saw beautiful flowers. He heard the trickling notes of an organ. He whispered into Silk's ear: 'They give a chap a jolly good send-off here, don't they?' Silk frowned, so Langham said no more. Silk probably hadn't got the chop. It was different for him.

After that, proceedings were just a blur. Zoë appeared, in an awfully pretty dress, and so did the bishop, in a kind of ball-gown, both there to see him off, presumably. It all went on and on. At one stage he was high in the roof, looking down, watching himself going through some kind of ceremony. Answering questions. Could it be a customs examination? Seemed unlikely. He felt light-headed. He shouldn't be at this height without oxygen. Bad for the brain. He came down to earth at a hell of a lick and made a perfect three-point landing. Not possible. He looked at his feet and counted them. Not three. See what oxygen starvation does to you? At that very moment the train came in. He felt its mighty power rumble up through the soles of his shoes. It was playing Mendelssohn's Wedding March, gale force ten. It was so loud that it blew him out of the cathedral.

4

He got carried along by a tide of congratulations. When the bridal party arrived at Bardney Castle House he knew he was married. Everyone was happy, so he joined in the fun and agreed with what they told him. But after a while he grew very tired of shaking hands and smiling. He wanted to be alone with Zoë. Where was she? Gone to change her clothes. An extraordinarily tall man gripped his elbow. 'Saw you admiring our cathedral,' he said too loudly. 'Fascinating place. I wrote a book about it.'

'Ah.' Langham got his elbow back. 'Fancy that.'

'Fifty-seven thousand square feet. Diocese was huge, you see. Reached from the Humber to the Thames. First cathedral was finished in 1092.'

'Good show.'

'Burned down in 1141,' he boomed. 'Major restorations were necessary, of course.'

'Yes. If you'll excuse me –'

'Worse followed.' He had Langham's elbow again. 'Disastrous earthquake in 1185. Whole structure largely destroyed.'

'Look, I must go, so –'

'Hugh of Avalon! Became bishop. Started rebuilding.'

'You're bloody deaf, aren't you?'

'The nave is thirteenth-century. The style is Early English.'

'Let me go or I'll kill you.' The pulses in Langham's head were pounding. This deaf maniac couldn't hear him and wouldn't release him, he kept barking on about a copy of Magna Carta kept in a cathedral chapel, so Langham snatched a bottle of champagne from a passing waiter and would have cracked it on the man's head if Pug Duff hadn't taken it from him. Others appeared: Silk, Tom Stuart, Jonty, Happy Hall, the MO, and they hustled him out of the room, along a corridor, away from the crowd.

'You're spoiling the party, Tony,' Stuart said. 'And you're letting the side down.'

'Mind your own bloody business.' Now he was nine years old.

'It is our business,' Duff said. 'You damn near put up a very large black, back there.' He waved the champagne bottle, and drank from it.

'Give me a swig.'

'Not likely. You don't deserve it.'

'Don't *what?*' He almost choked on rage. 'I nearly went for a Burton this morning. Lost the kite at five thousand, pulled out at a hundred! Bloody good job I did, or you bastards wouldn't be getting pissed now.' He lunged for the bottle, and missed.

'Wasn't a hundred,' Jonty said. 'More like five hundred. I was there.' He yawned. 'I had every confidence in the pilot. He knew what he was doing.'

'No I bloody didn't.'

'I blame the kite,' Happy Hall said. 'Lousy heap of scrap.'

'I blame the weather,' Silk said. Who cared? He certainly didn't. He wandered over to a window. The overcast had gone. A lazy sun shone in a soft blue sky.

'My theory is different,' the MO said. 'I don't believe you really wanted to get married, and now you're disappointed that you didn't get the chop.' He shrugged.

'I think he's bats,' Silk said. 'I know his family. They're all bats.'

Langham had turned away. He was looking at the parkland.

'If you don't want her, I'll have her,' Jonty said. 'Anything for a friend.'

'Pigeons,' Langham said, and pointed. 'Fucking pigeons.'

'Definitely pigeons,' Silk said. 'But otherwise engaged.'

'They were all over the cockpit.' Langham was calm now. 'I couldn't see for feathers. I'm going to kill those pigeons.'

'Good,' Duff said. 'We'll come with you.'

The butler was not surprised. Killing pigeons was one of the amenities at Bardney Castle. He supplied shotguns, and the airmen roamed the park for twenty minutes, blasting the innocent sky and even knocking down a few sluggish birds.

When they went indoors, Langham seemed much better. 'Try and get some rest,' the MO said to him.

Lady Shapland overheard this. 'What an absurd suggestion,' she said. She was dancing with the Under-Secretary of State for the Colonies. 'That boy is going to fertilise my daughter if he has to gird his loins every hour on the hour all through the honeymoon.'

'I rather think that girding the loins has an opposite effect,' her partner said.

She wasn't listening. 'I need an heir, Henry. He'd better not be firing blanks or I'll have him annulled.'

'You can't annul a bridegroom, Philly.'

'Just watch me. Stand and deliver, that's the name of the game.'

'My stars, Philly, you're full of zip. You wouldn't like to govern Nigeria, would you?'

Langham was dancing with Zoë. The shock of survival had passed; he was beginning to see its advantages. 'I nearly killed my crew this morning,' he said.

'Only nearly? I nearly slipped in the bath. Nearly broke my neck. Nearly spoilt your day.'

'Poor show. I don't like the sound of that bath. In future we shall bathe together. That's my decision, as an officer commissioned by His Majesty King George the Sixth. I'm jolly good at decisions.'

'Silko doesn't think so, darling.'

'Silko is the most stupid man I've ever met.'

'He thinks I'm making a great mistake. He said I should have married him.'

'Well, there you are. Pure stupidity on two legs. He should be an exhibit in a travelling circus.' They waved and smiled at Silk, who was dancing with a bridesmaid. 'That's a pretty girl.'

'This is heaven.' She stopped so that they could kiss. 'If you ever leave me I'll kill you.'

'Can't kill me if I've got the chop.' Not a clever remark; he was sorry he'd said it. 'Anyway, the circumstance won't arise. That's another of my brilliant decisions. Who's that tall bloke over there?'

'Giles Palfrey. Retired banker. Why?'

'He kept shouting at me. I nearly killed him, too.'

'Dear me,' she said. 'Another failure. You're really rotten at killing people, aren't you, darling?'

'Utterly hopeless,' he said, and felt much better for it. Sometimes it paid to lose.

The dance ended. He went looking for champagne, and met the bishop. 'At one stage today I feared you were about to expire,' the bishop said. 'I've never administered the last rites during a wedding service, and I'm not sure I know the drill. But you're looking much better now.'

'Thank you. I've been married all afternoon, and I think I've got the hang of it. I've discovered that sometimes it pays to lose.'

'Highly unlikely. In my experience of matrimony, if you think you've won, you've lost, and if you think you've lost, you really have lost.'

'Oh. Well, in that case, I'll settle for a draw.'

'Then you're disqualified.' The bishop smiled cheerfully and patted Langham on the shoulder. 'Remember those rules, old chap, and you should have a straightforward run to the grave.'

STRANGLE THE BUTLER

1

The couple took their brief honeymoon in London, in Albany. It was her idea. 'Lincolnshire is dreary,' she said. 'We shall get more than enough of it soon.' They went by train, first class. He slept most of the way. In the taxi from King's Cross, she said, 'You were dreaming, darling.'

'Was I?' He thought about it. 'Yes. I met my father.'

'Didn't you tell me he was dead?'

'Yes. But so was I, you see. Dead as a doughnut.'

'Dodo, darling. Dead as a dodo.'

He frowned. 'My father wouldn't make that sort of mistake.'

She saw that it disturbed him. 'Darling, dodo or doughnut, it really doesn't matter. They're much the same.'

'Doughnuts don't die. It's absurd. So I couldn't have been dead.'

'Of course not. Was it all a joke, d'you suppose?'

'Maybe. My father used to like playing practical jokes, but still ...'

'A practical joke about death is carrying things a bit far.'

'Yes. Anyway, I hate doughnuts. If they serve doughnuts in Heaven, I'm not going.' He had shaken off the dream and was cheerful again.

They spent most of the next three days in her apartment, and much of that time in bed.

On the evening of the second day, as they shared yet another sexual triumph, and separated, they lay with their fingers linked, letting the sweat cool their bodies. 'You're not a woman,' he said amiably, 'you're an animal.'

'Goody. I've always wanted to be a blue-assed baboon. They have such fun.'

'I doubt if even baboons keep up our sort of pace. I'm not complaining.'

'Good. Neither am I, darling.'

'It's just that you have a way of looking at me, and when you do, I get a slight pain down below. In my wedding tackle, not to put too fine a point on it.'

She propped herself on an elbow and studied his collapsed penis. 'We haven't put too fine a point on it, dearest.' She raised it with her index finger. 'You've got oodles of wear left in you.'

'What a comfort you are. All the same ...'

'You're suffering from chronic shortage of gin, my sweet.' She slipped out of bed. 'Gin cures all. If Hitler drank gin he wouldn't be in such a frightful paddy with everyone.'

While she was away, he thought about D-Dog and the rapidly magnifying patch of Lincolnshire that had so nearly become a large crater, burned black all around. The picture came to him less often, but it still caused a kick in his heartbeat. He had wondered about telling Zoë, realised it would mean explaining stabilized yaw, and decided against it.

She came back with the drinks.

'Something rather odd happened during our wedding ceremony,' he said. 'Cheers ... I had the sensation of being high up, near the roof, watching myself get married.'

'I've had that. Not for years, though. How did you get down?'

'Oh ... sideslipped, with full flap and a touch of rudder. By the way, you ought to know: I've made my will.'

She almost said, *But you're broke*. Instead she said, 'How thoughtful, darling. Anything special in it for me?'

'Um ... the castle. And my lucky mascot. Never fly without it.'

'Marvellous.' She snuggled against him. They linked arms and sipped each other's gin. She didn't point out that if she ever got his lucky mascot, it couldn't have been very lucky. Nobody said being in love meant being honest.

2

Rafferty gave him permission to live out. Bardney Castle was only a fifteen-minute drive from Kindrick. He bought a lemon-yellow

Frazer-Nash two-seater for ten pounds from an army officer who was being posted to Egypt. It seemed in style.

Owning a big house was rather like getting his commission. It had been good for the ego to be saluted wherever he went; now it was gratifying to be lord of this manor. Gardeners stopped work and doffed their caps. The staff smiled at the dashing young pilot as he headed for the lawns, a pair of black Labradors at his heels. He'd borrowed the dogs from the gamekeeper, but who cared? He enjoyed chucking bits of branch for them to chase. It was a hoot. The whole thing was a hoot.

Obviously he asked some of the boys to come over for a meal. No point in a splendid hoot unless you can share it. Tom Stuart came with Silko, Tubby Heckter and Jonty Brown. Langham planned to be outside to meet them when they arrived, but the blackout curtains in his suite got stuck. It took two servants and a stepladder to sort out the problem, and that was when the butler knocked on the door, entered, stepped aside and announced, 'Squadron Leader Stuart.'

'Bloody hell,' Langham muttered, and hurried forward with an unhappy grin, too late to stop the butler announcing the other three names. 'Honestly, I don't normally do this,' Langham said. Stuart gave a brief nod which made it obvious he was not impressed.

They met Zoë, and in the flurry of getting drinks and making small talk, the atmosphere improved. She told some amusing stories about the castle's alleged ghosts and eccentric owners. The butler announced that dinner was served. They trooped into the next room and in a gut-freezing instant Langham knew that this was all a terrible mistake. The table was too big, the plates were gilt-edged, there were battalions of crystal wineglasses and regiments of silver cutlery. The candelabra blazed. The napkins had been woven by virgins and monogrammed by the Royal School of Needlework. It was too rich for a bunch of bomber pilots.

'Just dry toast for me,' Tubby Heckter said. 'I'm on a diet.' Not a funny joke.

Servants eased the chairs forward as the guests sat, in case someone pulled a muscle.

Artichoke soup was served. Scallops in cream were served. Tournados Rossini were served. Banana soufflé with hot chocolate sauce was served. Tiny savouries tasting of bacon were served. A large ripe Stilton was wheeled in. Many wines had come and gone.

Port circulated. None of this made conversation easier.

Zoë was the problem: she didn't understand their shop, and they weren't interested in her life in London. As the endless meal wore on, she grew bored, stopped trying, became remote. The butler's presence didn't help. He saw, and oversaw, everything. At one point Jonty Brown used the wrong knife, and realized it, and felt so guilty that, in his confusion, he drank half his finger-bowl. It was a silver finger-bowl, very handsome. Anyone might have done the same.

They didn't linger over coffee. Langham went down with them and saw them leave.

Zoë was preparing for bed when he got back to their suite. 'Dull bunch,' she said.

'Well, they've just had a hard day.'

'Poor creatures. I've just had a hard evening, so don't expect me to feel sorry.'

'You certainly found it hard just to look interested.'

'Well, you looked ghastly. You kept grinning like a maniac.'

'I was trying to distract attention from your breasts.' He threw his shoes into a corner. 'Did you have to wear something so revealing?'

She peeled off her slip, and squared her shoulders, all for his benefit. 'Oh dear. And I thought you liked them. Silly me.'

He flung his shirt into the same corner. 'If you want to know the truth,' he said, and got rid of his trousers in the same direction, let the maids pick them up, that's what maids were for. 'I spent the whole bloody evening wondering why you and I were wasting our bloody time on that bloody silly food when we had better bloody things to do.'

'Too much bloody,' she said, 'and not enough fucking. Come here.'

So that was all right. For a while.

Next morning he arrived at the aerodrome to get a message to report to the Flight Office.

'Poor show,' Tom Stuart told him. 'Not our style.' His words were as flat as old pennies. 'Don't do it again.' He pointed to the door. Later, on the airfield, Langham met Jonty Brown and Tubby Heckter. 'I apologize,' he said. 'All a mistake.' They looked at each other. 'Have we been introduced?' Jonty said. 'Get the butler, Tubby. Throw this fellow out.' They walked on.

That left Silk. Langham sat next to him at lunch. 'It was a disaster, wasn't it?' he said. Silk nodded. 'Less fun than German measles,' he said. 'And more expensive than the Battle of the Somme.'

Langham stirred his soup. 'Nothing I can do about it now,' he said.

'Strangle the bloody butler,' Silk said. 'That would be a start.'

For the first time, Langham found himself reluctant to drive home at the end of the day, and when he neared Bardney Castle it loomed like a fortress. But that could just have been the blackout.

Zoë was on the phone to friends, probably in London. After ten minutes he said, 'Can't that wait?' but she seemed not to hear him. He took a bath. While he soaked, he counted the towels. Twelve towels of various sizes. Absurd. Nobody needed twelve towels.

He used one towel, and put on a dressing gown. She was still on the phone, and curled up in a way that suggested a long chat. He counted to twenty and took the receiver from her hand. 'Military priority,' he told the caller. 'This line is requisitioned.' He hung up.

'Goodness! Enter the caveman.' She fluttered her eyelids. 'Kind sir, if your passion is so strong, you need only ask.'

'Forget sex.' Part of him felt a sudden, deep dismay at this folly, but he pressed on. 'Last night was a big mistake.'

'Your idea to entertain, darling.'

'Yes, but not like *that*. Far too grand, too ambitious. They thought I was showing off. All that pomp and ceremony.'

'Someone has to serve the food.'

'Not the point. The boys want to relax when they go out, have a good time. Darts at the pub. Draught Bass, pickled eggs.'

'Look around you, my sweet. This isn't a pub. You really can't expect chef to make pickled eggs. He was with the George Cinq in Paris, for heaven's sake! And before that he trained at Claridges. *Claridges*, darling!'

'Who's boss here? Him or me?'

'He'd leave, darling. And Mummy would never forgive us.'

'Fine. You eat here with chef, and I hope you're both very happy. I'm off to a chic little transport café where they do an exquisite sausage and mash with lashings of Daddies Sauce.'

He got back late. She was asleep. He got up early, before she was awake. He accelerated down the drive, tyres spitting gravel. He got a glimpse of the house in his wing mirror, small and getting smaller all the time.

3

Group HQ ended 409's stint on standby. Now some other squadron would be bored rigid, waiting for shipping strikes that never came. The Wingco checked with the Met man and ordered night-flying training.

Langham phoned Bardney Castle and left a message: *Duty calls, shan't be home tonight.* As he hung up, he realized that he could do this any time he liked, whether he was flying or not. How would she know? Briefly, he felt free. No longer trapped. Yet that feeling was unsatisfactory too, and as the hours went by he couldn't get her out of his thoughts: a mixture of lust and longing and sour resentment. In the end he phoned the Castle again. She was out. No message. Bugger.

Night-flying was routine stuff. It annoyed the chicken farmers of Lincolnshire, but nobody got killed.

Next day, half the Hampdens got serviced while the crews practised escape drills in the other half; and Langham wondered why his wife hadn't telephoned the Mess. He felt weary, went to bed early, slept poorly.

At breakfast he sat with the 'A' Flight boys. They were arguing about second sight. 'I had an uncle,' Happy Hall said, 'brilliant water-diviner he was, which proves nothing, but he could pick winners like shelling peas, provided he never backed the horse. If he backed it, then it lost.'

'That's nothing. I can back losers,' Tubby Heckter said. 'I'm very gifted in that respect. Do it without thinking.'

Langham asked Happy, 'What would happen if your uncle backed the horse to lose?'

'It would win, of course. But he never did. Too honest.'

'I knew a flying instructor in Rhodesia who had second sight,' Jonty Brown said. 'Uncanny, the things he knew. Trouble was, his first sight was rubbish and he flew into the Chimanimani Mountains.'

'Which he didn't foresee,' Silk pointed out, 'so his second sight wasn't all that hot, was it?'

'Doesn't follow,' Tom Stuart said. 'Second sight doesn't mean you can change the future.'

'Happy's uncle could, by backing the horse,' Silk argued. 'And Jonty's instructor could have changed his flight plan.'

'Waste of time,' Jonty said. 'He'd have flown into Mount Inyangani instead. He told me so.'

'The future's coming,' Happy said confidently. 'You can't stop it.'

'Jane has lost her knickers again,' Pug Duff said. He was reading the strip cartoon in the *Daily Mirror*. 'I predicted that yesterday.' Nobody responded. Jane's clothes fell off very readily. 'And for my next trick, I predict absolute mayhem on the rugger field this afternoon.' That got their attention. 'Didn't you know? Rafferty's arranged a match with RAF Ossington. He thinks we need bucking up. Black Mac is our captain. The team's on the noticeboard.'

'Don't tell me ...' Langham began.

'You and Silko are playing.' Duff jabbed at a length of bacon until he forked it and held it up like a trophy. 'The blood wagon will be in attendance.'

At noon, a greasy drizzle began to fall. Langham couldn't eat lunch. He sat in the Mess and watched the team from RAF Ossington enjoy steak and kidney pie. They looked big and hard. Silk got on with his meal. 'No point in dying hungry,' he said. 'Anyway, Black Mac's put you and me in the front row of the scrum. A chap can hide in the scrum. I played there for years at Clifton and never touched the ball.'

Langham wasn't listening. 'Look at that hulking great giant,' he said. 'What a bruiser.'

'Don't worry. Black Mac will take care of him.'

Five minutes after the kick-off, Silk lost his lunch. Black Mac got the ball and charged head-down into a crowd of players. His shoulder walloped Silk in the stomach before Silk could dodge. He crawled to the touchline and threw up. He got to his feet, spitting the last foul-tasting fragments. 'Good man,' Group Captain Rafferty called. 'Better out than in.'

'I think I've injured something, sir,' Silk wheezed.

'Nonsense. If you quit we'll be a man short and then we'll never win. I say! Uncle!' The adjutant was refereeing. Rafferty waved his umbrella until Uncle stopped play and allowed Silk to return.

'For Christ's sake, man, keep out of my way!' McHarg told him. 'Pull your finger out. We've got a scrum. Get in there and *shove*.' Silk joined the scrum alongside Langham, who had a split lip. 'I hit his elbow with my face,' Langham said.

Black Mac continued to collide with them whenever they were

near the ball, and often when they were not. At half-time they left the rest of the team and limped over to the referee, who was standing alone, sucking a bit of lemon. 'Look here, Uncle,' Silk said. He showed the cuts on his shins, the scrapes on his body, the purple bruise that had half-closed an eye. 'Tony's just as bad.'

'I'm worth,' Langham lisped. His cut lip had swollen. Rain washed blood down his chin.

'It's a man's game,' Uncle said brusquely. His boots were a size too small; he knew all about pain. 'Ossington have always been a dirty lot. Don't worry, I'll watch out for foul play.'

'It's not them. It's Black Mac,' Silk said.

'Nonsense.' Uncle walked away. But after a minute he summoned McHarg. 'You really mustn't hit your own men, you know. That's foul play.'

'Not a bit of it. I read the rules last night. It's only a foul if you hit an opponent.'

'Really?' Uncle was startled. 'But look here ... I mean, what's the point? It won't help us win.'

'It might. Those two are awful lazy. They need a wee tickle to make them run.'

In the second half, Silk and Langham ran shamelessly away from their captain. They ran as far and as fast as possible. If by bad luck someone passed the ball to them, they immediately kicked it and ran the other way. This saved them from further serious damage. Ossington beat Kindrick by forty points.

Black Mac had stamped on Langham's right foot, so Langham used the accelerator cautiously as he drove to Bardney Castle. Zoë was shocked by the sight of his split lip. It had swollen enormously, forcing him to talk out of the side of his mouth.

'Darling! You look *dreadful*. What happened? Have you been in a fight?'

'In a manner of speaking.' He winced as she helped him out of his greatcoat, and her face twisted in sympathy. He noticed this and realised he could do better than rugby injuries. 'I wish I could tell you about it. Deadly secret, I'm afraid. Get shot at dawn if I say a word.' He tried to smile and his lip split again. The trickle of blood horrified her. She sent for ice.

'Have you seen a doctor? Yes, of course you have. Silly question. I knew you must be flying when you didn't phone me. You've been on operations, haven't you? No, you mustn't tell me. You're so calm! It must have been awful.'

'Well, getting in a panic never helps.'

Ice arrived. She wrapped some in a towel and he held it against his lip. He thought she looked even lovelier when she was worried about him. 'What can I do?' she asked.

'Whisky. The MO gave me some magic ointment for my various bumps and bruises, but it can wait.'

They held hands by the fire while he sipped whisky, awkwardly, through the corner of his mouth. Then she insisted that he show her all his injuries. 'All right,' he said, 'but it's not a pretty sight.'

He stood naked while she gently applied the MO's healing balm to his knocks and scrapes. Her open admiration, and the warmth of her touch, actually made him feel heroic. He wondered it if it was like this in days of yore, when a noble warrior returned from battle to his grateful maiden. Then what? Did she express her appreciation in the usual way?

She was thinking: *I never expected war to be like this. I suppose they fly somewhere and get involved in violent dogfights, or something* ... What she said was: 'One piece of equipment is still in good working order.'

'So it is. That's jolly lucky, isn't it?' He held her by the shoulders and they kissed.

'Are you quite sure, darling? You must be exhausted.'

'Not a bit. Never felt better.'

She put her arm around his waist and guided him to the bedroom. Because of his injuries, she made him lie on his back while she eased herself into position on top. He was impressed by her suppleness. Nobody mentioned pickled eggs.

4

Silk and Langham were young and healthy. Their injuries soon healed. Whenever he met them, McHarg asked if they were fit. 'The Group Captain wants me to take a team to Ossington,' he said, grinning like a shark. 'He wants revenge! He's a devil for revenge, is Rafferty.'

'I'd sooner bomb Berlin in broad daylight,' Silk said.

McHarg cackled in his odd, high-pitched fashion. 'That's what we like to see! Fighting spirit!' He walked away. A passing airman saluted him, and he returned the salute with such fervour that the man looked around for a cause.

'One of us has got to shoot him,' Langham said. He spun a coin and lost. 'I can't. I'm a married man.'

'How's Zoë?'

'Too much on her own. Gets bored.'

'Not by one of the gardeners, I hope. That's a joke, Tony.'

'Christ, it had better be.'

McHarg was in his office, reading an Air Ministry publication on the safe storage of tracer bullets, when he got an urgent summons to the operations room. A medium-sized flap was on. Two submarines, or perhaps the same submarine twice, had been spotted about fifty miles off the east coast. Group wanted six Hampdens in the air urgently, bombed up and fuelled for a long patrol. 'High explosive,' the Wingco said. 'Six two-hundred-and-fifty-pounders per kite. How soon?'

'Half an hour,' McHarg said, and ran from the room.

He took the first vehicle with a key in the ignition, the MO's Morris, and drove fast across half a mile of grass to the bomb dump. The huts where the armourers worked were empty except for three airmen playing brag. 'Where's everyone?' he roared, and saw the clock and knew: they were eating their bloody midday meal. He telephoned the Airmen's Mess and the Sergeants' Mess, ordered every armourer back on duty double-quick.

The three airmen were starting up the tractors, hitching on the bomb-trolleys, shouting, running. McHarg headed for the dump and stopped. Outside the entrance lay row upon row of shiny olive-green two-fifties. The stencilled idents said HE. No need to winkle the damn things out of the depths of the dump, then. Stroke of luck. Should save ten, fifteen minutes.

Armourers were turning up on bicycles and in trucks. He quickly got them loading the trolleys. The flight-sergeant armourer arrived on his motorbike. 'Anti-sub patrol,' McHarg told him crisply. 'Six kites, six two-fifty HEs per kite. Impact pistols. Get cracking. Wait! What were those stores doing outside the dump?'

'Getting cleaned, sir. The casings were all sweaty, we've been scraping the crystals off and –'

'Use 'em! You've got twenty minutes to take-off.'

The flight sergeant was soon back. 'We'll need more time, sir. Six two-fifties is a tight squeeze on some of these kites. Getting the bastards dead central so they lock into place ...' He sucked his teeth.

'Nothing new. Done it before.'

'Time is what I'm talking about, sir.'

'You're wasting it, standing here.'

As if to confirm this, they heard the harsh bark of Pegasus engines being tested. Soon the noise died as the ground crews cleared off and left bombing-up to the experts.

McHarg got in the Morris and drove to the nearest Hampden and watched. He knew the flight sergeant was right. Loading a bomber couldn't be rushed. The chain of trolleys had to be backed precisely under the belly so that each bomb could be winched up until it sat nicely in its carrier. It had to be secured with clamps that gripped it and held it rigid. Provided everything was dead central the carrier could be locked into place and a light would come on to indicate this. Then the whole procedure was repeated for the next bomb. The more bombs, the less space to work in. The armourers scraped their knuckles and cursed, but they did not rush.

Thirty minutes was up. McHarg said nothing.

He moved from Hampden to Hampden. He stopped at the fourth aeroplane: P-Peter. The flight sergeant was kneeling under it, his head and shoulders inside the bomb bay. McHarg walked over and squatted beside him. The concrete hardstanding was wet. Oil splashes had left twisted rainbows in the puddles. The flight sergeant, without looking at him, said, 'This carrier's totally fucked, sir.' He got out to let McHarg see.

The carrier was cockeyed. Something or someone had bashed it, knocked it out of shape and now it wouldn't slot into its space. That was one thing. The other was the bomb. Parts of it were lightly coated with yellow crystals. So were the other bombs in this bay.

'They're sweating,' McHarg said. 'Every bleeding one's sweating.'

'Yes sir.' The flight sergeant sounded sick. 'I was told they were all scraped, but obviously they weren't.'

'By Christ, I'll have someone on a charge for this. I'll have someone's guts.'

'We can change this load, sir. Get these off, put others on. Take twenty minutes if we go flat out.'

McHarg sat on his heels. He could see Rafferty and the Wingco standing near the control tower, watching. Outside the crew rooms, aircrew were sitting on the grass, watching. 'Not fucking likely,' he said. 'No daft bomb is going to make me look stupid. Get your head in here. If we ease off the clamps a wee bit, that'll give us some slack so we can give the carrier a dunt, straighten it out. Are you ready?'

They were standing awkwardly, legs braced, bodies twisted. Perhaps one of them slipped on the oily concrete. Perhaps one of them loosened a clamp too much, and the sudden weight of two hundred and fifty pounds of bomb was more than the other clamps would bear. Perhaps the volatile crystals made a damaging bang when the casing hit the concrete, or maybe the impact pistol triggered the Amatol, although it should have been safe. But what is safe? Nothing is ever totally safe. The bomb went off and the rest of the load exploded too, and everyone in or near the control tower saw P-Peter erupt like a small volcano. Men two hundred yards away were knocked flat. The nearest Hampden was blown over. Other aircraft were damaged by chunks falling from the sky. The blast stopped the church clock in Kindrick. A maid in an upstairs room at Bardney Castle House saw the pink glow made by six hundred gallons of burning petrol, and heard the boom, and was too frightened to tell anyone.

The Wingco managed to get four undamaged bombers into the air. They patrolled their sector of the North Sea and saw nothing but an upturned lifeboat. The sea was rough, visibility poor, it might well have looked to someone like the conning tower of a U-boat. They bombed it anyway, and came home, landing well away from the deep black hole that had once been the concrete hardstanding for P-Peter.

ONE CIVILIAN, NOW DEAD

1

T he court of inquiry, chaired by an air vice-marshal, adjourned in order to attend the funeral. There were seven coffins: five armourers plus an engine fitter and a bowser driver who had been standing too near. Most of the coffins were supplemented with sandbags to make a respectable weight. Those of McHarg and his flight sergeant contained nothing but sandbags: synthetic funeral, in aircrew jargon. Still, it was an impressive ceremony. The skies were steel-grey and frost coated every blade of grass. The church clock showed seven minutes past one. 'Shades of Rupert Brooke,' Bins murmured to Uncle as they waited for the pallbearers. 'Stands the church clock at thirteen oh seven? And is there haggis served in heaven?'

'Poor taste, old boy.'

'Yes. But irresistible.'

The air vice-marshal departed next day. There had been little evidence to examine and no close witnesses to question, so his report was bound to be pretty brief. The hole got filled in and within a week the scorched grass was decently covered by light snow.

This was not enough to stop flying, and late one afternoon Silk was making his approach to Kindrick, sinking gently to seven hundred feet, when he saw a farmhouse whose chimney was smoking and nearby a cottage whose chimney was not.

He told Langham, who called there on his way home. A farm labourer had been conscripted by the army and his wife had gone to live with her mother, so the cottage was empty. When she saw it, Zoë was surprisingly enthusiastic. 'It's a sweet little cottage. The furniture's quite impossible, and we'll need someone in to clean, but I'll take care of that. Extraordinary wallpaper, darling.'

'I think that's Mickey Mouse. The pictures don't quite join up, do they?'

'We'll have it painted eau de nil. Burgundy curtains, don't you think, darling? And an oatmeal carpet. Let's blend in with the countryside. I shall buy jodhpurs, lots of jodhpurs.'

Furniture vans and decorators came and went for a week. Then the couple moved in, none too soon. Winter began dumping snow. It took the ground crews all day to clear a landing strip, but the wind had all night to bury it in drifts. 409 did little flying until February 1940.

2

Christmas was a happy time. Zoë gave a string of parties; all the officers of 409 visited the cottage at least once. Away from the pomp of Bardney Castle she was a different person, bright, lively; everyone envied Tony; some tried to replace him. No luck. 'You're awfully sweet,' she would say, 'and I'm terribly old-fashioned.' Sometimes, when the party ended, she told him of these approaches. Later, he told Silk.

'Boot the bastard in the balls,' Silk suggested.

'Why? He didn't do any harm. Anyway ... I never thought I'd say this, but to tell the truth, there are times when I wouldn't mind having an understudy. I mean to say: twice a night, every night. What happens when the well runs dry?'

'Lay off, then. Don't be so damn greedy.'

'It's not me. It's her.'

'Oh.' For Silk, this was an entirely new concept. 'So she wears the trousers.'

'Half the time she wears bugger all. And I'm only flesh and blood.'

In mid-January, Langham drove home to find the cottage empty. He sat around, waited, got slightly drunk. The farm had a phone; there were people he could call who might know something. He went to bed, telling himself that if she had fallen in the snow and frozen to death, it was already too late, there was nothing he could do. Was that callous? Blame the war. He slept badly, told nobody she was missing, and next night she was there, waiting, with a box of oysters and a dozen lemons. 'For you,' she said.

'I hate oysters. They taste like death.'

'You must eat them, darling. I've been to see this brilliant special-ist in Harley Street, Guy Chard-Cox. He swears by oysters. I'm having two dozen a day sent here. Guy says it's what you need to do the trick.' She gave him Guy's business card.

'Chard-Cox,' he said. 'That's a joke, surely.'

'Guy can't help his name. He doesn't mind if people laugh, as long as he helps make babies.'

'You didn't tell me you were going to London.'

'I didn't expect to stay overnight, only I met some chums and anyway what does it matter? The important thing is to get me preg-gers. I know you're trying, but ...'

'This is your bloody mother's idea, isn't it?'

'My bloody mother's in New bloody York. Now *listen*, darling. Guy's had a look at me, nothing wrong he says, might be a good idea to cut down on the gin, but when I told him you were a Spitfire pilot he said stress is a funny thing, like shell-shock in the last war, once a man gets anxious then his octane rating goes down and he stops firing on all cylinders. That's how Guy explained it.'

By now he was pale with anger. He went outside and got logs and came in and hurled them on the fire. Sparks exploded.

'I am *not* under stress,' he said, too quietly.

She poured a very small gin with a huge amount of tonic, and looked at him over the rim. 'You *sound* under stress,' she said.

'I'm monumentally pissed off with your Harley Street quack. There's a difference. And I'm *not* a Spitfire pilot.'

'Darling, I couldn't tell Guy I was married to a man who flies Hampden bombers. He'd think you were a bus-driver.'

It was a joke. He thumped the table so hard that the gin bottle bounced. 'I need that drink more than you do,' he growled, and tried to grab it, which led to a friendly fight with inevitable physical contact, so they forgot the drink and went to bed. Later he ate six oysters. *Couldn't do any harm,* he thought.

3

Silk was a frequent visitor, and that helped. He sometimes brought along one of the Waafs from the station, but rarely the same girl twice. They had all been lectured by the senior Waaf Officer on the folly of falling in love with aircrew. 'You will be pregnant and he will be dead,' she said. They were not stupid. They noted the crashes, and they kept their distance. Zoë liked Silk because he made her laugh and if he offended anyone, hard cheese. One night, at supper, he boasted that he had designed Waaf's knickers for the Air Ministry. 'We called it Operation Passion-killer,' he said. 'My design won because it had triple-strength elastic and extra gussets. You don't know what gussets are,' he told Langham, 'but we tested my knickers on one hundred randy Canadian aircrew and they couldn't make a hole in them even when they worked in shifts.'

'Canadians in shifts,' Zoë said. 'Pure cotton, I hope. Perhaps a little *appliqué* around the neckline. One bare shoulder. No jewellery, of course.'

'Gusset ...' Langham had a dictionary. 'Interesting. It comes between 'gush' and 'gusto'.'

'Don't we all?' she said.

Silk had brought a Waaf sergeant, very pretty, very tough. 'Men are just jealous,' she told Zoë. 'Half the squadron wear silk stockings when they fly.'

'What do the other half wear?'

'A look of grim determination,' Langham said. He clenched his teeth and thrust his jaw.

'That looks like constipation, darling.'

'Quite impossible,' Silk said. 'At Clifton, constipaggers was a worse crime than buggery. We got dosed with syrup of figs quite ruthlessly.'

'I grew to quite like the taste,' Langham said.

'You just split an infinitive, darling.'

'Did I? The stuff's still working, then.'

When their guests had gone, Zoë said: 'Silk's awfully funny, isn't he? And sexy, too. I find bad taste very provocative, don't you? I wish you were less respectable, my love. Why can't you talk dirty and galvanize me into dancing naked in the snow?'

'Do my best.' He frowned and thought hard. 'All right. Here goes. Um ... Nipples. Wet bathing-suits. Contraceptive devices.' She shook her head. 'More nipples. Blue-assed baboons.' Still no success. 'Reinforced gussets?' he suggested. 'Rumpty-tumpty?'

'You're hopeless.'

'Personally, I find the phrase "rumpty-tumpty" very stimulating,' he said. 'Also hanky-panky and tutti-frutti.' He wasn't going to galvanize his wife. She galvanized herself without help, twice nightly.

4

The snow stopped in January, thawed, and fell again more heavily than ever. By mid-February it had vanished for good. The Wingco was eager to get 409 back in action, and Tom Stuart wanted to make it clear to everyone that married men got no special treatment. For days, Langham was too busy to go home. Zoë hated being left alone in boring Lincolnshire and when he turned up she nagged him to get a posting nearer London. 'No can do, old girl,' he said. 'Haven't you heard? There's a Phoney War on.'

'That's not funny. I'm going to cancel the oysters. You're never here.'

However, the war was becoming slightly less phoney. Experts at Bomber Command had analysed the heavy losses suffered in those attempts to attack enemy shipping near Wilhelmshaven, long ago in September, and they had decided that flak did all the damage. Obviously the aircraft went in too low. So, one week before Christmas 1939, on a fine, cloudless day, twenty-two Wellington bombers flew to Wilhelmshaven. They kept close formation, still supposedly the best defence against fighters. They attacked at thirteen thousand feet, supposedly too high for German flak to reach. Both beliefs were wrong. Flak split the formations, and Messerschmitt fighters ripped into their flanks. Twelve Wellingtons were shot down, most of them in the flames of their own petrol. Three limped home and made crash-landings. Of twenty-two bombers, only seven landed safely.

A loss of 68 per cent: that was the bad news. The good news, for 409 Squadron, was that daylight ops by Hampdens near the enemy coast were now definitely out; and self-sealing fuel tanks could be expected soon. Meanwhile, there were raids by night to drop leaflets.

These ops were codenamed Nickels. For the first time, Hampden crews flew over Germany, sometimes as far as Hanover, Osnabrück, Cologne, even the industrial thickets of the Ruhr. Everyone in 409 flew Nickels. The leaflets were a farce, they all knew that, but the trips were real enough: four hundred miles or more over a total blackout to a dot on the map, dump the bumf, turn round and fly back to the dot you left seven or eight hours ago: no picnic. Especially when people you couldn't see were trying hard to kill you. It wasn't like a cross-country navigation test around England, where every aerodrome had a beacon flashing its code letter, and you could ask for a fix if you got lost, and land at a friendly field if you got hopelessly lost. Silk's navigator was a new boy called Trevor Nimble, not yet twenty, a mathematician who had gone up to Oxford and quit after a year in order to join the RAF. He'd done a dozen cross-countries by night and never got even slightly lost. He could take star shots from the astrodome faster than any man Silk knew. The crew liked him because he played jazz on the violin and because his father was Sir Stamford Nimble, governor of Fiji. Trevor brought a touch of class to their kite, S-Sugar.

Their first Nickel was to Bremen.

This was an easy introduction to enemy territory. The River Weser flowed through Bremen, turned right and broadened into a long estuary. Find the estuary and you had a signpost to the city.

Silk took off at one a.m. and began the grind across the North Sea.

He climbed to eight thousand feet and ice began to form on the wings. Soon it was on the propellers and they were flinging splinters of ice at the cockpit. He went lower, found warm air at two thousand and stayed there. The hours passed peacefully. A half-moon shone through scattered cloud and showed a sea that looked like wrinkled black leather, as usual. His navigator gave him course corrections from time to time, nothing major, just the odd degree, until eventually Nimble navigated S-Sugar to within a mile of Heligoland, a rocky island fifty miles from the German coast, stuffed with flak batteries and heavy machine guns.

The barrage was so violent, like being caught in a firework display, that Silk took a couple of seconds to react. Then he banked steeply, dived to sea level and opened the throttles wide. Red and yellow tracer chased him.

Well, at least Nimble now knew exactly where they were. He gave

Silk the wrong course for Bremen. They never found the Weser, never found Bremen. Silk flew in circles, got hounded by searchlights and harassed by flak, and finally he dropped the leaflets on Rotenburg or Lüneburg or maybe Cloppenburg, who could tell, and turned for home. Nimble sent him across the north of Holland. The Dutch shelled S-Sugar all the way to the coast. It was dawn, and Nimble identified another definite landmark. The course he gave Silk was so wrong that Silk ignored it and steered himself back to England, to Lincoln, to RAF Kindrick.

Later, Tom Stuart interviewed Nimble, and sent him to the Wingco.

'If it's any consolation,' Hunt said, 'you're not the first, nor the last.'

'I was all right until Heligoland, until the flak, sir.' Nimble was still too bewildered to be miserable. 'After the flak I couldn't make my brain work. Each time I asked it to do something, it backed away. It was like ...' The comparison was foolish, but it was all he had. 'Like trying to see something through frosted glass.'

Hunt looked at the navigator's maps and records and calculations: shambles. 'You should have told your skipper.'

Nimble just shook his head, totally defeated. 'Nothing worked, sir.'

His bags were packed and he was off the camp by noon. Silk said goodbye for the crew. 'Not your fault,' he told him. 'Just one of those things.' Nimble nodded. It was all he could do to nod. Not yet twenty, and an utter failure. Thank God father was in Fiji.

5

'As it's your birthday,' Tom Stuart said, 'we've decided to let you bomb Germany.'

'It's not my birthday, sir,' Langham said.

'Oh dear. Air Chief-Marshal Ludlow-Hewitt, C-in-C Bomber Command, has blundered again. Whatever shall we do?'

'My mistake, sir. Of course it's my birthday.'

'Hallelujah. The Hun has had the gall to bomb British soil. You may have read about it while you were looking for Jane in the *Daily Mirror*. Attacked our ships in Scapa Flow, missed, blew holes in the Orkney Islands. Also, unfortunately, in one civilian, now dead. The

Roosevelt Rules are suspended while we visit the island of Sylt, which is the closest German equivalent to Scapa, and destroy the seaplane base at Hornum, which has no civilians. This will teach the Hun a lesson while showing the Yanks what decent chaps we are. Full bombload – incendiaries and HE – and before you ask, the answer is no, there will be no Long Delay pistols on the HE.'

Langham nodded gratefully. 'I know he's gone to wherever it is that armourers go,' he said, 'but I miss the bastard. Silly, isn't it?'

Stuart led a mixed formation from 'A' and 'B' Flights. They couldn't fail to find Sylt: it was the last German island before Denmark. No blackout in Denmark. In any case, thirty Whitley bombers had been given first crack at Hornum, followed by twenty Hampdens, so the place was very excited. A score of searchlights carved up the night, flak erupted all around, coloured tracer spiralled and bent, incendiaries twinkled on the ground, HE went off like little flashbulbs. Yet, apart from an occasional dull *bok-bok*, the only sound was the engines. Interesting.

The Air Ministry told the BBC and the BBC told the world that, in the biggest operation of the war so far, Bomber Command had knocked seven bells out of Hornum. The following day, Germany's Propaganda Ministry flew a bunch of American journalists to Sylt, and they reported that Hornum was largely intact. *Germany Calling*, the English-language radio channel, made the most of this.

'Showed the Yanks the wrong island!' Rafferty scoffed. 'That neck of the woods is stiff with Hun islands. Damn-fool reporters got bamboozled.'

'We dropped twenty tons of high explosive and twelve hundred incendiaries,' Bins said. 'They can't *all* have missed.'

'Pity it wasn't Berlin,' the Wingco said. 'I'd like to see Mr Goebbels get out of *that*.'

'At least he knows the eagle has teeth,' Rafferty growled.

The MO opened his mouth and then closed it. The group captain noticed. 'Yes?' he said.

'Oh ... I just wanted to mention the gunner in P-Peter, sir. LAC Davis. He took some shrapnel in the face. Lost an eye, I'm afraid.'

For a long moment Rafferty didn't move, didn't blink, stared at the MO but pictured instead the gunner searching the night sky over Sylt until the last image one eye would ever see was the shellburst that destroyed it. How horrible. What courage. 'Take me to him,' he said.

6

Immediately after the Hornum raid, 409 was again placed on standby, with all aircraft fuelled and bombed up. This kind of flap was becoming very common. 'It's spring,' Bins explained to Jonty Brown. 'Lambs gambol and warriors gamble. That's a play on words. You wouldn't understand, being a Rhodesian.'

'It's not spring in Rhodesia. It's autumn. You wouldn't understand, being a penguin.' A penguin was anyone with wings who didn't fly.

The flap lasted twenty-four hours. It was afternoon when 409 was stood down and Langham drove home. Zoë had read what the newspapers said about Hornum. 'Did you go on this beano?' she asked. 'How thrilling. What was it really like?'

'Hard to say, dear. Couldn't see much, because the searchlights were rather blinding. Then we dropped some parachute flares and they made it even worse. Dazzling.'

'The *Daily Express* says you delivered a knockout blow.'

'Do they? Awfully sweet of them.' He yawned. 'Sorry. I've been up all night. Can we go to bed, d'you think?'

'And Mr Chamberlain says that Hitler has missed the bus.'

'So I heard. I can't honestly see the Fuehrer travelling by bus, can you? Not his style.'

'But if there's a sort of ceasefire or something, you could get transferred, darling, couldn't you? Lots of aerodromes are on the edge of London and – '

'Let's talk about it later. Bed calls.' He made for the stairs, and stopped. 'Aren't you coming?'

'Sleep, darling, sleep. Get your strength back.' That had never happened before.

It was night when he woke. Below, people were talking. Zoë laughed. He pulled on trousers and a sweater and clumped downstairs, feeling thick in the head and sticky in the mouth. 'What's up?' he said.

She was playing cards with a man who looked thoroughly at home. He had more curly sandy hair than the RAF would allow, sky-blue eyes, freckled forehead, generous lower lip. Aged under thirty. No jacket. Checked shirt open at the neck, revealing more curly sandy hair. Shoulders like a wrestler. Hands like pianist. Smile like a villain. Was that Shakespeare? Sounded like him.

'Darling, this is Flemming Vansittart. He's teaching me bridge.'

They shook hands. The man had a grip like a blacksmith. So much for the pianist idea. 'She shows great promise,' Vansittart said.

'Promise, promise. Sit down, please. Promise. Yes, I remember. She promised me something once.' Langham warmed his backside at the fire. 'Probably forgotten it by now.' He wasn't making much sense and he didn't care. It was his house, he could say what he bloody well liked.

'You need a drink, my sweet. Flemming's from Holland.'

'Dutch! Your lot keep trying to kill me. With shells. Sodding great anti-aircraft shells. Not very nice, is it?'

Vansittart spread his arms in apology. 'I live here now. This part of England is similar to Holland, so I advise landowners. I'm an expert on reclamation.'

'I bet you are,' Langham said vigorously. 'Moment I laid eyes on you, I said to myself, look out, there's a bloke doing a bit of reclamation.'

'Don't be silly, darling.' She gave him a large gin. 'Drink up your nice medicine and you won't be so grouchy.'

'We're going out to dinner,' he told Vansittart. 'Soon as I get some shoes on. Pity you can't come, but you can't.'

'No we're not. Flemming brought some lovely steaks, so he's staying for supper.'

'You'd better cook 'em too,' Langham told him. 'She's a disaster in the kitchen and I'm too pissed. Good cook, are you?'

'How else could I survive in this country?' he said happily. Langham began to feel defeated. 'This gin is *flat*,' he complained, and drank more. 'Flat as bloody Holland.'

Vansittart turned out to be a very good cook. He was also amusing and interesting about his travels in exotic parts. Langham reacted by addressing him formally. 'Look here, Mr Vansittart,' he began.

'Please: call me Flemming.'

'If you insist. Got a better idea. Call you Flem, for short. Okay, Flem? Good old Anglo-Saxon word, Flem.' After that he said Flem every time he spoke. The Dutchman did not seem offended. Nothing upset him. Nothing disturbed his flow of conversation. He had a habit, when he wished to make a point, of reaching towards Zoë as if to gently tap her arm, yet never quite touching her. Once he turned to Langham and did briefly squeeze his wrist, for emphasis. The wrist tingled long after.

Vansittart embraced Zoë when he said goodbye. Langham escorted him to his car. 'A most enjoyable evening,' Vansittart said. 'Thanks for the steaks,' Langham said, 'and stay away from my wife or I'll break your neck.'

Even that didn't disturb him. 'I think you have misread the situation,' he said. 'Your charming wife has absolutely no sexual interest in me nor I in her. You, however, are a different cup of tea.' He got into his car. 'You appeal to me enormously.' The same half-moon that shone on Sylt now shone on his smile. Langham's pulse leaped twenty points. He slammed the car door. As the car pulled away he kicked the rear wing.

Zoë was in the bathroom. 'You rather overdid the Flem joke, darling. I mean to say, it's not a very pleasant word, is it?' She began brushing her teeth.

'He's as queer as a coot. Did you know that?'

She didn't hurry. Brushed every tooth. Rinsed the basin.

'Of course I did. Wasn't it obvious?'

'Not to me. How could you tell?'

'We'll talk about it tomorrow. Come to bed, darling.'

'No, I think I'll read the papers. You get your sleep, dear. Get your strength back.' He went downstairs, telling himself: *Two can play at that game, missy.*

They didn't talk about it next day. They lunched at Bardney Castle and drove to Lincoln and did some shopping. She bought him a pair of dark glasses, silver frames, very lightweight, to baffle the German searchlights. He bought her a little porcelain boxer dog, its muzzle on its paws, half-asleep. It delighted her; she had never had a pet, she said. They went to the pictures: Errol Flynn and Flora Robson in *The Sea Hawk*; ate a quick supper in a restaurant; drove home and went straight to bed. This time there was no need for invitations.

'Goodness,' she said. 'That should be enough for one small baby. I thought you would never stop.' He smirked in the darkness. Normal service had resumed.

DUTY, GENTLEMEN!

1

April 1940 was a busy month at Kindrick.

It began with a Tannoy message that crackled and droned throughout the camp as men walked to breakfast. 'Attention. All code-letters for aircraft have been changed in order to improve communications with the French Air Force. With immediate effect, A-Able is changed to A-*Ingénieux* and B-Baker to B-*Boulanger*. C-Charlie has been deleted. D-Dog is now D-*Chien*. E-Easy is E-*Facile*, et cetera. A full list is being circulated. Anyone requiring assistance with French pronunciation, report to the Orderly Room.'

It was the first of April. The adjutant was only mildly amused. 'Dafter things than that are going to happen before this war is over,' he told Bins as they sat down to porridge and kippers.

'You can't stop progress,' Bins said. He had no time for practical jokes. He was more interested in the *Times* crossword.

The adjutant considered trying to find out who the joker was and decided he had better things to do. There was the problem of Black Mac's Bentley. McHarg had left no will, and he had no next of kin. The safe thing would be to hand it over to some gloomy department of the Air Ministry. Rafferty disagreed. 'They don't know it exists. What they don't know can't harm them. Raffle the beast.'

'Risky, sir. Suppose some bolshy erk wins it? One minute he's sweeping out the hangars, next minute he's driving to the Naafi and half the camp's saluting him.'

'Good point. Officers only, then.'

Rafferty won the raffle. 'Bugger,' he said and donated the Bentley to 409, to replace the crew wagon. Silk refused to use the Bentley. 'It

111

brought me nothing but trouble,' he said, 'and look what happened to Black Mac. I'd sooner walk.'

'Superstition,' Langham said. 'You surprise me, Silko, an educated twerp like you. That Bentley's perfectly safe, as long as you remember to walk nine times around it backwards and spit on the tyres.'

'It's bad luck,' Silk insisted.

The first two crews to be taken to their Hampdens by Bentley were on Nickel ops. The Met man's predictions turned sour, and fog covered much of Europe. One crew made a forced landing in Holland, thinking it was Kent, and got interned. The other crew, short of fuel, bailed out over a mountainous corner of Lorraine and were lucky to end up in a French hospital. 'Double bugger,' Rafferty said. It didn't make him feel any better, and it didn't solve the problems of navigation over Europe in foul weather.

On the other hand, losses were good for promotion. Rafferty and Hunt recognized leadership when they saw it. Before long, Pug Duff was a flight lieutenant.

2

The Phoney War seemed to be over on April 9, 1940, when Germany overran Denmark and captured the main Norwegian ports and airfields, including Oslo. Allied forces hurried across the North Sea to fight for Norway. 409 Squadron rejoiced. It had been a long winter: months of training, and then the grind of Nickels, stooging around Germany for the doubtful pleasure of bombarding the enemy with paper. Now he had replied with high explosive, so at last there was the prospect of Bomber Command being turned loose to do the job it was designed for, and actually bombing something on land, anything, just as long as it blew up and hurt the Hun. 409 couldn't wait to do its stuff.

And then Bins told them that the Phoney War was not entirely dead, except in Norway. Elsewhere in Europe, the Roosevelt Rules still applied. No bombs on the enemy mainland, where civilians might get hurt.

However, the German army was shipping men and supplies from Kiel to Oslo as fast as it could. That part of the Baltic, Bins pointed out, is rather cramped. Ships had to pass through narrow channels between the large islands of Denmark. So 409 would drop magnetic mines in those channels.

As usual, the group captain ended the briefing with words of encouragement. 'Minelaying has been codenamed Gardening. Mines are Vegetables, very special weapons, very secret. Hitler must not get his sweaty hands on a Vegetable. If you can't drop it, or fly home with it, then crash the kite. No half-measures. Point your bomber at the nearest mountain, open the throttles, bale out, and wait for an extremely large explosion as you float down. Duty, gentlemen! Duty.'

At first, Gardening was a pleasant eight-hour trip. Sometimes a crew would go to the pictures in Lincoln, get fish and chips, return to Kindrick, take off before midnight and be back with the dawn for a good breakfast. After a week, Bins had good news: four German troopships had struck mines and sunk with devastating loss of life. 409 liked that. However, nothing is static in war, and German flak ships appeared in the Channels. Bins constantly stressed the importance of accuracy when Gardening. First the pilot must find a landmark and make a long, straight, timed run, quite slowly, letting the aeroplane sink gently to about two hundred feet, the navigator counting down the seconds to the precise spot. The mines fall and make silent splashes, white on black. The navigator makes a note in his log. The pilot opens the throttles and begins to climb. That was the standard procedure and that was what Happy Hall did. A flak ship blinded him with searchlights and boxed him with shellfire and sprayed him with tracer and turned the Hampden into blazing scrap in ten seconds. In twenty seconds the Baltic had received the remains and quenched the fire. The searchlight died.

At first the bomber was overdue; then missing. 'Sitting in their dinghy, I expect,' Pixie Hunt said. 'Who knows?' *Germany Calling* claimed to know. The announcer – already famous as Lord Haw-Haw – stated in his bogus upper-class drawl that the German navy had destroyed a Hampden bomber. 'Easily said,' Hunt grunted. Later, Lord Haw-Haw gave the serial number of the bomber, found on wreckage floating in the Baltic. 'Gentlemen of the RAF stationed at Kindrick in Lincolnshire should not trespass in

German waters,' he added. Hunt had nothing to say about that.

The next day, Langham drove home through a perfect, placid, warm English spring morning. The top of the Frazer-Nash was down. Healthy country smells blew in and out of the car. His backside still ached, his eyes itched and wouldn't stop blinking, his mouth remembered the taste of oxygen, and he was happy to be alive. A rabbit fled ahead, and he touched the brakes until it found safety in a hole in the hedge. Well done, bunny.

Zoë came out to meet him. 'Look,' she said. Their apple tree was in blossom.

'What a clever girl you are.'

She put her hands on his shoulders and examined his face. The impressions left by his helmet and oxygen mask were very faint but she knew where to look. 'Did you have a good night at the office, darling?'

'Usual routine, sweetie. Took off, stooged about, landed.'

It was what they always said.

He sat at the garden table and ate an enormous breakfast: eggs, bacon, mushrooms, fried potatoes, pork sausagemeat, racks of toast, coffee in a half-pint tankard. She snacked from his plate and told him the local gossip. He smiled and nodded. Part of his mind was still five hundred miles away, near the Danish port of Middelfart, good for a laugh at briefing but no joke when D-Dog broke cloud at six hundred feet and the rain was so heavy that Jonty Brown couldn't tell if they were over land or water. The flak batteries didn't hesitate. They splattered the night with red and yellow shellbursts. Jonty saw gun-flashes reflected in water. 'There's the channel!' he shouted. 'Not bloody likely,' Langham said. His right hand opened the throttles as his left hand hauled back the stick. D-Dog raised her nose and climbed through the scattered fragments of a dying shellburst. The turmoil of air rocked the wings and shrapnel punched ragged holes in the cockpit Perspex. Rain howled past observer and pilot. Then D-Dog was back in the clouds. Eventually Jonty found an unguarded stretch of channel, they dropped their mines and flew home, sometimes in drenching rain, sometimes above the weather where the air was arctic and ice formed inside the cockpit. Always Langham was sitting in a raging gale.

And now here he was, drowsy in the sunlight, tossing bits of toast for sparrows brave enough to swoop on the table, and admiring his wife's splendid legs while he wished his left arm would stop twitching. He put his left hand in his pocket and told it to behave. Zoë was talking about a clever seamstress who was making her some heavenly tweed slacks for the country.

'What's wrong with your jodhpurs?'

'Everyone's wearing jodhpurs, darling. And they don't suit everyone. Haven't you noticed?'

His fingers found a spiky lump of metal in his pocket and he took it out. 'I thought you might like to have this. Sort of keepsake.' She fingered it and made a face. 'Just shrapnel,' he said. 'Found it on the floor of the cockpit when we landed.'

'It's so ugly. It's vicious.'

'I suppose so. That's its job, to be vicious.' He took it back and held it against the sun, between finger and thumb, like a gem. 'Missed me, though.'

She saw the sharp, twisted metal so near his face. 'It's hateful,' she said. 'Get rid of it.' He threw it, hard, out of the garden, into a bramble patch. 'Best place for it,' he said.

They went to bed, as they always did when he came back from a night op, and he was asleep while she was still closing the curtains. He awoke alone. She heard him moving about, and came upstairs. They went back to bed and held each other, skin against skin. She could feel his heart beating. Nothing aroused him; nothing. 'Never mind,' she said.

'I must have left it in Denmark. It's a tragedy. Like *Hamlet*.'

'No, it's not. It's nothing like that.'

He put his head deep under the bedclothes. 'You're absolutely right,' he said. 'Doesn't look a bit like Hamlet. In fact it bears rather a close resemblance to Polonius. Wrinkled and bent.'

'Be patient, my love. Next time will be twice the fun.'

They lay side by side. She stroked his leg with the sole of her foot. 'Happy Hall got the chop,' he said.

'Oh. Did I meet him?'

'He was at the wedding. He was a good type.'

There was nothing more to be said about that. She listened to the frightful silence of Lincolnshire and wished it was London. He realized that his left arm had stopped twitching, and was glad.

NO IMPROVEMENT

April ended. Langham's problem did not. He blamed the strain of nightly Gardening ops. Zoë gave him iron tablets to suck.

The fight for Norway was obviously lost. Many of 409's crews were not sorry to see it end. The Danish Narrows had become too hot. The North Sea was a long haul for a Hampden trudging home with flak-damage and casualties on board; and sometimes the casualties, wrapped in parachutes against the freezing air howling down the fuselage, died before the Hampden landed.

409 got stood down. Langham took Silk in the Frazer-Nash to a country pub, the Black Swan. They sat beside a canal and drank beer and read newspapers. 'What a monumental cock-up,' Silk said.

'Censored, too. The truth must be worse. If possible.'

'I'll tell you what's worse. I've been given a different navigator. Gilchrist. The matinée idol.'

'He can't be as bad as that bloke you sacked. Name like a fairy.'

'Nimble. He wasn't stupid, he was duff. Flak made him freeze. This Gilchrist's a Brylcreem boy. He should be flying Spits.'

'You don't like him.'

'He hasn't got the balls for bombers.'

'He stood up to Rafferty, though. That took balls.'

'No, it took galloping stupidity. He hadn't been here ten minutes and he put up a black! Who needs a comedian for a nav? Gilchrist's been kicked from kite to kite. He's a bloody jinx. Now the Wingco's dumped him on me. The Wingco hates me.'

'Christ Almighty,' Langham said. 'You're in a foul stinking temper today, Silko.'

Silk grunted. He was leaning forward, elbows on knees. He watched a pair of wild ducks fly along the canal, lower their flaps and undercarriage, and make a perfectly greased landing. 'Wish I could do that,' he said. 'Yesterday I bounced like a bloody kangaroo.'

'Everybody has bad days.'

'Yeah. What worries me is, I didn't care. Shitty landing, and I didn't give a tiny toss.' He took out a coin. 'And here is the tiny toss I didn't give. Remember this?'

'That's your lucky penny.'

'It's been on every op I've done.' He spun it and caught it. 'Heads or tails? What are the odds?'

'Evens, of course. Fifty-fifty.'

'Yeah. But suppose you call heads nine times in a row and you win all nine. Now ...' He tossed again, and covered the penny with his hand. He looked Langham in the eyes. 'Still fifty-fifty?'

'Logic says yes, but ...'

'But you're not convinced.' Silk threw the penny in the canal. 'Fuck luck. The chop is the chop is the chop. End of story.'

They finished their beer and walked along the towpath. 'You need some leave,' Langham said.

'Leave book's closed. I asked Uncle for a week's compassionate to go and see *Gone With The Wind*, and he said the squadron's awfully short of compassion right now, try again next year.'

Silk was jaunty again. Langham relaxed a little. 'Still, the loss of the lucky penny bothered him, and he tried to persuade Silk to do something about Gilchrist, encourage the man, teach him some tricks of the trade.

'I don't leave anything to luck,' Langham said. 'I check everything in advance. I go over the flight plan with Jonty, and he gives me a copy of all the course bearings. He writes the numbers big, too, in case I can't see very well. Suppose Jonty gets knocked out? Over the target, say. I want the course for base in my hand, not down the other end of the observer's tunnel. And I do an intercom check every seven minutes. A gunner's no damn good if his oxygen tube's come unplugged. I always have short gunners, five-seven, five-eight, because they can handle the guns in their little cupolas better than a big chap whose knees and elbows get in the way. And everybody in my crew can find his way anywhere in the kite by feel, in total darkness ...'

He had a dozen other precautions. At the end, Silk just shrugged and said, 'Well, bully for you, Tony. Now tell me what you do when the unknown happens. Stabilized yaw, for instance.'

'Refer to Pilot's Notes.'

They turned back. 'How's your sex life?' Silk asked. 'Can you find time for a cup of cocoa between orgies?'

'Awfully decent of you to ask. It's not good news, I'm afraid. My half of the bargain has gone absent without leave. It's been acting with what drill sergeants call mute insolence.'

'No lead in the pencil?'

'Scarcely a pencil, sometimes.'

'Better see the MO.'

The more Langham thought about it, the less he liked the idea. The MO was good at fractures and frostbite but he was a bachelor, and he had a strange and cynical sense of humour. He might attempt Freudian therapy. He had a couch in his office. Not bloody likely. Langham went to his flight commander and said he had urgent business affairs to sort out in London, and Tom gave him twenty-four hours' leave. He caught an express from Lincoln and was in Harley Street by late afternoon. He told the receptionist he was Zoë Herrick Herrick's husband. Twenty minutes later he was shaking hands with Guy Chard-Cox. He had prepared a sober, intelligent statement on the train; now it vanished like steam. 'No sex,' he said. 'My plonker won't rise to the occasion any more.'

'That must be quite infuriating.' Chard-Cox was forty-odd, slim, bright-eyed, square-jawed, the opposite of the pompous consultant Langham had expected to meet. 'So many things can sabotage our reproductive system that it's a miracle we are here today. Take spermatorrhoea, which is a discharge of seminal fluid that occurs independently of voluntary sexual excitement.'

'I think I would have noticed that, don't you?'

'Of course. How about circumcision?'

'I noticed that long ago.'

'So we can rule out phimosis. Splendid. Let's see … Constipation sometimes causes pressure on veins, thus irritating the sexual organs … No constipation, good, good. You must tell me your secret. So many of my patients are bound solid.'

'Terror helps.'

Chard-Cox smiled. 'I'm sure it does. There's an unhelpful condition called intertrigo, or chafing. No chafing? Excellent. Congenital syphilis I'm sure the RAF would have detected. How about dropsy? A hydrocele, which is just a bag of liquid, forms in the scrotum and may result in varicose veins on the spermatic cord.'

'Would I be aware of it?'

'You would. Furthermore you'd be extremely unlucky. The condition is usually confined to elderly men in the tropics.'

'God help us. Not exactly Rudyard Kipling, is it?'

'No. I wonder ... There's a problem called pressure palsy, sometimes known as crutch paralysis. Can we consider the flying suit you wear? Is it strapped very tightly around the groin? Enough to produce a loss of sensation? No? Forget crutch paralysis, then. Perhaps Raynaud's Disease might apply. It concerns prolonged chill or frostbite leading to gangrene of the extremities. The question arises: do you fly your Spitfire in icy conditions for long periods?'

'Yes and no. It's not a Spitfire, it's a Hampden bomber. And I often fly for hours when the outside temperature is down to thirty or forty below and my extremities, as you call them, are colder than a witch's tit and even smaller. But all that was happening long before I got married, so ...' He spread his hands.

'Delete Raynaud. I was sure your wife said Spitfires.'

'It's a long story.'

'Yes, of course. Sherry?'

There was a pause while they went through the ritual of pouring and sipping. 'Your wife told me a lot about her mother. Lady Shapland has quite a powerful personality, hasn't she? Seems always to get what she wants.' Langham couldn't argue with that. 'What do you really want? Do you really want to be a father?'

Langham hid his face behind his hands.

'Perhaps you were never given much choice,' Chard-Cox said.

Langham made a muffled grunt.

'So when you made love to your wife ...'

'I was a stud.' Langham dropped his hands. He felt very tired. 'I was doing it to satisfy the old bitch.' That wasn't the whole truth but it was near enough.

'Almost as if she were there beside you.'

'Urging me on.' Langham swigged his sherry. 'Like one of her bloody silly racehorses.'

They talked for a further ten minutes, but really everything had been said. Langham picked up his hat. 'What you might call blindingly obvious,' he said sadly.

'It happens all the time,' Chard-Cox told him. 'Not that it's any consolation. But it's a start.'

He took the train back to Lincoln, dozing, waking to rehearse in his mind what he was going to say to Zoë, dozing again. He drove to the cottage, arrived refreshed by the night air, and found his wife finishing supper with Flemming Vansittart and Silk. They all seemed very happy. 'Hell's teeth! You again,' he said to the Dutchman. 'Believe me, you won't get anywhere with *him*.' He pointed at Silk. 'He only sleeps with red-headed twins. Anyway, I'm still going to break your neck.'

'Surely not,' Flemming said. 'I'm just about to make the crêpes Suzette.'

'Sit down, darling. If you break Flemming's neck I'll break yours. Have some cassoulet, it's delicious.'

'Flem made it, didn't you, Flem?' Silk said. He was more than slightly drunk. 'Bloody good cook. Have a drink, don't be so bloody miserable.' He poured a glass of red wine.

'Did Flem make this too?'

Upstairs, the lavatory flushed. 'He certainly made *that*,' Zoë said. They laughed. Langham didn't understand. Silk's new popsy came down the stairs and got introduced. Langham tasted the cassoulet. Superb. Zoë asked him where he'd been. 'Nowhere near Holland, thank Christ,' he growled. They found that hilarious. He gave up.

Later, lying in bed, he said: 'I can't see what you see in that pansy.'

'Simple, darling. If he hadn't mended the hole in the roof, you'd have rain dripping in your face. If he hadn't done something to the WC, we'd be squatting in the bushes. You haven't been here to help, have you? And I like Flemming. It's nice to have someone to talk to. Just talk. I don't have sex with my friends. And you seem to have lost your boyish charm lately, haven't you?'

He was too tired to argue. He thought: *Tomorrow morning we'll sort it all out*. But next day he couldn't find the words; and in any case his leave was over.

He told Silk about going to Harley Street. 'The quack thinks that Zoë's mum is the nigger in the woodpile,' he said. 'The more she leans on me, the more I back off.' Silk nodded. 'Interesting,' he said. That was all. What more was there?

WE SHAN'T SEE HIM
IN A HURRY

1

When the Luftwaffe bombed the heart of Rotterdam for no good military reason and killed nine hundred Dutch civilians, then at last, finally, irrevocably, the Roosevelt Rules were scrapped and 409 flew to German cities and dropped, not leaflets, but bombs.

Actually some Hampdens carried bombs *and* leaflets. With Hitler conquering more of Europe than Napoleon or Charlemagne or Genghis Khan had managed, and far faster, this was an odd time to urge the German people to change their ways. Soon the Luftwaffe would be dropping leaflets on England, showing Churchill with a Tommy-gun and denouncing him as a gangster. Churchill was quite flattered, and the British liked the picture. Either way, bumf was bumf. It changed nothing.

But the air war, which had started so sluggishly, took off in a rush. Bombers of all types attacked railways, bridges and road junctions: vital links between Germany and the battlefront. By the time the bombers arrived, the battlefront had usually moved on. So the attack was switched to German industry. 409 Squadron learned new names in the Ruhr area: Gelsenkirchen, Dortmund, Castrop-Rauxel, Bochum, Mülheim, Krefeld, Wuppertal, many more. They were also sent to bomb Hamburg, Bremen and Cologne, familiar from Nickel trips. Bins briefed them on the oil installations to be hit, and Rafferty encouraged them to make every bomb count because the enemy must, by now, be running out of fuel. Bomber Command redoubled its attacks as the fighting threatened Dunkirk. The German army did not run out of fuel. Dunkirk fell. Maybe someone in the Ministry of Economic Warfare had got his sums wrong.

So ended May 1940, and June was just as hectic. Germany now had Holland, so the RAF no longer needed to make a great dog-leg to avoid neutral territory. That knocked a couple of hundred miles off a trip to the Ruhr and places like Cologne and Aachen, and it saved a further two hundred on the homeward journey. This was important in June and July. The nights were at their shortest. The northern sky was never completely dark. An incoming bomber was silhouetted for the benefit of German night fighters.

There was no such thing as safety in numbers. Each Hampden from 409 flew as an individual. Its crews decided when to take off, which route to follow, whether to bomb from high or low, sometimes what bombs to carry. Even when Group ordered 409 to send a whole Flight to hit a single target, the trip was a long and solitary experience for each crew. They might see another bomber caught by searchlights, or the flash and flicker of its bombs; but when they dumped their own load and made the long journey home, they rarely saw another machine until perhaps they had crossed the English coast and somebody else might be glimpsed in the moonlight, heading for the same base.

Ops were like that: long hauls when usually nothing went very wrong. Occasionally everything failed. It happened to Tubby Heckter and his crew, over Bremen. Flak smashed his compass and ruined his altimeter. Fog blanked the English coast. He was lost, and much lower than he thought, which was why he flew into the balloon barrage at Harwich. A cable sawed a wing off. The wreck burned so brightly that the fire brigade easily found it, even in the fog. And a week later, 'B' Flight's commander, Micky Byrd, failed to return. Just vanished. Next day, Pug Duff was an acting squadron leader, commanding the Flight. 'Who better?' Hunt said; and Rafferty agreed.

2

'Tell your batman to press your best uniform,' the Wingco said. 'You're going to be presented with your own personal aeroplane.'

'Yes, sir,' Langham said. 'I don't understand, sir.'

'Your rich mother-in-law has donated a Hampden to the nation. It's to be called the *Lady Shapland*. The ceremony's tomorrow, in front of the control tower. The bishop will bless the kite. The Press will take pictures. You will smile.'

'I like D-Dog, sir. I don't want another kite.'

'What you want is totally irrelevant. Remember that journalists twist everything, so tell them that Lady Shapland is a wonderful woman. Otherwise keep your mouth shut.'

Langham found Silk having a shower after playing squash, and told him the news. Silk was impressed. 'How much does a Hampden cost?'

'God knows. She probably sold Worcestershire to raise the cash. It's easy for her.'

'Ah.' Silk watched as Langham thrashed the air with the racket. Air whistled past the strings. 'Do I detect a note of bitterness?'

'Well, it's pure bloody blackmail, Silko. She won't let me rest until she's a blasted grandmother, will she? First she bullied me, now she's trying to bribe me. I didn't get married, I got bought and sold in a cattlemarket. Why doesn't the old bitch get into bed with us? Then she can kick me in the balls until I do the dirty deed.'

'Kicking you in the balls won't help. Biology was never your top subject at Clifton, was it?'

They strolled back to their rooms.

'Funny thing,' Langham said sombrely. 'Father used to worry that I might run amok and get some girl pregnant. Now I've got the opposite problem.'

'It makes no sense,' Silk said. 'I've only seen Zoë fully dressed, and even so she makes my flybuttons pop. You get her in bed, stark naked, and nothing happens? You've got a knot in your dong.'

Suddenly Langham was angry. 'You think you can do better?' he snapped. 'Okay, go ahead, she's yours.'

Silk gave a snort of amusement, but he saw it was no joke. 'Thanks awfully. I've got my hands full with that new Waaf, Brenda.'

'Not a hope in hell. Come on, Zoë likes you, she's said so. Five minutes is all it takes. Be a pal.'

Silk thought about it. Part of him was shocked and dismayed. A larger part wanted to jump at the chance. Unlike many pilots, Silk had lost his virginity, but it had been a rushed and disappointing business in a railway carriage between stops, and he wanted more. He wanted fireworks. Sex with Zoë would blow his socks off. 'What does she say about it?' he asked cautiously.

'Nothing. I haven't asked her.'

Now Silk was shocked and bewildered. 'It's all your idea?'

'Look, you know the score. I can't give her what she wants. You can. Then I'll be off the hook, don't you see?'

'You make it sound so simple. Just one problem: you're married and I'm not.'

'Who cares? Once the lights are out, Zoë won't know the difference. All cats are black in the dark.'

'I can't believe we're discussing this. It's absurd.'

'Don't say no, Silko. Think it over. Sex with Zoë is fun,' Langham said miserably. 'It really is the most tremendous fun.'

3

The ceremony of donating, naming and blessing the bomber was a great success. The sun shone. The entire squadron paraded. The band of the RAF played. Lady Shapland wore a dress of sky-blue silk topped off with a clever hat modelled on an RAF forage cap. Zoë wore a short coat and skirt of white linen with a scarlet headscarf and knocked her mother dead.

Various people made brief speeches: an air marshal, the Secretary of State for Air, Group Captain Rafferty. Lady Shapland named the Hampden after herself. The Bible is notoriously thin on aeronautical advice, so the bishop made the most of Isaiah, chapter forty, verse thirty-one: 'They that wait upon the Lord shall renew their strength; they shall mount up with wings as eagles; they shall run, and not be weary; and they shall walk, and not faint.' He blessed the Hampden, and prayed that those who flew in it would smite the ungodly. The Wingco led three cheers and everyone except the air marshal flung his cap in the air, a pre-arranged spectacle for the benefit of Press photographers. Finally the officers and guests went to tea in the Mess.

An hour later, Langham's smile ached. Philly took him by the arm and steered him outside. 'The British wouldn't know a real sandwich if it bit them in the ass,' she said. 'Those little triangles are pathetic. How you guys ever won India beats me. We'll take a walk.'

They strolled over to her Hampden. 'Why did you do it?' he asked.

'For fun. Why else? Speaking of which, Zoë tells me you two are having trouble in the sack.' He nodded. 'You don't play Hide The Salami any more. Did used to. Don't now.'

He walked away, kicked a tyre, came back. 'There are some things you can't buy. Not even you.'

Her eyes widened. 'If you can't cut the mustard, that's cause for divorce and I can buy *that* in ten seconds, don't kid yourself, sonny.' She snapped her fingers. He saw that her hand was trembling. A pulse in her throat was throbbing furiously. One thing he had learned to recognize was fear. This woman was afraid. What a surprise.

'Why make such a fuss?' he asked. 'You've got a son in Africa, haven't you? Rhodesia? Tell him to do his ghastly family duty.'

'He can't. When he was eighteen he had cancer of the testicles. Lucky to live, but he's not a man any more. Men are so damn *weak*.'

They walked on. For the first time in a month, he felt calm. 'You're a selfish bitch, Lady Shapland,' he said. 'You've always got what you want, and it's never enough. You'll never see fifty again, will you? And you're desperate for Zoë and me to breed, so your whole rich stupid life won't be a waste.'

'Congratulations, kid. I just cut you out of my will.'

'There you go again. We speak different languages. You've bought a Hampden. So what? We lose a couple of kites like this one every month. Go ahead, buy another kite, buy two, it won't replace eight dead men.'

'They're young, they don't know what they're losing. It's harder when you get older. You'll see.'

'Highly unlikely.' He spoke so crisply that she was silenced. They walked back to the Mess.

4

That night he was on ops. The target was Gelsenkirchen but industrial haze blotted out the Ruhr valley and Jonty got hopelessly lost.
Langham prowled around at fifteen hundred feet, searching and
failing, breathing the chemical stink of a thousand factories. Even the
searchlights were baffled by the pollution. In the end he gave up and
went home via Schiphol aerodrome, which he could see clearly, and
he bombed it instead. Everyone bombed Schiphol. It was the dustbin
for leftover bombs.

Still, the crew had earned their bacon and eggs, which they never
got. Fog was thick over East Anglia, Kindrick was closed, Langham
got diverted to West Raynham, cancelled, diverted to Feltwell, cancelled, and ended up at Abingdon in Oxfordshire, a big Operational
Training Unit. Bombers were packed all over the field. No breakfast.
They slept on blankets in a hangar. It was midday before they landed
back at Kindrick. There was a flap on, reports of a German battleship in the North Sea, all crews to briefing, all Hampdens bombed
up. Soon that got changed to mines: Gardening at Rotterdam. Fresh
briefing. Then the mines came off and the bombs went back on
again. No briefing. Nobody cared any more. Too much climax and
anticlimax. At nine p.m. the whole shambolic op was scrubbed.
Everyone cheered and headed for alcohol except Langham, who
drove home through the mild and scented evening air.

He was met at the garden gate by a delirious boxer puppy. It
barked endlessly, scattering spittle, and leaped at his legs. 'Get off,
you brute!' he shouted, waving his cap at it. The dog jumped, trying
to bite the cap. This was fun.

'Don't do that, darling,' Zoë called. 'He's just being friendly.'

'Make the bugger shut up, then. I've got dirt on my bags.'

She hurried down the path and clipped a leash to the dog's collar.
It stopped barking and began chewing her shoes. 'He's pure boxer,'
she said.

'He's pure menace. What's he doing here? You're not looking after
him, I hope.'

'No, he's mine, I bought him.' As they walked to the cottage the
dog lunged to left and right, desperate to eat a flower or catch a moth.
'Heel, boy! Heel, I say!' Encouraged, the dog lunged more fiercely.

'You bought him. Why?'

'Oh, because. You take him, darling. My hand hurts.'

They went in. He tied the leash to the leg of a sofa. The dog raced away and was stopped, choking. 'It can't stay here,' he said. 'It's completely batty.'

'No, he's not, he's sweet! Don't you remember, you gave me that little porcelain boxer?' It was on the mantelpiece. 'I'm all alone here. I need a friend. What's the matter?'

Langham was sniffing, slowly turning, searching. 'Something smells in here. A peculiar stink.'

'It's not his fault, my love. He's just a little doggie, you mustn't blame him if he …'

Langham was scrutinizing several dark patches on the carpet. 'The damn thing's crapped everywhere,' he said. He saw more. 'There isn't anywhere it hasn't crapped.'

'It's not his fault, and besides …' She took a small bottle from a shelf and quickly sprayed the darkest patch. 'There. Now I've covered up the nasty smell, so everything's all right, isn't it?'

His nose twitched. 'What is that stuff?'

'Chanel Number Three.'

He laughed so much that he had to sit down. The dog stopped chewing the sofa leg and began chewing his shoe. 'Has this hound got a name?' he said.

'Of course he has. I call him Handyman, because he's always doing little jobs about the house.' That was even funnier. She smiled. It was a long time since she had seen him so happy.

'He seems to have a taste for feet,' Langham said. 'What have you been feeding him on?'

'Jam doughnuts, darling. And beer. I read somewhere that dogs like beer.'

Now Langham was too exhausted to laugh. 'Jam doughnuts,' he said. 'Beer. My poor sweet angel. You don't know anything, do you?'

'Well, daddy would never let us have pets when we were children.' She sat on his lap and unbuttoned his tunic. The puppy fell asleep with his mouth full of shoelaces. After a certain amount of kissing, she said, 'Handyman's not the only stinker here.'

'That's honest sweat.'

'I'll run an honest bath for you. Stay there.'

The bath smelt powerfully of exotic oils and essences. 'This isn't

127

Chanel Number Three, is it?' he asked as he eased himself into surprisingly hot water. No answer. His skin tingled in a way that he hadn't felt since winter afternoons at Clifton, rubbing pungent embrocation on his shoulders before rugger matches.

After a couple of minutes he found himself looking at an erection. He splashed it, but it didn't go away. After ten minutes it was taller than ever. He stood up and watched it. Fresh air made no difference. 'Come and look at this,' he called.

She came in. 'Well,' she said. 'There's a thing.' She flicked it gently with a fingertip. It shivered like a flagpole in a wind.

'You don't sound surprised.'

'Well … promise you won't be angry, because … the fact is, Flemming gave me some special bath salts. He said a handful might help but I'm afraid my hand slipped and the whole boxful went in.'

'Flemming.'

'Yes. He told me he trained as a vet.'

Langham looked again. 'I don't know whether to laugh or cry.'

'Come with me.' She led him out of the bathroom. 'I'll see if I can find a good home for it.'

5

Next morning it poured with rain. Handyman liked that. He romped around the garden and came in, soaking wet and muddy. 'Who cares?' Langham said. 'Worse things happen upstairs. Tubby Heckter bought it, for instance.'

'Yes, I know. Silko told me last night. I mean yesterday. Some time, anyway.'

'Good type, Tubby.'

He chopped up a tin of corned beef with a handful of broken biscuits. Handyman wolfed it down and fell asleep. Now there was no reason to stay, so reluctantly he drove back to camp. His front wheels carved up the puddles and flung them aside.

Silk was, at first, astonished. 'Three hours?' he said. Then he was sceptical. 'I don't see how that's physically possible,' he said. Finally he offered his congratulations. 'It makes a nice change to hear some good news.'

'And she's bought a puppy to play with when I'm not there. Bliss reigns.'

'Damn good show.' Silk nodded and smiled, and kept nodding. 'Yes. I suppose this means your ... um ... offer, proposition, solution, you know what I mean, is now ...'

'Stone dead.'

'I would never have gone ahead with it, anyway.'

'Yes, you would, you liar.'

'Well, only for your sake.'

'Have you no shame?'

'Three hours,' Silk said. 'It makes you think, doesn't it?'

That afternoon the rain cleared and Silk went up for a night-flying test. His Hampden flew perfectly until he came to enter the landing circuit and the undercarriage refused to go down. The hydraulic system had a fault, obviously. The back-up system was a bottle of compressed air. It didn't work either. The pilot could pump the undercarriage down, by hand. The pump handle was locked solid.

Silk flew out to sea, burned up some fuel, came back and used up most of the rest. The control tower cleared the circuit. He got the crew into their crash positions. He made his final approach as slowly as possible. Everything felt normal; he found it hard to believe there were no wheels waiting to take the bomber's weight. Then he was skimming the ground, and the belly ploughed into the turf, he heard the scream of tearing metal, the propellers sent up a green blizzard that turned brown, and Silk's head got flung violently, savagely, from side to side.

Everybody escaped. The next thing Silk knew, he was in the MO's office, talking to both of them. If he looked at only one MO, that man drifted away and there were two again. It went on for hours. The MO thought he might have concussion. Double vision could be a symptom. Silk got packed off to a hospital in Cambridge. They specialized in this stuff.

His eyesight cleared up after two days but they kept him for a week. When he got back to Kindrick he reported to his Flight Commander, who was not Tom Stuart but a new squadron leader called Frank Fender. 'I've just taken over,' he said. 'Stuart caught a packet coming back from Hanover, night fighter probably, badly wounded. I believe he made a forced landing on a fighter field in Kent. We shan't see him in a hurry.'

'Good God,' Silk said. 'Fancy old Tom ... Anybody else?'

Fender opened a file. 'As I said, I've just arrived. Let's see ... Tony Langham bought it over Osnabruck. Flak. That's all.'

Silk went to the adjutant's office. His legs felt like stilts. 'Why didn't anyone tell me, Uncle?' he said.

'Don't be bloody silly, Silko,' the adjutant said, gently. He reached for the whisky bottle he kept in a desk drawer for occasions like this. There was always one chap that you thought would never get the chop. It had been the same in the First War. One chap would always come back, and when he didn't, it was worse than dying. Uncle had seen it a dozen times. Silk looked stunned, like a boy who had walked slap-bang into a telegraph pole.

PART TWO

Risk Creates Optimism

BEWARE INTRUDERS

1

409 Squadron's death toll was typical. During the summer and autumn of 1940, more aircrew were killed in Bomber Command than in Fighter Command. But it was Fighter Command that gripped the attention of the British people, because summer 1940 was the time of the Battle of Britain. When it came to newspaper space, Hampdens bombing Germany could not compete with Spitfires and Hurricanes clashing with the Luftwaffe over England.

At the height of the Battle of Britain, a bus came down from London to RAF Bodkin Hazel, a fighter aerodrome in Kent.

The bus brought Air Vice-Marshal Thurgood and an aide, Squadron Leader Perry, plus foreign correspondents from the United States, Scandinavia, Switzerland, Brazil, Canada, Russia, Spain. They were there because, increasingly, foreign newspapers and magazines were sceptical of British claims that Fighter Command was defeating the Luftwaffe. Some said that Air Ministry press releases were pure propaganda, written to boost morale, not to be taken seriously, especially when it came to claims of enemy aircraft destroyed.

Well, Bodkin Hazel was at the sharpest end of the fighting, and Thurgood introduced the journalists to squadron and flight commanders. Fortunately, there was a scramble to intercept raiders and the visitors saw a mass take-off. Not all the fighters returned. 'They probably landed elsewhere to refuel,' Thurgood said. 'Happens all the time.'

When he had debriefed the pilots, the Intelligence Officer joined the journalists. Flight Lieutenant Skelton was in his thirties, tall, with a beaky nose supporting horn-rim glasses. His forehead was domed, his cheekbones were wide, his jaws narrow. His nickname was Skull. 'Any luck?' someone asked.

'One Heinkel 111 definitely destroyed,' Skelton said. 'One possible.'

The journalists made notes, but they were disappointed. Twelve Hurricanes took off. All they got was one lousy Heinkel.

'To reach the bombers, our chaps often have to smash through the German fighter screen,' Thurgood pointed out.

'Any losses?' an American asked.

'One Hurricane,' Skelton said. 'The pilot baled out.'

'Even Steven, then.'

For a final question-and-answer session, the correspondents assembled in a lecture room. Thurgood brought Skelton along for good measure.

Everyone had been impressed by what they saw; nevertheless, their questions were still very pointed. What was the proof that the Air Ministry's scores were right? If so many German planes had been shot down, where were all the wrecks? According to the RAF, most of the Luftwaffe had been destroyed, but the raids seemed to be getting bigger, didn't they? Thurgood did his best but the longer it went on the more his answers sounded like excuses, which annoyed him. He resented having to deny allegations of false accounting at a time when the very survival of his country was under threat from a foreign dictator who had made a trade of dishonesty.

The meeting dragged to an end. He knew he had not convinced them. The room emptied until only a couple of the correspondents remained, asking the same old questions in different words. Thurgood forced a smile. 'If you think so little of our claims,' he said, 'why not go to Berlin and check theirs? The Lufwaffe's scores are absolutely preposterous!'

One of the journalists looked at Skelton. 'D'you have an opinion?' he asked.

'Undoubtedly the Luftwaffe's claims are inflated,' Skelton said. 'It's a natural phenomenon. High-speed combat invariably has that effect. Airmen are not ideal witnesses. Risk creates optimism, and optimism creates –'

'Wait outside, Skelton,' Thurgood said stonily. When the journalists had gone, he recalled Skelton and blasted him for his interfering stupidity. The Intelligence Officer was unmoved. 'I'm sorry if I embarrassed you, sir,' he said. 'But what the Luftwaffe claims is beside the point. Proving them wrong doesn't prove us right. If we believe our own lies we merely deceive ourselves and, by so doing, we aid the enemy. Surely that's self-evident.'

'Don't preach to me, flight lieutenant.'

Skull twitched his nose and made his spectacles bounce. 'Preaching assumes moral alternatives, sir. War allows us no such choice. We cannot award a fighter pilot his kill just because we feel he *deserves* it. The truth –'

'Get out.' Thurgood sounded sick, and looked even sicker. Skelton hesitated. The air vice-marshal grabbed the nearest weapon and hurled it at Skelton's head. It was a half-pint bottle of ink, government issue, short and chunky, and it should have cracked his skull. It missed by an inch and smashed a framed portrait of the King in RAF uniform. Ink drenched the wall. Squadron Leader Perry seized Skelton and hustled him out and kicked the door shut behind them. 'You maniac,' he said. 'Bugger off and hide! Understand? *Hide.*'

Skelton could not move. 'Luther,' he said. 'Martin Luther chucked his ink-horn at the devil and missed.' He saw the look in Perry's eyes and he turned and trotted off.

Next day the air vice-marshal picked up the telephone and had an amiable chat with an old friend in Air Ministry.

'Chap doesn't strike me as Fighter Command material,' Thurgood said. 'Too long-winded. Beats about the bush. Full of waffle.'

Skelton was posted as an instructor in Intelligence to a Flying Training School in Aberdeenshire. It was called RAF Feck. 'What's it near?' the adjutant asked him.

'Absolutely nothing.' Skelton was examining a map. 'Unless you count a village called Nether Feck.'

'Come on, Skull. It's got to be near *some*where exciting.'

'Germany seems closest.'

The adjutant came over and looked. 'Mmm,' he said. 'Slightly off the beaten track.'

'It's Siberia, Uncle. I'll die up there.'

'Nonsense. The Scots are great fun. You wait and see.'

Skull went off to pack. The adjutant telephoned his opposite number at Feck, supposedly to confirm Skull's posting but actually to find out something about the place. 'What can I tell you?' the other man said. 'Nine months of fog and three months of snow. That's Feck.'

'Doesn't sound very thrilling.'

'We make our own entertainment. Ping-pong and funerals, mainly.'

RAF Feck trained pilots to fly twin-engined aircraft. Mostly these were Blenheims.

In the fighting over France, Blenheims got shot down by the score. Clearly, something better was needed. Large numbers of Blenheims were made available for training units. This was just as well. At Feck, a day without a crash was cause for mild surprise.

At first, the scale of these losses shocked Skull. After a while he got to know a senior instructor, and he asked what caused them.

'Usually we never know,' the man said. He looked tired. 'I have a few theories. For instance, power is intoxicating. We give these boys an aeroplane. Last year they were riding a bike. Now they've got fifteen hundred horsepower at their fingertips. They go solo, they can't resist flying too fast or too low, or banking too hard. Power seduces them, you see. But one tiny mistake gets magnified by all that power. It only takes a second to lose control.'

'Can't you weed out the dare-devil types?' Skull asked.

'All pilots have a streak of dare-devil. Otherwise they wouldn't be pilots, would they?'

Skull remembered the sober and experienced pilots he had known who had chosen to fly underneath bridges for no sane reason that anyone could identify. Some had died. 'It seems such an idiotic waste,' he said.

'Well, there are other reasons for crashes,' the senior instructor said. 'Some pilots lack faith. They don't trust their instruments. They fly by the seat of their pants, and the physical sensations they feel, or think they feel, tell them they're climbing when the instruments show they're diving. Or they're convinced the aeroplane is turning when the instruments show otherwise. And so they kill themselves.'

Skull was beginning to be sorry he'd asked.

'Flying is a very unnatural affair,' the senior instructor said.

Skull could not blot out the dull thump of a distant explosion, the klaxon summoning the crash crew, the hammering bell of the blood wagon; but he did his best to ignore them. They weren't his business. His business was in the lecture room, explaining the why and how of Intelligence. The trainees were not especially interested. They were eager to fly, to qualify, to get to an operational squadron before something went horribly wrong and the war ended. So he lectured them as he used to do at Cambridge, speaking to a crowd of bored undergraduates who were as relieved as he was when they were free to go off and play games.

In his spare time he went bird-watching, as far as possible from Feck. He took his leave allowance one day at a time, drove to St Andrews, browsed the university library and indulged in an orgy of reading. When spring came, he went into the hills and did some trout fishing. It was an odd life. The newspapers told him about the Blitz. Heavy bombing had reached as far north as Glasgow. But Skull's war was confined to RAF Feck, and there seemed no reason why Air Ministry should find a need for his services anywhere else; until one day a signal curtly ordered him to proceed to London. No explanation.

2

'They've bombed the Sheldrake,' Champion said. 'The *bastards.*' For a moment the shock left him breathless.

'I'm surprised that you're surprised,' Skelton said. 'The rest of London's been blitzed. Why not your club?'

Champion recovered and strode forward. ARP barriers shut off Pall Mall but his wing commander's rings got him through. Skelton, only a flight lieutenant, followed.

'Just look,' Champion said. 'Some idiot Kraut pilot hasn't the wit to find the docks, so he drops his stupid bomb on the Sheldrake. I mean, just look. I'm on the wine committee.'

'Past tense, surely.'

'Bastards. Absolute bastards.'

A man approached them, an elderly man made to seem older by a covering of dust and a smear of dried blood on his temple. He had a soldierly bearing. 'Mr Champion, sir,' he said.

'Good Lord, it's Tizard. Are you hurt, man?' To Skelton he said: 'One of the club servants ... This is a sad sight, Tizard.'

'Indeed it is, sir. But we've saved the club silver. And two can play at this game, sir. I served in the last show, and take it from me, sir, the Huns haven't got our backbone. You know me, sir, I'm not a vindictive man, but I hope the RAF blows Berlin to smithereens.'

Champion patted his shoulder. 'Good man, Tizzard ... Well, we shan't get any lunch here, shall we?'

'The Army and Navy Club has offered our members its hospitality during the emergency, sir.'

They walked to the Army and Navy.

It was springtime, but the air smelled of bonfires: city bonfires, stinking not of dead leaves but of charred linoleum and half-burnt mattresses, tinged with the harsh aroma of dead fireworks. It was eight months since the Blitz had first introduced Londoners to this smell. Now they scarcely noticed it.

The two officers said little until they sat down to lunch.

Ten years before, Champion had been an undergraduate at Cambridge and Skelton had been his tutor. They had disliked each other. Skelton was a youngish history don; his special interest was Tudor Puritan sects. Champion did not take the Puritans seriously. He was not stupid but he was lazy. Sometimes his essays manipulated facts in order to suit his views. Skelton found that intolerable. What made it worse was Champion's bland indifference when he got found out. 'If you were an accountant,' Skelton told him, 'you'd be in prison.'

'Quite a few Puritans went to jail.'

'For their beliefs. You distort those beliefs.'

'If they were alive, they might find I'd improved them.'

'And if you want to write fiction, then change your degree. Read English.'

Champion wrinkled his nose. 'They're all pansies. They all wear mauve socks.'

'So do I, occasionally. Write me an essay on the effects of bigotry on Tudor clothing. You'll find it quite startling.'

Champion found it damn dull. Skelton amused him: he was too donnish to be true, under thirty yet already developing a scholarly stoop. He wore tweeds as faded and shapeless as a poor watercolour. During tutorials he propped his head on his hand. He had a lank moustache. His glasses were horn-rimmed and heavy. Skelton was practising to be an old man, thirty years ahead of his time.

Champion thought this a waste of life. He knew what he liked about Cambridge: rowing in the college eight, drinking beer in pubs, and flying Gloster Gamecocks with the University Air Squadron at weekends. Reading history was just a way of enjoying three good years. He got a middling degree, went down, and never came back. There were many like him, all easily forgettable, and Skelton forgot them.

Some years later, Skelton had a short and shattering love affair. He thought of quitting the university, the country, perhaps the world. His load of yearning and contempt and rage was so great that it left him weary and helpless. Not knowing why, he did something absurd: he enlisted in the RAF Volunteer Reserve. With his feeble eyes they'd never let him fly, so it was all pointless. The RAF welcomed him and gave him a uniform. At weekends and at summer camps it trained him to be an Intelligence Officer. He shaved off his moustache, stood up straight, and looked ten years younger. To his surprise, Intelligence was as interesting as history and airmen were more entertaining than dons. Eventually he learned to salute without embarrassment. He even forgot the bloody woman, sometimes for weeks at a time.

When war broke out he was called up at once. He served with a fighter squadron until he got banished to RAF Feck. The signal from Air Ministry that ordered him to proceed to London told him to report to Wing Commander R.G.T. Champion.

He was on the train, doing the *Times* crossword, when the faded memory of a mediocre undergraduate drifted into his mind. Surely it couldn't be *that* R.G.T. Champion? A wing commander? But it was.

Soup was followed by whitebait, with a deliciously crisp white Bordeaux.

'I assume you're paying for this,' Skelton said. 'That bottle alone would take my pay for a week.'

'Lunch is taken care of, old chap. Tell me: what do you know about Bomber Command?'

Skelton looked hard at Champion. 'You know I know damn all about Bomber Command. If you wish to tell me something, I suggest you do so without preamble.'

Champion ate some brown bread. 'You haven't changed, have you? I remember how you always crossed out the first paragraph of my essays.'

'With good reason. You were clearing your throat, arranging your thoughts, such as they were. What *are* your thoughts?'

'I think you're wasted up at RAF Feck. This is a bomber war, and it's going to be huge. We're the only fighting force that's hitting the enemy where it hurts, which is in his homeland. The army can't, neither can the navy. Bomber Command is unique. So we need the best brains. We're developing very big, very powerful aircraft, hell of a bomb-load, colossal range, phenomenal accuracy ...'

Champion spoke enthusiastically, while Skelton finished his fish and enjoyed more wine.

'That's what's going to settle Jerry's hash,' Champion said. 'We've got the winning hand. If you get on the bandwagon now, the sky's the limit, believe me.'

'Bandwagons don't fly. Muddled speech reflects muddled thought.'

'Listen: bolt a couple of Rolls-Royce Merlins onto a bandwagon and it'll fly like a bird. Or a Wellington. Which is now the best bomber operated by any air force anywhere. Ever been inside a Wimpy?' Skelton shook his head. 'Now's your chance,' Champion said. '409 Squadron recently switched from Hampdens to Wellingtons. They need an extra Intelligence Officer. They're at RAF Coney Garth, in Suffolk. Not far from Cambridge, actually.'

'Why are you persuading me? Why not just post me there, and have done with it?'

They paused while game pie was served and Champion tasted a Côtes du Rhone and gave his approval. 'If we drink enough,' he told Skelton, 'we might be able to digest the inscrutable contents of this pie ... Now then. This is a special job. 409 is a pukka squadron. Their kites are standard Wimpys, they fly the usual pattern of ops. But they have the best bombing record in the Command.'

'Somebody must be top. Maybe 409 are lucky.'

'Forget luck. The figures prove –'

'Oh, figures.' Skelton polished his glasses and squinted at Champion. 'The numbers game. Are these the same figures that proved Fighter Command destroyed the Luftwaffe twice over, last year?'

Champion sighed. He put down his knife and fork. Speaking softly, he said: 'I have access to intelligence summaries at the very highest level. Allow me to assure you that 409 Squadron are supremely good at their job.'

'Splendid. I'm not supremely good at mine. You wouldn't want me to lower their standard.'

'We want you to find out how they do it, what makes them different. Pin-point the special qualities of 409 and maybe we can bring all the other squadrons up to their standard.'

'Ah! Now I understand.' Skelton pushed his plate aside. 'C-in-C Bomber Command wants to be able to say that all his squadrons are above average.'

Champion smiled happily. 'I knew I was right. Your mind works differently. You'll see things with the clear eye of an outsider, things that everyone else takes for granted.'

Skelton grunted. 'And what do I do with these startling insights?'

'Bring them to me when you're ready.'

Skelton suddenly grew tired of the whole discussion. 'Those people over there are eating treacle tart,' he said. 'Get me a large portion, with cream, and I'll go anywhere you like. But I think you're making a mistake.'

They took coffee in the smoking room. 'Why aren't you flying?' Skelton asked. 'You're still young enough.'

'One prang too many. Some of our pre-war bombers were frankly ropey.' He tapped his head with a teaspoon. 'The quacks grounded me.'

'Rotten luck.'

'One door closes, another opens.'

They went into Piccadilly. The sky was a fragile blue. The barrage balloons flying from Hyde Park scarcely moved in the breeze.

'It looks like another blitzy night,' Skelton said. 'Will Jerry be back, d'you think?'

'Yes. And no doubt Jerry is asking himself the same question about our chaps. Would you like to know the answer?'

'Please.'

'The answer,' Champion said, 'will be thunderous.' He smiled like a vicar announcing the next hymn on Mothering Sunday.

3

Skull drove into RAF Coney Garth at four p.m., in the middle of a fair-sized flap.

Aircraft were droning around the circuit. Vans and trucks were shuttling from hangars and workshops to Wellingtons parked at the perimeter. The Tannoy was chanting a string of messages. Skull had had an apple for lunch; he was looking forward to tea and toast in the Mess. Obviously that could wait. An airman showed him where the Ops Room was. Two armed Service Policemen guarded it. They admitted Skull only when 409's Senior Intelligence Officer came to the door and told them to.

He was a Squadron Leader with a shiny head, thick moustache and busy eyes made bigger and busier by powerful spectacles. 'Bloody glad to see *you*,' he said, almost accusingly. 'I've lost a pilot officer and a Waaf sergeant, one posted, one gone down with flu, so that leaves me and Corporal Hawkins, and Group has changed the target *twice* since noon. What? Anyway, I've got everything sorted out now. Can you take over here? I haven't eaten since breakfast. What's your name?'

'Skelton.'

'Of course. You're Skull. I'm called Bins. Right, I'm off.' He got into his tunic; Skull saw an Observer's half-wing, much faded. 'Final briefing, seventeen hundred hours.' The door banged behind him.

Skull, thought Skull. *How did he know about Skull?* One of the mysteries of RAF life was the way nicknames went ahead of a posting. 'What's the target?' he asked.

'Mannheim, sir,' Corporal Hawkins said.

Everywhere Skull looked there were telephones. Some were labelled with initials that meant nothing to him. 'You'd better start explaining –' he began, when a phone rang. Hawkins answered it. *Mannheim*, Skull thought. *Where the devil is Mannheim?* A map of Germany covered half a wall and he began searching. Another phone rang. The Sergeants' Mess wanted to know when the aircrew sandwiches should be ready. Skull said Corporal Hawkins would call them back. He fended off the next two calls in the same way and then got a brisk Scotsman on the red phone. Instinctively, Skull knew it would be a mistake to offer him a corporal; on the other hand the man spoke too fast and used strange words. 'Say again, please,' Skull said. 'This is an awfully bad line. I missed half of that. Who are you?'

'NLO.'

'Still not good. Perhaps if – '

'NLO. Naval Liaison Officer, for Christ's sake. Can you hear me now? Can you write? Then write this: convoy three seven green new position ...' Skull wrote hard.

Phones kept ringing. When Bins returned, Skull had a small stack of messages to give him. 'Anything crucial here?' Bins asked. Skull thought. 'Um...' he said. He couldn't remember what half the messages were about. Bins turned to Corporal Hawkins. 'Got the target file? Good. Let's go.'

The squadron was sending six Wellingtons to Mannheim; there were thirty-six aircrew in the Briefing Room. Skull listened carefully to the squadron commander's description of the target, what it manufactured, and precisely where, and just how it helped the German war effort. Other officers took over. A stream of information came thick and fast – petrol load, bombload, take-off time, diversion airfields, signal codes, recognition signals, alternative targets – until Skull let it wash over him. He looked at the crews. He had expected them to be older than fighter pilots; instead they seemed younger. Many gunners and wireless ops were twenty at most; probably only eighteen or nineteen. He saw pilots with schoolboy faces. He glanced back at the squadron commander: awfully young to be a Wingco. Three rings on his sleeve went halfway to his elbow. Skull felt curiously remote from this scene. He was nearly forty: a very old man to the crews. They laughed at something Bins was saying about searchlight concentrations. Skull missed the joke but he smiled anyway.

'Any questions?' Bins said.

'Who else is on this raid?' someone asked.

'Only Wellingtons. Thirty-odd kites. If you see something over Germany that's not a Wimpy, shoot it down.'

'What about convoys? Can we shoot at them?' a pilot asked. There was groaning and whistling.

'Only one convoy,' Bins said. 'Northbound off Cromer, so it should be well away from you. Anything else? No? Then it's weather time.' He handed his pointer to the Met man.

'Thank you. The predicted winds,' the Met man began, and paused.

'Are *wrong*,' the crews all said, and laughed. He smiled sadly and waited for their chatter to fade.

'Old squadron tradition,' Bins murmured to Skull. 'Brings them luck.'

'About convoys,' Skull said softly. 'There may be more up-to-date gen in one of those messages I gave you.'

'Nothing crucial, you said.' Bins was searching the notes. 'God damn it all to hell. A *new* convoy. Bloody damn and buggery.'

'Surely it's not too late – '

'Not the point. Corrections are bad form. The chaps don't like them.'

'Oh dear.'

'You've put up a black, old boy.'

When the Met man finished, Bins announced new convoy information: on the outward flight it would be northward, off The Maze; returning, northward off Thorpeness. 'Avoid it,' he said. Nobody laughed at that. 'A final reminder: beware of intruders. The Hun likes to prowl around East Anglia. You're never home until you're home.'

A voice at the back said, 'Pity the bloody convoys can't shoot down the bloody intruders.' That won a rumble of approval.

Briefing ended. A group captain wished them luck. The crews stood up and waited while the briefing officers left.

Outside, the Wingco paused to look at the sky. Two layers of broken cloud, at greatly different heights, were moving in slightly different directions. 'A spot of fog early on, to keep the intruders away,' he said, 'then clearing in time to let our chaps get down. That would suit me nicely.'

'Alas, fog is not normally so obliging,' the Met man said.

'It's been some time since an intruder got a kite, sir,' Bins said.

'Is it? I'm not so sure. If we find a German cannon-shell in a wreck, does that mean the Wimpy got hit over Germany, staggered home and fell to bits in the air? Or did an intruder clobber it over King's Lynn just as the crew relaxed?' Nobody had an answer. 'Jerry's bloody cunning. I wish I knew what his tactics are.'

'We use intruders, too, sir,' Skull said.

The Wingco's head rotated like a hawk locating a sparrow. 'What's that got to do with the price of apples?'

'If our intruders are successful over France, sir, perhaps we should ask them to tell us *their* tactics.'

The Wingco grunted. He pointed to the Operations Officer, who had kept himself in the background, 'Some fool has parked a Lagonda in my space outside the Mess. Tell the adjutant, would you?' He strode away.

The Ops Officer said softly, 'Nobody on the squadron owns a Lagonda.'

'I do,' Skull said.

'Well, you've just put up a black. Move the bloody thing, fast.' He hurried after the Wingco.

'How was I to know?' Skull asked.

'Well, you know now,' the Met man said.

'A Lagonda,' Bins said. 'That's a bit rich, for a flight lieutenant.'

'My aunt gave it to me. She can't get the petrol, Lagondas being large and thirsty.'

'Pug Duff drives an MG,' the Met man said. 'Not large. Quite small, in fact. Like him. Lots of zip. Also like him. I'd say you've put up a considerable black.'

'Nothing new,' Skull said. 'When's dinner?'

4

By sunset, the sky had cleared, with just a few faint scribbles of yellow cloud at great height. The air was mild. A breeze barely ruffled the grass. Skull and the Ops Officer stood outside the Operations Block and watched time pass.

The Ops Officer's name was Bellamy. He stood as if he were at ease on a parade ground: shoulders squared, hands linked behind his back, feet at ten-to-two, calves braced. He was a squadron leader with a pilot's wings, and he was twenty-six. Bellamy had been in the RAF since he was sixteen, and he would have felt uncomfortable standing in any other way. He was lean and spruce, and he always looked alert.

'Curious, sir, isn't it?' Skull said. Unlike Bellamy, he was slightly round-shouldered, and he wore his uniform as if he were looking after it for a friend. 'Here we are, doing this, and they're over there, doing exactly the same. Wouldn't it be odd if one day both sets of bombers met in the middle?'

'Highly unlikely,' Bellamy said. 'They usually cross the Channel from bases in France, Belgium maybe. We nearly always go out over the North Sea.' He stopped. What he had said sounded like an arrangement, even an agreement. 'Not on the cards.' End of discussion.

Airmen were lighting a row of gooseneck flares, which dimly outlined the flare-path. 'We'd better stooge over to the caravan,' Bellamy said. They walked to his car. 'Have you a nickname?' he asked. 'Intelligence Officers usually do.'

'I'm Skull, sir. Short for Skelton.'

'Drop the "sir", Skull. Save it for formal occasions.'

They set off. 'Have you a nickname?' Skull asked.

'It used to be Butcha, because I looked so young. Butcha is Hindustani for boy.' Bellamy did not smile; he rarely smiled unless he thought smiling would improve morale. 'Complete change of cast since then,' he said. 'Nobody remembers that stuff.'

The caravan was really a four-wheeled trailer, painted a bold chequerboard all over, parked near the take-off end of the flare-path. A Perspex dome, big enough for a man's head, was fitted to the top.

Around the perimeter, Wellingtons were starting up and pilots began testing their engines. Each roar grew and grew until it had the harshness of a challenge. As it fell away, another challenge took over.

Two airmen stood up when the officers climbed into the caravan. One man was in charge of an array of radio equipment; the other was wearing earphones. 'Anything yet?' Bellamy asked him.

'R-Robert's got trouble with the oxygen, sir,' the man said. 'They're changing some bottles.'

'Thank you.' Bellamy took the headset and stepped onto a wooden box. Now his head was in the dome. 'Give Flight Lieutenant Skelton a set, please. I want him to hear this.'

At first Skull heard nothing but the slush of atmospherics. The radio operator gave him a chair and poured him some coffee. Then a voice said: 'E-Easy to Sandstorm.'

'Sandstorm receiving you, E-Easy,' Bellamy said.

'E-Easy, request permission to taxi.'

'You may taxi, E-Easy.'

After that a steady stream of requests came from other captains: J-Jig, F-Fox, B-Baker, M-Mother, R-Robert. Then the first Wellington asked clearance for take-off. 'You are clear for take-off, E-Easy,' Bellamy said. His head slowly swivelled as he followed the bomber. Skull freed one ear to listen to the charging bellow.

'E-Easy airborne at nineteen oh five,' Bellamy said. The airman wrote it down. There was a long pause while Bellamy watched the navigation lights get smaller and higher, before he gave the next Wellington clearance. Nobody seemed in a great hurry. It took twenty minutes to get the flight away. 'Thank you,' Bellamy said as he returned the headset. 'Jolly good coffee,' Skull told the radio operator.

They drove back to the operations block. 'So what happens now?' Skull asked.

'Oh, the usual. Dinner in the Mess. I believe there's a good film at the station cinema. Charles Laughton.'

'I meant the raid. I was surprised we didn't wait to see them in formation.'

'Not a hope. The chaps tried night-flying in formation last year. Wellingtons collided with tedious regularity. Awfully dark up there.'

'So each bomber makes its own way to the target. And then bombs individually?'

'Yes.'

'Doesn't that multiply the risk of error?'

'Quite the reverse. It multiplies the chance of success. Fly as a group, and if your Master Navigator goes wrong, everyone goes wrong.' Bellamy spoke crisply. He did everything crisply; he believed it was crucial that everyone understood exactly what to do, or men died unnecessarily. 'This isn't like Fighter Command,' he said. 'This isn't smash-and-grab in the sky and then home to pick up your popsy. Bomber Command is in the long-distance business of delivering high explosive by the ton, to the door. We think about it very carefully.'

'Yes, of course.'

'Have you met the station commander? Group Captain Rafferty. Grand chap, fine leader. Come on.'

They went in. Rafferty was standing in the middle of the Ops Room, whirling a black telephone by its flex. Three Waafs, seated at desks, watched him. 'Ask me what I'm doing,' he said to Bellamy.

'Yes, sir. What – '

'I'm trying to strangle this raving fool on the other end.' Rafferty caught the phone and shouted into it: 'Listen! I don't want your excuses and I don't need your apologies! Simply tell the airman who endangered R-Robert that if he ever installs a faulty oxygen bottle again I shall personally ...' He jammed his shoulder against the phone and put his hands over the ears of the nearest Waaf. 'I shall personally seek him out and ram it up his arse.' He removed his hands and hung up the phone. 'You didn't hear that, did you?' he asked a different Waaf.

'Yes, sir.'

'Well, you didn't understand it, did you?'

'Yes, sir.'

'Disgraceful. Who's this?'

'Flight Lieutenant Skelton,' Bellamy said. 'New Intelligence Officer.' Skull saluted.

'Ah-ha.' Rafferty perched his backside against a table-map that half-filled the room. 'Oh-ho. Mr Skelton.' He put his head back and stared down his nose. 'Did D-Dog get away on time?'

'It did,' Bellamy said.

'I hear you escaped from Fighter Command, Mr Skelton.'

'I was expelled, sir.'

'I thought as much. Air Ministry recommended you very strongly. Always a bad sign. What did you do?'

'I raped an air vice-marshal,' Skull said.

Bellamy's teeth clenched but the Waafs didn't even blink. Neither did Rafferty. 'What with?' he asked.

'The truth, sir.'

'I bet that hurt. Well, this is a different world. Many years ago, people asked me to fly fighters, do all that tomfoolery at air shows – formation aerobatics, wingtips tied together with ribbon. Make the crowd go *Ooh-ah*. I chose bombers. Never regretted it. A chap can have a real career in Bomber Command. Bombing is what aeroplanes are *for*. The rest is frills.'

'I quite agree, sir,' Skull said. 'The trouble with Fighter Command is it's all smash-and-grab in the sky and then home to pick up your popsy.'

'Huh.' Rafferty stared at Skull, stared so hard that Bellamy chewed his lower lip and hurt himself. 'Huh,' Rafferty said again. 'Well, I'll be in the Mess.' He went out.

'I'll show you where we do the interrogations,' Bellamy said.

They went through a corridor to an adjacent hut. Long trestle tables, many wooden chairs, Air Ministry posters defaced by aircrew impatient to tell their story and go for their bacon and egg. Bellamy kicked a chair aside. 'You just put up a black,' he said. 'The groupie won't forgive you in a hurry.'

'For what?'

'Smash-and-grab in the sky. Home to pick up your popsy. That's *his* line. Bad enough that you stole it, but you threw it in his face! Poor show, old chap. Very big black.'

'If I stole it, you stole it first.' Skull couldn't take this seriously.

'Not where he could hear me, for God's sake.' Bellamy rapped his knuckles on the table.

'Well, he should be flattered.'

'Listen: these things matter. Rafferty doesn't like Intelligence Officers. He thinks they get in the way. Frankly, I agree. A man who hasn't flown has no right to question aircrew.'

'I've flown. Went to Le Touquet in September 1939, in a Bombay troop-carrier. I was sick.'

'Take my advice: don't mention it here,' Bellamy said grimly. 'It won't improve your credit.'

'What will?'

Bellamy wanted his dinner. 'Fly on ops and get shot down in flames,' he said. 'The chaps will respect you for that.' He left. Skull hurried after him, and just got a lift to the Mess.

5

Despite changing some bottles, R-Robert still had oxygen trouble. Only the navigator was affected, but that was more than enough to worry the whole crew. If the navigator couldn't think straight, they might end up anywhere. France. Poland. The Alps.

The first hour was simple. They crossed the North Sea at five thousand because there was cloud at six thousand and the pilot wanted to get a good pin-point fix on the Dutch coast.

The fix was positive: Walcheren, on the point of the Zeeland peninsula. It placed them twenty miles east of track: twenty miles off course. That might mean several things. Maybe the predicted winds had changed. Maybe a weather front was late. Or early. Maybe the navigator's threes looked like his eights.

Or maybe the compass wasn't feeling very well.

The pilot was Gilchrist, the ex-actor. It was a long time since he had put Rafferty straight about Shakespeare. Now he was a veteran, on his twenty-sixth op. Soon coloured beads of flak began reaching for the Wellington. The pilot climbed into cloud and out of it, and kept climbing to fourteen thousand feet, by which time everyone was breathing oxygen.

Twenty minutes later the wireless op spoke on the intercom. 'Something's wrong with the nav, skipper.'

'See what it is,' Gilchrist told the second pilot.

He went back and found the navigator lying beside his chair, with the wireless op kneeling beside him, fixing his oxygen tube to a fresh bottle, turning the supply up to maximum. No effect. The second pilot squeezed the tube and found a blockage: ice crystals. He crushed them, and within seconds the navigator stirred. They got him back on his seat. They had to hold him: he was as limp as a pillow. He stared at the chart on his table. The course he had been plotting became a wobbly line that trailed to the edge and fell off.

Gilchrist went down to eight thousand, where they could all breathe normally. The navigator drank some coffee.

'How d'you feel?' the second pilot asked.

'Better.' There was dried blood on his face. He must have banged his head when he blacked out.

'Can you take a star shot?' Gilchrist asked.

'I can try.'

'Flak behind, skip,' the rear gunner said.

'Thank you. And searchlights ahead.' A small forest of lights had sprung up, restlessly slicing the night. 'No loitering here, I think.' He banked the bomber through a quarter-circle and climbed away. In five minutes they were all back on oxygen.

'New course, skip,' the navigator said. 'Steer one seven five degrees.'

'One seven five. How far to target?'

'Couple of hundred miles. I'm working on it.'

'Good show. Everybody else, watch out for fixes.'

But the German blackout was total. The navigator went to the astrodome and tried to take star shots. He took so long that Gilchrist told him to forget it. 'Damn stars keep jumping about,' the navigator said. He went back to his charts, and saw tiny sparks wandering at the edge of his vision. He decided not to tell the pilot.

The wireless op moved to the astrodome and searched for fighters. An hour passed: an hour of steady, battering noise and broken cloud. By dead reckoning they were over Mannheim. But nothing had changed: empty sky above, deep blackness below, patchy cloud between.

'Bugger this for a lark,' Gilchrist said. 'Can't anybody see the Rhine?' Mannheim was on the Rhine. 'Bloody great river, full of water. It's got to be down there somewhere.' Nobody answered. 'We'll go down and take a dekko,' he said. As he began a wide spiral the wireless op said: 'Bombs exploding, starboard.' The yellow splashes were very small. Mannheim turned out to be thirty-five miles away. Thirty-five miles off course.

'Bloody winds,' the navigator said. By then he was in the nose, squinting through the bombsight. His tiny sparks were still wandering.

6

Later the RAF called it debriefing. In 1941 it was interrogation. The station commander and the CO attended but the Intelligence Officer did the work.

Skull stood behind Bins and watched him work. The first crew home was J-Jig, at 0120. After more than six hours in the air they were both weary and chirpy, glad to get a mug of coffee with a slug of rum in it.

The first questions were the crucial ones. 'Did you reach Mannheim?' Yes. 'Did you identify the target?' The navigator (and bomb-aimer) said it was as plain as day. 'Did you bomb the target?' Absolutely. Right on the nose. Piece of cake. 'I saw the bombs go in,' said the rear gunner. 'Bull's-eye.' Bins wanted more detail: time on target, colour of explosions, any secondary explosions, any fires, colour of fires … Then he whizzed through a dozen items: flak, fighters, searchlights, sightings of other bombers going down, decoy fires, any technical problems, weather, winds …

'Predicted winds were wrong,' the pilot said. 'We got blown east until we got a fix on the Rhine south of Mainz. Then it was easy.'

They were restless. Bacon and eggs waited: best meal of the day. Bins said, 'Anything else I should know? No? Thanks. Well done.'

'Damn good show,' the group captain said.

Bins took care of M-Mother, then F-Fox and E-Easy. Everyone was pleased: all the Wellingtons had landed. The crews of B-Baker and R-Robert came in together. There was a rush to get to Bins' table. B-Baker won. R-Robert went to an empty table and dragged out the chairs as noisily as possible. 'Shop!' the pilot called. He pounded the table.

'You know the drill,' Bins said to Skull. 'Keep it brief, make it snappy.' He gave him an interrogation form.

Gilchrist didn't wait to be questioned. 'Found Mannheim. Recognized the target. Bombed the AP.' Skull looked puzzled. 'The what?' he asked. 'Aiming Point,' the pilot said. The others put on expressions of comic disbelief: the bloody IO didn't know what an AP was! 'Rear gunner saw our bombs straddle the target,' Gilchrist said.

'Two d's in "straddle",' the rear gunner said.

'You're very kind,' Skull said.

'No fighters. Usual flak. Nothing special at all,' Gilchrist said. 'Whole trip was a doddle.' Some of the crew were standing up.

'I suppose the Rhine helped,' Skull said. 'It runs dead straight out of Mannheim for about two miles, is that right? The perfect landmark.'

'Perfect,' the navigator said. He was feeling much better. 'Coming out, we flew straight up the Rhine.'

'Interesting.' Skull made a note. 'And the oil tanks beside the river: were they on fire?'

'Not half. Burning like blazes.'

'Flames reflected in the water?'

'That's right.'

The crew of B-Baker were clumping out of the hut.

'I'll finish off here,' Bins said. 'Anything else you want to tell me? No? Thanks. Well done.'

'Damn good show,' the group captain said. Gilchrist and his men hurried out. Rafferty and Duff followed them, leaving the Intelligence Officers to write up the operational report.

'Don't gossip with the chaps,' Bins told Skull. 'Ask your questions, get the gen, *finish*.'

'I wasn't gossiping.'

'I heard you chattering about flames reflected in the Rhine. Nobody gives a damn. The chaps want their meal. God knows they've earned it.'

'I was curious to know if they remembered seeing burning oil tanks alongside the river north of Mannheim, that's all.'

Bins put down his fountain-pen and looked at him. 'There are no oil tanks on the Rhine north of Mannheim.'

'R-Robert saw them burning like blazes.'

Bins found a bit of blotting paper and cleaned the nib. He drew a perfect circle to make sure it worked. 'Look,' he said. 'First day on the squadron and you've put up three large blacks. For Christ's sake don't do any more damage. This job is tricky enough already.'

'Shall I make us some cocoa? At RAF Feck my cocoa-making was highly commended.'

While Skull made cocoa, Bins found R-Robert's report and obliterated the bit about burning oil tanks. In the margin he wrote *Irrelevant jocular remarks*, and initialled it.

7

S-Sugar was the oldest Wellington on 409 Squadron.

She had taken a lot of knocks: slashed by shrapnel, wrenched by storm-force winds, dumped on bumpy runways by pilots who were ten feet higher than they planned to be. Also baked, soaked and frozen by the British weather as she sat at dispersal. But Wellingtons were designed to take punishment. She was still strong enough to haul a load of bombs to Berlin, provided all her bits worked.

When a new crew arrived at RAF Coney Garth, Pug Duff gave them S-Sugar and told the pilot, Jeremy Diamond, aged twenty-one, ex-medical student, that he had two weeks in which to knock his crew into shape. 'Fly all the hours God gives,' Pug said. 'Don't wait for sunshine. Good weather teaches you nothing. Learn in the rain.'

Diamond did just that. After a week, he took off and flew east, on a navigation exercise plus bombing practice. Over the North Sea the weather turned foul.

The radio was receiving yards of harsh static and nothing else. The demons of cumulo-nimbus bounced the bomber until the navigator was too sick to do his job. Diamond climbed until he was above the weather, at nine thousand. He turned back, reached the coast and found the bombing range. Nine thousand was far too high. He went down until the navigator said he could see the targets through the bomb-sight. Diamond didn't believe him, the nav sounded weak, maybe he was still sick; so Diamond banked the Wimpy so that he could look down and see for himself. Just as he banked, the nav said, 'Bombs gone.' Which meant the bombs had swung sideways with the Wimpy. Too late now.

Diamond turned north, hoping to escape the weather, but the weather went north, too. He tried to climb above it, and the wings iced up. The more he climbed, the worse the ice, until the Wimpy was labouring. He had to go back down into the muck. The port engine packed up and now he couldn't maintain height even if he wanted to. He was searching for a hole in the cloud when he scraped the top of a Yorkshire hill that should have been thirty miles away, and he terrified himself. Ten seconds later he flew into another, bigger hill.

New boys began at the bottom. The sprog crew got the worst kite. Why waste a good Wimpy when you could waste a duff one? It was only common sense.

8

Rain was still falling next day. It fell on RAF Coney Garth as the adjutant showed the station commander an order from Group. The order directed Rafferty to arrange an appropriate visit, without delay, to a civilian who had been accidentally bombed.

'You go and see the fellow,' Rafferty said.

'No fear,' the adjutant said. 'Not my pigeon, sir.'

'Be a sport, Douglas. You're awfully good at this sort of thing. Honeyed tongue, and so on.'

'Honey's on ration, sir. So is tongue, come to that.'

'Every bloody thing's on ration. Except bleating civilians.'

In his flying days, Rafferty's nickname had been Tiny. Now his presence was even more massive. He was afraid of very few things, but one was angry civilians. 'Why don't we send Pug?' he suggested. 'It's his squadron. I'm just the bally caretaker here.'

'Squadron's on ops tonight.'

'Send Bellamy, then. He's not flying.'

'Bellamy's giving the briefing.' The adjutant paused, and played his ace. 'It seems this chap is a former MP, sir.'

Rafferty gave in. 'I'm not going alone,' he said.

'Well, Skull's available. Used to be a Cambridge don. Never lost for words, although I can't say I understand them all.'

Rafferty perked up. 'Skull can do all the talking. I'll just …' The adjutant shook his head. 'Well, I'm damn well not going to apologize.' Rafferty muttered. 'Sod 'em all.'

They went in his official car. An airman drove. Skull had brought a file. 'The complainant is Major-General Count Blanco de Colossal-Howitzer-Bombardment, sir,' he began. Rafferty stared. Skull said. 'I cannot tell a lie, sir. I made that up.'

'Drop the "sir", Skull. And the jokes. Who is this blasted civilian?'

'Brigadier Piers Barriton, MC. Used to drive racing cars. Tory MP for ten years. A widower. Owns a farm with a large sanctuary for sea birds. He claims that both the farm and the sanctuary were bombed.'

'We'll see about that.'

'The brigadier has one other passion. Fly-fishing.'

'Boring bloody nonsense.'

'True. But as we have some time, you might like to know the difference between a March Brown, a Greenwell's Glory and a Tupp's Indispensable.'

'Damn-fool names. All right, fire away.'

Brigadier Barriton met them at the front door of his farmhouse. He was in his sixties, angular, slightly hunched, with cropped white hair. Two dogs sat on the doorstep: orderlies awaiting orders. Rafferty introduced himself and Skull. The brigadier did not offer to shake hands. 'You'll want to see the bombs,' he said. His voice held a trace of Scottish Highlands. A trace of granite.

The further they walked, the muddier it got. The visitors had not thought to bring gumboots. The fields were flat and there was little to be said about them. Rafferty gave up trying to keep his trouser legs clean and he plodded behind the brigadier. Skull's attempts at conversation got nowhere. 'Wonderful skies in these parts, sir,' he said. 'Do you paint, at all?' Barriton shook his head. 'Neither do I,' Skull said sympathetically.

Rain had passed, but the sky was overcast and Rafferty could see a squall heading their way.

The first bomb was lying on a sack. Rafferty recognized 409 Squadron's colours. All their practice bombs were painted yellow, with a red fin. Still, the brig didn't know that, did he? 'This is a job for the experts,' he said. 'It may well be German.'

'I doubt that.' Barriton rolled it over with his foot. Stencilled down one side was 409 SQDN HOT SHOTS. 'It struck that Dutch barn yonder. Went through the roof and made a mess of a ton of turnips. The other bombs are widely scattered.'

'You will be compensated in full,' Rafferty said.

'Tell that to my breeding gulls.' He set off again.

It was half a mile to the sanctuary. Rafferty and Skull looked at sea-birds circling mudflats, creeks and stretches of reed, with the grey North Sea beyond. Soon a thin rain began to fall. 'It's taken me ten years to persuade those particular birds to nest here,' Barriton said, 'and now you go and bomb them.'

Rafferty was more interested in the black squall racing towards them. Young Diamond must have run into weather like this. Foul, turning worse. 'Accident,' he said. 'I'm sorry.'

'You think I'm making too much of this,' Barriton said. 'Well, I fought the Hun and I know one thing. Germany will not be beaten by accident.'

Nobody spoke on the way back.

By the time they reached the car, the group captain's feet were squelching inside his shoes; but that was not what angered him. Rain dripped from his nose as he watched the brigadier shut the dogs in a shed, and turn and stand, waiting for his visitors to go.

'Sir!' Rafferty said. It was so explosive that he paused to control his feelings. 'Sir ... I came here to apologize for a mistake, and I've done so. But I will not apologize for the hazards of war. Nor will I allow

you or anyone to belittle the men I'm proud to lead. War is dangerous. Accidents happen. Brave men die. No doubt you knew a few.'

'More than a few.'

Rafferty gestured at the wet horizon. 'You love your sea-birds, sir.
Bully for you. I love my aircrew. Some of them disturbed your birds.
The birds may come back. But the crew of that bomber will never
come back. That's all I have to say, sir.' He was about to leave when
Skull stopped him. Barriton had opened the farmhouse door and was
standing aside, waiting for them to enter.

Rafferty sat in the kitchen, near a coal-burning stove as big as a
sideboard, and watched his stockinged feet steam. Barriton gave
them towels, and made tea. Rafferty was silent; Skull talked easily.
He noticed Peter Fleming's *Brazilian Adventure* on a bookshelf, and
praised it, which led to piranha fish, and to scorpions, and desert
travel, and crusader castles. Barriton had something to say about
them all. One topic led to another. 'Fame is over-rated, if you ask
me,' Skull said. He picked up a tin of St Bruno tobacco. 'Everyone's
heard of St Bruno, but who was he? Come to that, who was the great
Greenwell?'

Barriton's face changed; the boy in the man showed through. 'Do
you fish?' he asked.

'Not as often as the group captain.'

Rafferty cleared his throat, and tried to remember the difference
between a March Brown and a Tupps' Indispensable. Barriton said:
'Take a look at my Greenwells. There's no decent trout fishing in
East Anglia, so fly-tying is the next best thing.' He was opening
drawers and pulling out trays lined with yellow felt. Trout flies were
lined up like gems in a jeweller's. 'What d'you think of that one,
group captain?'

'My goodness,' Rafferty said. 'That's something. That really is
something.'

'I hope that makes him happy,' Rafferty said. They were in the car,
heading home. 'These trousers will never be the same again.'

'You handled him beautifully.'

'Bloody retired pongo. Bloody blimp. Bloody has-been MP. Never
flown in his life and he's got the brass gall to be sniffy about our
training methods.'

'He's a lonely old man.'

'Lucky for him. If he'd been younger I'd have flattened him. Men like that haven't got the faintest idea what Bomber Command's about.'

'Few people do.'

'They don't know what courage and strength it takes to go on hammering the Hun, night after night. Brave men in Bomber Command. None braver than 409. Give 'em the chance, and they'll make Hitler look silly.'

Skull watched the countryside go by. 'All the same,' he said, 'S-Sugar missed the bombing range by ... well, by rather a long way.' Rafferty looked at his watch. 'And how did they end up in Yorkshire?' Skull asked.

'Won't this damn car go any faster?' Rafferty growled. The driver put his foot down.

'You did jolly well with his Greenwell's Glories,' Skull murmured.

'It's about time you called me "sir" again,' Rafferty told him. 'Straighten your tie. Do up your tunic. You look a complete shambles.'

RANDOM HAVOC

1

While Rafferty and Skull were heading westward, two civilians were driving roughly north, aiming for Coney Garth. Rollo Blazer was a film cameraman; Kate Kelly was his sound recordist. Their route was rough because after they left London they got lost. All the signposts in England had been removed a year ago, during the invasion scare. Kate had a map but until they knew where they were, it was useless. Every road they took twisted and wandered. And the rain blotted out any landmarks.

Rollo Blazer stopped the car at a T-junction. The wipers cleared the windscreen and revealed a high barbed-wire fence, a wet field and a sky loaded with cloud. Then a gust rocked the car on its springs and lashed it with rain and the wipers had their work to do all over again. The car was misting up. Kate used a headscarf to wipe the windscreen. 'We must be in Suffolk by now,' she said.

'Why? What does Suffolk look like?'

She wiped the windscreen again. 'Looks wet.'

'Left or right?'

'Damn good question.' A truck arrived behind them and gave a rasping blast. 'Right,' she said.

The truck followed them. Rollo saw an entrance to a field and swerved into it. The truck charged past. He killed the engine. 'Say what you like about the Blitz,' he said, 'it filmed well.' Ahead stretched soggy grass and sky: dark green and grey. 'You know what that's going to look like on the screen. Cold porridge.' He took a Leica from a bag and focused on a passing bird. 'Look, a fly in the porridge,' he said.

The wind was still gusting. It battered the grass and made the barbed wire shriek.

'My mike is ready to hate this place,' Kate said. 'It's all screaming and howling.'

'That's the fly. It's drowning in the porridge.' Someone knocked on his window. He wound it down. Four RAF policemen looked at him. All wore revolver holsters, and one had the holster open and his hand on the gun. 'Identify yourselves,' he demanded.

'I'm Alfred Hitchcock and she's Vivien Leigh,' Rollo said.

'Keep your hands where I can see them,' the policeman said. 'You're both under arrest.'

'And about time too,' Rollo said. 'I'm bloody starving.'

It was the wrong thing to say but he delivered it well. Long ago, Rollo Blazer had been a promising young actor, talented and handsome, until he threw it all away.

His curse was his restless imagination. The off-stage life of a character intrigued him. At rehearsals he kept asking: 'What's the story behind the story?' It irritated the cast. 'For fuck's sake, Rollo,' an old actor told him, 'the audience don't give a damn what happens off-stage. You can exit and convert to Satanism and strangle your grandmother, for all they care.' Next night, in Act Two, Rollo entered on cue and said, 'I've converted to Satanism and strangled my grandmother, does anybody care?' Then he spoke his usual lines. For the rest of the performance, whenever he came on stage the audience was unusually alert. Rollo met the old actor in the wings. 'You know,' he murmured, 'I think they do care.' The man gave a wintry smile. 'Any fool can chuck a brick through a stained-glass window,' he said. The curtain fell and Rollo was sacked.

He was glad. The prospect of a long run bored him. What next? He'd had bit-parts in a few short movies. It was fun but the money was pitiful. He borrowed twenty-five pounds from an aunt who thought he was twice as handsome as Leslie Howard, and gave ten to a cameraman to teach him how to shoot movies. This was 1930, when many a worker got a pound a week. Rollo learned a lot for his tenner. With the other fifteen he bought a slightly damaged Sunbeam Talbot and had it painted red. Red for Blazer.

The car became familiar at low-budget shoots on locations around London. Rollo said he was freelancing for movie magazines. He helped carry equipment, he watched and learned. One day a cameraman fell sick. Rollo volunteered. He wasn't expert but he was cheap, and the film was already over budget. The director kept him on.

By 1939 he was a veteran of the British film industry. All the easy charm of the slim young actor had gone: he was stocky, even stubby, and his right shoulder sagged from carrying cameras. Rust-red hair was greying about the ears; freckles dotted his nose and cheekbones. At the corners of his eyes, years of squinting into a thousand viewfinders had left arrowhead tracks. He was thirty-four and divorced. He came across many attractive women and some who were beautiful, but if he thought too much about any of them the scar on his scalp itched.

Rollo had married an actress called Miriam. It was meant to be a union of minds and souls as well as bodies, but from the first they fought. While he was an actor they fought about the difference between good and bad theatre. When he became a cameraman he despised the theatre and they fought over that. No blood got shed until their final fight. She threw plates. Most women cannot throw straight, or far. He dodged a couple and then realized that he was safer standing still. She missed and missed. He leaned against a wall and laughed because he genuinely found the scene funny. 'You've seen too many B-movies,' he said. 'People only do this in the movies.' That made her furious, and her fury made her miss him by an even wider margin. He was laughing so much that his ribs hurt. She rushed at him with the last plate and smashed it on his head. When she saw blood trickle down his face, she ran from the room and from his life. He needed six stitches. Ever afterwards, if he laughed too much or if the sudden sight of a delightful woman flustered his loins, the scar itched. Rollo Blazer took this as a warning. He had no intention of remarrying. Too old.

In the summer of 1939, Paramount wanted him as second cameraman on a production of *Robin Hood* to be shot at various British castles. On the day that Britain declared war, an assistant producer phoned him. 'Head office just pulled the plug,' he said. 'It's cancelled.'

'Splendid. Peace in our time, after all,' Blazer said. 'Chamberlain will be pleased. Have you told Hitler?'

'Glad you can see the funny side of it. You're not on contract, Rollo, so we don't owe you a bean. Just calling to say goodbye.'

161

'This is not the Robin Hood spirit.'

'And Hitler isn't the Sheriff of Nottingham. What d'you reckon you'll do now?'

'God knows.'

Thirty-four was the wrong age in 1939. Not old enough to have fought in the first war and not young enough to fight in this one. Men ten years younger than Rollo were being sent home by recruiting officers and told to wait. In any case, uniforms didn't excite him. Sailors got drowned, soldiers got blisters, and airmen had to fly. Rollo disliked heights and distrusted aeroplanes. When a friend in the Ministry of Information told him that its Crown Film Unit needed a cameraman, he knew at once that this was the way to serve his country.

He did his best. He filmed the British Expeditionary Force going cheerily off to France. He shot patriotic filmlets about what to do in an air raid, the correct way to wear a gas mask, how to use a stirrup pump on an incendiary bomb. It was hard to make the Phoney War exciting when it produced nothing but the blackout. How could you shoot the damn blackout? Then the war became real and he filmed what was left of the British Expeditionary Force, grimy and weary, many without weapons, a few without clothes, as they got off the ships from Dunkirk. He knew his footage would never get past the censors. They wanted shots of grinning Tommies, giving the thumbs-up. He filmed the dazed anger of a beaten army because it was history; it deserved to be filmed.

For a few weeks he shot training films for the Home Guard. How to make a Molotov cocktail. How to stop a German tank by stuffing a potato up its exhaust pipe. How to garrote a stormtrooper with a rabbit-snare. Then Crown sent him to cover what Churchill was calling the Battle of Britain.

The battle was unfilmable. For one thing it was two or three miles high, virtually invisible; for another, it was spread all over the south and east of England. If Rollo gambled and went to Essex, the battle that day was over Kent. If he went to Kent, the cloudbase was down to a thousand feet. Once he was lucky: the fighting was right above him and the sky was clear. Sometimes the sunlight flashed on a speck of metal. It was like watching very tiny minnows in a very clear stream. Machine-gun fire was like a stick rattled along a railing in another street. He shot what he could. Spitfires landing, Hurricanes taking off. A high mesh of contrails, as pretty as Chinese writing on blue paper. Nothing an audience would look at for more than fifteen seconds. Everyone was talking about invasion. Rollo abandoned the air war and explored the South Coast.

Wherever he found the army doing anything interesting, he got ordered away. He showed documents to prove he worked for Crown Films, but they did not satisfy lieutenants and captains fresh from France where much sabotage had been done by Nazi parachutists dressed as nuns. Nobody had actually met a nun-parachutist, which showed how lethal they were: they killed on sight and left no witnesses. The best shot that Rollo could get was a profile of a sentry on a clifftop, from which he pulled back to reveal that the soldier was overlooking the empty Channel.

In 1940, a lot of newsreels used that clip as shorthand for the invasion that never came. Rollo came to despise it. 'Cliché,' he said. 'Bad cinema. Movies should move. That's just a lousy piece of celluloid.'

2

In place of the invasion came the Blitz.

The raiders came by night in wave after wave. London was so near the Luftwaffe airfields in Belgium and northern France that sometimes the Heinkels and Dorniers and Junkers made two trips, returning to stoke up the fires they had started. Next morning, cameramen roamed the smoking streets. Rollo was in bed, asleep. He had been up all night, catching the action.

Nobody at Crown asked him to do it. He went out because he couldn't resist it, and because he reckoned someone should record the death of a great city, even if nobody survived to see his film. All the experts had calculated that the bombers must kill and maim hundreds of thousands of people. Warsaw and Rotterdam had been flattened like sandcastles; why not London? Each evening, as he left his Chelsea flat, Rollo was reconciled to the thought that, if and when he came back, there might be no flat and no Chelsea.

It didn't happen. London was not obliterated. It was thoroughly spattered with high explosive, and sometimes the spatterings merged to destroy whole streets, but more often the bomb-strikes were as thoughtless as raindrops. It was no safer to stand in Hyde Park than it was to sit in the Café de Paris. There were stray craters in the park, and one night the Café de Paris got blown to blazes, along with the band, the singer and the customers.

Random havoc.

The phrase come to Rollo Blazer at the end of a long night of wandering devastation, when he realized that this military operation had no plan, no system, no shape. The bombers might skip one street and strike the next: kill here, spare there. Or neither. Or both. Or some other witless combination. All these shuddering blasts and blazes added up to an idiot tantrum: random havoc. He was on his way home when he turned a corner and saw a doubledecker bus standing on its nose in a hole, quite upright. He filmed it and thought: *You could bomb every bus route in London every night for a year and this wouldn't happen again. Two years. Ten.* A church clock began to chime and it could not stop. The bell was cracked. It sounded old and weary and touched with despair, and it made a perfect soundtrack. In fact it was beyond perfection, the sort of cinema you wouldn't dare put in a script in case it looked corny. This wasn't corny, it was heartbreaking, it was the world turned upside down and tolling its own death. What made it utterly heartbreaking was the knowledge that it wasn't even cinema, because Rollo wasn't shooting with sound.

His boss at Crown was an ex-advertising man called Harry Frobisher. Frobisher hadn't slept much, he'd had to walk most of the way to the office, and when he arrived Rollo Blazer was waiting, asking for a sound recordist to work with him.

'I don't need your sound,' Harry said. 'Shoot mute, I'll dub in my own sound. Fire bells, bombs exploding, anything.'

Rollo told him about the bus and the church. 'You can't dub that,' he said. 'You haven't got a cracked bell on record.'

'If I need it, I'll send someone to record it.'

'Too late,' Rollo lied. 'Delayed-action bomb in the crypt. Whole place is a heap of rubble now.'

Frobisher was a bulky, untidy man with a lumpy, warty face, the kind that no barber would want to shave. His mouth was permanently set in a slight twist that made him look as if he had just made an unwise decision. He was stuck with his face. He didn't care what people thought of it. If it made them nervous, too bad; he got on with running his section of Crown Films. He ran it well.

Rollo wasn't nervous but he knew when to say nothing.

'I'm short of good soundmen,' Harry said. 'Also short of lunatics. Only a maniac would work with you. You should be dead by now.'

'I'm very careful,' Rollo said. 'I always wear a tin hat.'

'Come off it. I've seen your stuff. It's terrifying. Even mute, it scared me.'

Rollo was pleased. 'Imagine what sound would add.'

'You haven't got a storyline.' Harry left his desk and went to the window. 'Bombed buildings. People are sick of seeing bombed buildings. I can see two from here. Three.'

'I've got human interest. Firemen, wardens, coppers. It's a film about London. I just want the audience to hear the voice of London.'

'This isn't the only Blitz, you know. Liverpool, Plymouth, Bristol, Coventry, Southampton, Birmingham, they're getting hammered too. Why don't you go and film them?'

Rollo scratched his stubbled jaw. They both knew it was an unfair question. It came from weeks and months of bottled-up fear and anger generated by living in a city always under attack and helpless to defend itself, except by flinging up a vast number of anti-aircraft shells which didn't seem to deter the raiders and which fell in the form of whistling, jagged shrapnel that clattered off rooftops and roads and broke windows and occasionally struck and killed a wandering Londoner.

'We're supposed to be boosting morale,' Harry said 'Do your worst, Fritz – London can take it. That sort of thing. What you've shot looks like hell on earth.'

'Well, it is hell. But hell perfectly framed and in sharp focus and steady as a rock. Now, with sound –'

The window panes vibrated noisily to the curt grunt of a distant explosion. Harry picked up a pair of binoculars. 'Lambeth,' he said. 'Or maybe Camberwell.' He focussed on a column of smoke, climbing and bending with the wind. 'Five hundred kilograms, probably. Jerry does it deliberately, you know, to put the wind up the rescue squads.'

'I know.'

'Puts the wind up *me*, I don't mind admitting.'

'Be grateful to the bomb-disposal squads, then. Hell of a good story there.' Rollo yawned and stretched. 'Of course it comes best from their own lips.'

Harry put the binoculars back. 'You never give up, do you? Okay. If we've got anyone crazy enough, you can have a sound recordist.'

'You won't regret this, Mr de Mille,' Rollo said. 'The German box office alone will be worth millions.' Harry wasn't listening. 'Film those bomb-disposal guys while they can still talk and you can still shoot,' he said. 'Now leave. You stink like a bonfire.'

Later that day, Rollo got a message from Frobisher: *Try Freddy Kelly*, with a Hammersmith address. It was dark by the time he rang the bell. A youngish woman said she was Freddy Kelly. Now that was a surprise.

Even in 1940, when women were replacing men in all sorts of jobs, Rollo had never known a female sound recordist. He didn't like the idea, and when he looked at this example he didn't like the example. Not nearly ugly enough. Good-looking young women were a pain and a nuisance during filming: that was his experience. They couldn't write clearly, couldn't add minutes and seconds, lost things you asked them to keep, and banged their nails in the clapperboard. They whispered and giggled when you wanted silence. Worst of all they distracted the attention of men who had jobs to do. That was the ultimate sin: women were not serious about filming. The better they looked, the worse they behaved. Freddy Kelly was a tallish blonde, hair short and shaggy, with the kind of face that made greengrocers put an extra apple in her bag, free. Arms and legs to match. Two bumps on her chest, as God intended. Hopeless. No use to anybody.

He stopped just inside the house. He knew she would make a scene, so he might as well say it and go. 'You're not what I want,' he said.

'Well, you're not what I want,' she said. 'But who said life was fair?'

They went into the living-room and did not sit.

'Nothing personal,' he said. 'Let me explain –'

'No, let me explain, I can do it faster. First, I haven't got the strength and this is a tough job, I might hurt myself. Second, I haven't got the experience and this is a difficult job, tricky sound, I wouldn't know how to handle it. Third, I'm young and innocent, the

166

men can't swear while I'm around and that bloody well pisses them off. Fourth, I need a separate lavatory or I burst into tears. Fifth is usually something vague and embarrassed about the curse.' She spoke calmly and easily. 'There,' she said. 'Have I covered everything?'

'Why call yourself Freddy?'

'Same reason Archie Leach calls himself Cary Grant. To get the work.'

Rollo looked at framed photographs on the mantelpiece. He recognised some people: directors, cameramen, actors. She wore slacks and a leather flying-jacket; she blended in with the men. 'Why work with me?'

'It's what I do for a living.'

'Living? Filming the Blitz? You want to die?'

'It hasn't killed you yet.'

That convinced him. She was too cocky, too mouthy. 'You're not strong enough,' he said. He picked up his hat.

'You're probably right. Look: before you go, do me a favour, please. Just carry that table into the kitchen for me.' It was a dining table, square, thick, mahogany, with legs like tree-stumps. 'Please.'

It wasn't a favour, it was a challenge. A sensible man would have smiled and walked away. Rollo felt tricked and it made him angry. He grabbed the table and heaved. It felt chained to the floor. He staggered two paces and couldn't make three. The table hit the floor with a crash that made the blackout blind slowly roll up. She switched off the lights. In the darkness he sprawled on the table. Tiny stars cruised about his vision. 'Your sodding table,' he said. 'It's buggered my back.'

'Well, you didn't bend your knees enough, did you? It's lucky I've got two strong shoulders. Your camera goes on one and my sound stuff on the other.'

He slid off the table and sat on the carpet. Faintly, like a dog howling in a distant village, a siren sounded; then, like other dogs, other sirens copied it.

'Hadn't we better be going?' she said.

It was a small raid: a dozen aircraft. Confused by thick cloud and rain, they bombed the suburbs and left. Scattered damage. Nothing there for Rollo. He took his female soundman to a pub.

'So what's your real name?' he said.

'Kate. Kate Padaszczlavski. From Wloctawek.'

'And where the hell is Wloctawek?'

'Between Torun and Krosniewice. Poland.'

'Oh. *That* Wloctawek.'

'My dad came here from Poland. Nobody can pronounce Padaszczlavski, so I took mum's maiden name. Kelly. From Ballyduff. What else can I tell you?'

Rollo drank some beer. 'You scared of bombs?'

'Who isn't?'

'Good. Scared tells you when you're in the right place. Death makes great movies.'

She cocked her head. 'Death plus a big budget.'

'Money's no object. We've got hundreds of bombers, thousands of bombs, a city in flames. Makes *Gone With The Wind* look like a smoky chimney.'

'Begorrah,' Kate said. 'As they say in Wloctawek.'

They worked the Blitz for the rest of the winter and into spring. They made a good team. Both were Londoners; Kate had grown up in the East End, Rollo was at home in the West End. They filmed the destruction of entire communities in the slums and the burning of famous landmarks in Soho and Mayfair and Knightsbridge and Chelsea. Kate had a nose for trouble. One terrible night, when Rollo was black with smoke and wet with spray from firehoses and ready to quit, she persuaded him to walk up the Strand and down Fleet Street. St Paul's cathedral was pink as salmon in the glow from the buildings burning on three sides. They filmed it from the roof of an abandoned pub. The soundtrack collected the woof and thud of guns and bombs, and the steady rumble of collapsing roofs and walls. 'Eat your heart out, Selznick,' Rollo said. A week later they were shooting in the London docks. A fire-float pumped a pattern of high, white jets onto an oil storage tank, trying to cool it. 'Pretty picture,' Kate said. While Rollo was filming, a stick of bombs hurried down the dockside and the blast knocked them over. When they got up, the oil tank was belching flames. Rollo wiped dust off the lens. He filmed blazing oil spreading across the water until it surrounded the boat and in the end he was filming white jets spouting out of waving red fire.

'Did you get that?' he asked

168

'I got the oil fire,' she said. 'Sounded like an express going through a station.'

Smoke was coming down like a rich black fog. Soon it blotted out the fire-float.

Rollo and Kate were not callous, nor greedy for sensation; too much sensation came their way, unsought. The Blitz was a thing of terror, shot through with agony and heartbreak and the obscenity of casual maiming and killing. They saw this. They saw things that sickened them so much that they couldn't film any of it. On the other hand, it was all happening and therefore, nausea permitting, it deserved to be filmed. They were ready every night. As soon as the first rusty groan of the first air-raid siren began to climb towards its roller-coastering wail, they felt what everyone felt: a gut-tightening dread. Here comes death. But they also felt a keen professional interest. Rollo was right: death made great movies.

They filmed fires and explosions, and the people who fought them and survived them. They got stories from a policeman wearing a cape that had been stiffened by a shower of molten lead; from a woman saved after two days under the rubble of her home; from ambulance drivers who drove on tyres shredded by broken glass; from rescue workers, and wardens, and sappers who dug out and defused unexploded bombs. The Blitz went on and on. Many people who took shelter saw no point in coming to the surface: they lived in caves and cellars and disused tunnels. Rollo and Kate filmed them too. Perhaps such people were right, for towards the end of spring the raids grew heavier. After the night of 19 March, 1941, *Germany Calling* said that more than four hundred bombers raided London. Nobody argued. On 16 April it was over six hundred; three nights later, over seven hundred. One bomber, a Heinkel 111, made a mess of some deer in Richmond Park, but not before it had killed its own crew. Rollo and Kate were lucky that night; doubly lucky. They filmed it, and it missed them.

Kate saw it first. 'Look up there,' she said. The Heinkel was lazily spiralling down a searchlight beam as though each was hypnotized by the other. Rollo filmed, and tried not to breathe. He knew this was one of the classic shots of war. A wing spun away, and the bomber exploded. Pieces fled into the night. Each piece trailed flame. A man said, 'Jesus Christ Almighty.'

The searchlight was nearby; and when, after a few seconds, the beam vanished, the night seemed huge and the burning bits looked tiny. Soon they too disappeared. Rollo lowered the camera. 'Did you get that voice?'

'Yes.'

'Sounded as if he'd seen a miracle.'

'Yes.'

'You can't script stuff like that. You can script the words but not the voice. It makes that shot universal. You could watch it in China or Brazil and still get the same kick.'

The raid was fading away, the guns giving up as the bombers turned south and droned towards home. The clouds above parts of London were as red as dawn, but dawn was still two hours away.

They stowed their equipment in the car. Rollo started the engine.

'If that fellow saying "Jesus Christ Almighty" isn't on the sound-track I'm going to kill you,' he said.

'You kill me, I'll tell the union and they'll get your name taken off the credits.'

'Credits?' he said. 'Credits. I never thought about credits.' *Filmed by Rollo Blazer*. The idea kept him quiet for several minutes.

3

London was huge; it could afford to lose several hundred acres. It could even afford to lose its great buildings. The House of Commons was wrecked: seven bombs had blown it apart. Westminster Abbey was hit. So was Buckingham Palace, and the Tower of London, and the British Museum, and every railway terminus, and five hospitals, and all the churches in the City, and more. It was a long and gloomy list.

Everywhere Londoners looked they saw the ruins of landmarks in their everyday lives. What the Luftwaffe had done yesterday it could repeat tomorrow, and the next night, and go on repeating until the long-threatened invasion came. In the shattered shopfronts, hand-written signs said *Business as usual – London can take it*. The tired faces of the customers told a different story. To make matters worse, there were precious few luxuries in the shops. Rationing hurt.

For about a year now, in all of Europe, only Britain had stood against Germany and Italy. Defiance was a noble attitude, but it was lonely and painful and tiring, and many people wondered how it was going to win the war.

4

The Heinkel corkscrewed lazily down the searchlight beam, as if the light were winding it in. Abruptly it flung its little wings away and then it exploded. Bits of aeroplane fluttered, trailing flames. Noise of the explosion arrived, like a door slamming. The searchlight went out. The flames made bright scratches in the night.

The tail of the film flapped through the projector, the screen went blank white, the overhead lights came on.

'What did that man say?' Gunnery asked. 'Right at the end?'

'He said "Jesus Christ Almighty,"' Harry Frobisher said.

Delahaye yawned; it was stuffy in the viewing room. 'Might run into trouble with the Church over that,' he said.

'People swear in the Blitz,' Gunnery said.

'Of course they do,' Delahaye said. 'They say worse things than "Jesus Christ Almighty". But we're not going to repeat them in the cinema, are we?'

Timothy Delahaye was Minister of Information. The Crown Film Unit was one of his responsibilities. Normally he was happy to leave the running of Crown to its head, Blake Gunnery, who knew all about film. Gunnery's mother, widowed in the First War, had married an American film producer and raised Blake in California. At twenty-five he came back to England, made a string of successful B-movies, and then rashly invested all his money in an avant-garde production, a dark political thriller full of revolutionary camera-angles, exactly what Thirties audiences didn't want to see. Gunnery went bust. He still had one asset: the baronetcy which he had inherited from his father. When the top job at Crown Films became vacant, Timothy Delahaye was among those who interviewed him. The baronetcy clinched it. Gunnery never used the title, but he could obviously be depended upon to serve the State.

'Leaving blasphemy aside,' Delahaye said to Gunnery, 'this Blitz stuff is quite brilliant. How much is there?'

'Forty-seven reels.'

'Golly. The man deserves a medal. Some of his shots made me want to run for my life.'

'Those poor devils couldn't run,' Gunnery said. 'Firemen and so on. Had to stand and fight. Stand and die, some of them.'

'Well, there it is.' Delahaye made an it's-all-over-now gesture. 'We can't use any of it. Not a foot.'

'I'll have it locked in the vault. Double-locked.'

'Very wise. How will your man Blazer react?'

'He'll throw a fit, Minister,' Frobisher said. 'Come at me with the paperknife, I expect. He believes he's shot an epic. London, bloody but unbowed. That sort of thing.'

'So he has,' Delahaye said. 'It'll be a masterpiece one day. When we've won the war, and we can look back with pride at this ordeal by fire, that will be the time to let our people see Blazer's film. Not now.'

'Sir, the Blitz is a victory of a sort,' Frobisher argued.

'No, it's not, Harry,' Gunnery said. 'It's a kick in the teeth.'

'Yes.' Frobisher remembered images from Blazer's footage. 'Yes, I suppose you're right.'

'So where do we stand?' the Minister said briskly. 'The nation's morale has taken a pounding. First Dunkirk, then the Blitz. We need a damn good morale-booster. Something to make people feel good about the war. Good about democracy. What would cheer up the average man in the typical air raid shelter?'

'Only one thing that I can think of, Minister,' Gunnery said, 'and that's knowing that the RAF is bombing the living daylights out of Berlin.'

Timothy Delahaye picked up a phone. 'Get me the Air Ministry,' he said. 'Air Commodore Russell in Press and Public Relations.'

'The RAF isn't bombing the daylights out of Berlin, sir,' Frobisher said.

'It will be,' Delahaye said. 'By the time you've finished with it.'

5

Tim Delahaye and Charlie Russell were distant cousins and old friends. Each knew what the other's job involved, and neither felt any need to be especially sympathetic. They met in the Minister's office, which on that particular morning had a fine view of heavy rain.

'One good thing,' the Air Commodore said. 'It helps to lay the dust.'

'Yes. Last night's raid. We had a few bombs, didn't we? A few incendiaries?'

'A few hundred. And if you've got me here to complain that the RAF can't shoot down Jerry bombers, I don't want to hear it. We do our best.'

'I know you do, Charlie. But look here. The Blitz has been going on for seven or eight months, and people are fed up with it. We need a victory.'

'Try the Army and Navy Stores. Try Harrods. Try prayer.'

'Bomber Command is a kind of a victory.'

Russell sniffed.

A man brought in coffee on a tray, and left. Delahaye poured. Russell stroked the coffeepot with his finger. 'Solid silver,' he said.

'My father bequeathed it. Damned if I'll leave it at home to be bombed.'

'I'm lucky to get a chipped china mug, in my office.'

'Don't take this amiss, Charlie, but you don't seem frightfully bullish about the Royal Air Force today.'

'Don't I? Well, I'll back it to the hilt. What I *won't* do is embarrass anyone – from the CO to the erk who sweeps out the hangar – with a lot of overblown propaganda.'

'Has that happened?'

'The Battle of Britain. Not your fault, Tim, but by the time it was over, the public thought every RAF fighter pilot was a Greek god who went up before breakfast, knocked down a brace of Dorniers, did a victory roll and said it was a piece of cake.'

'With a modest smile.'

'The chaps didn't like it, Tim. Didn't like being called "Glory Boys". They knew it was all balls.'

'Yes.'

'So no more glory boys. Flak and fighters are bad enough without coming back to bullshit.'

'Quite agree. That's why I want my chaps to make an absolutely honest, accurate film about your best Wellington squadron.'

Russell made a sour face. 'C-in-C Bomber Command doesn't like film crews wandering around his bases. They jeopardize security. One bloody cameraman filmed a Guest Night in the Mess. You can imagine how the boys reacted. They debagged the adjutant. I had hell's own job getting the negative.'

'It won't be that kind of film.'

Russell shook his head. 'Bomber Command can be very sticky. Believe me, they won't budge.'

'Let me pass on a piece of news,' the Minister said. 'The Royal Navy has given permission for a major feature film about the exploits of one of its destroyers.'

'Oh?' Russell became very alert. 'Which one?'

'HMS *Kelly*, commanded by –'

'Mountbatten. The king's cousin.'

'Noel Coward is directing and starring. The film will be a great hit. The navy will look very good.'

'The bloody *Kelly sank*.'

'Amid scenes of the most tremendous pluck. The Admiralty are very excited about it.'

'Trust the navy to blow its own bugle. They hate the RAF, you know. They wouldn't rest until they got the Fleet Air Arm away from us. And now their damn ships fire at our chaps all the time. Utter bastards.'

'The army is planning a big film too, set in North Africa.' Delahaye brushed biscuit crumbs from his fingers.

'That's crazy,' Russell said. 'The army is *losing*, for God's sake.'

'Laurence Olivier is a Commando officer. Rex Harrison is an expert in Intelligence. Margaret Lockwood plays a fearless nurse. Good cast.'

'Good at what? Running backwards? Rommel's twenty miles inside Egypt.'

'Backs-to-the-wall stuff, Charlie. The army's always been good at that.'

'The army hates us too. After Dunkirk it wasn't safe for an airman to go into an army pub. The brown jobs reckon we let them down. All balls, of course.'

'I know, I know. But please think about it. Did you see Olivier in *Wuthering Heights*? Quite brilliant. And I know the navy are very serious about HMS *Kelly*. Just imagine. Mountbatten. Noel Coward.'

'The fellow's a pansy.'

'He'll be a very gallant pansy. All the nice girls love a sailor.'

'Enemies everywhere,' Russell said bitterly. 'And I don't mean Hitler.'

That afternoon, Russell phoned Delahaye and said Air Ministry was fully in favour of a film about Bomber Command. 409 Squadron, based at RAF Coney Garth in Suffolk, had the best record of any Wellington squadron.

'Fine.'

'I can get you David Niven. He was excellent in *Dawn Patrol*. He's in the army, but they'll lend him to us. David Niven's better than Noel Coward, don't you think?'

'It's not that sort of film, Charlie. This is a documentary. Real men, real action. Crown Films will make it. They're part of my little empire.'

'We'll need to see the script.'

'Of course you shall. You can have a bit part. Bring your own brush and you can be the erk who sweeps out the hangar.'

'Ha bloody ha,' Russell said. He had set his heart on getting David Niven to play a bomber pilot: skilful, ambitious, charming, unafraid. Another disappointment. War was all disappointment.

6

Rain made everything worse.

When Rollo was a boy, summer holidays were always in Cornwall. It always rained. That couldn't be true, but it was how he remembered it. Bad enough being small: no money, no power, no freedom to go anywhere without adult permission, and no money to do anything when you got there. And then it rained. Cornwall turned granite-grey. The sky seemed to sulk, dragging itself heavily and gloomily out of the Atlantic. A day of rain was a slow death in wet sandals.

When he became a cameraman, the first thing Blazer reacted to when he awoke each day was the light. Good light meant a good day's shoot, if they were shooting outdoors. Rain was the most depressing sound. That nibbling, speckling patter on the windows put him in a bad temper, whether he was filming or not.

Now the rain was the second sound he heard when he awoke.

He had been up all night, driving all over London with Kate, searching for something different to film and finding the same old smoking craters and shattered buildings. To make it worse, rain kept spotting the lens. A wasted night.

He fell into bed at seven. A shrill bell drilled into his brain. He hated waking up. He saw the clock and detested the time: eleven twenty. He loathed the rattle of rain on the window. The bell stopped. Whoever tried to phone him had quit. Thank God. He dragged the covers over his head and *Fucking hell*! the bastard hadn't quit and it wasn't the phone, it was the door. He stumbled through the flat and opened it. His wife was there. Ex-wife. Miriam. Weeping. No, not weeping. That was rain dripping down her face. 'I was afraid you were out,' she said.

'I was out.' He plucked at his pyjamas. 'This is my outerwear.'

'I'm sorry.' Maybe she was crying a bit, too.

'Not half as sorry as me.' She had a suitcase. 'Oh, shit,' he said.

'I couldn't think where else to go.'

'I could.' They went into the kitchen. 'Salvation Army. Scotland Yard. Your mother's place.'

'She's dead. Died four years ago.'

He sat down and immediately stood up: the fly on his pyjama pants had flared open. His raincoat lay nearby. He put it on. *What's the matter with you?* he asked himself. *She's seen it all before, a thousand times.* She was drying her face with a tea-towel. 'Are you unwell, Miriam?' he asked.

'No.'

He waited. 'Well, if you're not going to tell me, I'm not going to ask.'

'You never knew what sacrifices I made for you, Rollo,' she said. 'I gave –'

'Stop!' he shouted. 'Don't say you gave me the best years of your life. I can take the Blitz, and I can take cheap dialogue, but not both together.'

She filled the kettle with water. That simple action amazed him: it was as if she had never been away: what gall! 'There's no gas,' he said. 'They've turned it off. A bomb.' She struck a match, and the gas flowered obediently. 'What a cow you are,' he said. 'You can't stay here.'

'I've been bombed out.'

'Well, obviously.' Rollo kicked her suitcase. 'I didn't think you were selling lavatory brushes. You still can't stay here.'

Miriam simply looked at him. Her hair was damp; she tucked it behind her ears. She seemed five or six years older, and this disappointed Rollo until he did the arithmetic and realized she *was* five or six years older. So was he. Bloody hell.

'But I really need to stay here,' she said.

'There's no damn room! You're not my wife, I don't have to feed and clothe you and keep you in household crockery to smash on my head. You told me to go to hell, remember? Well, I went to hell and here I am, slightly grilled and smelling of sulphur but otherwise happy in my hell-hole, and you can't have it!'

'You don't understand,' she said.

He threw a cup at her, and missed by a yard. She flinched, and smiled sadly. 'Christ Almighty!' he roared. 'Don't you remember *any*thing? If you stay here, one of us will kill the other before sunset. We hate each other, Miriam.'

'But I've nowhere else to go.'

He pulled the raincoat over his head and closed his eyes. He said: 'I can't see you, so you don't exist.' The raincoat stank of blitzed buildings. *Ah, happy days*, he thought.

'House two doors away got hit,' she said. He heard her making tea: the hot rush and bubble of water into the pot. 'Next door wasn't safe. They pulled it down and half my house came down with it.'

A milk bottle clinked, a teaspoon rattled. He wanted a cup of tea. More than that, he wanted to chuck her into the street. In the movies men got chucked into the street all the time. Why not a woman, for once? The phone rang and she picked it up.

'It's for you,' she said.

'Of course it's for bloody me.' Now he had to come out of hiding. 'Look: go and stay in a hotel, Miriam. I'll pay, if I must. Hullo. Rollo Blazer speaking.'

It was a brief conversation.

'That was the office,' he told her. 'The boss wants to see me. Drink up. I'll drive you to a hotel.'

'There's Desmond as well,' she said. 'He's been living with me. As a paying guest, so to speak.'

'Spare me your feeble euphemisms, Miriam. If the bugger's your boyfriend, say so. Do you fuck each other?'

She nodded. He thought he saw a tiny smile of pride.

'Well, you can do it in the gutter. This is a very small flat. I need every square inch.'

'Desmond's waiting outside. We came in his car.'

Rollo raised his arms and howled like dog. The effort was tiring and soon he had to stop. She was still there, sipping tea, watching. 'Cover yourself up, Rollo,' she said. 'You know the neighbours can see in, and it's not a pretty sight.'

'If I come back and find bloody Desmond in this bloody flat I'll bloody kill the pair of you.'

He shaved and dressed, and went out to his car. The rain had stopped. One other car was parked nearby, and a man stood beside it: a naval officer, tall, broad, very bearded. He was carrying a pair of gloves, and he made a jaunty little salute with them. Rollo nodded. As he drove away he wondered what the chap saw in Miriam. Then he wondered what he, Rollo, had seen in Miriam. Whatever it was, it had turned out to be an optical illusion.

He put it out of his mind. Quite soon he would be back in the real world, the world of film. It was a reassuring thought.

7

'Warmest congratulations,' Blake Gunnery said. Frobisher was working on the cork. Rollo Blazer smiled modestly. The cork ricocheted off the ceiling. Frobisher made haste to pour. 'There are few privileges in my job,' Gunnery said, 'but one is seeing the work of true genius, and another is toasting its creator.'

They clinked glasses and drank. Blazer drank deep; this was

breakfast. Or lunch. 'The real heroes are out there,' he said.

'Let's drink to London,' Gunnery said, and they did.

'It's literally unforgettable,' Rollo said, 'because it's all on film.'

Frobisher gave him more champagne. 'Not all,' he said. Rollo glanced up, but Frobisher was looking at Gunnery.

'A year ago, during the Battle of Britain,' Gunnery said, 'Churchill told us men would look back and say: "This was their finest hour." I wonder what men will say when they look back on the Blitz?'

'Eight horrible months,' Frobisher said confidently.

'Not quite a massacre,' Gunnery said. 'The word *carnage* suggests itself. You've seen more of it than anyone, Blazer. Would you find *carnage* acceptable?'

Rollo thought of some of the things he had seen. 'It's not too strong.' His glass was full again.

'Some of the raids ...' Gunnery shook his head. 'Unspeakable. Right? Nobody should be asked to stomach ... I mean to say, in all decency, isn't it beyond all ...?' Rollo found himself nodding. 'I'm so glad you agree,' Gunnery said. 'There's no middle way, is there?'

'We can't show your Blitz film,' Frobisher said.

Rollo had sensed the coming punch, but he could find no words, only an angry noise. 'Hey, hey, hey,' he said. It was not enough. 'Hey.'

'Rollo, my friend,' Frobisher said. 'You've shot forty-odd reels of brilliant horror movie. People won't go to the cinema and pay to see that kind of horror. They can stay at home and see it for real. For free.'

'Not everybody,' Rollo protested. 'Millions don't live in cities, they've never heard a bomb drop, they don't *know* – '

'And they would prefer not to know,' Gunnery said. 'You are aware of Mass Observation? Their researchers go all over Britain with their clever questionnaires, and they get surprising answers. Yes, folk in the provinces are sorry for Londoners, but not all *that* sorry. There has always been a feeling that Londoners are a snotty lot who deserve to be cut down to size.'

'I don't believe nobody cares.'

'And of course you are right,' Gunnery said. 'People feel very badly about the Blitz, not just on London but on Liverpool, Coventry – well, you know the list. They feel very badly indeed.'

'Mass Observation,' Harry Frobisher said. He had moved away and was looking out of a window.

'Demoralization of the civilian populace is a major aim of the Blitz,' Gunnery said. 'It has had a large degree of success. Now, I put it to you: should we reinforce Hitler's success by publicizing it in the cinema?'

'Not bloody likely,' Frobisher said.

Gunnery emptied the bottle into Rollo's glass but only an inch of fizz came out. 'Somewhat symbolic of British morale.'

'That's exactly why we need a Blitz film,' Rollo insisted. 'To show that Jerry did his worst and – '

'And sometimes we panicked,' Frobisher said. 'The Blitz wasn't all guts and gallantry.'

'Ninety-nine per cent was.'

'Let's not quibble,' Gunnery said. 'The government blundered badly at the start. Trying to stop people sheltering in the Underground stations made them very angry, especially in the East End. There was trouble.'

'People marched from Stepney to the Savoy Hotel,' Frobisher said. 'They didn't see why the rich should be warm and safe in the cellars of the Savoy while the poor got blown to bits in street shelters. That was censored, of course.'

Rollo said nothing. He had filmed street shelters. He knew how they stood up to bombing: not at all well.

'Not that censorship helped,' Gunnery said. 'You're not supposed to know this, but during the Blitz the army lost a lot of men through desertion. Worried about their families. Newspapers told them nothing. Phones didn't work.'

'That was nobody's fault,' Rollo muttered. 'Bombs smash things.'

'People are brave and they'll take a lot,' Frobisher said. 'But the fact is there was a danger of plague in London in some of those stinking tunnels used as unofficial shelters, and after Liverpool got bombed there were riots and looting, and when Churchill visited Bristol he got booed.'

'He got cheered,' Rollo said. 'I saw it on a newsreel.'

'And booed. That bit got censored.'

'The decision has been reached,' Gunnery said. 'The best thing we can do about the Blitz is leave it quietly alone until the war is over.'

Rollo swallowed his dregs. 'I'm obviously wasting my time here,' he said, 'I might as well go off and join the Grenadier Guards.'

'Certainly not. A man of your talents? Unthinkable. No, we have an urgent project that's exactly right for you. I want you to go and make a film about RAF Bomber Command.'

Rollo was astonished. 'Me? Why me? I hate aeroplanes.'

'But you love your country. And right now, Bomber Command is the only part of the Armed Services that is regularly dropping high explosive on the black heart of the enemy.'

'People need to see that,' Frobisher said. 'Seeing it will do them good. It'll build up their morale.'

'The squadron we've chosen is in Suffolk,' Gunnery said. 'Keep the same soundman, if you like. Can you be there tomorrow?'

Blazer thought of his ex-wife and of Desmond, her so-to-speak paying guest, spreading themselves in his flat. 'I'll go today,' he said.

'Splendid. Now let me explain the story.'

TRUTH ALWAYS HURTS

1

The Service Police took Rollo and Kate to RAF Coney Garth and put them in the guardroom. They were given mugs of tea while the Duty Officer was found. He was a sprog pilot officer, totally out of his depth when shown identity documents allegedly from the Crown Film Unit. 'You should have been notified,' Rollo told him. 'We expected to be expected.'

'I have no orders concerning you.'

He went away, consulted the adjutant, and spent an hour on the phone to London. He finally tracked down Blake Gunnery, who called Air Commodore Russell. 'Another cock-up,' Russell said. After a decent interval, lengthy signals from Air Ministry clattered out of the teleprinter at RAF Coney Garth, and the civilians were released.

'A word of advice,' the Duty Officer said. 'Don't make jokes to RAF policemen. Security is no laughing matter in Bomber Command.'

'Can I have my car back?' Rollo asked. 'All our film gear is in it.'

'That's up to the group captain.' The Duty Officer knew from the adjutant that Rafferty had returned in a thoroughly bad temper. 'And he's unavailable at present.'

He drove them to the officers' quarters. 'Mr Blazer's room is here. Miss Kelly is staying at the Waafery.' This startled her. 'All the Waafs live over there.' He pointed to a distant cluster of pine trees. 'The policy is strict separation. Rather a long walk, I'm afraid. A bicycle is useful.'

'Oh no. That's impossible,' she said. 'We work as a team, you see. We've never been separated since the day we married.' She ruffled

Rollo's hair. 'Happiest day of his life,' she told the Duty Officer. 'I have to keep reminding him.'

'What lies you do tell,' Rollo said.

The Duty Officer looked at his clipboard. 'Mr Blazer and Miss Kelly. That's my information.'

'I keep my maiden name for professional purposes. Haven't you got married quarters? A place this size ...' her left hand fluttered, the one with the wedding ring.

Recently, Bomber Command had decided that aircrew wives should not live on the base; it divided their husbands' attention: bad for morale. The Duty Officer took Rollo and Kate to married quarters and installed them in a house. Rollo looked out of an upper window. Nothing was happening; the aerodrome was a desert. 'Is it always as quiet as this?' he asked.

'Good God, no. Ops have been scrubbed. The chaps have gone to town. Newmarket, Bury St Edmunds. I'll get your suitcases sent over. You can have dinner in the Ladies' Room adjoining the Mess. I'm afraid the Mess is strictly men-only.' He left.

She was testing the springs of a creaky double bed. 'You may kiss the bride,' she said.

'A word of advice. Don't say it unless you mean it.' They sat on opposite sides of the bed and looked at each other. He thought: *Why risk it?* She thought: *Do I mean it?* She said: 'Nobody knows what they mean until they hear how it sounds.'

He blinked three times. She knew what that meant: he didn't understand and he was too tired and hungry to think more about it. 'You were pretty slick with that wedding ring,' he said.

'I carry it for protection. It scares away wolves.'

His scalp itched a little, and he touched the scar, for luck. 'You think you're smart,' he said. 'Well, I've got news for you. You *are* smart.' He stood up. That was enough for one evening.

They had dinner in the Ladies' Room, alone, and went to the camp cinema. Most seats were empty. They sat near the MO, who seemed half-asleep. While they waited for the lights to go down, Rollo introduced himself and Kate. 'Pretty dull today, wasn't it?' he said. 'We're in the film business. Came here looking for action.'

'I'm in the piles business.' The MO spoke blankly. 'I don't need to look. Aircrew come to me. All that sitting. Hours and hours.' His eyelids closed, and then flickered open. 'Any time you want to film piles, I'll show you the best in Bomber Command.'

The film turned out to be a dull comedy. Rollo and Kate left halfway through. By ten they were in bed and asleep like any old married couple.

2

Next morning, Rafferty felt much better. After all, he'd torn a large strip off that carping old pongo, Barriton. The sun shone. He'd had a signal from Air Ministry that bucked him up, no end. He got Air Commodore Russell on the blower and confirmed it: 409 had been chosen to star in a film.

He'd served with Charlie on the North-West Frontier of India, dropping bombs on fanatical tribesmen to teach them not to get bolshy with the British Raj. 'We had some bloody good fun in the Khyber Pass, didn't we?' he said.

'You and I put the wind up the Fakir of Ipi, all right. What a frightful blighter he was. Thought he was safe in his mountain stronghold.'

'Nobody was safe when you were around, Charlie. Man, woman or mountain goat.' They laughed until it hurt.

'This cinema-thing,' Russell said. 'Get it right, Tiny. There could be bags of kudos in it.'

'You know 409, Charles. Bull's-eye every time.'

Rafferty asked the Wingco to pop in, and gave him the good news. 'Feather in the cap, eh? They could have picked any squadron in the Command, and they chose yours. Once in a blue moon, Air Ministry gets it right. Congratulations, Pug.'

'Thank you, sir. A film, you say. For training purposes?'

'No, no, no. A *real* film. It'll be shown in the cinema, Pug! In every bally cinema in the land. In the world, probably.'

'Except Germany, sir.'

'Don't bet on it, old boy. I'm sure the Luftwaffe will want to see it. I think it's time we met these movie-makers, don't you?'

Rafferty asked his secretary to find them. She was Sergeant Felicity

Parks, without doubt the prettiest Waaf on the base. Rank had its privileges.

Rafferty was surprised to find that the Crown film crew consisted of two.

'I'm cameraman, writer and director,' Rollo said. 'She records sound and corrects my spelling and makes the sandwiches.'

'Very economical,' Rafferty said.

'You don't need a mob to shoot a film. Hollywood thinks you do, but everyone in Hollywood wears jodhpurs and cravats.' Blazer was in a faded brown corduroy suit. Kate was in grey slacks and an old navy peajacket. 'We'll melt into the background, group captain. You won't even know we're here.'

'I doubt that ... Well, here's the set-up. Strictly speaking, I look after two squadrons, but one operates from a satellite field down the road. They fly old Fairey Battles which tow target drogues for trainee gunners to shoot at, deadly dull. Don't bother with them. *Here* we have 409 Squadron with Wellingtons, led by Wing Commander Duff. A crack outfit, if I say so.' He pointed to a large board on the wall behind his desk. It listed the names of German cities, beginning with Wilhelmshaven. A second board was already half-full. '409's score-card. Tomorrow there should be another name. Bomber Command hasn't rested since the day war was declared.'

Rollo read, and was impressed. 'Is there any town you haven't hit? Stuttgart, Berlin, Magdeburg, Stettin, Hamm, Osnabruck ... Berlin again. You really like Bremen and Hamburg, don't you? Also Kiel and Cologne and Hanover and ...' He gave up.

'It's fair to say that 409 has made its mark,' Pug Duff said. His modesty was enormous. 'And not just in the Third Reich. We attack French targets too: Lorient, Boulogne, Brest. Some of the boys even popped over to Italy, once. Bombed Turin.' It sounded like a bank-holiday excursion. 'Enough about us. Tell me your plans.'

'We're here to catch the action,' Rollo said. 'Film the flying, capture the guts and the gallantry. The idea is to show people exactly what Bomber Command does. No actors. Real airmen. No glamour, no ballyhoo, no propaganda. Just the real thing. We want to film the truth as it happens. Couldn't be simpler.'

'Can I get something straight?' Kate asked. 'A wing commander is a squadron commander?'

'Correct,' Duff said.

185

'So what does a squadron leader do?'

'A squadron leader is a flight commander.'

'Satisfied now?' Rollo said to her.

'It's how Bomber Command operates,' Rafferty said. 'We're big business. RAF Coney Garth is more than a mile square. Airfield, a thousand yards long. Personnel total twelve hundred.'

'It's going to be tough to squeeze all that into the frame,' Rollo said. 'Perhaps we could start by taking a look around the station. Get an overall impression.'

Rafferty agreed. 'Jolly good idea. We'll lay on a guide.'

'Unfortunately I have business to attend to,' Duff said. 'Let me see … I think Flying Officer Lomas is free this morning.'

Handshakes all round. The visitors went away with Sergeant Felicity Banks to find Lomas.

Rafferty was in good spirits. 'They seem to know their business, don't they? And they don't want to interfere with your duties, which is nice. I can't see any problems, can you?'

'Piece of cake, sir.'

3

Flying Officer Lomas was a lanky, bony six-footer, aged twenty-two. He was nicknamed Polly, because he had a nose like a parrot. His right arm was in a sling.

'Enemy action?' Rollo asked.

'In a manner of speaking. Playing rugger in the Mess, with a cushion for a ball. Got trodden on by Beef Benton, stupid clot. Cracked a wrist.'

He showed them around the station: a great number of brick buildings linked by asphalt paths.

'Tell me something,' Kate said. 'What's the worst part about bombing Germany? The absolute worst?'

'Weather. Winds, cold, fog.'

Rollo glanced at Kate. 'That's going to look damn dull on the screen,' he said.

'Most bomber ops *are* dull,' Lomas said. 'Fly there, bomb the target, fly home. Six hours in the air and you end up with a numb bum. Would you like to see the airfield?'

RAF Coney Garth was restlessly busy. There was always a Wellington warming up or taking off, or cruising around the circuit, or landing. Groundcrew came and went, on bikes, in vans or trucks. The Tannoy never ran out of information. 'Ops tonight, am I right?' Rollo said. 'Tell me what's happening.'

Lomas laughed, and looked away. 'All terribly hush-hush, I'm afraid. Do you know Ginger Rogers? Working in films must be jolly interesting.'

On their way back he met a young pilot officer, as ruddy as a ploughboy. 'This is Harry Chester,' Lomas said. 'Not a bad golfer. Completely hopeless in a Wimpy.' They chatted. Chester glanced at Kate as often as he dared.

'You look like the dangerous sort,' she said. 'What's the most dangerous thing you've come across in 409?'

Chester grinned. 'Oh, riding the Grand National, without a doubt. It's a game we play in the Mess on Guest Nights and suchlike. You put a sofa on its back and ride into it on a bicycle, flat out, so you go flying over the top. Whoever flies furthest wins. Damned hairy! Good fun, though.'

They thanked Lomas and Chester, and said goodbye.

'They won't talk,' Rollo said. 'Why won't they talk? We're not the enemy.'

'And we're not members of their club,' Kate said. 'We don't belong here. That's why.'

'Well, it's not bloody good enough.'

The business that Pug Duff had to attend to involved a fight.

Every aircrew officer had a number of airmen whose conduct and welfare were his concern. In Flight Lieutenant Silk's case the men were in the Motor Transport Section. One of them, LAC Piggott, had allegedly caused an affray in the guardroom while signing out of camp. Now Piggott and Silk were in front of Wing Commander Duff, who was trying to decide whether or not this was a court-martial offence. He was reading Piggott's statement. 'You say you entered the guardroom and the SP on duty, Corporal Black, declared,

"Hullo, Manky Piggott, you Welsh bastard. How much petrol you stole today?" Is that correct?'

'Sir.'

'So you hit him.'

'He poked me with his pencil, sir.'

'So you hit him.'

'I hit him *back*, sir. He poked me first. Self-defence, sir.'

'He's got a fractured jaw.'

'Slipped an' fell, sir. Bashed 'is face on the floor.'

Duff clenched his teeth. He looked at Silk. 'Extreme provocation and defamation, sir,' Silk said. 'Piggott isn't Welsh, he's Scottish. And the term "manky": highly offensive, sir.'

'It means scruffy, dirty, squalid. That's what Piggott is. You're known as Manky Piggott from end to end of this camp, aren't you?' Piggott couldn't find a helpful answer, so he stayed silent. Duff massaged his brow. Airmen must not hit policemen. Corporal Black was all mouth and no brain. Piggott was a good mechanic, and Coney Garth was short of mechanics. Policemen were two a penny. What mattered most? Operational efficiency. He looked up.

'Many things have gone wrong this morning, Piggott. Things your manky brain never even considers. For instance, I've got three Wimpys unserviceable. Last night, they could fly. Today: no damn good. I've just heard that Group wants volunteers for some new cloak-and-dagger squadron. Bang goes my best crew, I expect. All our bombsights have got to be re-calibrated, yet again. There's food poisoning in the Sergeants' Mess, for God's sake. Those bloody silly moles are back, digging holes in the flare-path. There's a funeral for Pilot Officer Diamond and the rest of S-Sugar to be arranged. And you're in trouble once more. Not a happy list, is it?'

'No, sir.' Piggott sounded genuinely worried.

'Then consider yourself extremely fortunate. Loss of pay and confined to camp for twenty-eight days. Next time: the glasshouse.'

Piggott saluted and marched out, well satisfied.

'Bloody idiots.' Duff threw the papers into his out-tray. 'That includes you, Silko. You're still running your petrol swindle, aren't you?'

'Not a swindle, Pug. Bloody good value.'

'Bloody quick cremation. One day some sprog PO will fill his Austin Seven with hundred-octane juice and go out in a blaze of glory.'

'I had the Frazer-Nash converted. She loves aviation gas.'

'I don't care. Look: do me a favour and remember that the Waafs' letters are censored. All women lie, I know, but … What do they see in you? You're bloody *scruffy*, Silko.'

'Scruffy, but not manky.'

'Can't you leave the poor girls alone?'

'That's rich, coming from you. Don't forget I knew you in Elementary Flying Training. You humped anything that would lie still for five minutes.'

'Ancient history. Beat it, I've got work to do.'

'Three minutes, sometimes. Is it true you've got the lead in this MGM epic?'

'What epic? It hasn't been officially announced yet.' Duff couldn't disguise the satisfaction in his voice.

'Everyone knows,' Silk said. 'Security here is a disgrace.'

In the afternoon, Rollo and Kate separated. Rollo tried to talk to the mechanics, with no success. If he looked in a hangar, a flight sergeant with a spanner ordered him away. He wasn't allowed anywhere near a bomber on the perimeter. 'There's a flap on,' a fitter told him. 'Don't hang about. A prop might chop your head off.'

Kate went elsewhere and sought out unemployed aircrew who might like to go for a walk and discuss ops. After a couple of hours she returned to married quarters. Rollo was in an armchair, rubbing his scar with the eraser end of a pencil, and scowling at a foolscap pad. 'Any luck?' he said.

'Yes and no. I met three lonely lads. One poor boy just lost his mum. Died of injuries she got in the Blitz. I held his hand. The other two said flying is boring and did I feel like a quick roll in the hay? Not in so many words, of course.'

'Bastards. I hope you told them you're happily married.'

'My poor feet.' She sat on the floor and rested against his legs. 'You're so innocent, Rollo. They want their mothers. Haven't you ever read Freud?'

He waved Freud away. 'I don't want to know about it. Go and see the MO, he'll give you some special double-strength vulcanized condoms made out of Russian tractor tyres. I've got a script.'

She took the pad and read. 'Bombs,' she said. 'More bombs.'

She turned a page. 'Oh, look: another bomb.'

'Use your imagination, Kate. 409 is all about bombing, okay, so we tell the story *from the bomb's point of view*. It arrives at the base, overhears scraps of conversation, all about the next op. The big day comes, it's towed out to a Wimpy, someone chalks a message on it, "To Hitler from 409" or something, and we take off. Finally: climax! Picture this: a black screen slowly opening, dividing in half. We're in the bomb bay. Looking past our bomb, at Germany, miles below. It falls.' He whistled down the scale. 'Bombs gone! We watch, and watch, until bang! Target erupts. Doors close. End of film.'

'End of career, more likely.'

'What's wrong with it?'

'It stinks. Nobody loves a bomb, Rollo. Nothing interesting happens in a bomb dump. This tells me zero about 409. Where are the people? Twelve hundred people here, and you show me a bomb.'

'You're a cruel, cruel woman.' He tore up the script. 'All right. You want people, I'll give you people. That sergeant Waaf, Felicity Somebody, she's got to be in this film. I see her in the Operations Room, sitting by the phone, waiting for the last Wellington to return. Courage personified.'

'She's not Ops. She's Admin,' Kate said.

'She's stunning. And nobody will know the difference.'

4

Rollo met the Wingco in his office. 'Problem,' he said. 'This film isn't about *things* or *places,* it's about *people*. But every time we try to talk to your people, they clam up.'

'Oh dear.'

'Frankly, I could get more information out of a bomb.'

'Well, that won't do.'

'We need them to tell us what it's like to do their job. I mean, *really* like. All the details, good and bad. So we'll have something to build a framework with.'

'Aircrew are a modest lot, Mr Blazer. It's not done to brag in the

RAF. Makes chaps uncomfortable. Still, leave it to me. I'll sort something out.'

Duff sent for his two flight commanders and explained the need for complete cooperation with the film crew. 'This movie is to be absolutely honest,' he said. 'Nothing phoney. They want to know exactly what it's like to be on a bomber squadron. As it's a film, I suppose they want action. A few gory details wouldn't do any harm.'

'They'll wet their knickers if they hear the truth,' said Squadron Leader Pratten. He was Australian: chunky, balding, with a deeply corrugated forehead.

Duff said, 'Well, I wet my knickers often enough when we were bombing those invasion barges last summer.'

The other squadron leader was a tall Cornishman called Hazard, a permanently serious man who only removed his pipe in order to eat or sleep. 'It's not easy to get the boys to talk,' he said. 'You know how they feel about shooting a line.'

'Nobody else will be present. All I want is the truth, and bags of it.'

'Even if it hurts?' Pratten said.

'The truth always hurts.'

Next morning, the Wingco told Rollo that a few aircrew had agreed to discuss some of their memorable experiences. Rollo was delighted. 'All in total confidence,' Duff said. Rollo put his hand on his heart.

They used a quiet office, empty except for a few chairs. 'Coffee and biscuits have been organized,' Duff said; and left.

The first man was a flight-lieutenant pilot, nothing special to look at, medium build, forgettable face. He said, 'I'm told you're interested in the sort of stuff one never hears on the BBC or reads in the papers. Well, I saw this happen. Over Munster. Heavy flak, very concentrated, you could smell it. The searchlights found a Wimpy, not from 409, and they coned it.' His hands made a cone shape, fingertips touching. 'So all the flak batteries plastered it and soon it was on fire.' The more he spoke, the softer his voice. 'I was counting the parachutes. Bins always wants to know. Somebody came out of the top, probably the nav, maybe the wireless op. Anyway, he smashed straight into the tail. The Wimpy has a very high tail-fin, you've seen it, I expect. Tall and sharp. Then the pilot got out. Exit in the cockpit roof. Not easy, with all that clobber we wear, but he got out. Now he's in the slipstream, a hundred and fifty miles an hour and it blows him against the radio mast. The poor bastard is hooked around the mast. And the speed's going up because his Wimpy's going down. If he gets off the mast, the tail's waiting.' The flight lieutenant stood up. 'And all as bright as day.' He nodded goodbye and went.

'He didn't finish,' Rollo said.

'He told us all he knew,' Kate said.

Next was a wireless op, not yet nineteen, with two scraps of toilet paper on his chin where he'd cut himself shaving, not having practised much. He had a lopsided grin to match his bent teeth.

'Over the target, see,' he said. 'Can't remember where, they all look the bloody same to me. Doesn't matter, anyway. Nobody can see the ground, too much haze. Must have been the Ruhr. Skipper says, drop a flare, so I plopped one down the flare-chute and the bloody thing gets stuck! And ignites! That's half a million candle-power! I'm blinded, I'm choking on smoke, Jerry can't believe his luck, he's chucking flak at us with both hands, and the crew's screaming at me to do something.' He found the memory very funny.

'You're here, so you must have done something,' Rollo said.

'Yeah. I put my leg in the chute and stamped down hard. That shifted the bugger. Nearly chopped off the family jewels, too. Long chute, short legs, goodbye goolies!'

'But you got back all right,' Kate said.

'Some of us did. The rear gunner bought it. Lump of shell cut his head off.'

He was followed by a sergeant pilot with the ribbon of a DFM. 'Short and sweet. We were doing an NFT. Night-Flying Test,' he said before they could ask. 'The port prop fell off. Whole airscrew just flew away, still spinning. Quite pretty. The manufacturers tell you a Wellington can fly with one dead engine but unfortunately nobody had told that aeroplane and she flew like a brick. Thank God the rear gunner saw an airfield, about the size of a cricket pitch. A small cricket pitch. I managed to put her down first time, just as well, because there wasn't going to be a second. Hit a Tiger Moth, flattened it. Wiped out the undercarriage on a wall. Carried on at speed across a ploughed field. Starboard wingtip just missed a farmer on a tractor. Matter of inches. Finally stopped. We all jumped out quick, and when I looked back he was still ploughing!' He shook his head. 'I dream about that farmer sometimes. Silly sod.'

He was replaced by a rear gunner with an untidy scar which

wandered from his left ear to the corner of his mouth. The rest of his face was handsome.

'I'd better explain about the doors.' He had a soft Irish accent. 'When you get into the rear turret, you shut the doors behind you. They're like those bat-wing doors you see in westerns, only they're steel and they fill the space altogether. It's to stop any cannon shells flying up the fuselage, if a night fighter catches us. Anyway, we'd bombed Kiel, we were always bombing Kiel in them days, and on our way home, crossing Holland, the flak got us and knocked the bejesus out of us and damaged the doors so they wouldn't open. Now I'm trapped. My parachute's in a container on the other side of the doors, there's no room for it in the turret. Intercom's dead. For all I know the rest of the crew are dead too, and George is flying the kite. The autopilot?' They nodded; they'd heard of George. 'Nobody was dead,' he said. 'The wireless op got the fire axe and chopped the door down. Took him an hour. Now we're over England. The Wimpy's shaking like a wet dog. The pilot says bale out, so we jump. Never jumped before. It's as black as sin. Rough landing, but it didn't kill me, unlike some. Then I'm captured by a Home Guard who wants to shoot me for being a Jerry, or a member of the IRA, he doesn't care which. I got taken to a railway station, put on a train to London, crossed London by Tube, took two trains to get here, and everywhere – *everywhere* – the RTOs, that's Rail Transport Officers, wanted to see my travel warrant. One long argument. No warrant, no travel, they said. And when I got here the Equipment Officer said I'd have to pay for losing my parachute.'

They waited. 'And did you?' Rollo asked.

'I told him I'd kill him first, and he seemed to lose interest.'

Men came and went for the rest of the morning. A pilot described a near head-on collision with a Ju 88 over the North Sea: a quarter of a million cubic miles of air to play with, and two machines chose the same spot. 'Just think,' he said. 'If we'd hit, nobody would ever have known. Except us, of course.' A navigator spoke of what he called 'the unspeakable': ditching in the sea. There was a ditching drill but pilots never discussed it; obviously they couldn't practise it, and it would never happen to them. Same with the dinghy drill. Crews weren't interested. The RAF had an air-sea rescue system but first of all they had to find you. While they were looking, you were sitting in your little rubber dinghy, and if the kite had been shot-up, chances were the dinghy had holes in it. If you weren't found soon, you wouldn't last long. 'Soaked to the skin, freezing cold, scared stiff,' he said. 'The North Sea just sucks the life out of you.'

'You've done it,' Rollo said: 'You know.'

He nodded. 'No fuel, both engines quit together. Stroke of luck: the moon came out, so the pilot could see the waves. You've got to ditch *towards* the waves, tail-down, or you sink like a stone. We got into the dinghy okay. Fifty miles off-shore, I reckoned. The predicted winds were all to cock, as usual. We were only five miles from England. By dawn we were on the beach, got blown there. Minefields everywhere, but we didn't know, we walked past them. God looks after idiots and aircrew. Well, sometimes.'

A wireless op had a story about Pranging Irons. These were bits of scrap metal that crews dropped on Germany. He personally dismantled an old motorbike and dropped it, piece by piece. Also two bricks and a rusty chamber-pot. 'A jerry for the Jerries,' he explained.

'D'you think they got the point?' Kate asked.

'Hope so. It had "Made in England" on it.'

When he left, Rollo said, 'Maybe we can use that. Nice bit of light relief.'

'It's pathetic. He's like a schoolboy blowing a raspberry.'

'Well, most of them *were* schoolboys not so long ago.'

'He's dropped the jerry. It's gone. What are you going to do? Buy another?'

'I might.'

'Yeah? What happened to truth? Not changing anything?'

'This is the truth. We'd just be underlining it.'

A pilot came in and talked about low flying: strictly forbidden and everyone did it, often on NFTs. If he came back from Germany and got diverted to another field because of fog, he always returned to Coney Garth next day at treetop level. Hedgetop level. He had a wireless op who'd got chopped from the pilots course. Mouthy. Cocky. Pain in the arse. 'I put him in the front gunner's position, in the nose.' The pilot said. 'Then I flew really low. Flew *below* the trees. Flew into a damned great quarry. He saw the rock face coming straight at him. Then – throttles open, stick back, up and away. I'm told his underpants were not a pretty sight.'

Rollo thanked him, and saw him to the door.

'You could use that,' Kate suggested. 'Very dramatic.'

'He's totally mad,' Rollo said. 'What's your excuse?'

There were more experiences: the sergeant pilot who ate a dodgy pre-op meal of savoury mince and had the squits all the way to Hanover and back, along with his crew; the rear gunner who fired off all his ammunition at a twisting, dodging night fighter until he realised it was the Wimpy's moon-shadow on cloud; the wireless op who had been posted to 409 from a squadron where two bombers had been shot down by RAF night fighters; and others. The last man to appear was Flight Lieutenant Silk.

They were impressed by the age of his uniform and his genial attitude. 'I bet you know Hedy Lemarr,' he said.

'Never had the pleasure,' Rollo said.

'Damn. I bet someone five bob you did.'

'I suppose I could lie.'

'Tell you what. You lie for me and I'll lie for you. I'll tell you about a pilot called Sam Blackett who reckoned that it was safest to fly where the flak was thickest.'

'Was he right?' Freddy asked.

'Apparently not. Damn! That was supposed to be a lie.' Silk hooked a spare chair with a foot, dragged it nearer, and rested his feet on it. 'I've got Cary Grant's autograph, you know.'

'This has been a strange morning,' Rollo said. 'I don't know what to believe.'

'Oh, believe it all. I'm sure it's true. Why should these chaps invent anything?' Silk was serious. 'The facts are horrible enough.'

'But we can't use them. My notes are a catalogue of disaster. This can't be the story of Bomber Command, can it?'

'It's just Pug Duff's little joke. I trained with Pug, we got our wings together, he's a bit tight-arsed since they gave him a squadron but he means well. He doesn't want you to turn 409 into a bunch of farts with handlebar moustaches. Types who say "Wizard prang" and give a chivalrous salute to the dying Hun as his Messerschmitt goes down in flames. Pug can't stand horseshit. Bullshit is different, there's always bullshit in the RAF, but horseshit is waste, it's killing crews for nothing. We pick up these dreadful terms from visiting Yanks.'

'Yanks?' Kate asked.

'American air force officers. They attend briefings from time to time, in civvies of course. Awfully decent types. Never chew tobacco.

We've got a Jamaican gunner in 'B' Flight and so far the Yanks haven't tried to lynch him at all. *Awfully* decent.'

'Look, Mr Silk,' Rollo said, 'I don't know what the hell's going on here, and I don't see how I can make a film about 409. It's too big, too complicated, too technical. Have you any advice?'

'Get in a kite,' Silk said. 'Go on an op.' He shook hands with them and strolled out.

'Why are you looking like that?' Kate said. 'It's the obvious thing to do. It's been obvious to me ever since we got here.'

'Hey, just wait a damn minute. Blake Gunnery never said anything about going on an op. Harry Frobisher never told me – '

'You don't like flying, do you?'

'It's just not ...' Rollo searched for the right phrase, and failed to find it. 'It's not my cup of tea,' he said. That sounded feeble.

'Well, how the hell did you expect to get shots of these Wimpys bombing Germany?' Kate demanded.

'There are ways and means.' That sounded even more feeble. 'For a start, I could easily show one of the crew how to use the camera. It's not difficult. And they can't be busy all the time. It would just take them a couple of minutes and – '

'Cobblers! That really is horseshit.' They glared at each other.

'All right,' Rollo said. He was pink with rage. 'If that's what you want, if that's what'll make you bloody happy, then I'll fly on a goddam op. I'll film the lousy raid. Try and stop me.'

'Don't make me responsible,' she told him. 'You took on this job, not me. If you think you can film 409 without flying, then do it. But don't blame me if it's a turkey.'

'I just don't see the point in getting killed, that's all.'

She let him have the last word; they both knew it was only noise. They said little until they were on their way to the Ladies' Room for lunch, and they paused to watch a Wellington take off. 'Someone told me that thing weighs fifteen tons,' Rollo said. 'God never meant fifteen tons to fly.' The Wellington came unstuck and climbed and tucked its wheels away. 'It's like making Big Ben fly,' he said. 'It's not natural.'

Late that afternoon, when all the NFTs had been done and the crews had been briefed and the Wimpys bombed up, the op was scrubbed. It left a sour taste of anticlimax. Poor show.

5

Rafferty used his authority and got Mr and Mrs Blazer out of the Ladies' Room and into the Officers' Mess. He headed off any objections by declaring Kate to be an honorary man. They were also permitted to attend briefings.

Rollo said nothing to anyone about taking part in an op. He decided to sleep on it, and reach a definite decision next day. He slept badly and woke up, hot and sweaty, at four in the morning. Once, when he was a small boy, he had tried to walk along the top rail of a wooden fence, and slipped, and fallen astride the narrow plank. The agony had so drenched his body that for a while he gave up hope of life. Now he felt the same despair.

At breakfast, Kate found a place among some pilots. Rollo sat opposite Skull. 'I'm thinking of going on an op,' he said. 'First time, for me. Never flown in a plane. I expect you've been up dozens of times.'

'Once,' Skull said. 'Frightful experience.'

'Ah.' Rollo waited, but Skull had nothing to add. 'I thought I ought to find out what it's like,' he said. 'After all, it's the reason we're all here.'

'Not all of us,' Skull said. 'You're free to leave. You can go back to London any time you like.'

Briefly, their eyes met; then Rollo looked away. He was comparing the hell of going up in a Wellington with the purgatory of going back to share a flat with Miriam. Not much to choose between them.

He was still undecided when he tried to see the Wingco and was told he'd have to wait. Urgent meeting in progress. 'Is the squadron on ops tonight?' he asked, and got a polite smile in return. Bloody silly question.

Duff had called a meeting with his Flight Commanders, the Engineer Officer and the Intelligence Officers. Rafferty attended too.

Duff began speaking quietly, but his left shoulder was hunched in a way that everyone recognized. Somebody had pulled the Wingco's chain.

Air Ministry, he said, had ordered – and Command had confirmed – that, as soon as possible, cameras must be installed in all bomber aircraft to record the strike of bombs. Hitherto only a very few Wimpys had carried cameras: the ones with the best crews. That was acceptable. Now every kite had to bring back pictures. 'They don't trust us,' he said. 'They're happy to send us hundreds of miles over Germany through flak as thick as pigshit, but they don't trust us to report the results. They think they know better. They sit in their fat fucking offices, drinking sweet tea, and pass judgement on my crews, based on a lot of fuzzy *snaps*.' He gave himself the luxury of hammering that word.

'The boys won't like it,' Hazard said. 'They'll think they're being spied on.'

'Of course they're being spied on,' Pratten said. 'Why install a camera unless you don't trust the crew?'

Group Captain Rafferty belched softly and pressed his stomach. 'Let's get all our ducks in a row before we start shooting.' He slipped a peppermint into his mouth. 'I take it you have no objection to reconnaissance photographs of the target being taken next day.'

'No objection, sir, and no faith in the outcome,' Duff said. 'The pilot's too high and his camera's too small.'

'They got some very clear pictures of invasion barges in the Channel ports a year ago,' Skull said.

'Easy. A blind man with a box Brownie could've done it,' Duff sneered. 'But send the buggers to a hot spot like Hamburg or Cologne or Dortmund ...' He shook his head.

'You don't see much detail from fifteen thousand,' Hazard said, 'and fifteen thou is where you'd better be. Or more.'

'Show us your snaps, Bins,' Rafferty said. 'I know you're itching to.'

Bins passed around some ten-by-twelve prints. 'A bit dated, but they prove the point. Vertical photography doesn't always reveal much. A building could be gutted by incendiaries but if the roof hasn't collapsed, it looks intact.'

The Engineer Officer was examining the dates stamped on the backs of the prints. 'My God, these are ancient. They must have been taken with the Old F.24 camera, eight-inch lens. Nowadays the photo-recce kites use a new camera. It's got a twenty-inch lens.'

'So what?' Duff said. 'The bigger the camera, the greater the error.' This astonished the Engineer Officer. He looked at Rafferty, who offered him a peppermint. 'I'll tell you what really gets on my left tit,'

Duff said. 'Air bloody Ministry not only doesn't trust my crews, it doesn't even trust Bomber Command with its own pictures! The Photo Reconnaissance Unit is in Coastal Command!'

'When did a flying-boat last bomb Berlin?' Hazard asked. Their laughter encouraged him. He waggled his pipe.

'Forget Coastal. Forget their PRU.' Duff tore one of the prints into scraps. 'Only one thing matters here. Operational efficiency. Christ knows the bombing run is hairy enough, holding her straight and level until you can stuff the nose down and vanish. Well, now we can't. Now we've all got to *remain* straight and level, and drop the photo-flash and wait and wait until the bombs explode and the flash goes off. *Then* we can vanish.'

'I've seen my bombs explode,' Pratten said. 'Flames and smoke, flames and smoke. What more is a photograph going to show?'

'Tell your crews that a camera has one eye and no brain. They have two eyes and great experience. I'll take their word over a twenty-inch lens any day of the week.'

The meeting ended. Duff was still hunched and frowning when Rollo Blazer was shown in. 'I've got to film an op,' Rollo said. 'I've got to fly in a Wimpy on a raid.'

'Why not?' Duff said. 'Air Ministry is very keen on taking cameras on raids. There's an op tonight, Bremen. We often go to Bremen. Very juicy target. You'll see lots of flak.'

Rollo felt a great surge of relief. Now it was all out of his hands. He was part of the machinery of Bomber Command. It would send him to Bremen and, God willing, bring him back again, and nothing would be required of him except to shoot film and do as he was told. He felt fit and strong and surprisingly brave. 'Good show,' he said.

Duff was picking up his telephone when he remembered something. 'I take it you passed your medical,' he said.

'Medical? I don't need a medical. Fit as a flea, me.'

'No medical?' Duff replaced the phone. 'You're not going to tell me that Crown Films sent you here, to go on ops, without a medical examination?'

'It was all a bit rushed, I'm afraid. Does it matter?' Rollo saw Duff's lips compressed into a thin line and knew that it mattered a lot.

He met Kate in the ante-room and said he wouldn't be allowed to fly until he passed a comprehensive medical. 'It seems that altitude 'does bizarre things to the human body,' he said. 'They're afraid I might break wind and blow my boots off and kill someone.'

'You're very chirpy, all of a sudden.'

'Why not? It's only a matter of life and death.'

Rollo went to Sick Quarters at two o'clock, and he was still there at three.

The MO began with his medical history. Any trouble with the heart? The bowels? Throat? Lungs? Respiration in general? Any difficulty in breathing? Persistent coughing? Problems with the nasal passages?

'I had croup when I was a kid,' Rollo said. 'Highly dramatic, it was. The doctor fainted when he saw me.'

'Croup, you say.' The MO thought about it. 'Croup. Have you got your tonsils?'

'Damn. I left them in Tunbridge Wells. I was only six at the time. Kids are so careless. If I'd known you wanted them – '

'Be quiet.' The MO used a tongue-depressor and peered down Rollo's throat. 'My Christ, that's a mess. What did they use, garden shears?' He looked at Rollo's tongue. 'Texture and colour remind me of my bedroom carpet. Take your clothes off.'

'All of them?'

'Should I brace myself for some hideous abnormality?'

Rollo stripped. His chest disappointed the MO. 'Breathe in. Out. In, and take a deep breath and hold it. A *deep* breath, I said ... Good God, is that the best you can do?'

'It's kept me alive so far.'

'I said hold it.'

'I can't talk *and* hold my breath.'

'Then shut up.'

'I'll shut up when you stop asking questions.'

'Take a deep breath and hold it while I count to thirty.'

Rollo collapsed at fourteen. The MO took his pulse and blood pressure. 'You have the cardio-pulmonary system of a ten-year-old boy,' he said.

'Then give it back to the little sod,' Rollo wheezed.

'Goodness, how droll. Are you sure you've never had rheumatic fever? Fainting fits? Breathlessness? Palpitations?'

'The worst thing that happened to me was the Blitz. I survived that, didn't I?'

'Give me a sample of urine. After that we'll put you on the treadmill, and then you can blow up a few balloons. If you're still conscious, we'll get down to some serious tests.'

At the end of an hour Rollo got dressed. The MO sat at his desk, hunched over his notes. 'Give it to me straight, doc,' Rollo said. 'Will I ever play the violin again?' The MO didn't look up, didn't smile, didn't respond. The silence lengthened and Rollo wished he'd kept his mouth shut. He could hear his pulse throbbing. It didn't sound strong. Or steady.

'Well, you're not fit for aircrew duties,' the MO said.

'I'm not going to carry out aircrew duties.'

'I'm aware of that. What concerns me is how your somewhat battered system would respond to conditions of minus thirty degrees Fahrenheit at, say, twelve thousand feet, for several hours.' He reached a decision. 'I need a second opinion. I'm sending you to an RAF aircrew assessment centre. They have specialist equipment. Not far from here. Tomorrow morning, probably.'

BANG LIKE RABBITS

1

Six Wellingtons were going to Bremen. Rollo and Kate sat at the side of the briefing room. He worked out camera angles in his head; it took his mind off flying. She looked at the faces until she noticed an air gunner watching her and she felt guilty, he should be paying attention, this was serious stuff; and she turned away. Much of the serious stuff meant nothing to her. Bins talked about primary and secondary targets, using much jargon. Skull talked of spoofs and decoys. Pug Duff had something to say about what made Bremen so important: aircraft factories and a yard that built U-boats. Specialists gave complicated advice about navigation and signals. Finally, the group captain said Bremen was about the size of Liverpool, and he didn't need to remind everyone what the Luftwaffe had done to Liverpool. Now 409 had a chance to return the compliment, and flatten a few U-boats too. Good luck.

When Rafferty left, a civilian in a well-cut dark blue suit went with him. Good haircut. Broad moustache, neatly trimmed. 'He's a Yank,' Rollo murmured to Kate. 'Wears a wedding ring. Zip fly on his pants. Very clean fingernails. Got to be a Yank.' Rollo felt better, knowing that he wasn't flying. Tomorrow was a year away.

The next time they saw the blue suit was at dusk. By then, everyone knew he was Colonel Kemp, assistant air attaché at the American embassy. He was one of the group standing at the end of the flare-path, next to the Flying Control caravan, waving off the bombers.

A cold wind had arrived from the northernmost part of the North Sea, and Skull noticed that Kate was hunched and shivering. 'Come inside and have some coffee,' he said. 'You two should see the maestro at work.'

They sat in the caravan and watched Bellamy send each Wellington on its way. His head in the plastic dome slowly swivelled as the engines thundered and faded. 'We'll shoot him from the outside,' Rollo said softly. 'Medium close-up, lit from below. Wonderfully theatrical.'

'Sure,' Kate said. 'Why not stick a rose behind each ear?'

'I'm not changing anything. Just illuminating the truth.'

The last bomber took off. They thanked Bellamy and left.

Skull lingered until the two airmen had gone. 'Perhaps I'm chasing moonbeams,' he said. 'After all, this isn't my subject. I just wonder if it's altogether wise to control operational take-offs as you do, by radio.'

'Standard procedure,' Bellamy said. 'Simple and quick.'

'Yes ... The thing is, I was in Fighter Command last year, and during the Battle of Britain the German air force used to assemble large formations over the north of France. Fighter Command got early warning of this, because we had experts listening to the enemy radio traffic.'

'And you think the enemy is listening to ours.'

'It crossed my mind.'

'Having made that short journey, please let it travel on. Bomber Command would not have allocated a channel unless it was secure.'

They went out and Skull nearly lost his cap to the wind. 'Isn't that a rather dangerous assumption? Presumably Jerry didn't realize we were reading his radio traffic during the Battle.'

'Then Jerry's an ass. That's why he lost the Battle. Get in, I'm freezing.' Skull recognized that tone of voice. Discussion over. He got in and they drove away.

By now the first Wellington was crossing the coast at Aldeburgh, where the long blunt bulge of Orfordness, ringed by water, made an unmistakeable landmark. Normally they would fly deep into the North Sea, past the Friesian Islands, and turn south for a quick dash to Bremen, but the Germans had built such a thick belt of guns and searchlights along their coast that 409 was experimenting with a different approach to the target: an overland approach. They would take a direct route, fly east across Holland, and hope to sneak into Bremen behind the flak barrier. It might be the safest way. And if it wasn't the safest, it was the quickest.

Within an hour, T-Tommy was back.

The pilot was Beef Benton, famous on the squadron for being able to drink a yard of ale in thirteen seconds. 'Tommy just didn't want to go,' he told Bins. They were alone. 'First I lost power in the port engine. Couldn't maintain height. Ran into cu-nims and suddenly there's ice everywhere, including the carburettors. Went lower to lose the ice and got stuck at eight hundred feet. Tommy refused to climb. Ice damaged the elevators, perhaps. I don't know. That was when the navigator told me he'd forgotten half his charts. Then some ships began shelling us, ours or theirs, who knows? I decided to call it a day. Or a night. Whichever you prefer.'

Benton had a meal and went to bed and twenty minutes later was roused by the duty NCO. He dressed and reported to the Wingco. Duff said the Engineer Officer couldn't find anything wrong with T-Tommy. He'd fired up the engines and tested the elevators. 'Do you still want to bomb Bremen?' he asked. 'Tonight?'

Benton looked around, in search of an answer, and saw Colonel Kemp sitting in a corner. *What a shitty question*, he thought. *Say no and I'm chopped. Say yes and it'll be daylight before we clear the enemy coast.* 'I always wanted to bomb Bremen, sir,' he said.

'Take S-Sugar, the reserve kite. Your crew's waiting.' Benton saluted and went out. 'See what I mean?' Duff said to Kemp. 'Red-hot keen.'

2

'That's not Bremen,' Silk said.

'Yes it is, skip,' Woodman said. 'Right a bit.' He was the navigator of D-Dog, which made him the bomb-aimer too. He was lying in the nose, looking through the bomb-sight at a slice of Germany two miles below. 'I can see the river. More right.'

'Lots of German towns have rivers,' Silk said.

'Flak behind us, skip,' the rear gunner said.

'Best place for it.'

'Right,' Woodman said.

'Flak's closer.' The gunner's name was Chubb. The intercom

lightened and heightened men's voices. Chubb was nineteen and sounded fifteen. 'They've got our height, skip.'

'Left, left,' Woodman said. 'Steady.'

'Going down.' Silk put Dog into a shallow dive and levelled out at nine thousand.

'Now I can't see a damn thing,' Woodman said. Broken cloud had arrived to blot out much of the ground.

Everyone could see flak but it was scattered and distant, no bigger than the sparks of fireflies and lasting about as long. There were searchlights in the area but they had to find holes in the clouds.

'Not Bremen,' Silk said. 'Too quiet.'

'I definitely saw the river,' Woodman said.

'Couple of fires, over on the right,' Campbell said. He was the wireless op but now he was in the astrodome, looking for fighters.

'Decoys. Wrong colour,' Silk said. He saw a wide canyon in the clouds and turned and flew into it. 'See anything, Woody?'

'Smoke. Yes, smoke. Something's burning down there.'

A mile ahead, five searchlights were hunting. Flak flickered, red-white, vanished, returned elsewhere. Soon rags of smoke fled past the cockpit.

'I can see bomb-flashes, skip,' Chubb said. 'Somebody's bombing the place.'

'Can't help that, my son. It's still not Bremen.' Silk closed the bomb doors. The searchlights were bigger and busier. 'Going round again.' He banked Dog and opened the throttles.

Nobody spoke. Circling the city would take about eight minutes, and at the end they would make another approach, straight and level to give Woodman a chance, and give the German gunners another chance, too. Going round again meant making a series of timed runs on various bearings. Silk had a second pilot, an Australian called Mallaby, who helped him with the circuit. After the last turn, Mallaby said: 'If this isn't Bremen, why are we bombing it?'

'I'm not taking the bombs back. And Woody goes all huffy if he doesn't get his way.'

'It's Bremen, all right,' Woodman said. 'I can see the bridge. Smoke's worse.'

'Bomb doors open.' The Wellington vibrated as the slipstream snatched at the bomb doors.

'Left, left, steady. Left. Good. Steady at that.' The cloud was thinner now. 'Coming up … Coming up … Bombs gone.' The bomber reacted with a bounce. 'Steer three four eight. Goodbye, Bremen.'

'Three four eight,' Silk said. 'Next time we do this, the kite will have a camera, and the bomb run will go on and on …' He counted to fifteen. 'See anything, Chubby?'

'Yes! Spot on target! Lovely grub.'

Woodman climbed out of the nose and went to his navigator's table. He worked on his charts and gave Silk a new bearing. 'Eleven minutes to the coast,' he said.

'That's nice. They told me you died in your sleep, Badge.'

'Correct, skip.' Badger was the front gunner: the coldest, bleakest place in the aircraft, with nothing to look at but the onrushing night and maybe, one day, just the briefest glimpse of a night fighter. Hour after hour of searching until the eyes ached for rest, just a few seconds, ample time for a black Messerschmitt to sidle up and blow D-Dog apart. Badger's eyes never rested. Silk never nagged. If he spoke, it was only to check that the intercom worked.

A light mist coated Coney Garth and they were over the flare-path before the glim-lights were visible but Silk put Dog on the grass without trouble. When he climbed down the ladder from the hatch in the nose, the night air smelled sweetly of aviation fuel and crushed clover. Five hours and a bit.

The truck came to take them to interrogation. Badger banged his knee on the tailgate and swore. 'You want to take more care, Badge,' Silk said. 'It's bloody dangerous, this bombing lark.'

3

Bins wrote fast. It was one of the things that made him popular with the crews. When four Wellingtons landed within minutes of each other, they knew they could depend on him to whiz through his questions and let the chaps get to their bacon and eggs without delay. He didn't need Skull. Skull was with Pug Duff and Colonel Kemp, ready to answer any questions the American might have.

'Thank you,' Bins said to the crew of K-King.

'Damned good show,' the group captain said. Six pairs of flying boots thudded to the door. Bins saw Flight Lieutenant Pearson and crew, wrote 'B-Beer' on a fresh form and said. 'Did you reach Bremen all right?'

'Certainly did.'

'Find the target?'

'Yep.'

'Hit the target?'

'Bull's-eye,' Pearson's navigator said.

'Direct hit,' the rear gunner said. 'I saw the bombs go in. Spot-on.'

Bins ran through some routine questions about defences. 'Nothing special,' Pearson said. 'Usual stuff. The cloud helped us. No fighters.'

'Thank you,' Bins said. 'Damned good show,' Rafferty told them. Another crew lumbered forward: Pilot Officer Chester's Q-Queenie. 'Reach Bremen?' Bins asked.

'Just put "same again", Bins,' Chester said. 'Found it, bombed it, left it in flames, came home.' He smiled happily. 'Just another day on the night shift.'

'So you definitely hit the target? The U-boat yards?'

'Straddled 'em,' Chester's rear gunner said. 'Made one hell of a mess. They won't be building any subs for a long time.'

'Anything special about the defences? No? See any aircraft attacked, coned, in trouble? No?' The crew stood silent, eager for food. 'Jolly good. Thank you.'

'Damned good show.'

Bins took care of U-Uncle, sent them away, and saw Flying Officer Silk waiting. This time he refilled his fountain-pen, took off his glasses and polished them, wrote 'D-Dog' on a form and had a sudden longing for a whisky and water. He could taste it, almost smell it. 'Now,' he said, 'tell me your news.'

Silk was scratching the inside of his right ear with a match, and simultaneously trying to catch a small white moth with his left hand. He wasn't even looking at Bins.

'Cloud was a bit of a nuisance,' Woodman said. 'We went round twice and I found the target second time, next to the river. Couldn't miss it, really.'

'I saw them go in,' Chubb said. 'Spot on target. Lovely grub.'

'Wasn't smoke a problem? You were one of the last to bomb.'

'Must have got blown away,' Woodman said

'Strong winds,' Mallaby added.

'Anything else of interest?'

'Plenty of flak, and all in the wrong place,' Badger said. He was half-turned, ready to go.

'No night fighters?'

'That's right,' Silk said. 'And we didn't bomb Bremen, either.' The moth had got away. He switched the match to the other ear.

Bins leaned back, hands linked behind his head. The wireless op, Campbell, found a chair and sat down, heavily. 'Should I cross all this out?' Bins asked. An air-extractor stopped whirring and the atmosphere seemed flat. Dead.

'Please yourself,' Silk said. 'I've been to Bremen umpteen times. I know what it's like. It's got German navy gunners. They bang like rabbits. Very hot, very accurate, very fast. Not like tonight. Tonight's gunners couldn't piss down their right legs in a flat calm.' He spoke mildly.

'If not Bremen,' Bins said, 'then where?'

'Oldenburg, I expect.' Silk strolled over to a wall map of northern Germany. 'Thirty miles west of Bremen. On a river.'

'Bremen's four times the size of Oldenburg.' Bins wasn't arguing; just giving the facts. 'Oldenburg hasn't got any U-boat yards. No docks, to speak of. It's like Bath Spa.'

'Explains the feeble flak,' Silk said.

The Wingco cleared his throat. 'The target was burning when you got there?' he asked. Silk nodded. By now all his crew were sprawled on chairs, bored, resigned, impatient, hungry. 'So here's the question,' Duff said. 'We sent six Wellingtons, and four crews say they clobbered Bremen, so how come you're so sure you bombed Oldenburg?'

'I reckon the forecast winds were wrong. The Met man predicted thirty miles an hour from the east, but the actual winds at ten thou were sixty or seventy. Ten-tenths cloud over the Dutch coast, so nobody got a pinpoint when we crossed. We never reached Bremen. Blame the wind.'

'I saw docks,' Woodman said, 'and I bombed docks.' The rear gunner nodded vigorously.

Rafferty decided this had lasted long enough. 'Well,' he said, 'if Oldenburg ever had any docks, they've gone for a Burton now.' It was a joke.

'Doubt it,' Silk said. 'With those winds, at that height, we probably hit the suburbs.' He had stopped scratching his ear. He struck the match and everyone watched it burn. He licked his fingertips and there was a soft sizzle when he held the match by its blackened head and let the flames eat up the stem.

'Thank you,' Bins said. The crew were at the door when Rafferty called, 'Damned good show.'

4

It was three in the morning. Rafferty and Duff took Colonel Kemp to the Mess for a nightcap or two. 409 had a tradition that the bar never closed until the op was finished and all crews were accounted for, one way or the other.

'Cheers,' Rafferty said. They clinked glasses. 'Death to all tyrants, hands across the sea, et cetera.'

'Another damn good raid,' Duff said.

'I have a question, if I may,' Kemp said. Rafferty gestured, urging him on. 'About Wellington S-Sugar. The reserve plane.' Not all American voices twang like guitars. Kemp's had the husky warmth of a cello. 'How often does that sort of thing happen?'

'Boomerangs,' Duff said. 'They fly off, and all too soon they fly back. Known as "early returns" on some squadrons. Here, they're boomerangs and the chaps know I won't tolerate them.'

'Infectious,' Rafferty said. 'One crew turns back, next time it's two, then four.'

'I jump on it with both feet,' Duff said.

'I've visited squadrons where they talk about "hangar queens",' Kemp said. 'Aircraft that are always unreliable. Cure one fault, here comes another.'

'Our servicing is second to none,' Duff said. 'No kite is perfect, of course. A captain can always find a reason to turn back if he looks hard enough. 409 teaches him to find several reasons to press on.'

'Pug's a press-on type,' Rafferty said

'Success breeds success,' Duff said. 'I don't know what boomerangs breed.'

209

'Twitch,' Rafferty said.

'Something else puzzles me,' Kemp said. 'That pilot who insisted he bombed Oldenburg. You didn't ask him *why*. I mean, if he knew Bremen was thirty miles away ...'

'Ah, well.' Rafferty chuckled. 'That's Silk.'

'He's the joker in the pack,' Duff said. 'Most experienced pilot on the squadron, flew Hampdens before we got Wimpys, now he's halfway through his second tour of ops, scruffy as hell, should be a squadron leader but he doesn't give a damn for anything or anyone. I don't argue with Silk. Waste of breath.'

'But if he doesn't care,' Kemp said, 'why does he carry on flying?'

'No option,' Rafferty explained. 'He volunteered to fly. He finished his first tour. Now he's got to finish his second.'

'Silk's a pain in the arse,' Duff said, 'but the boys like him. He's 409's mascot. As long as he hits the target, I don't care if he talks balls.'

Ten minutes later, Silk walked in and Kemp went over and introduced himself. He had never seen such old eyes in such a young face.

Silk's conversational style managed to sound brisk and pessimistic at the same time. 'You don't look like an American,' he said. 'Have you met Hedy Lemarr? Dorothy Lamour? Veronica Lake? Lana Turner? The one in the swimsuit?'

'Esther Williams. No. May I buy you a drink?'

'Nobody's met Hedy Lemarr. Makes a chap wonder why we went to war. You can't buy drinks, you're not a member. Two pints of embalming fluid,' he told a Mess waiter. 'And a plate of stale whelks. I can't eat fresh whelks,' he told Kemp. 'They're too volatile. I expect you're the same.'

'I'm afraid I've never eaten a whelk.'

'Neither have I. Cancel the whelks,' he told a different waiter.

Kemp waited. Silk seemed to have reached an end. 'I was at the debriefing,' Kemp said. 'You had a different slant on tonight's raid, compared with the others.'

'Oh well ... Six kites. Wasn't much of a raid, was it? Does it make any difference whether we miss Bremen, or Oldenburg? Half the bombs are duds, anyway.'

Two beers arrived. 'Whelks won't be stale till tomorrow, Mr Silk,' the waiter said woodenly, and went away.

'Help me out here,' Kemp said. 'Bremen's very heavily defended, and it's not far from Oldenburg. Couldn't you see its searchlights? The Germans knew you were in the area.'

'What searchlights? Jerry doesn't show us where he is unless we bother him. Why should he? Makes more sense for him to hide in his lovely blackout and let us stooge overhead and go on our way. Lost.'

Kemp rubbed his jaw. 'Now I know you're joking.'

'Colonel, if I took this job seriously I'd be as barmy as Pug Duff. Let me give you a potted history of the bombing war. To begin with we flew low, five or six thousand feet. At night, in decent weather, full moon, we could map-read our way across Germany. Not much flak. But Jerry machine guns became a nuisance. So we flew higher. Can't map-read so well now. Then, heavy tracer. Five hundred rounds per gun per minute, reaching eight thousand and going off bang. So, we flew higher still. Now, we can't pick out anything except big landmarks. Lakes, rivers, erupting volcanoes. Jerry chucks in light flak. His 3.7-calibre stuff can fire a shell every three seconds. Up we go again, ten thousand, twelve, more, because Jerry's also got an 88-millimetre weapon, very nasty, and now we're so high the navigator can't find a pinpoint on the ground, can't check the predicted winds, can't take a star-shot through cloud, and all his dead-reckoning calculations are up the spout because the stupid pilot keeps changing course when the flak gets so close he can smell it. So where are we?'

They drank their beer.

'One bloke got so lost he bombed Yorkshire,' Silk said.

'But many German cities *have* been bombed,' Kemp said. 'The Germans themselves admit that. You even bombed Berlin.'

'They say Yorkshire looks a lot better for it.'

'Well ...' Kemp stood up. 'I appreciate your help, flight lieutenant.'

'Don't believe anything Pug Duff tells you. He lies like a rug.'

Kemp went back to Rafferty and the Wingco. 'I bet he told you nothing works,' Duff said. 'Ops are a nonsense. Am I right?'

'Pretty close.'

'Silk enjoys being bloody-minded. After flying, it's what he does best.'

Kemp got four hours' sleep. At eight-thirty, as he was going into the Mess for breakfast, he met Skull coming out. 'My stars!' he said. 'You fellows work long hours.'

211

'Actually I'm rather late. The others are at their desks by now. The squadron may be on ops again tonight, and our planning starts early.'

'Seems to pay off. Washington is very impressed with the way you fellows keep pounding the Nazis. Bomber Command is a bright light in a gloomy world.'

'It's a big battle. There's plenty of room for two.'

Kemp nodded. They both knew he couldn't discuss America's neutrality. 'Explain something to me, would you? Last night, before the party broke up, didn't somebody say the reserve plane, S-Sugar, was a total loss?'

'Yes. Flak damage over the German coast. She came down in a field in Essex and caught fire. The crew got out. Some casualties, I believe.'

'I see.' Kemp didn't sound convinced. 'The reason I ask is I caught the BBC news just now. They say a force of Wellingtons hit the U-boat docks at Bremen and, quote, none of our aircraft was lost, unquote.'

'That's right,' Skull said.

'Yet one is wrecked. In Essex.'

'But not lost. An aircraft is lost when nobody knows where it is. We know precisely where S-Sugar is.'

'I must remember that.' They shook hands. 'Good luck.'

'I recommend the kippers,' Skull said.

JINX POPSY

1

By ten o'clock, ops were on: a rubber factory in Hanover. The weather in Suffolk was good, but by midday ops were scrubbed. The high winds that 409 had met on the way to Bremen were circling around a deep low-pressure system that had settled on central Europe. The Met men predicted foul weather in Germany, becoming abominable later. 409 was stood down for two days. Urgent servicing could be done. Cameras could be installed. Aircrew could get pissed.

None of this made any difference to Rollo. He had been driven, in Rafferty's car, to the aircrew assessment centre, and now his head was being X-rayed from five different angles. An ear, nose and throat specialist had decided that his sinuses and associated cavities deserved closer scrutiny.

'I'm just a passenger,' Rollo told the X-ray technician. 'I'm not going to fly the bloody plane. What's all the fuss about?'

'It's about your cranial orifices. You know how your ears pop when you go up a big hill? Some people can't fly because their head won't tolerate changes in pressure. The pain sends them berserk. Now, keep absolutely still, please.'

Rollo was placed in a waiting room while they developed the plates. A medical orderly came in and asked for a sample of his urine. 'If that's got anything to do with sinuses, my plumbing is in big trouble,' Rollo said. The orderly nodded soberly and went away.

Time passed. Rollo practised holding his breath, and got up to twenty seconds. A male nurse opened the door and called his name. Rollo followed him down a series of unfamiliar corridors and finally arrived at a dental surgery.

The dentist was as big as Rafferty but far friendlier. 'Just as well we took these snaps, Mr Blazer,' he said. He held up the X-rays. 'I've never seen such sinuses. Perfect in every respect! Nothing to worry about there. But *here* ...' He pointed to the end of the jawbone. 'Just look at that wisdom tooth! I mean to say, it's in a bad way, isn't it?'

'Oh, hell and damnation,' Rollo said.

'Better have it out, don't you think? We certainly can't pass you as fit to fly with that tooth. Have it out, old chap. What you haven't got, can't harm you. That's the RAF's dental policy.'

Rollo took the X-ray from him. The wisdom tooth had roots like an oak tree. He desperately wanted to discuss alternative solutions, but his mouth had stopped working. He was trapped.

2

The obvious thing for Silk to do was get a haircut. His hair was so thick that it bulged out around the sides of his cap. Hazard kept telling him it needed cutting. But the barber on the base was a butcher, so that meant driving to Bury St Edmunds, where there was a man who understood hair. Too bad he didn't understand people. His hobby was collecting postage stamps. No: his real hobby was talking about them, endlessly, tediously. Silk forgot about a haircut.

He had a golf club, good condition, one previous owner, collided with a Hampden in eight-tenths cloud over Krefeld. If he could find a golf ball he could whack it around the aerodrome. He was scrabbling in the back of a drawer when he pulled out a photograph, several photographs, some taken outside a cathedral, others at a wedding reception, and one taken during a briefing by Pixie Hunt at RAF Kindrick. Pixie of the piercing eyes. Well, Pixie was gone. They were all gone. Silk burned the snaps in an ashtray. 'I don't wish to discuss it,' he said aloud, to nobody.

He drove out of camp in the Frazer-Nash. 'Nobody left it to me,' he said. 'I won it in a raffle. Kindly leave the room.'

He stopped at the first village he came to. It had a pub, the King William, and he wanted a pint of beer, but if he went inside they would all look at him, at his wings, at his face, and nobody would say anything until some stumpy-toothed, bald-headed farm labourer came up to the bar for a refill and said, 'Day off today, then?' And Silk would agree, he wasn't actually flying at that particular moment, and the man would say, 'I was at the Somme, you know. Not like this, it wasn't.' You couldn't go into a pub without meeting a boring old fart who told you how lucky you were, not dying of trenchfoot at the Somme.

So Silk went to the village shop instead. Bought a small loaf, two apples and a bottle of milk. Sat on a bench at the edge of the village green. It was a big green, and some boys were playing cricket. *How frightfully English*, he thought. *Pub, church, cricket, and here comes a haywain with a couple of immensely patriotic cart-horses*. The batsman took an almighty swing and hit the ball higher than the elms. It fell about ten feet short of Silk and bounced over his head. A boy came running.

'This place is worse than Bremen,' Silk said.

The boy fetched the ball and trotted back. 'What's Bremen like?' he asked.

'Not cricket.'

The boy looked at him, decided not to risk another question, and returned to the game. The sun shone, the church clock sounded the hour, and another bloody haywain came around the corner. Silk felt totally out of place. He tossed the food into the car and drove away.

After a mile or so he reached a wood. Nothing majestic; just a tangled mass of silver birch, ash, sycamore, a few beech, the occasional oak. He liked trees. He enjoyed watching the top branches wave in the wind and hearing the whispered conversation of the leaves. That was a thoroughly sentimental idea and one which he would never have mentioned to his crew. They were in Newmarket, flashing their half-wings at floozies in pubs. He'd seen enough uniforms for a while. Enough floozies, too. A gap in the wood looked as if it might be a track, so he turned into it. The Frazer-Nash mowed down grass and thistles, and after fifty yards he stopped. This was as good a place as any to eat his lunch.

Food made him drowsy. He curled up in the back seat of the car with his hat over his eyes and fell asleep.

The usual dream came along. He half-rolled the Wimpy, a pointless manoeuvre and strictly forbidden by the manufacturers. Now the kite was upside-down and everything was falling off the instrument panel: first the boost gauges, then the flap control lever and the altimeter and the air speed indicator and more; they all dropped to the roof. Without them, he couldn't land. But he didn't care. He'd had this dream many times before, he knew that landing was impossible when inverted, so there was no point in worrying. One small problem. How to drop the bombs? Damn things were a nuisance, get rid of them. He pulled the jettison control lever and it came away in his hand. Fat lot of use that was. He dropped it and it fell past his face. Damn. They'd make him pay for it. He'd signed for this kite, and what you lost, you paid for. Sure enough, here was the Engineer Officer, poking him, what a mannerless bastard. Silk took a long time to wake up, and it wasn't the Engineer Officer. It was Zoë. Well, that couldn't be right. He let his eyelids close. Back to sleep. 'Come on, Silko,' she said. 'Hit the deck.'

Gradually he became completely awake. She was kneeling on the front seat, looking like an angel who had missed too many hairdressing appointments. A rather weather-beaten angel. In a grubby green sweater with a hole in the elbow. 'That's the navy,' he said. 'We never hit the deck. Our batman wakes us with a nice cup of tea.' He sat up and scratched his ribs. 'It is you, isn't it?'

'What an asinine question, even by your standards ... Oh, look. Milk.' She drank from the bottle.

'You never used to touch the stuff.'

'Things have changed. You've changed. You've got more lines than Clapham Junction.' She traced the map of his face with her fingertip. His face enjoyed it.

'This is a thumping great coincidence, isn't it?' he said.

'No. Quite the opposite. Let's go for a walk.'

They took a path into the wood, and Zoë explained. She said that she had been looking for Silk. First she found out that 409 was at Coney Garth; then she hung about the area, hoping to catch sight of him. She had a push-bike, and today she'd seen the Frazer-Nash and hoped it was him driving.

'Of course it was me,' he said. 'Nobody else drives it.'

'Somebody else might. Remember how you got it.'

'Goodness. You *have* changed.'

She had followed the car on her bike, lost it, seen it leaving the village, lost it again, and searched the lanes without much hope – he was probably miles and miles away – until she noticed the wheel marks in the grassy track.

'Bluebell, the Girl Detective,' he said.

'Don't laugh. It's taken me ten days.'

'Zoë, my sweet. What's wrong with the telephone? Call the Officers' Mess. Send me a postcard. Ask at the Main Gate, and I'll come and meet you.'

'There's something else. I'm on the run from the police.'

That had to be a joke. 'Dear Zoë,' he said. 'I'm finding it very difficult to concentrate right now because, in the words of the popular song, as time goes by, woman needs man and man must have his mate, that no-one can deny. Certainly not me. But it's never as simple as that, is it, and in a nutshell, I haven't got a French letter on me.'

'Poor Silko,' she said. 'Why are men so *slow*? I was ready the minute I saw you in the car. And the only protection I need is your tunic to lie on. Forest floors can be dreadfully lumpy.'

Already they were undressing. 'Later, you must tell me about the police,' he said. 'Much later. Next month will do.'

Later, of course, was too soon; as it always is. The keener the desire, the quicker the anticlimax. One quick glimpse of paradise from the mountaintop, Silk thought as they walked back to the car, and then God tips you over the edge. Still, better than no glimpse at all.

He put her bike in the back of the car, reversed to the road, and drove until they saw a tea garden. A small girl brought a large teapot and a plate of scones with a jar of plum jam.

'It's been nearly a year,' Zoë said. 'Feels like ten.'

'He might be a prisoner-of-war. Cock-ups do occur. It's not impossible.'

'He's dead, Silko. I knew as soon as I opened the door and saw the adjutant. Stone dead.'

'Where did you go?'

'London. Albany. You didn't write.'

'Couldn't think what to say. You weren't interested in the squadron, and anyway life was just ops, and more ops. You didn't write, either.'

'I had too much to say. Life became very messy, Silko, and it was all my fault. First, I was pregnant. No surprise. God knows Tony tried hard enough.'

'I did my little best, too.'

'Forget that.'

'What! Never.'

'The baby was born in March. Anthony Charles Hubert. Greedy little savage. Chewed on my breasts until they were raw. I'd got engaged to Hubert at Christmas, he was a fighter pilot ...'

'Big mistake. They're cowboys.'

'Well, he's a dead cowboy. Shot down over France. Then something strange happened to me, I began to hate the baby, so I gave it to Mummy.'

'Makes sense. She's the one who wanted it.'

'And Mummy's living in Dublin, so there aren't any problems about food rationing. Or bombing.'

'No? Jerry bombed Ireland twice. By mistake, of course. I'm told it doesn't hurt so much when you get accidentally killed.'

'Hey.' She rapped his knuckles with a knife-handle and he spilled his tea. 'If you know my story so well, *you* tell it.'

'Zoë, you've ruined these trousers.'

'I've cleaned them. What a shambles you are, Silko ... Anyway, after the baby went away I met a wonderful Norwegian pilot called Rolf and we both wanted to marry and a week later – gone. Failed to return, nobody knew what happened. That was when I decided I must be a jinx popsy, and I gave up men. Then I met someone at a party who asked me to work for a refugee charity, raising money. He was a Czech count and they had nice offices in Belgrave Square. The chairman was a Polish baron and I worked for the director. He was a Hungarian prince. They made me treasurer because I'm English and according to law ... I can't remember the details and it didn't seem to matter because it was a charity and nobody was working for pay, we were raising lots of money for a really good cause, I just signed documents when I was asked to, a pure formality they said, and about a fortnight ago I turned up and the office was empty and all the money had gone. It seems that I'd authorized it. The police were banging on the front door, so I did a bunk through the back window. There's a warrant for my arrest.'

Silk made a guess, and said, 'How much is missing?'

'A quarter of a million pounds.'

He winced. His guess had been twenty thousand. 'When you say you're on the run...'

'I've got Rolf's revolver. He was supposed to take it whenever he flew, but he gave it to me, in case I got attacked in the blackout. I drove to Suffolk and ran out of petrol and when a policeman asked to see my identity card I told him to stick 'em up.'

'You actually said, to a British bobby, "Stick 'em up".'

'Yes.'

'Bizarre. Was it loaded?'

'Probably not. How does one find out?'

'I take it he stuck them up.'

'Yes. So I stole his bike. That's it in your car. He wasn't a real policeman, just a Special Constable. They don't count, do they? He was quite small, too. I managed to lower the saddle. That was lucky, wasn't it?'

'And where are you living?'

'I'll show you.'

They drove back, past the aerodrome, up narrow lanes, into a dirt track that led eventually to a small, broken-down bungalow over-looking a lake. Marshy scrubland was all around. No house was in sight. 'I think people used to come here to shoot duck,' Zoë said, 'but the bombers scared the ducks away.'

They went inside. There was a hole in the roof and a strong smell of mildew. The only furniture was a sagging sofa, covered with blankets. He saw a revolver hanging from a nail, took it down, checked it. Empty. A cardboard box had some tins in it. 'Pilchards,' Zoë said. 'I'm getting rather sick of pilchards.'

'Can't your mother do something? She's got millions. Or that peculiar Dutchman, Flemming Thingummy.'

'Vansittart. I think he's gone to Holland to be a spy.' She picked at what little was left of the wallpaper. 'Anyway, what could he do? I transferred the money, I'm guilty in law, even if someone pays it all back. I'm bound to be arrested.' The last bit of wallpaper fell. 'You're awfully clever, Silko. Can't you think of something?'

'I've got one idea. But we've already done that.'

'Ages ago.'

'True, true.'

'Let's say it was an air-test. To make sure none of the screws were loose.'

'What a clever, beautiful girl you are.'

The sofa creaked, but none of its screws came loose. A Wimpy on its final approach made the windows vibrate. Silk and Zoë had heard it all before, and they concentrated on enjoying themselves, since the rest of the world wasn't being much fun.

3

Rollo lay on a bed. The dentist sat on a tall stool, watching him. The male nurse stood alongside.

'The body is a wonderful machine,' the dentist said. 'Take blood, for instance. First it cleanses the wound, then it coagulates and seals up the hole in the body, and all the while it keeps searching for hostile bacteria which may have taken the opportunity to sneak in, and if it finds any, it bumps them off. Meanwhile, of course, the blood is also engaged in its epic journey around the body which keeps us alive. Man has invented nothing so clever as blood.'

Rollo leaned sideways and spat a heavy gobbet of the stuff into a basin. The nurse came forward and wiped his mouth with a towel and went back to his place.

'I almost forgot to mention another quality of blood,' the dentist said 'It's non-toxic. You can swallow it quite safely.'

Rollo was very tired. The anaesthetic had almost worn off but he was dozy. There was a hole in his jaw the size of a bucket, and he kept having to empty it.

'And here's another thing,' the dentist said. 'Is it pure chance that blood is red? The perfect symbol for danger, isn't it? The body has a good reason for everything, and that includes colour. Imagine yellow blood. Or green! Well, duty calls. Give him another aspirin in thirty minutes,' he told the nurse, and left.

There was nothing to look at but the ceiling. Nothing to hear but the thud of his pulse. One side on his face felt as if it had been clubbed. Rollo grew accustomed to the pain. Without realising it, he drifted into sleep, and woke up choking on blood. After that he knew there was no point in trying to stay awake. If his body disagreed, it would wake him up, choking and spitting. That was another thing blood was good for: waking you up. The dentist had missed that one. Rollo dozed off again.

The room was in dusk when he opened his eyes, not because he was choking, but because the nurse was lifting him by the shoulders, making him sit up. Automatically, Rollo spat into the basin.

'Jolly good,' the dentist said. 'Look: we're going to put a couple of stitches into that cavity. Knit the edges together. Try to stop the bleeding.'

Rollo got off the bed. He raised a finger. Big speech coming. 'What's the rush?' he said. 'I've still got a pint left.' They were kind enough to smile, although they had heard it before. They had heard everything before.

4

The signal came from Command and said: *Report King's College Cambridge 1800 hours in civilian clothes. Authority: R.G.T. Champion, Group Captain.*

Skull got the Lagonda filled up with RAF petrol and wore the only decent suit he had, an Irish thornproof tweed of such a dark green that it looked almost black. Two years in uniform made him feel naked without a hat, so he borrowed a bowler from the adjutant. His sudden release from Coney Garth turned the day into a holiday. He sped west and was in Cambridge by three o'clock. He strolled along the Backs and enjoyed the calm beauty of the university during the Long Vacation. Cambridge was at its best without undergraduates, Skull thought. A pity it couldn't be a permanent arrangement.

At six he walked into King's, and the Porter's Lodge installed him in the room of an undergraduate called Cooksley, reading medicine. Skull had a bath and he was browsing through Cooksley's books when Champion knocked and came in. 'We're dining at High Table,' he announced.

'I bet you didn't know that bone marrow comes in two colours, red and yellow,' Skull said.

'Here's a gown for you.'

'Not striped, you understand. Either red or yellow. The red marrow makes blood cells. That's reassuring, isn't it?'

'We'll be late.'

Skull followed him. 'How the blood cells escape from the marrow and enter the arteries was not revealed. Possibly in the next chapter.' He noticed that Champion's suit, of charcoal-grey flannel, had been generously tailored to enhance the shoulders. 'You look bigger,' he said. 'But of course you're a group captain now.'

Champion said, 'We're here to meet a chap called Butt. David Bensusan-Butt. You've never heard of him. He's only twenty-seven but he's private secretary to Professor Lindemann and Lindemann is Churchill's personal adviser on weapons and science and the like. This means that Bensusan-Butt is in the Prime Minister's office. He's a civil servant but they're not all stupid and Bensusan-Butt's got a brain like Battersea Power Station. He's a King's man. That's why I got you both here, away from London. He'll be more relaxed here.'

'Relaxed about what?'

'Good question. Bomber Command has plans. It needs to be twice as big, maybe four times as big. However, we've got enemies in the War Cabinet. My spies tell me that Lindemann has ordered Bensusan-Butt to do a deep analysis of Bomber Command and award marks out of ten.'

Skull was introduced to the man and they talked briefly, not about the war. Skull got an impression of warmth and wit, of an intense energy, and of someone who knew exactly how each sentence would end before he began it. Then they went into Hall and were seated too far apart for conversation. Skull thought: *Champion wants to run the show. This should be interesting.*

When dinner ended, Champion did not linger. He led his guests to his rooms, which were much more spacious than Cooksley's. Champion's influence had evicted a professor of clinical biochemistry. Such raw power both impressed and depressed Skull.

'No piano, I'm afraid,' Champion said, and murmured to Skull, 'Mr Bensusan-Butt is an excellent pianist.'

'Purely for pleasure,' his guest said. 'Some play squash, I play Haydn. Incidentally, can we drop the Bensusan? Butt is enough. David is even better.'

'Splendid,' Champion said. 'I'm Ralph, and Skelton is ... well, Skelton is Skull. Very apt. He's my tame brain in the field of battle.'

Skull had been adjusting the blackout curtains. Now his head turned slowly. 'What did you call me?' he said.

Champion should have apologized, but he had only recently been made up to group captain and he could not apologize to a flight lieutenant. Instead, he bustled about, offering drinks: brandy, port, whisky, Madeira?

'I wouldn't mind some coffee,' Butt said.

'Of course. Skull, be a good fellow and make some coffee.'

'No.' It was said calmly but firmly.

Champion frowned. 'Are you allergic to coffee?'

'No.'

Champion looked at Butt with mock-despair. 'Mutiny. Is it like this in Downing Street?'

Butt smiled. 'We are all mutineers in Downing Street. The Prime Minister gets restless when he is surrounded by harmony. War is not a harmonious business.'

'Well, Bomber Command has never shirked a chance to stir up trouble.' Champion went into the kitchen and filled a kettle and put it on the stove and came back. 'People forget that Bomber Command has been operating against the enemy since the very first day of the war. Whenever the weather allowed we've hammered him in his own backyard. No other Service can claim that.' He went out. Rattling and clinking were heard. He came back with a loaded tray. 'No coffee. Is tea all right? As I was saying, the Command hasn't had full credit for its efforts throughout almost two years. Shipping strikes, Nickels, Gardening, and then the Battle of Britain which was really *two* battles. The fighter boys did their stuff but who sank all those invasion barges? Every Channel port from Antwerp to Dieppe – Ostend, Dunkirk, Calais, Boulogne – all through last summer, night after night, walloped by Bomber Command! And when Hitler dropped the first bombs on London, it wasn't Spitfires that flew to Berlin the next night and gave the Germans a fright. Which is what Bomber Command has been doing ever since. Night after night. Is there a Focke-Wulf aircraft factory in Bremen? Fine. We'll send a hundred bombers and blast it. That's just what we did last January. Target destroyed. What's next? And so we've continued. We know Nazi Germany is suffering. You can't drop a four-thousand-pound blockbuster on Bremen without giving Hitler a headache.'

Butt poured the tea. 'I have a feeling that was a preamble,' he said.

'Throat-clearing,' Skull said. 'Delete paragraph one.'

'If you double the size of Bomber Command, you quadruple its destructive power,' Champion said. 'How? By overwhelming the German defences. *Quadruple* the size of Bomber Command and you can utterly devastate the German war machine ...' He raised a hand to dramatize the point. '... without the need for a land invasion of Europe.'

Butt sipped his tea.

'That's the view from the top,' Champion said. 'But it's the squadrons that do the real work, isn't it? 409 Squadron at Coney Garth is one of the best. What is their formula for consistent success? Our eminent sleuth has the answer.'

Champion meant to flatter. Skull felt he was being patronized. This made no difference to Skull's answer but it sharpened his tone of voice. 'There is no formula,' he said, 'because there is no consistent success.'

'That's the trouble with academics,' Champion said. 'They will quibble about words. If you don't like "consistent", how about "conspicuous"?'

'The term I most dislike is "interrogation",' Skull said.

'It's what we do to pilots after an op,' Champion explained to Butt.

'It's what we *don't* do to them,' Skull said. 'Interrogation suggests a degree of mental toughness. A rigorous examination of performance. That's not what happens. A crew's report is accepted at face value, and rarely challenged. Interrogation is a poor method of measuring success.'

Champion had an instant answer. 'Then it's just as well we don't depend too heavily upon it. One infallible indicator of Bomber Command's effectiveness is the enemy's response, and I don't think that even you, Skull, would dispute the evidence of flak damage which our bombers bring back.'

'Yes, it's evidence,' Skull said. 'But of what?'

'That the Hun has been stung! We've laid waste so many of his cities that flak, searchlights, night fighters are top priority over there!'

'Oh, I doubt that. The Russian front is Hitler's top priority.'

'And Russia desperately wants us to keep bombing, to take the pressure off her. When the other man gets mad, you know your punches are hurting, and I've seen the German newspapers. They get very upset at Bomber Command.'

'Proves nothing,' Skull said. 'Our newspapers made gloomy reading during the Blitz, but they didn't make the German bombers any more effective.'

'Thank God for that!' Champion was brisk; he seemed to be enjoying the exchange. 'You were in London in the Blitz?' he asked Butt, who nodded. 'So was I. Skull was in Scotland ... Ask any Londoner, Skull. He'll tell you whether the Blitz was effective or not. Bombing hurts, old chap. It's already hurt Berlin. Given time we'll flatten it.'

'Hitler didn't flatten London.'

'He made a mess of it.'

'Of a small part of it. Measured on the map, only one yard in ten of Greater London is covered by a building. Inevitably, most bombs fell in the ninety per cent that is open space.'

'Such as railways? All the London termini got hit. Does your open space include churchyards? That would explain all the Wren churches that we lost. Did the Germans waste those bombs?'

Skull took his glasses off and polished them with his tie. 'It begs the question,' he said, and squinted hard at Butt, 'that this war will be won by bombing churches.' He put his glasses on, and made a little act of locating Champion. 'Ah. There you are.'

'Well, it certainly won't be won with debating tricks,' Champion said. 'There's nothing tricky about high explosive. If the Luftwaffe can destroy Coventry, we can destroy, say, Hamburg.'

'Coventry wasn't destroyed. Just because Goebbels says so, doesn't make it true. I've heard too many of our pilots say they annihilated the target, and next week they got sent back to annihilate it again.'

'Repairs,' Champion said. 'Salvage work'.

'You can't repair annihilation. People are too casual with words. Coventry wasn't destroyed. Its *centre* was severely damaged. Its gas and electricity and water supplies were cut. Some factories were hit. But by far the greater part of Coventry was still standing next day, and all the factories were back in action within weeks, some within days.'

'They were indeed,' Butt said. 'However, we don't want the Germans to know that. How did you find out?'

'Intelligence. A Waaf in my section comes from Coventry.'

'Ah. And what conclusion do you draw from all this?'

Skull puffed out his cheeks. 'Not a conclusion, but a suggestion. If the Luftwaffe couldn't destroy Coventry, perhaps we shouldn't be too cocksure about destroying Hamburg.'

'Too late,' Champion said cheerfully. 'We've already made a start. And we've also knocked down large chunks of Kiel, Bremen and Wilhelmshaven. How can I be so cocksure of this? Because neutral businessmen see it and tell us. Foreign journalists make reports. Travellers *travel*, Skull. In and out of Europe.'

'Travellers. I see.' Skull felt that he had been sucked into playing verbal ping-pong for the amusement of an audience of one, and he was growing tired of it. 'I trained to be a historian, and historians are suspicious of travellers' tales. Men like to excite their listeners. The traveller visits, say, Dusseldorf and sees one bombed street. When he returns to Sweden he tells what he saw and soon there is a report headed "Devastation hits Dusseldorf", from which it is but a short skip and a jump to believe that Dusseldorf is devastated.'

'Jolly good!' Champion applauded, briefly. 'The strategic bombing campaign as seen through the eyes of a Swedish news editor. That's more than I had hoped for.' To Butt he said, 'He really is awfully clever, isn't he?' To Skull he said, 'Thank you, flight lieutenant. Most enjoyable. I don't think we need keep you up any longer.' Skull shook hands with Butt. At the door, Champion said, 'You must lunch with me at my club, old chap.'

'If I must,' Skull said.

Champion came back and poured himself a whisky. 'I like old Skull,' he said. 'He's got a mind like a rugger ball: you never know which way it will bounce. Of course, his weakness is he sees everything at squadron level. He can't take the broad view. I brought him along to act as a sort of devil's advocate. Not bad, was he?'

'Not bad at all,' Butt said.

'Now to serious business. Bomber Command's the only weapon we have which can seriously damage Germany. That's hard fact. And you don't need the brains of an archbishop to see that the more bombers we build, the sooner we win. Or have I overlooked something?'

'Tell me more,' Butt said.

5

Next morning, Silk bought some food at the village shop: bread, salad stuff, two Chelsea buns, four pears, lemonade. Everything else was on ration. He drove to the broken bungalow and Zoë wasn't there. He sat by the edge of the lake and watched dragonflies perform manoeuvres that were strictly banned by the manufacturers. After a while she appeared, very wet. 'I found a bubbling brook,' she said. 'Had an all-over wash. How the rabbits stared. Golly, such red tomatoes.' She ate one. She sat beside him.

'What's that funny smell?' he asked. 'It smells like carbolic soap.'

'That's because it is. All the best outlaws use carbolic, darling.'

'It smells awfully coarse. Us bomber pilots are terribly sensitive, you know. Pug Duff cries at dog shows.'

'Don't believe you.' She stretched out so that her head was resting on his lap. 'Tony wasn't sensitive. Tony was an animal. Sometimes I had to bite him on the neck to make him stop.'

'Are we talking about the same chap?' No answer. Her eyes were closed. 'How often did you bite his neck?'

'Once.'

'What a shocking liar you are. I was going to ask you to marry me but ...'

'Jinx popsy, remember?'

'Balls. I'm on my second tour. I'm jinx-proof.'

'I won't marry you, Silko.'

'Too late. I withdrew the offer ages ago.'

'You don't really love me. You just covet my body.'

'You coveted mine first.'

'I did, didn't I?' She smiled at the memory. 'Men are so slow.'

Silk thought about that. Was he really slow? Often, during the past year, he had thought about Zoë, about finding her again. Why hadn't he done anything? Because he was slow? Or because he hadn't expected to survive his first tour? Thirty ops had been too many for most crews. After that, instructing ham-fisted student pilots in clapped-out Wimpys had been a chapter of accidents. He had no right to survive that, either. Nobody on the squadron had ever finished a second tour. It was one reason why he kept putting off having a haircut. Or getting a new uniform. Or buying a book. Fancy going to all that trouble and then getting the chop. Wasted effort. And now, as it turned out, Zoë had come looking for him, which probably proved something, but Silk didn't care what it was. He preferred to sit and enjoy the feeling of her head in his lap while he watched the dragonflies do their stunts. How long was a dragonfly's tour of ops? Bloody short, judging by their frantic antics. That was nice. 'Frantic antics,' he murmured. She didn't move. Sound asleep.

Zoë wanted lunch: a real knife-and-fork lunch, not tomato sandwiches and lemonade. Silk told her she looked like a gypsy princess and no respectable hotel would serve her. 'They'd better,' she said. But she brushed her hair.

They drove across Suffolk. At every crossroads or junction, she pointed and that was where he went. He felt a sense of happy irresponsibility, but he also felt hungry. 'Are we going somewhere special?' he asked.

'Oh, yes.'

'Zoë, you're completely lost.'

She kissed him on the cheek. 'And Tony said you were thick. You're not at all thick, Silko.'

After many more turnings, she suddenly pointed at a white-stucco hotel. 'There,' she said. Silk parked, and they went in. A middle-aged woman sat at reception. She wore a straw hat with a rose tucked into the band and she was knitting a scarf, using the biggest needles Silk had ever seen. They were like chopsticks. 'Hullo,' Zoë said. 'We'd like lunch, please.'

'Can't be done. We don't do lunches, not since my chef got called up by the army.'

'Oh.' Zoë fished a chequebook out of a skirt pocket. 'In that case I'd like to cash a cheque for fifty pounds.'

'So would I.' She hadn't stopped knitting.

Zoë took the revolver from her other skirt pocket. 'If you don't give me fifty pounds, I'll shoot this man.'

Silk put his hands up. 'She's quite mad,' he said. 'I'd pay her, if I were you.'

'If I had fifty pounds,' the woman said, 'I'd be at the races.'

'It's a real gun,' Zoë said. 'Look: give us the money and we'll *take* you to the races.'

She put down her knitting. 'He's a nice boy,' she said. 'What good would it do to shoot him?'

'Ten pounds.' Zoë opened the chequebook. 'It won't bounce, I promise.'

'I'll tell you what I'll do. I'll let you have a room and bath, and a plate of ham sandwiches, for the afternoon, for a pound.'

'Done,' Silk said, and lowered his hands.

'It's not like this in the movies,' Zoë said.

'I was your age once,' the woman said. 'I know what it's like to be young. I eloped with an Italian count when I was nineteen. We ran away to Gretna Green and the blacksmith married us, but it turned out he wasn't an Italian count, he was a vacuum-cleaner salesman with a wife in Cardiff. Still, he was lovely in bed.'

Silk gave her a pound.

'Use any room,' she said. 'A hotel with no meals doesn't get many guests.'

'I'm on the run from the police,' Zoë said. Silk groaned.

'I get the occasional deserter staying here,' the woman said. 'They're no trouble. D'you like mustard?'

Zoë picked the room. They lay on the bed, comfortably naked in the afternoon sunshine, and ate ham sandwiches. 'She didn't play the game,' Zoë said. 'What if the gun had gone off accidentally?'

'It's empty, you juggins.'

'She didn't know that. She might have killed you.'

'I think you confused her. Why did you say you would shoot me? We came in together, we were friends.'

'Who else could I shoot? Not her. Women don't shoot other women, do they? Anyway I bet if I'd been a man, James Cagney for instance, she'd have found fifty pounds. It's not as if I'm robbing anyone. My cheque's good. The money's in the bank.'

'Zoë, my sweet, if you want fifty quid, write me a cheque and I'll cash it for you. You don't need a gun.'

'Perhaps. It's all become a bit of a bore, hasn't it?' She got mustard on her fingers, and wiped them on his thigh.

'What a slut you are, Zoë.'

'Yes. Go on. More like that.'

'Slut. Floozy. Tramp, trollop, tart. Strumpet. Bitch. Double slut. Super bitch.' She was on top of him, laughing as she kissed him, smearing mustard from her lips to his. Without looking, he reached sideways and put the remaining sandwiches on a side-table. That was the hard work done. Now it was all uphill to the mountaintop.

A DIFFERENT POINT
OF VIEW

Constance Babington Smith was a beauty with brains. Her father, Sir Henry, had been private secretary to the Viceroy of India. Her mother was the daughter of the ninth Earl of Elgin. Her eldest brother was a director of the Bank of England. In the 1930s she became very interested in flying. Eventually she was such an expert on all aspects of aviation that she wrote a regular column for *The Aeroplane* magazine. When war broke out, she was commissioned in the Waaf and joined Coastal Command's Photographic Reconnaissance Unit. It was based at Danesfield, a mansion in Buckinghamshire. That was where David Bensusan-Butt went.

'I'm told you know more about interpreting air reconnaissance pictures than anyone else,' he said.

'Actually, that's quite likely,' she said, 'because until recently I was the only one here who was doing it. But I'm sure the Germans must have something similar.'

'It's a subject I know absolutely nothing about.'

'Good. That means you start with an uncluttered mind.'

For the rest of the day she showed him what to look for, and how to find it, in photographs of Germany taken by high-flying aircraft. He learned much about camouflage, shadow, bomb damage, fire damage and smoke. He used magnifying glasses of various size and complexity. Next day he came back and practised his skills.

'It makes a change to meet someone like you,' she said. 'I sometimes think the various Commands don't have much faith in our Unit. Unless our interpretation confirms what they already think, they're likely to ignore it.'

'What about photographs of the target taken by our bombers at night? Can you help me with those? I imagine that flak and search-lights are a problem.'

He came back again. By now they knew each other well enough for him to ask the name of the delicate perfume she always wore. '*L'Heure Bleue*,' she said. 'By Guerlain. I slosh it on, in case an air vice-marshal looks in. This uniform is fearfully masculine, don't you think?'

'In your case, not for one instant,' he said. His utter honesty made it sound like a vote of thanks.

FACT ISN'T TRUTH

1

Rollo spent two days and nights at the assessment centre. Even with stitches to reduce the hole in the gums, his blood was slow to form a permanent clot. He drank beef tea through a straw, listened to the radio, thought about 409 and wondered what an op would look like through a viewfinder. Then, at last, the dentist said he was satisfied. Rafferty's car arrived.

Kate was impressed when she saw him. Half his face was still swollen. 'You look as if you nearly had mumps and then changed your mind,' she said. 'That's a mump you've got there. One mump.'

'You feeling strong?' Rollo said. He took the wisdom tooth, wrapped in a square of bloody lint, from his pocket, and showed it to her.

'Oh my God ...' She turned away, repelled and fascinated at the same time; and sneaked a last look. 'That's not a tooth, it's a fang. What a size! No wonder your face is so beat-up. D'you want a drink? I do, after that.'

'Too early. They've rationed my booze. What's been going on here?'

'Not much. 409 was stood down until today. Plenty of hustle and bustle now, so my guess is ops are on tonight.'

After what he'd been through, flying didn't frighten Rollo. It couldn't be any worse than having a wisdom pulled out. He wanted to get on with it. He asked for an urgent meeting with the Wingco and the group captain. Within an hour, he and Kate were in Rafferty's office with Pug Duff. Rollo told them it was time to decide on casting.

Rafferty was puzzled. One Wimpy was much like another, he said, and so were the crews. Rollo said he had noticed a black man on the squadron. Duff identified him: Sergeant Palmer, from Jamaica, rear gunner in T-Tommy, damn good type. 'I'm sure he is,' Rollo said, 'but there's a problem with trying to film a black man on a dark night. All you see is the eyes.' Rollo's jaw was still stiff. His voice was flat. He sounded tough. 'Also there could be difficulties when the film gets shown in America. You know what they're like over there.'

'Forget T-Tommy,' Duff said. 'How about B-Baker? No niggers, and Joe Pearson's a damn good pilot.'

'Isn't he from up north?' Rollo asked. 'Yorkshire accent?'

'Salt of the earth,' Rafferty said. 'Done twenty ops.'

'I can't gamble on a bloke with a funny accent,' Rollo said. 'Half the audience won't take him seriously, and we'd need subtitles in America. It's got to be someone who speaks good English.'

'Which rules out the Australians, Rhodesians and Canadians,' Duff said. 'And the Irish.' He took a long, hard look at the point of his pencil. 'At a pinch, I suppose, I could do the job myself.'

This frightened Rollo. Duff was far too short to play the hero, but Rollo wasn't brave enough to tell him so. He was grateful when Kate pointed out that the film was supposed to be about a typical Wimpy crew. 'You're the CO, sir. You plan the ops. We can't very well have you briefing yourself, can we? You're a chief, not an Indian.'

'Flight Lieutenant Silk?' Rollo suggested. 'His English is good.'

'And he's guaranteed to say the wrong thing,' Rafferty said. He snapped his fingers. 'I know the man for you. Why didn't I think of him before? Flying Officer Gilchrist. C-Charlie.'

'We could do a lot worse,' Duff agreed. 'Gilchrist won't say the wrong thing. Mostly he won't say anything at all.'

'Now that he's got a whole lot of ops under his belt, it's knocked some sense into him,' Rafferty said. 'When he came here, he was a bit of a pansy.'

'Used to be an actor,' Duff said.

'We all make mistakes,' Rollo said; which amused them.

He found Gilchrist and told him that C-Charlie had been chosen to be filmed during an op. Gilchrist's only response was to nod. Rollo suggested they go to his married quarters, to discuss the technical aspects. Gilchrist nodded.

Kate was there. When Rollo introduced them, she said: 'I know you. I saw you in *How Like An Angel*. You were very good.'

'Thanks.' He made half a smile. 'Long time ago.' The half-smile died.

'I need to put together an outline for a script,' Rollo said. 'A good documentary has a shape, it tells a story. This is the story of an op, obviously. But where does it begin?'

'Oh … high in the sky. A photo-recce kite does a quick dash over Germany. Some penguin at Command sees the snaps, finds a target, gives it to Group, Group gives it to 409, the Wingco gives it to me.'

'So the target's the key. Find it, hit it, beat it. That's our story. Right?'

'Other things can happen.'

'Sure, sure.' Rollo heard himself. He sounded too slick, too casual. 'What sort of things?'

'Mistakes. A Wimpy explodes when it's being bombed up. That's happened. Wimpys collide on the perimeter track. Might lose an engine on take-off. Big bang, then.'

'Let's assume none of that happens,' Rollo said. 'For the sake of brevity.'

'Also happiness,' Kate explained. 'This film is about winners. You take off, no disasters. What next?'

'Reach the coast. Watch out for intruders. That's German night fighters. Might not even be Jerry. I remember when a Spitfire shot down a Hampden.' Rollo put his head in his hands. 'I suppose it seemed a good idea at the time,' Gilchrist said. Nothing changed his quiet voice.

'Nobody gets shot down,' Kate said. 'It must be true, it's in the script. What's next?'

'Enemy coast. Belt of lights and flak.'

'Good,' Rollo said. 'The beast at bay, spitting fire and fury. 409 sails through the storm. That'll make a great sequence. Then?'

'Depends on the target. Another hour if it's Dortmund. Two hours to Stuttgart. Three to Chemnitz. More flak. Night fighters. I've seen kites blow up. Big flash.'

'Let's cut to the chase,' Rollo said. 'Hitting the target. Is that the climax of the whole op? You aim, you drop – boom, up goes the factory.'

'Does it?' Gilchrist said. He raised an eyebrow.

'If it doesn't,' Kate said, 'something's gone wrong, hasn't it?'

'Maybe it does, maybe it doesn't. From ten or twelve thousand feet you can't always be sure. It's like Guy Fawkes' Night down there.'

Rollo did the sum in his head. Twelve thousand feet was about two miles. 'I can't focus on something two miles away, *at night*!' he complained.

'Neither can the flak batteries,' Gilchrist said. 'That's the whole idea.'

'Let's forget the target for a minute,' Kate said. 'We can always come back to it later.'

'We often do.'

'What about the trip home? What are the problems now?'

'Weather.'

'I can't film rain at twelve thousand feet.'

'Shut up, Rollo. What about the weather?'

'Unpredicted winds bugger up the navigation. Electrical storms bugger up the instruments. Icing buggers up the whole aeroplane. Ice inside the cockpit, sometimes.'

'I can film that,' Rollo said.

'Fog is worst.'

'Nobody can film fog.' Rollo went to the bathroom.

'At the end of a long op, fog is a bitch,' Gilchrist said. He was talking more freely now. 'The station's clamped, you've got to divert, your fuel's low. I was on an op last winter. Dusseldorf. Came back, fog everywhere. Twenty-two bombers crashed in England that night. Twenty-two.'

Rollo returned. 'Not strictly true,' he said. 'I *can* film fog, but it looks very boring. Fog at night, even more so. Listen: I had a better idea. Suppose you get hit by flak. Not you personally. Just a near-miss, enough to make a few holes and prang one of the crew.' He saw Gilchrist's eyes widen. 'Not killed,' Rollo said. 'Just put out of action.'

Gilchrist looked at Kate. 'What happened to the happy film?'

'He's a happy casualty,' Rollo said. 'A mere flesh wound. In the leg, say. He makes a complete recovery, I promise. Now tell me: what's his job? Everyone's important, sure, but you've bombed the target, you're halfway home, who can you do without? For a short time?'

'Second pilot.'

Rollo frowned, picturing the scene. 'He sits next to you, doesn't he? Too risky. We can't panic the audience, not now when you're nearly home. Who's next?'

'Wireless op, I suppose.'

Rollo had questions to ask about pain-killing injections, but there was a knock on the door. It was Silk and Zoë. 'I wonder if you could hide Mrs Langham for a few days,' Silk said. 'She doesn't eat much. Pilchards, mainly.'

'He smuggled me into camp under a sack in the back seat of his car,' Zoë told them. 'I'm on the run from the police.'

'Are you serious?' Kate said.

'Ask anyone in Suffolk,' Silk said wearily. 'They'll confirm it.'

2

Ops were changed before lunch. The bombs came off; mines were loaded, but only onto two aircraft. Group wanted two Wimpys for Gardening, and Gilchrist's C-Charlie was not one of them. 409 relaxed.

Rollo heard all this from Squadron Leader Hazard, one of the flight commanders. 'Damn,' he said. 'Just when I was getting keyed up.'

'Never bitch about a scrub. It could be the op where you get the chop.'

'I know, but … it's unsettling, isn't it? I feel … let down.'

'I'll tell you what's worse. In the kite, engines warmed up, ready to taxi, and *then* the scrub signal. I've seen men get out of the aeroplane and throw up. Doesn't pay to think when you're aircrew. How's your tooth?'

'Better, thank you.' Rollo had given up telling people that the pain came from a hole and not from a tooth. Compared with ops and scrubs, what was a bloody silly hole?

The afternoon was empty. Rollo got approval to film a typical briefing session. He had a sandwich for lunch, and wrote a script. Normally a briefing lasted half an hour; Rollo scripted five minutes. He showed it to Rafferty and Duff.

'This can't be right,' the Wingco said. 'I'm supposed to send my crews to bomb some vital oil tanks, and you want me to tell them to go in *low*. Not bloody likely! Minimum of eight thousand. Ten's good and thirteen's better.'

'I expect Mr Blazer has a reason,' Rafferty said.

'Every good film needs a good villain,' Rollo said. 'Ours is the target. The audience must *see* that target. Okay, they see photographs of it at the briefing, good, now they know which particular dragon 409 Squadron has to slay. But unless they see the actual target *through the eyes of the crew*, the audience hasn't completed the experience. We want our audience to identify with your crew, to share their achievements. Which it can't do from thirteen thousand feet.'

'Vital oil tanks,' Duff said. 'According to this, they're heavily defended.'

'Spare yourself, Pug,' Rafferty said. 'They don't exist, do they, Mr Blazer?'

'Not in Germany. Bins found this nice shot of the river Severn.' He showed them an aerial photograph of a sweeping bend, with a road and railway. 'Those round things are genuine oil tanks.'

'Someone in the audience is bound to recognize this place,' Duff said.

'We've flopped the negative. Left-to-right becomes right-to-left. We're calling it Krumingen. Everyone will believe it's in Germany. Later on, when there's a full moon, a kite can fly me over the Severn, I can shoot the moonlight on the water, we flop the neg, Bob's your uncle. C-Charlie's found its target.'

'Dashed clever,' Rafferty said.

Duff grunted, and looked at the script again. 'This is like no briefing I've ever attended. You've given Bins four lines. I've got eight. That's more than nav, signals and Met put together. The group captain's got the last word, and very brief it is.'

'I based it on what you usually say. Slightly condensed, that's all.'

'I suppose you want us to memorize this stuff,' Rafferty said.

The crews filled the briefing room. Rollo and Kate got some establishing shots, then filmed the entry of the briefing officers, then stopped filming for a rehearsal.

It went badly. Duff began by describing the importance of the target and the method of attack. His body was stiff, his eyes stared straight ahead, he looked grim and he sounded tense. Bins was next. He explained the target photograph, speaking in a stop-go monotone which lacked all conviction. Armaments, Signals and Met had little to say and seemed glad of it. Finally, the group captain delivered his little pep talk with a total lack of pep.

'They're terrible,' Rollo whispered to Kate.

'They're not actors. They're worried about their lines.'

'That was excellent,' he announced. 'Very professional.' He asked those with speaking parts to come with him into the next room, and he rehearsed them in private. 'Don't worry about saying the exact words, just say what comes naturally. A little warmth, a few gestures, a touch of gusto?' He smiled broadly, but he was the only man who did. The second rehearsal was a very slight improvement. They returned to the briefing room. Rollo urged the crews to look more interested. 'This information is all for your benefit,' he reminded them. 'Feel free to react.'

He filmed the third effort.

Duff delivered his opening remarks again. It was an important target and would be heavily defended. Crews should go in low, to be sure of accuracy. He ended with the usual words: 'Any questions?'

A pilot raised his hand. 'How low is low, sir?'

'As high as you like,' Duff said. That earned a small cheer.

Later, when the Met man said, 'The predicted winds ...' all the crews chanted, 'Are wrong!'

Rollo made a mental note to edit out the interruptions. But there was nothing he could do to improve Rafferty. The group captain slumped at the sight of the cine-camera. His words were hesitant and his voice was dull. He wished them good luck as if they were taking his last sixpence.

3

Zoë couldn't leave the house, so Silk and Gilchrist came to supper. Rollo did the cooking. It was sausage and mash, with bottled Bass.

'My potato has lumps in it,' Kate said.

'That's nothing,' Silk said. 'My sausage doesn't know whether it's coming or going. See? You can eat either end. Not simultaneously, of course.'

'You must have an interesting job,' Gilchrist said to Kate. Duty done, he went back to his food.

'Well, it's interesting to watch Rollo win the war,' she said. 'We came here to film a typical crew on a typical raid. So far he's picked the best crew, with the best-looking pilot. He wants the Wimpy to go in really low so that he can get nice clear pictures of the target. Did I forget anything?'

'Kate's a romantic,' Rollo said. 'She thinks you just point a camera at the world and you get the truth.' He was quite unworried.

'I did forget something,' she said.

'Fact isn't truth. Truth is something you *discover*.'

'I forgot the wireless op. Rollo's going to shoot the wireless op in the leg, if he can get a gun.'

'I've got a gun,' Zoë said.

'Empty,' Silk said.

'Only because you emptied it, darling. I've got lots of bullets.' She took the revolver from her skirt pocket.

'Why?' Kate asked.

'She keeps it not to shoot people with,' Silk said. 'Special constables, hotel receptionists, me. Nothing personal, you understand. Zoë won't shoot you, too, if you ask nicely.'

'You're such a lovely chump, Silko.' Zoë kissed him on the cheek. 'It's for my own protection. The police gave it to me. The Special Branch. In case I bump into any Irish revolutionaries and they start any funny business.'

Kate said, 'So you're not on the run from the police?'

'Sometimes I am.' She smiled, reassuringly. 'It depends.'

'Wait a minute,' Silk said. 'What about the charity, the fraud, the quarter of a million?' He had stopped eating.

'That was all a trick to catch the IRA. It was a subterfuge.'

'Ah,' Gilchrist whispered. 'Subterfuge.' The word gave him great pleasure.

'But this is *Suffolk*,' Kate complained. 'What the hell's the IRA doing in Suffolk?'

'Frightfully hush-hush, I'm afraid.'

'You said you came here looking for me,' Silk said. 'What was that – another subterfuge?'

'Everyone's so angry,' Zoë said. 'What is everyone so angry about?'

'Your pack of lies,' Silk told her. 'Just give me the facts, for God's sake.'

'Fact isn't truth,' Rollo said, too complacently, which started the argument all over again.

4

The Met man was up with the dawn and liked what he saw. The sky was empty and the breeze was light. It would be a day for farmers to bring in the harvest and armourers to bomb up the Wellingtons. Later he talked to his colleagues at Group. An anticyclone covered the British Isles. The rubbish that had recently clogged the skies of Germany was probably gone, pushed south over the Balkans. The Met man went out and flew his weather balloon, estimated visibility, recorded atmospheric pressure, and told Pug Duff what the Wingco had known as soon as he opened his bedroom window. Ops tonight.

Orders came through from Group while the sun was still burning the dew from the grass. Six aircraft to attack Essen.

That took some of the shine off the day.

Every target was dangerous but some were worse than others. Rotterdam had its attractions; so did St Nazaire and Boulogne and Le Havre. None was in Germany and all were on the coast, so it was possible to get in and get out fast and avoid most of the flak. Enemy ports like Emden, Wilhelmshaven, Hamburg and Kiel were hot spots but they didn't require hours of flying over Germany. It was the deeper ops – Brunswick, Kassel, Frankfurt – that brought a thoughtful silence to the briefing room when the city was named.

The silence was prolonged if the target was south of Munster and north of Cologne. This was the Rhineland, Germany's industrial powerhouse. Twenty towns crowded so closely that, from the air, they formed a sprawling, smoking mass of production called, simply, the Ruhr. Bomber Command crews came to christen it 'the Happy Valley'. After Berlin, the Ruhr was the most heavily defended place in Germany. The last time 409 raided it, one Wimpy was shot down and all the others struggled home, trailing tatters of fabric. 'Roofed with flak,' was how a pilot described the Ruhr at night. Essen was in the middle of the Ruhr. Wellington C-Charlie was on the op.

The Wingco waited until noon, just in case Command changed its mind, before he had the Tannoy request Mr Blazer's presence in his office. 'I just want to confirm that your trip is on,' he said. 'Flight Lieutenant Gilchrist's C-Charlie will carry one bomb less to Essen, to compensate for the weight of you and the film equipment.'

'Good show,' Rollo said. 'What's so special about Essen?'

'Krupp's steel works. Peach of a target. Gilchrist will tell you the drill for take-off. Pay special attention to your parachute. It's got three handles. Pick it up by the wrong handle and you'll fill the kite with acres of silk. Well, good luck.'

A VERY LARGE BLACK

1

Colonel Kemp had been impressed by 409. He admired the clipped and matter-of-fact speech of the officers at briefing, and the quiet confidence of the crews' reports at interrogation. These were no war games. This was the real thing, and he felt privileged to meet men who risked everything to damage the enemy and made no fuss about it and might be dead tomorrow.

He called Charlie Russell, who ran Press and PR at Air Ministry, and said he'd very much like to go back. Russell looked at the golden sunshine and gave himself a day off. He collected Kemp from the embassy and drove to Coney Garth. He made sure that Kemp was happy in the Mess, talking to the flight commanders, and he went to see Rafferty.

'You've had this movie-maker chap from Crown Films for some time, haven't you?' he said. 'I get nothing out of Crown, and of course the Ministry of Information tells me sod all, it's full of nancy-boys who sleep in a hairnet, so I thought I'd stooge over here and ask how the film's coming along.'

'You couldn't have chosen a better day, Charlie. We're on ops tonight and the cameraman's in a Wimpy. It's Essen. He's pleased as punch.'

'Essen.' The air commodore went for a slow walk around the room. 'Essen means ... Krupp's? Thought so. Fancy that. Essen.'

'He wants action shots. Flak and stuff.'

'From what I hear of Essen, he'll be able to get out and walk on it.'

Rafferty detected a lack of enthusiasm. 'All the more exciting, surely. He keeps saying he wants to show an op as it really is.'

'A Wimpy going down in flames. Will he show that? No. Won't show Essen either, unless by a miracle a gale springs up and blows away all their industrial fug. And if the Huns create their usual smokescreen, he won't see many bomb strikes. Of course, it's your decision, Tiny.'

'Not too late to change, Charlie.'

'Entirely up to you. All I'm saying is Essen is a bloody dangerous target, and if this fellow gets killed trying to film a supposedly first-class squadron in action, then 409 will have put up a very large black.'

'Point taken.'

'And here are two other things that are none of my business. Colonel Kemp is here. There are Americans like him, air attachés so-called, hanging around Bomber Command bases everywhere.'

'Jolly good type, I thought.'

'Yes. They see, they hear, they report to Washington. The American people think highly of our precision bombing. Not like the Nazis, who bomb indiscriminately, and hit towns, civilians, schools, hospitals, women and children. No mercy at all. By contrast, the RAF only bombs military targets. We *never* bomb civilians. Now, Kemp is going to be present at today's briefing.'

'Ah. You'd like Bins to …'

'The IO? Yes. Get him to stress how crucial it is to bomb Krupp's and Krupp's alone. No risk to innocent civilians, Tiny. Of course the last thing I want to do is interfere.'

'Quite. And there was another matter you wished to discuss?'

Russell wandered away and looked out of the window. 'You've got another IO called Skull. I hear worrying things about Skull. He seems to enjoy picking holes in the crews' reports after ops. That's bad for morale. I'm an outsider, of course. You must do as you see fit. But please keep your Skull away from my Colonel Kemp.'

'Nothing easier, Charlie,' Rafferty said. 'Consider it done.'

The group captain met the Wingco after lunch and they agreed on all points. What was gratifying was the way all three solutions interlocked.

They told Rollo Blazer he was not going to Essen. Inevitably, he asked why; the man was a civilian, after all. 'Operational reasons,' Duff said. Rollo had no answer. His fate was postponed. He didn't know whether to feel disappointed or not. He felt helpless, and went away.

They sent for Bins. He understood his orders at once. 'While you're here,' Rafferty said, 'how is Skull fitting in? Any problems?'

'He knows his job. I wish he'd stick to it, sir. He can't leave well alone. As you know, we still drop Nickels from time to time. I just found him with a handful of leaflets, translating the German and ridiculing the contents. That's the sort of thing he does.'

'Send for him, would you, Bins?' Rafferty said. 'And tell him to bring the leaflets.'

Skull arrived, and was surprised to be offered a seat. Rafferty was not normally so cordial to junior Intelligence Officers. The Wingco was already straddling a chair, nibbling at a thumbnail without much success. There was little to nibble. Bins retired to a corner and folded his arms.

'What d'you make of that bumf?' Rafferty asked.

'It's simple-minded, sir. It's a crude attempt to subvert German morale with threats of increased bombing. It assumes that German resistance is weaker than ours. Not very clever.' He stopped. Rafferty wasn't listening.

'You have just quoted from a secret document, flight lieutenant. Have you got permission so to do?'

'You asked me what I made of it, sir.'

'I never told you to read it, let alone translate it and analyze it. Are you aware that Nickels are covered by the Official Secrets Act?'

'It can't be secret if millions of Germans have read it, sir.'

'Who says?' Rafferty growled, and Skull was smart enough not to answer. 'You are in breach of the Official Secrets Act. That is a very, very serious offence in wartime.'

Duff abandoned his thumb and put it away for another time.

'I can't believe the charge would stand up in court, sir,' Skull said.

'Whether or not court-martial proceedings follow is for me to decide. I'm influenced by your general attitude to the war. Are you really putting your shoulder to the wheel, or are you just along for the ride? Let's take ops. What do you know about ops? I mean, really know. Only what you've heard. Is it right for you to question crews about something you don't understand?'

Duff said: 'Bins has been on ops.'

'Gunner in a Hampden,' Bins said. 'Kiel.'

'By chance, there's room for a passenger in C-Charlie tonight,' Rafferty said. 'Essen. Of course, you'd have to volunteer.'

Skull reviewed his options. It took him about three seconds. If he refused to volunteer, the news would be all over the station in an hour and the aircrew would treat him with amused contempt and life would be impossible. If he volunteered, death would be very possible. Also violent, terrifying and painful. 'The Ruhr,' he said lightly. 'It should be an illuminating experience.'

2

Skull was sick twice before C-Charlie crossed the English coast. It came as no surprise. The only time he had flown before this was to France in September 1939, in a lurching, bumping troop-carrier, and he had been sick then. This time he took several stout paper bags with him.

After throwing up, he had nothing to do.

In the hour before take-off, the second pilot had explained everything that Skull needed to know: mainly concerning emergencies. He showed him how to clip on his parachute, how to operate it, and where the parachute exits were; also the crash exits. They seemed unnecessarily small and badly positioned for men in bulky flying kit. Skull tried not to think of that. He was shown where the two portable fire extinguishers were stowed. He was shown his crash position: behind the main spar. 'Then there's ditching,' the second pilot said. 'I'll explain that if it happens.'

'Awfully kind. Have you any general advice? This is my first op.'

'Don't say anything unless you must. The skipper doesn't like chat.'

That was why Gilchrist's nickname was Chatty. Even his intercom checks were terse: just a word or two from each position: front guns, second pilot, nav, WOP, rear guns. The passenger added: 'Skull.' Then no comment, unless the nav gave a course change; and that was briefly said, briefly acknowledged. Skull lay on the crew bed, just a narrow bunk. The crew had no time to rest, so this must be for casualties, he decided. His brain was not accustomed to idleness. It calculated that he was lying directly above the bomb bay. An hour passed. The engine noise battered his ears like a continually breaking wave. He dozed.

The wireless op shook his shoulder and told him to turn on his oxygen. He clipped his mask shut and inhaled. His heart was thudding and his mouth was dry. The oxygen tasted of rubber and his nasal passages complained but after a while his heartbeat slowed and all his senses brightened. The engines seemed to be throbbing with a strange urgency. Perhaps that was in his head. He sat on the bed and, for no reason, sang a song: 'You'd be so nice to come home to' ... Why not? With his intercom mike switched off, nobody could hear him. He could scarcely hear himself.

A voice said, 'Enemy coast coming up.' That must be the front gunner. Skull took his oxygen bottle, went forward, re-plugged his intercom and stood behind the pilots. The instrument panel made a faint green glow. He discovered the air speed: one hundred and fifty-five miles an hour. Altimeter said fourteen thousand three hundred. Half as high as Everest. My goodness. The rest of the panel was a sprawl of gauges and switches and levers which he would never understand. He looked up and saw a band of searchlights, from far left to far right. Each moved slowly. They reminded him of reeds growing in a stream, pulled this way and that by the wandering current. It was all very soothing. Lots of coloured lights began to decorate the sky, climbing slowly, then suddenly fast, then falling away. Skull gripped the seat-back: C-Charlie was in a gentle dive. The searchlights were more intense, busier. Now they reminded Skull of Hollywood: of film premières, glamour, ballyhoo. Innocent fun. Lights sparkled on the ground. It was all very pretty. Soon Gilchrist had raced through the defended belt and blackness returned. C-Charlie climbed again.

Skull had a spell in the bomb-aimer's position, looking down. Nothing memorable happened. Once, he saw another aeroplane but it turned out to be the Wellington's moon-shadow on cloud. There was more and more cloud. He went back to the bed. The wireless op came and looked at him, so he gave a thumbs-up. The gesture felt theatrical and fraudulent, and he was glad the oxygen mask hid his face.

Another hour passed. Tedium, cold, the foul taste of oxygen, a hungry stomach but no appetite for food. And he'd have to endure all this again on the way back. Then, a sudden shout on the intercom and C-Charlie banked so steeply that he fell on the floor.

Now there was a lot of chat. From it, Skull guessed that another Wellington had loomed out of the night and Gilchrist had avoided it. Bins had said, at briefing, that sixty bombers would be over the Ruhr. When C-Charlie was level, Skull went forward.

Wherever he looked, he saw searchlights hunting in teams, and a continuous sparkle of flak. Some of the flak rippled in a straight line and vanished. Some climbed like a chain of rockets and fell away. Skull was amazed by the extravagance. *All it takes is one shell*, he thought. Gilchrist ignored the flak. He was talking to his navigator, discussing the absence of landmarks. The problem was industrial haze, made worse by cloud. The nav claimed that dead reckoning put them over Gelsenkirchen, which meant Essen was to the south-west. The front gunner was pretty sure he'd seen Mulheim, so Essen must be east. Gilchrist asked the rear gunner what he could see. 'Fuck all, skip,' he said. 'Some bastard's dropped a flare and the haze is worse than ever.' Gilchrist decided to fly on.

When Skull smelled the harsh tang of cordite for the first time, he wanted to turn and run. Cordite meant the shell had exploded bang in front, on the same level, not long ago. Men down there were trying to kill him, and getting close to succeeding. He felt weak, and sat on the main spar. All the time, Gilchrist was holding his fatuous conversation with the crew about the layout of the Ruhr. They went on and on and bloody on. *Wasn't that Duisburg? More like Oberhausen. Well, this is Mulheim, then. Could be Bochum, skip. So we passed Gelsenkirchen? Sod this haze …*

Skull stood up and was horrified to see how much worse the flak was. Nothing could fly through that, it was madness. And still the discussion went on. He had a parachute, he knew the exits, he could leave, now. The Wimpy rocked like a boat in a swell. 'Turbulence,' Gilchrist said. 'There's a kite ahead. We'll follow him.' Skull had to sit down again. After a minute, Gilchrist said: 'Ah … poor devil. You should see this, Skull.' He got up, weak at the knees. Far below, searchlights coned a Wellington. Flak chased it, tickled it. Flame streaked from a wing and the aircraft exploded. 'Log that, would you, nav?' Gilchrist said.

He found Essen because, he said, he recognized the smell. A peculiar chemical stink, he said, that only Essen produced. The nav crawled down to his bomb-aiming position. Gilchrist lost height, circling widely, until Skull could see light flak bursting all around. *Quickly, quickly, drop the bombs*, he thought. The nav said he was sure he recognized the steel works, but too late, C-Charlie had overshot. Someone said it looked more like Gelsenkirchen. 'We'll go round again,' Gilchrist said. Skull unplugged his intercom. 'I'll kill you, you incompetent idiot!' he screamed. Nobody heard.

Second time round, they dropped the bombs and held steady for the flash and the camera. Skull was shaking with cold. He tripped and fell on his way to the bed, bloodied his nose. A piece of shell had nicked the fabric beside the bed, ripping it away. He lay down and let freezing air crash against him. When C-Charlie landed at Coney Garth, Skull couldn't walk, couldn't speak. The blood wagon took him to the MO, who gave him a big sedative and a nice warm cot.

3

Zoë was bored with being cooped up in the Blazers' house, and she wanted to go for a walk. Silk brought her a pair of Waaf overalls and a bucket. 'Nobody ever stops a Waaf if she's carrying a bucket,' he said. 'Everyone assumes she's doing a job. Carry it in your right hand and you won't even have to salute.'

She tried on the overalls. 'Primitive,' she said. 'Barbaric. Quite odious. No thank you.'

'What's wrong with them?'

'They're an obscene joke. They make me look shabby.'

'That's the whole bloody point, you stupid woman.'

She gave them back. 'I can remember when you had a sense of style, Silko. Look at you now.' They were in the kitchen, and Kate was making toast for breakfast. 'He keeps proposing to me,' Zoë said. 'Look at that grubby uniform. Would you marry him?'

'Like a flash.'

'I look much sexier without the uniform,' Silk said. 'Isn't that right, Zoë?'

'Rather a coarse remark.' She nibbled some toast.

'Zoë can be pretty coarse herself,' he said. He was irritated: getting those overalls had not been easy. 'The rich are like that.'

'I'm not rich. I'm not on the run. And I want to see my friends from the old days. Jonty Brown and Tom Stuart and Tubby Heckter. Pixie Hunt, too.'

'Not at home to callers, sweetie. Got the chop, all of them,' Silk said. 'Finish your toast, we're off. I smuggled you in, now I've got to smuggle you out. Then I can bring you back in, legally. Why? Because you haven't been signed *in* at the Main Gate, so legally you can't be signed *out*.'

'That's utterly asinine.'

'You're the expert in that field.' He hustled her out, just as Rollo came downstairs. 'What was all that about?' Rollo asked.

'They're not in love,' Kate said.

'Neither are we. That makes two happy couples. She's stunning, isn't she?'

'Forget it, Rollo. She's mad and you're nuts. Think of the children.'

4

As soon as they were out of sight of the aerodrome, Silk pulled off the road and stopped. Zoë kicked aside the sacking and got into the front seat. 'I'm hungry,' she said. 'Where can we get a good black market breakfast?'

Sunlight streamed through ancient oaks and dappled the Frazer-Nash. A pair of hefty cart-horses wandered up to a fence and blinked at the visitors. In the distance, a thrush tried out variations on an original theme. It was a scene made for lovers. Rollo Blazer would have shot it at once, before he lost the light.

'What a ghastly woman you are,' Silk said.

'Abuse like that is slightly premature, darling. Save it until we're in bed.'

'You're worse than your bloody mother. At least she was honest about her greed. You can't be honest about anything, can you?'

'If we don't have breakfast, then we can't have sex. That's not blackmail, it's pure biology. And I was honest about those Socialist overalls. Too honest for you, Silko. Start the car, before I eat one of those charmingly rustic horses.'

Silk got out, and took the keys with him. It was easier to deal with Zoë from a distance. 'You lie about everything. I can't take that.

Everyone cheats a bit, but you … You never had a baby, did you?'

She was too hungry to argue, so she did the next best thing and gave a smile of childish innocence. 'How did you know?'

'Absence of stretch marks.'

'Clever Silko. Not so slow, after all.'

'And I doubt if your mother's in Dublin.'

'No. In Kentucky. For the racing.'

'And all that junk about charity funds and the special constable and being a jinx popsy was all junk.'

'No. I had a fling with a couple of pilots, both killed in action. Anyway, nothing really mattered after I lost Tony. Mummy did a bunk to America to escape the Blitz. Maybe I should have gone too. Everyone else was being frightfully patriotic and I honestly didn't give a damn. There you are, Silko: a bit of your foul honesty at last.' She got out of the car and stood with her face turned away from him. 'Why don't you ask me what I'm really doing here? I came looking for Tony, and don't tell me it was very foolish. I told myself that a hundred times. I honestly didn't expect to find you. You were a big surprise.'

'So you adopted me as a sort of substitute Tony. Is that the truth?'

No answer.

'I still don't see why you had to lie so much. You're such a fraud, Zoë.'

'And you're such a prig, Silko.'

That hurt. That drew blood. 'I don't mind being fucked about,' he said, 'but I can't stand being buggered about.' He checked his watch. 'Look: I'm on duty soon.'

He drove her to Bury St Edmunds railway station. Neither of them spoke until it was time to say goodbye. 'Has the squadron still got that lovely boxer dog?' she asked. 'Handyman? I gave him to 409 as a mascot.'

'Got knocked down in the road,' Silk said. 'Dead.'

Zoë looked him in the eyes. 'You couldn't even lie about that, could you?' she said sadly. 'You're hopeless, Silko.' She kissed him on the lips and walked away, leaving him feeling that he had found the truth and it wasn't worth the price he had paid, so he should have stuck with the lies.

Too late now. He got back to Coney Garth just in time to hear that he was on ops. Bloody Bremen again. Good. When all else failed, there was always bombing.

A WHOLE NEW SLANT

1

Rafferty always found time to visit wounded aircrew, but Skull wasn't aircrew and he had no serious injuries, so Rafferty asked the Ops Officer, Bellamy, to pop in and see the chap.

Skull was in bed, eating porridge. He was unshaven and the spoon seemed heavy. There was a small cut on his nose. Bellamy asked how he was feeling.

'Somewhat sluggish. The brain feels like ...' He gazed at the porridge, and finally shook his head.

'You're probably still a bit doped.'

'Sometimes I can smell flak. It smells strange. Pungent.' Speaking was like laying bricks: every word had to be found and placed. 'Flak is close when ...' He aimed his spoon at nothing. 'When you can smell it.'

'Still, you got back, didn't you? Takes a lot to stop a Wimpy.'

Skull licked the spoon and thought. 'Cold treacle,' he said carefully. 'Brain feels like ...' He yawned hugely. 'Feels like ... Damn. Forgotten again.'

'Treacle. Doesn't matter.' Bellamy took the porridge bowl from Skull's hand before he spilled it. 'You should get some sleep.'

'Flak. Horrible. We were lost, Bellamy. Stooged about, looking for ... um... Essen. Half an hour, in the flak, over the Ruhr. Big mistake.' Skull clutched Bellamy's sleeve. 'I know a better way.'

'I see. Well, I suppose you'd better tell me, so I can tell the Wingco.'

'Forget the damn target. Forget bloody Krupp's. Bomb Essen. Then – go.'

'Bomb the city? I honestly don't think that's on the cards, old boy.'

'The kites have to fly round and round. In all that flak.'

Bellamy took Skull's hand from his sleeve. 'Right, I've got the message. You get some rest.'

'A Wimpy blew up.' To Bellamy's horror there were tears on Skull's face. 'And we never even bombed Essen. We never even found Essen.'

Bellamy reported to Rafferty that Skull was exhausted and not making much sense. The sight of flak seemed to have unbalanced him. 'Kept babbling about making the city the target, the whole city. At least I think that's what he meant.'

'That's what happens when you put a Cambridge don in uniform,' Rafferty said. 'I don't want our tame Yank going anywhere near him. See to it, would you?'

Colonel Kemp was found in a hangar, watching a Wellington get an engine change. He knew of Skull's Essen op, and was impressed by it. He hoped the wound wasn't serious.

'Concussion,' Bellamy said. 'They're taking X-rays. Meanwhile, absolute quiet. No visitors, I'm afraid. Poor chap's incoherent at times.'

'Good Lord. What hit him? A shell splinter?'

'Nothing hit him. He tripped over the main spar and landed on his head. We warned him beforehand, but you know what these academic types are like. They live in a world of their own.'

Colonel Kemp nodded, and made a mental note: beware the main spar. He was determined to go on an op, and soon.

2

At Coney Garth, the group captain was king. Just the sight of four rings on a sleeve was enough to make a corporal square his shoulders and look alert. It was enough to make an AC2 scuttle out of sight. But at High Wycombe, in Buckinghamshire, group captains were small change.

High Wycombe was the headquarters of Bomber Command. Its

C-in-C, Air Marshal Sir Richard Peirce, had flown with the Royal Naval Air Service in World War One and gone on to build a solid career in the RAF. He knew very well that, having been given Bomber Command, he had to defend it. Whispers had reached him that the Prime Minister might be having second thoughts about strategic bombing, whatever that meant. Downing Street had asked for certain files and photographs to be sent to a civil servant, name of Butt, and that was bad enough, but this Butt was an economist by training, a youngster of twenty-seven, not long down from Cambridge. It was known that Butt had visited the PRU at Danesfield, several times, and not to ogle the delightful Constance Babington Smith, either. What the devil was going on? The chief of Bomber Command – an air marshal and a knight of the realm – couldn't very well ask young Butt what he was up to. However, there was no reason why Champion, not much older than Butt and also a Cambridge man, shouldn't continue the friendship begun at King's and invite Butt to lunch at his club.

The Sheldrake was a blackened ruin. They went to the Army and Navy Club, and ate in a private room.

'Security,' Champion explained. 'I'm just a dogsbody in operational planning, but you live and work in the throbbing heart of the war ... Look, I've got us a salmon, which has the great virtue of being off-ration, as does the salad. Not desperately exciting but ... is that all right?' Butt assured him it was more than all right. 'And this white Burgundy is quite sturdy,' Champion remarked, 'which is more than can be said of the French performance last year ... Oh dear. How horribly indiscreet of me. I never spoke.'

'Didn't you? I never heard.'

'Splendid. That makes us quits.'

Lunch was good, and Champion was not so clumsy as to spoil it by talking shop. It was only when they got to the coffee that he said, 'This reminds me of Skull. What a brain! Yet capable of such *naiveté*. You remember how concerned he was to give words their precise meaning? To him, a target is a target. Either you hit it or you miss it. If a raid doesn't succeed, it fails. Well, as you know better than I, strategic bombing isn't that simple.'

'Some raids are partially successful, you mean.'

'And some are doubly successful.' Champion sipped his coffee. He cocked an eyebrow at Butt, who was looking politely baffled. 'What

Skull couldn't fathom,' Champion said, 'because he's not a pilot, because he doesn't look beyond the words, is that Bomber Command aims to hit two targets with one bomb.'

Butt blinked a couple of times. 'We're talking about area bombing.'

'Exactly.'

'Perhaps we should say "approximately".'

Champion smiled. 'Or even "allegedly". My lords and masters at Command are no fools. They've never believed that *every* bomber hits *every* specific target, no matter what the crew may claim. Flak, cloud, smoke, different winds at different heights, an enemy search-light smack in the bomb-aimer's face – a dozen factors might spoil the attack. The difference is, this time last year pilots were told that if they couldn't find a specific target, they must bring their bombs back. Not any more. Now they *always* bomb a target, because the target is enemy morale, and they can't miss that.'

'Assuming that the target area is big enough.'

'It always is. For many months now, every military target we attack is in a German town. If we hit that specific target, hooray. If we miss it and hit the built-up area, three cheers for that, too. German factories are no good without German workers.'

'What do the bomber crews think of this?' Butt asked.

'The subject doesn't arise. We always give them a specific target.'

'I see. Perhaps you don't want to damage *their* morale.'

'What's important is we can't afford to upset the Americans. They still think we should bomb by daylight, to spare the civilians.' Champion looked inside the coffee pot. 'Idealism runs riot in America as long as it's not their aircraft getting shot down.' He topped up their cups. 'So when our crews are being briefed for an op, we use the phrase "industrial centre". It sounds like a factory but it covers the whole town.'

'And what you're saying is that not a bomb is wasted?'

Champion was pleased. Butt had grasped the concept very quickly. 'We have a motto in Bomber Command,' he said. '"Profitable target, in profitable surroundings". We're turning it into a fine art.'

'My goodness,' Butt said. 'That puts a whole new slant on things.'

'It puts the fear of death into German civilians,' Champion said. 'Morale is a very fragile commodity when Fritz hears the scream of a four-thousand-pound high-capacity blast bomb.'

'A fearsome weapon,' Butt agreed.

'The Prime Minister takes the credit. "Devastate the Nazi home-land." Isn't that what he said a year ago?' When Butt gave an inscrutable smile, Champion made an apologetic gesture. 'Or so I'm told. That statement was highly confidential. Officially, I know nothing. Of course you mustn't comment, and I should never have mentioned it. All the same, we're doing just what he wanted, aren't we? There I go again. Pay no attention, David.'

'Thank you for lunch, Ralph,' Butt said. 'I'm learning all the time.'

3

After the Essen raid, Gilchrist and his crew got to bed at dawn. The Wingco never even considered sending C-Charlie to Bremen. If Rollo Blazer wanted to film this op, it would be in another Wimpy, and by good luck Flying Officer Polly Lomas was fit again. His cracked wrist had healed; he would fly Q-Queenie. He was twenty-one but looked nineteen, had a bright smile and spoke good Home Counties English. Duff and Rafferty agreed that Lomas would take Blazer.

Rollo found Lomas standing next to Queenie at dispersal.

'Hard though I try, I cannot love this aeroplane,' Lomas said. 'Admire and respect, yes. But look at her: she's podgy. She resembles a pregnant sofa, doesn't she?'

'Never seen one,' Rollo said.

'She's a tough old cow, I don't dispute that. She's brought me home with scads and scads of fabric shot away and the wind whistling through her bones. Are you superstitious?'

'Um ... depends.'

'This is the third Queenie the squadron's had in three months. Some crews think the letter Q must be bad luck. Doesn't bother me. I'll tell you what does make me wonder. Wimpys have this famous geodesic design, this basketweave framework, and everyone says that's what makes the kite so amazingly strong. So why won't she spin? Nobody's ever spun a Wimpy. And survived, that is.'

Rollo looked at the pregnant sofa and imagined it spinning, and looked away. 'Who would want to spin her?' he asked.

'Me for one. Over Hamburg, we got coned. I tried every stunt I knew. Couldn't escape the cone. Spinning would probably have made matters worse, but what the hell, if intelligence doesn't work, try stupidity.'

'So how did you get away?'

'Luck. And Mackenzie.' Lomas took a little wooden figure of a kilted highlander from his pocket. 'I never fly without Mackenzie.'

'I thought you weren't superstitious.'

'Mackenzie's an each-way bet. Can't do any harm.'

Rollo should have gained strength from Lomas's breezy optimism. Instead, he trudged away, feeling suddenly drained of energy. He intended to walk back to his married quarters, but he soon knew it was too far. He changed direction, heading for the Mess, and stumbled as he turned. His legs were unreliable. His knees seemed to wish to fold the wrong way. His muscles were made of string. He didn't feel his face hit the ground, and so didn't know how lucky he was that it was grass and not tarmac.

The Tannoy summoned Mrs Blazer to the MO's office.

'He's not going to die. Not today, anyway,' the MO told her. 'But he's semi-conscious at best, so he can't answer my questions. Has he ever fainted before?'

'Only once, that I know of,' Kate said. 'During the Blitz. We were filming a big fire and a cloud of smoke came down on us and he passed out. Not for long, just a minute or so. I think he choked on the smoke.'

'Well, there was no smoke today. Has he ever mentioned diabetes? Vertigo? Low blood sugar?'

'No. None of those. Look: you examined him a couple of days ago. Didn't he tell you everything?'

'Men lie,' the MO said.

'Oh.' She felt helpless. Since they came to Coney Garth she had prepared herself to meet injury, bloodshed, men lost in action. But Rollo had simply collapsed in the open air. 'Haven't you got some idea what's wrong?' she asked. 'What are his ...?' She couldn't find the word. 'You know.'

'Symptoms. His temperature's high, he's got abdominal pain, there are shivering fits and some other signs that might indicate food poisoning. But ...'

255

'Toast and coffee. That's all he had for breakfast.'

'Yes. I checked with the Mess. And nobody else has gone down with food poisoning. There's another possibility. I can't prove it, but I suspect the dental extraction is behind all this.'

'That damn tooth,' Kate said.

'Not the tooth itself. However, there might have been an abscess in the tissues near the tooth. Maybe the extraction exposed the abscess. If it burst, and some of the pus escaped into the stomach ...' The MO shrugged.

'It would be like food poisoning?'

'Rather worse, I imagine.'

'Can you do anything for him?'

'The best solution is for his digestive system to pass this revolting matter in the normal fashion, as soon as possible. So we'll purge his bowels. By this time tomorrow his innards should be empty and the patient well on the way to recovery.'

'What if that doesn't work?'

'I've just had an idea. Why don't you pop down the corridor and have a chat with Skull? He's getting bored. I think he'll be fit for duty soon.'

Kate went off to see Skull. The MO telephoned Group Captain Rafferty. 'Mr Blazer is in a stable condition, sir,' he reported.

'Good. When I heard about him, my first thought was he'd got a bad case of twitch. He was due to go on ops tonight, with Q-Queenie. Wouldn't be the first chap to develop galloping cold feet, would he?'

'True, sir. But Mr Blazer is genuinely sick.'

'I see. Well, keep me informed.'

In the evening, Skull was wandering about Sick Quarters in search of company and conversation, when he stopped at an open door. Rollo Blazer was in bed. 'Hullo,' he said. 'What happened to you?'

Rollo whispered: 'Wrath of God.'

Skull went closer and saw that Rollo's face was as white as paper. 'I say ... Did you go on ops?'

'Did I?' Only Rollo's lips moved. 'No. Not me.'

Skull took the temperature chart from the bed-rail and examined it. 'You've been up and down like a kangaroo.' He replaced the chart. 'Not that I have any experience of kangaroos.'

He had nothing more to say, but it seemed discourteous to leave. He sat on the only chair. Rollo lay as still as a stone. Once, his eyes flickered towards Skull, but the effort was too much and they stopped trying. 'You went on ops,' he whispered.

'Yes, that's true. I did.' Skull realized that he was speaking strongly, as if it made up for Rollo's feeble voice. 'We went to Essen. Not a nice place. Other than that, I can't seem to remember anything of interest. Dreadfully cold, Germany, I do remember that. People said it would be hot, but my recollection is of extreme cold.' By now, Rollo's eyelids were almost closed. 'Well, I mustn't trespass on your hospitality any further,' Skull said. He left, treading softly.

4

By 1941 all Wellingtons had self-sealing fuel tanks. If a bullet holed a tank, escaping petrol reacted with an inner layer of rubber compound that lined the tank, the compound rapidly expanded, the hole was plugged. But nothing could seal a hole the size of a pumpkin.

Over Bremen, Q-Queenie got bracketed by heavy flak that tossed her about like a boy in a blanket. All the wing tanks were ripped open and the undercarriage came down. Soon the engines were coughing, and with the added drag of the wheels, Polly Lomas had to descend. He caught sight of moonlight glistening on concrete and was sure it was a stretch of autobahn. He made an excellent landing on what turned out to be a runway in a Luftwaffe airfield. The crew set Queenie on fire, as orders required, and the blaze brought German guards at high speed. Within minutes, Lomas and his men were in the bag.

At Coney Garth, D-Dog was the last Wimpy to return. Bins asked the usual questions and was relieved when Silk seemed to agree that they had bombed Bremen. 'Did you definitely hit the target?' he asked. Silk said: 'We did better than that. We hit two breweries and the naval officers' brothel.' Everyone laughed. Even Bins smiled as he wrote: *Target definitely hit*. 'Damned good show,' Rafferty said.

He waited up until it was impossible for Q-Queenie to be in the air. No distress signal. No reports from other airfields. Nothing from the Observer Corps. 'Let's turn in,' he said to Bellamy.

'Yes, sir. Just as well Mr Blazer didn't go with Lomas, isn't it? The chaps are becoming a bit leery of this film business. They think Blazer's turning into a Jonah.'

'Superstition,' Rafferty said. 'It's as bad as fact.' He went to bed.

5

Kate slept poorly, worried about Rollo. She wasted her anxiety. Late in the morning she got a message: Rollo was awake and insisting on seeing her. She found him sitting up in bed, eating scrambled white of egg and drinking sweet tea from a pint mug. 'What have I missed?' he asked.

'My God, you look awful. You look as if you've risen from the grave on a wet Wednesday in Stepney.'

'Do I? Well, I've risen, that's the main thing.' There was nothing in his voice but faint impatience. 'Come on, what have I missed?'

'Not a damn thing. The squadron got the day off today, so the crews are out playing cricket, and I've washed my hair.' She said nothing about the Bremen raid. No point in upsetting him.

'Q-Queenie,' he said. 'Got the chop, didn't she?' His flat voice made it sound even worse.

'For God's sake.' Kate was angry, and she walked away from him. 'You knew what you missed, so why ask?'

'Skull told me.'

'Of course he did. Intelligence knows everything.'

'The MO told Skull.'

'All in a day's work,' she said. 'Just another crew gone west. I'm beginning to hate this job.'

Rollo was eating steadily, and watching her. 'Can't quit now,' he said. 'Think of the première.'

'Yeah. Rollo's not dead, so it's all very funny.' She went out.

'Be ready tomorrow,' he said. 'Tomorrow I'll be in action.'

He was wrong. He recovered his strength remarkably quickly, but the MO made him stay in Sick Quarters for another day. Even so, he didn't miss anything. In the morning, 409 was on standby for Gardening at Rotterdam; then the target was changed to Brest; and at four p.m. the whole operation was scrubbed. Much waiting; no trade. There were many days like that.

Silk went to his room and wrote a note to Zoë which turned into a very long letter. He re-read the pages and despaired. What a lot of cock. The jokes were obvious, the emotions were cheap, and self-pity leaked between the lines. It was lust disguised as sentimentality. He tore the letter into small pieces, threw them into a waste basket, distrusted his batman and flushed the bits down the toilet.

He slept for an hour and took a shower. The evening looked beautiful. He saw vast, unlimited quantities of clean air and a honey-coloured sky getting ready to perform its grand finale, the stunning sunset. He skipped dinner and went for a walk with his golf club around the perimeter track. He reached the dispersal bays and he was halfway through his usual game, which involved chipping the ball over each Wimpy in turn, when Pug Duff drove by and stopped. 'Get in!' he shouted.

Silk played his shot and walked over to the car. 'British Museum, cabby,' he said, 'and drive like the wind.' He got in.

They went to the furthest corner of the field. 'Finest mushrooms in Suffolk,' Duff said. The grass was thickly dotted with them, as white as plates. 'You're lucky I got enough bacon for two.'

He had also brought a Primus stove, a frying pan, six sausages, half a loaf, and four bottles of beer. They cooked the bacon and sausages, and fried the mushrooms in the fat. By now it was dusk. Swallows zigzagged overhead, making flying look easy. Duff dragged the back seat from the car and they sat and ate out of the frying pan.

'Do you often do this?' Silk asked.

'Only when I can't stand the sight of the bloody squadron any longer.'

'I never expected you to make Wingco, Pug. Not with those puny little legs of yours. How can you kick people up the arse?'

'I take a running jump. And since we're opening our hearts, I never thought I'd find you in the awkward squad. Everybody's out of step except our Silko, isn't that right?'

Silk drank some beer, and wiped his lips.

'You make life bloody difficult for me,' Duff said. 'It's hellish hard work trying to boost morale when you come back and tell everyone the squadron just bombed Zurich.'

'I would never say that. I might say we *missed* Zurich.'

'Morale is crucial. And you keep chipping away at it.'

'Listen ...' Silk eased his backside. 'Night after night, op after op, crews tell Bins and Skull, yes, they found the target and yes, they hit the target. You know that's not always true.'

'Perhaps.'

'And the *crews* know it. They know who the bullshit-merchants are. How many Wimpys completely miss the target? Ten per cent? Twenty? Thirty?'

'No, no,' Duff said. 'That's incompatible with good morale. If my crews start to think their efforts are wasted, they'll stop trying. Confidence and efficiency go hand in hand. Determination is half the battle.'

'Jesus,' Silk said. 'You sound like Henry the Fifth on Benzedrine.'

'Never mind what I sound like. These chaps have got to believe in success before they can succeed. Don't you see that?'

'You've got a lousy job, Pug.' Silk ate the last fried mushroom. 'It's got so you wouldn't know the truth if it took its clothes off and got into bed with you. Let's talk about something else.'

'I dreamt about Sergeant Felicity Parks last night,' Duff said. 'What a stunner. D'you think she'd marry me?'

'I dreamt about her, too. After what she and I got up to, I don't think you'd want her, Pug.'

They talked until darkness. As they drove back to their quarters, a fog was beginning to creep across the field. That explained the scrub. Sometimes Group got things right.

BLAST WAVES

1

The MO told Rollo he was discharged, and gave him a small packet of pills. 'Benzedrine,' he said. 'Only if you go on ops, and then don't take more than one. Are you familiar with this stuff?'

'Vaguely.'

The MO smiled: a rare sight. 'Vague is not the word I'd choose. Benzedrine will make you so alert that you will amaze yourself with your sheer, staggering brilliance. Don't take Benzedrine lightly. Or vaguely.'

Rollo emerged into the beginnings of a full-scale flap. After days of stand-downs and scrubs, ops were on again. Group wanted 409 to make a maximum effort. An attack by an entire squadron was rare. The Wingco decided to go on this one. Gilchrist was on leave, so he took over C-Charlie. Then his phone rang for the fiftieth time and he learned that Mr Blazer was now fit to fly. Duff was pleased: a full squadron op, led by the CO! Just the occasion to be preserved on film for a grateful posterity. Always assuming any posterity would be left when this noisy carnage was over. He called Bellamy. 'Find a kite for Blazer,' he said. 'You know the drill. No plug-uglies, no stutterers, no maniacs.'

Bellamy had plenty of more important things to do. He ran through the list of pilots and eliminated most. He went to the remainder and tried to find a volunteer. He didn't expect any great enthusiasm and he didn't get any. As soon as a pilot said, 'Personally, I've got nothing against the chap ...' Bellamy knew what was coming: the other crew members thought Blazer would jinx the trip. Look what had happened to Polly Lomas. Bellamy was running out of names and hope when he saw Silk. 'My crew all think he's a Jonah,' Silk said, 'but I don't give a toss what they think. I'll take him.'

'Good. Fine.' Bellamy looked him in the eyes and saw a kind of battered tranquillity that worried him. 'No tricks, Silko. No jokes.'

'I was never more serious in my life,' Silk told him. 'As they say in the films.'

They found Rollo in the Mess, ordering a beer. 'Forget that,' Bellamy said. 'No alcohol before ops. I've got you a place in D-Dog tonight.'

Rollo's stomach muscles clenched. 'Lucky me,' he said. He had persuaded himself that he was brave, but now they were rushing him into it and he knew he was frightened of flying. His mouth seemed to be full of saliva. Even his body was betraying him.

'Grab your hat,' Silk said. 'We're doing an NFT.'

'Haven't got a hat.' Rollo looked around for rescue.

'Night-Flying Test,' Bellamy said.

'I know what it means.' They outnumbered him.

'D'you want a parachute?' Silk asked. 'If it doesn't work, you take it back and they give you another.' He gently steered Rollo out of the room. 'Very old joke, that. Past its best.'

Half an hour later, Rollo was sitting behind the main spar, sweating inside his flying clobber, looking at D-Dog shaking as if it was as frightened as he was. The front gunner was sitting beside him, reading a paperback western. Half its cover had been torn off. All that Rollo could see of the title was *Gulch*. It was like the inside of this Wimpy: slapdash, disorderly, cluttered. Everywhere he looked, bits of equipment were fixed to the sides and the roof. Behind them ran cables, tubes, wires. Even *ropes*. What were ropes doing in a bomber? The engines went from a roar to a howl. Rollo went from a sitting to a foetal position, hugged his parachute, closed his eyes. He knew D-Dog was moving. By closing his eyes really tightly and curling his toes, he was helping to keep the aeroplane in one piece. Forget it. Wasted effort. D-Dog was too heavy to take off. He opened his eyes. The bumps got harder. The gunner turned a page. Rollo started counting the seconds. He was going to die, so he was entitled to know exactly how long he'd lived. Then the awful thumping bouncing stopped, the engine note sweetened, and he realized that, for the first time in his life, he was flying.

Soon, the gunner stuffed his book in a pocket and went forward.

Rollo felt proud and ashamed at the same time: proud because he had conquered flight, and ashamed because he knew he should have done it long ago. Kate was right. This was the guts of the film. The rest was just trimmings. D-Dog was the hero. It was up to him to capture the courage.

He climbed over the main spar and stood behind the pilots. The noise was appalling.

After a while, the second pilot, Mallaby, noticed him and showed him where to plug in his intercom lead. At once the awful roar receded to a noise like surf. Then he heard Silk say: 'Welcome to the office. That's Newmarket below.' His voice was thin.

Rollo glanced down. Ah yes. Pretty little toytown. Piece of cake. 'I never thought the noise would be such a problem,' he said. Mallaby reached up and turned the intercom switch on Rollo's oxygen mask. 'Bloody noisy, isn't it?' Rollo said.

'The Pegasus-eighteen engine delivers nine hundred and twenty-five horsepower, and we have two of them, each about six feet from the cockpit. But really, the worst noise comes from the prop tips.' Silk pointed to the shimmering disc just to the left of his head. 'They're about two feet from my ear, at their closest. Spinning awfully fast, too.' He waved at the instrument panel. 'One of these dials tells us how fast, I forget which. Second pilot probably knows.'

'Oh, fearfully fast,' Mallaby said.

'But we're quite safe,' Silk said. 'The props hardly ever break. Anyway, Dog's covered in cloth, so that will protect us.'

Rollo was only half-listening. He was more interested in the way Silk used one hand to hold his oxygen mask over his mouth, in order to speak into his microphone. 'I can't see your lips when you do that,' he said.

'You won't hear my voice if I don't.'

'The point is, I don't see how I can film any chat between you two if half your mouth is covered up.'

'The cockpit's not a chatty place,' Mallaby said. The intercom accentuated his Australian accent. 'And when we go on oxygen you won't see anything except the eyes.'

'He has wonderfully expressive eyes,' Silk said. 'They speak volumes.'

Rollo decided to leave the chat problem until later. 'Is it all right if I take a look around the kite?'

Mallaby unstrapped himself and led the way. It was a short tour. Forward, and below the cockpit level, was the bomb aimer's position, looking down through a window in the floor. Good close-up possibilities here, Rollo thought, provided the scene could be lit. But the front gunner's position was out of sight, sealed off by a metal bulkhead. Mallaby opened it. The gunner and his guns filled the space, and a gale whistled through slots in the Perspex where the barrels poked out. Poor show. They went back, down the cluttered fuselage, past the navigator at his desk and the wireless op at his set. Essential jobs, but not exciting. The rear gunner was also invisible behind a steel bulkhead. And that was that. There was a bed to sit on. Mallaby returned to his office. Rollo sat on the bed and worried. Sometimes D-Dog flexed slightly, or twisted a little. Normally that would have frightened him. He ignored it. He had all the anxiety he could handle.

2

Rollo held a post mortem in Squadron Leader Bellamy's office. Kate and Silk were there; also the Engineer Officer.

Rollo said the difficulties of filming inside D-Dog made it impossible to follow his draft script, or indeed anybody's script. Dialogue in the cockpit was out of the question. Further back, the nav and the wireless op could make themselves heard, but only if they shouted, and you couldn't have people shouting all through a film.

'There must be a solution,' Kate said. She was no longer angry with Rollo. He'd been ill, fevered, confused. They were a team again; it was time to behave professionally. 'I've seen flying films where they have dialogue in the cockpit. Some guy comes in and tells the pilot the radio's bust and the pilot says do your best. They talk all the time.'

'Not in a Wimpy,' Silk said.

'I couldn't hear myself speak,' Rollo said. 'Those engines just beat your voice to death.'

'Well, that's what the intercom's for,' the Engineer Officer said.

'Everybody sounds *thin* on the intercom,' Rollo complained. 'Can't you make them deeper? More masculine?'

Bellamy had an idea. 'Why don't you forget the voices? Film the op, and then employ a commentator to describe what's happening.'

Rollo scowled. 'Might as well have *captions*, for Christ's sake.' Bellamy was offended. He remembered some urgent business, and left.

Kate pointed out that it was intercom dialogue or nothing. Rollo pointed out that he couldn't shoot film *and* record sound off the intercom. 'Then I'll do the sound,' she said. 'That's what I'm here for.' They both looked at Silk.

'Suits me,' Silk said. 'If that's what you want.' Now they all looked at the Engineer Officer. 'Leave me out of this!' he said. 'It's illegal, it's dangerous, and I'm going to have a pee.'

While he was out of the room, they made the decision. She wouldn't be the first woman to go on an op, Silk said. Many a Waaf had been smuggled into a Wimpy by her boyfriend. Everyone knew it happened. As long as nothing went wrong, nobody kicked up a fuss.

The Engineer Officer came back. 'We decided against it,' Silk said. 'I knew you would.'

'Next item,' Rollo said. 'Oxygen masks.' But there was to be no answer to that problem. The mike was in the mouthpiece of the mask, for obvious reasons. There was nothing to be done about the cramped shape of the cockpit, either, or the impossibility of getting a camera inside the gun turrets. Rollo hated abandoning the guns; they were his only chance of capturing real, close-up, explosive action. 'Couldn't I shoot over the gunner's shoulder as he lets fly at something?' he pleaded.

'All you'll get is a lot of dazzle. The turret's pitch-black.'

'We could fix up a little interior light.'

'No fear. I'm not illuminating my turrets for the benefit of a Jerry night fighter.'

Rollo had intended to ask for brighter lights inside the fuselage, and some tiny spotlights on the pilots' faces, but he knew when to quit. 'I guess I'll just have to grab whatever I can get,' he said.

'Look on the bright side,' Silk said.

Rollo tried, and failed. 'What bright side?'

'Port or starboard, take your pick, over the target. They chuck fireworks up, we chuck fireworks down, and nobody gets a wink of sleep.'

'You might find this useful,' the Engineer Officer said. He gave Kate an empty paint tin. 'It's a long trip.'

'Ah. How kind.'

'Not at all. When necessary, it can be emptied down the flare chute.'

'If you put out our incendiaries,' Silk said, 'the crew will never forgive you.'

3

David Butt's handwriting was neat and legible. His draft report was quite short. Constance Babington Smith read it; then re-read it.

'If Bomber Command sees this,' she said thoughtfully, 'they'll shoot you.'

He fingered the lobe of his left ear, and did not seem alarmed.

'And they'll miss you by a mile, if what you claim is true,' she said.

'Fact is fact,' he said.

'Yes, I agree. However, this report is a cookie, isn't it? And I'm trying to imagine what happens when you drop a cookie on the C-in-C, Bomber Command.'

'Good point. What do you think the response will be?'

'I think that blast waves will rock High Wycombe, shake the corridors at Air Ministry, and play merry hell with the War Cabinet.'

'Quite possibly. It's all out of my hands.'

For a moment they looked at each other. It was a curious occasion, possibly unique: two youngish, good-looking people, each highly expert but in different fields, each talking quietly and rationally about something which only they knew; something that would affect the course of a world war. 'Is there anything more I can do?' she asked.

'I'm hugely obliged to you already. I couldn't have got this far without the help of your Section. Essentially, mine is a statistical investigation. It all comes down to numbers. I'd be grateful if you would scrutinize my calculations and tell me if I've misplaced the decimal point.'

He went for a walk in the grounds. He was dead-heading a rose bush when she came out and gave him the pages. 'All correct,' she said.

Butt drove back to London, to his office in the War Cabinet Secretariat. In an hour he had a perfectly typed copy of his report.

He checked it twice, and went down the corridor and knocked on the door of Lord Cherwell, who was his boss and Churchill's Scientific Adviser. Cherwell had only recently been ennobled. He was better known as Professor Lindemann.

A lot of reports landed on Lindemann's desk. Long experience had taught him that the pages to look at were the first and the last. The first told you the purpose and the last told you the conclusions.

Page one said that Butt's report concerned his statistical investigation of RAF bombing of Germany on forty-eight nights between June 2 and July 25, 1941. He had examined one hundred separate raids on twenty-eight different targets. He had studied six hundred and fifty photographs taken during night operations, as well as operational summaries of Intelligence reports, and other information.

Lindemann turned to the conclusions. He raised one eyebrow, but only briefly.

Lindemann was a hard man. He understood flying. For twenty-five years he had studied aeronautics, and that included a spell as a test pilot. Without doubt he was a brilliant scientist, but he combined brilliance with a harsh and intolerant manner. He was often dismissive of other scientists, even contemptuous, if he disagreed with them. Now he gave Butt, who was half his age, the cold stare that might mean anything.

'Mr Butt,' he said. 'So that there may be no doubt in anybody's mind, least of all the Prime Minister's ... Your principal conclusion is that when Bomber Command attacked a target, two out of three aircraft failed to get within five miles of that target.'

'Average figure for Europe, sir. Not all targets were in Germany.'

'So I see. Targets in France produced better results, you say. Two out of three bombers got within five miles. But over Germany, results were worse. Only one bomber in four got within five miles. Do I understand you correctly? This is what you claim your investigations have found?'

'Yes, sir.'

'And over the Ruhr ...' Lindemann leaned back and gazed at the ceiling light for several seconds. When he spoke again, his voice was softer. 'Over the Ruhr, you say that only one bomber in *ten* got within five miles of its target.'

'Again, an average figure, sir.'

'Average. So it was sometimes *less* than one in ten?'

'When the moon was new and haze was thick, the proportion was one in fifteen, sir. Given full moon and no haze, it improved considerably. However, with the increasing intensity of anti-aircraft fire, the proportion worsened. The figures are on page seven, sir.'

'I am to inform the Prime Minister that, for as long as the RAF has been sending aircraft to bomb Germany, three out of four bombers have failed to find – let alone hit – their target. That is what you wish me to say, is it?'

Butt thought fast, and decided that he wasn't going to be bullied by Lindemann. 'I'm not competent to suggest what you should tell the Prime Minister, sir. But I think you should know that the full story of Bomber Command's effectiveness is worse than those figures indicate.'

Lindemann flicked through the pages. 'Over Europe, two out of three bombers fail to reach their target. Over Germany, three out of four. Over the Ruhr, nine out of ten. How can the picture be any worse, Mr Butt?'

'Sir, my investigation concerned the number of aircraft that were recorded by Bomber Command as having attacked their primary target. But on those raids, Bomber Command sent many aircraft which did not claim to have attacked their targets. I examined one hundred raids. Bomber Command sent a total of just over six thousand aircraft on those raids. Just over two thousand reported that they failed to reach the target, and so they were not included in my study. If we add to my findings this additional one third of all aircraft despatched – those which, by their own account, did not attack – then the conclusion must be that, of the total aircraft despatched, only one fifth reached their target. Therefore ...' Butt stopped. Lindemann had raised a hand.

'Enough, Mr Butt. In a nutshell: of every hundred British bombers that took off, twenty bombed the target and eighty failed. That's what you're saying.'

Butt thought: *You don't trap me like that.* 'My brief did not include the actual bombing of the target, sir.'

'If they reached it, why wouldn't they bomb it?'

'Sir, for the purpose of my investigation, the target area was defined as having a radius of five miles. This amounts to an area of over seventy-five square miles. Any bomb that fell inside that area was considered to have hit the target area.'

'Seventy-five square miles,' Lindemann said. 'A very large city.'

'Only Berlin covers such an area, sir.'

'Which means any other target area must consist of ... what?'

'Largely of open country, sir.'

'Fields.'

'Yes, sir.'

'Bomber Command has been killing cows.'

Butt hesitated. *He knows, anyway*, he thought. 'And aircrew, sir,' he said.

'Thank you, Mr Butt. We are all in your debt.'

Butt went out. Lindemann weighed the report in his hand. 'High explosive,' he said aloud.

4

Kate and Rollo attended the briefing. By now they were a familiar presence.

The target was Hanover.

Nobody cheered, but there was a slight feeling of relaxation. It could have been worse. It could have been the Ruhr, or a long haul like Frankfurt or Mannheim. Hanover was only about a hundred miles from the German coast. It meant a long slog across the North Sea, but 409 was accustomed to that.

The briefing followed its usual pattern. It would be a biggish raid: sixty Wellingtons and thirty Hampdens. Hanover contained several factories that were crucial to the German war machine and it was an important communications centre. The Aiming Point was the railway station, easily identified because the Masch See, a lake more than a mile long and shaped rather like a Yale key, pointed towards it. The Met man said there was a fifty-fifty risk of some electrical storm activity over the North Sea but it was moving away northwards and should be replaced with clear skies. 'The predicted winds ...' he announced and waited while they chanted their reply, before he said, 'Are south-westerly over Germany, thirty knots, becoming westerly, twenty knots, for your return over the North Sea. No fog is expected.' The Wingco warned them to be ready for heavy light flak and couldn't understand why they laughed. The group captain told them this was a chance to give Hitler a bloody nose, so strike hard. Good luck. And that was that.

The room emptied, until only Silk and Skull were left. Skull was collecting maps and photographs and Intelligence summaries.

'You remember the lovely Zoë? Langham's popsy?' Silk said. 'You went to one of their parties.'

'No.'

'Oh. Stupid of me. Of course, you weren't at Kindrick, were you? The thing is, Zoë turned up here last week, looking for me so she said, and that was very enjoyable, up to a point. Now she's gone back to London, but I can't get her out of my mind. Maybe I ought to ask her to marry me. What d'you think?'

'Ask her.' Skull rolled up a map and slipped a rubber band around it.

'Trouble is, she's such a terrible liar.'

'The truth is rationed like margarine nowadays. Was this briefing honest? Are the interrogations honest? Is the man Blazer honest? He lives in a world of make-believe. Are you honest?'

Silk wondered. 'Up to a point,' he said. He watched Skull cram papers into a file. Some got torn. 'Well, I'd better push off,' he said. 'Thanks for the advice.'

'I was lying,' Skull said. 'Not that it matters.'

5

Engines were briefly tested sixty minutes before take-off. After that, crews had to wait at their aeroplane. With nothing left to do, it was the worst hour of the day. Most men sat or lay on the grass, saying very little, thinking too much, some wondering how they came to volunteer for such a bitch of a job, and all pushing to the backs of their minds the knowledge that it was a stone-cold certainty someone, maybe not on this squadron, but someone, somewhere, was going to get the chop before tomorrow. It was a long hour that felt like punishment for no offence. Even Silk was subdued. And then, while nobody was looking, the minutes had sneaked by and the first engines fired. None of D-Dog's crew moved.

After a while, with engines all along dispersal joining in, Rollo asked Silk why he wasn't starting-up.

'Dog's last in the queue. I'm not going to waste fuel and risk over-heating the engines.'

'Last? I thought everyone took off in alphabetical order.'

'We're carrying the cookie. The four-thousand-pounder. It makes sense for us to go last.' He stretched and yawned. 'Pug Duff would never speak to me again if Dog fell on her face halfway down the flare-path and ruined the grass.' He strolled away.

Rollo went to Kate. She was bundled up in flying gear, all of it scrounged by Silk, and the warmth had made her drowsy. 'Wake up,' he said. How could she sleep at a time like this? 'We're carrying the cookie. It's a bomb as big as a bus.'

'I know. Micky Mallaby told me.'

He found the second pilot admiring the sunset. 'This cookie we've got on board,' he said. 'Why hasn't everyone got one?'

'Most of the Wimpys haven't been adapted yet. Their bomb bays aren't big enough. Haven't you seen a cookie? It looks like two big dustbins welded together, end to end.'

'I should have been told. I could have filmed it.'

'Dunno anything about that, mate. Ask Woody. He's got to drop the bloody thing.'

The crew were drifting towards the bomber. Rollo, now beginning to be excited by the news, intercepted Woodman. 'This cookie will make a hell of a bang, won't it?' he asked. 'I mean to say, four thousand pounds of TNT, that'll blow the railway station to bits, won't it?'

'If we hit it. A cookie's not a real bomb. It hasn't got a tail. It's got the ballistic properties of a brick shit-house. Might go anywhere. I'll be pleased if it lands within a mile of the AP.'

Rollo was discouraged, but not for long. When he was sitting next to Kate, behind the main spar, and D-Dog was taxying along the perimeter track, he said: 'If I can catch this cookie when it explodes, we could have the perfect climax. It'll look like the crack of doom.' He was so excited that he forgot to clench his toes when Silk took Dog roaring down the flare-path and, creaking and groaning under its load, into the early night.

6

There was still some light at four thousand. Rollo leaned into the cockpit and filmed Silk flying Dog. He shot the shimmer of a prop disc and changed focus to get the English coastline, far below. He thought the surf looked like toothpaste and the sea looked like oilskin. Black oilskin. Ten seconds of that was plenty.

Kate was taking a feed from the intercom and playing it straight onto the soundtrack. Rollo persuaded Silk and Mallory to say something technical, so they exchanged a few words about keeping an eye on the cylinder-head temperatures. When they finished, the nav gave Silk a new course: eighty-four degrees. Silk did something to the compass, and told everyone to watch out for night fighters. Rollo was pleased. It all added up to a nice little sequence: D-Dog, off to war.

He had seen the map; he knew that crossing the North Sea would take about two hours. No point in carrying a heavy camera all that way, so he put it in its bag. Already his knees ached slightly, from constant bending in order to soften the bumps and dips of flying. D-Dog was not a perfect platform for a cameraman.

At six thousand, and still climbing, Silk switched on the autopilot. Rollo took great interest. Outside, it was night; the only light in the cockpit came from the dials and gauges, a dim green glow, not enough to let him shoot this scene. Some other time, he thought.

Silk kept his hands on his thighs, and he never stopped checking the instrument panel. 'This is just testing,' he told Rollo. 'I don't trust George. George is a treacherous bastard. He's liable to go haywire, and then if you don't disengage him fast, he'll kill you. That's why we keep a fire axe here.' He pointed to the axe, at the second pilot's side.

'If George gets the hump, I chop through his hydraulics,' Mallaby said. 'Cut his bloody head off.'

'Crikey,' Rollo said. It seemed a feeble comment.

He watched the wheel on the control column turn an inch or so, one way or the other. Sometimes the stick wandered back and forth. The rudder bar was rarely still. 'George is a bit restless, isn't he?' he asked.

'No, that's Dog. She's a typical Wimpy, always bending and stretching. It affects the control runs. That's the cables going out to the wings and back to the tail. Dog twists, the controls move, George corrects. Busy man, George.'

'It's what makes the Wimpy so tough,' Mallaby said. 'She's all basket-weave. Alloy basketweave. The strength is in the shape. You can't break her back because she hasn't got a spine. Bloody clever.'

'But she does fidget,' Silk said. 'Isn't that right, Chubby?'

'Right, Skip,' the rear gunner said. 'She likes to wag her tail.'

'She does it to keep you awake.'

'It's like a fairground ride back here.'

'Chubby's always on the *qui vive*,' Silk said to Rollo. 'I know because every time he rotates his turret, his guns act as a little rudder and Dog does a little shimmy. And that's enough of George.' He disengaged the autopilot. 'I haven't got time to do that if we get jumped by a Hun.'

Rollo watched his face. Silk's eyes were always moving. He had a routine: he looked at the compass; then at the airspeed indicator; at the horizon; at the moon, which was just rising; at the sea; at other instruments, oil pressures, maybe, or fuel gauges, or engine temperatures; then back to the compass again. An endless check. And the op had only just begun. Rollo felt tired. He went back to the rest bed and sat beside Kate. All the interior lights had been dimmed until they were soft sparks in the dark. That must be how Silk wanted it.

He put his mouth close to her ear and shouted: 'I could do with some coffee.'

She shouted back: 'No coffee until we reach the North Sea on the way home. Otherwise – bad luck.'

Bloody hell, he thought. *Already she knows more than me.* Soon they climbed above eight thousand and everyone was on oxygen and the camera crew had nothing to do but look at the blackness and endure the bumps and shudders and the taste of wet rubber.

7

Group Captain Rafferty had a good dinner: brown Windsor soup, lamb stew with roast potatoes and leeks, apple pie and custard. He knew it was going to be a long night. Rafferty had a big body; it needed plenty of fuel. He had a second helping of apple pie.

409 Squadron would still be outward bound, over the North Sea. Rafferty left the Mess and looked at the weather. Ten thousand stars and not one wisp of mist. Good. *Don't let me down tonight*, he told the sky, *not with a maximum effort in the air*. Somewhere near Hanover, five hundred miles away, his opposite number in a Luftwaffe night fighter base was probably looking at the same stars and having similar thoughts. *Well, you started it, chum*, Rafferty told him. *Now watch Bomber Command finish it*. From the corner of his eye he glimpsed a shooting star come and go so fast that if you blinked, you missed it. Rafferty wasn't a poetic man but he thought he'd witnessed something symbolic, if only he could put words to it.

No, that was hopeless. He went indoors and found the adjutant. They went to a quiet corner of the ante-room and played draughts for a shilling a game. Uncle was good at draughts. Not slapdash, but he didn't brood either. Made his move, liked to attack. Rafferty approved of that. He lost seven shillings, fought back and was a shilling up, and then they decided to have a coffee break. 'Bring some for Mr Skelton too,' Rafferty told the Mess servant. To Uncle he said, 'He's been waiting nearly an hour for us to finish playing. Too well-mannered to interrupt, of course. My compliments to Mr Skelton,' he said to the servant, 'and would he be so kind as to join us.'

Skull sat at their table. He had a large buff envelope. They each made the usual polite remarks. The weather was praised. Coffee came.

Rafferty felt unusually friendly towards Skull. He still regarded him as part of the furniture, like all Intelligence Officers, useful but not essential; somewhere between catering and accounts. However, the man had been plucky enough to go on an op, which meant he'd had a whiff of grapeshot, whatever that might be, so he wasn't a dead loss. 'Greenwell's Glory,' he said. 'Remember that afternoon, Skull? You and your trout flies really bamboozled that dreadful brigadier. Best bit of Intelligence work you've done.'

'Thank you, sir. If my best contribution is to recognize trout flies, my efforts here would seem to be wasted.'

'It was a joke, old boy. Uncle was amused. Laugh, Uncle.'

'Ha ha,' the adjutant said. 'Ho ho.'

'There you are. Relax, Skull. Loosen your stays.'

'Was this a joke, sir?' Skull took three big photographs from his envelope and spread them on the table. 'The Essen raid,' he said. They were night shots, taken by the flash of a flare from a bomber. Written across each of them in red Chinagraph was a single word: *Unacceptable*.

'Pug Duff's writing,' the adjutant said.

'What does he mean?' Rafferty asked. 'The print's no good, or he doesn't like what's on it?'

'The latter,' Skull said. 'I asked him why, and he said they don't provide a true picture of bombing by 409 and the photographs must not be sent to Group.'

Rafferty put his glasses on and picked up a print. 'Where's the target?' he said. 'I can't see much detail. Is it blurred?'

'The target isn't there,' Skull said. 'There's no detail on that picture because it's mostly farmland. Pasture. Some forest.'

Rafferty studied the other two prints. 'Plenty of built-up areas here. Flak, too. Are those bomb-bursts?'

'Yes, sir. But not on Essen. This photograph was taken over Dorsten, a small town about twenty miles north-east of Essen. The other shows Solingen, another small town about twenty-five miles south of Essen.'

'And you suspect the worst,' Rafferty said.

'If those three Wellingtons hit Dorsten, Solingen and a field, they didn't hit Essen, sir, no matter what the CO decides.'

'Don't rush your fences, old chap,' the adjutant said. He stretched his legs and waggled his feet. 'One thing I've learned about war is never to assume that anything will work as planned, especially the equipment. How do we know that those cameras did their stuff properly?' He searched for his tobacco pouch. 'Maybe the Wimpys bombed Essen but the cameras clicked five minutes too late. A Wimpy can be twenty miles away in five minutes.'

'Or maybe they were five minutes too early,' Rafferty suggested.

The adjutant pointed his pipe at Skull. 'Never underestimate the power of the cock-up,' he said.

'On that basis, sir, we might as well disregard *all* photographs.'

Rafferty gave his most paternal smile. 'I wouldn't lose a moment's sleep if you did. I'll tell you what *would* upset me, Skull, and what I won't tolerate for an instant, and that's any chivvying and harassing of a crew because a photograph is at odds with their report. Those boys have been through seventeen different types of hell, all night long, they may have seen their comrades killed, and they don't deserve to face hostile questioning when what they really need is to have their morale reinforced.'

'You should know that, Skull,' the adjutant said. 'It's no picnic over Germany, is it?'

'None of that is relevant to the question of accuracy,' Skull insisted. 'We can't award a crew a direct hit on the target because we feel they *deserve* it, can we? Oh, Christ ...' He paused, and took a deep breath. 'This is exactly what got me kicked out of Fighter Command.'

'You're rambling, old chap,' Rafferty said. 'It's that knock on the head you got over Essen.'

'It was a nose-bleed.'

'Have a nap,' the adjutant advised. He was setting up the draughts board. 'You've been overdoing it again.'

8

D-Dog was the last Wellington to leave Coney Garth, so by the time she reached the German coast the others had stirred up the defences. Badger, in Dog's front turret, had no need to say, 'Enemy coast ahead.' Searchlights told that story. But he said it anyway. Being the first to spot landfalls was one of the few rewards of sitting in the coldest place in the aircraft. Silk acknowledged. 'Looks like Borkum, skip,' Badger said. His voice was as light as a ploughboy's.

Rollo felt stiff in the limbs and thick in the head. Kate was leaning against him, half-asleep. He saw Woodman get up from the nav's table and go forward. He shook Kate. They stumbled after Woodman, climbed over the main spar and re-plugged their intercoms. Now the cockpit area was very crowded. Woodman made space for them and pointed down. 'See that island? Shaped like a V? That's Borkum. Good pinpoint. Tells us we're on track.'

Rollo looked at the altimeter: over thirteen thousand feet. He looked again at Borkum. It was like a collar stud on a carpet. There were searchlights ahead, so the real coastline couldn't be far away. That might be worth filming. He fetched the camera from his bag, checked that it was loaded, no hairs in the lens, all correct, and by the time he got back to the cockpit the aeroplane was vibrating brutally. It was like being inside a bass drum on a bandstand.

He waited. Maybe this would pass. It got worse. He put the camera to his eye and everything was a fine blur. The thin sticks of searchlights were fat and fuzzy. He put the camera down and plugged in his intercom. 'Why is everything shaking?' he asked.

'I de-synchronized the engines,' Silk said. 'They're not making the same revs. Not speaking the same language.'

'It buggers up Jerry's sound locators,' Mallaby said.

'De-synch is good for your health,' Silk said.

'It's shaking the fillings out of my teeth,' Rollo said. 'I can't hold the camera still.'

'Let it shake, then,' Mallaby said. 'Shoot the truth.'

Was that a joke? Rollo couldn't tell. Both pilots were wearing their goggles, so he couldn't even see their eyes. He gave Kate a thumbs-down. By now Dog was over the mainland and searchlights were swinging briskly, prodding corners of the sky, standing still as if they had lost interest, then suddenly hunting again. The flak was colourful, more like festival celebrations than high explosive. Lights pulsed from the ground, red and yellow, some green; they were in no hurry until their final rush. Dog was above much of this, but plenty of star-shaped explosions reached her level. One of them burst alongside, maybe a hundred yards away, and Dog caught the fringe of the blast and lurched. Silk lost height and swung onto a new course. Rollo got a glimpse of more shellbursts, high up where they would have been. Then Dog was through the coastal belt. Silk pushed up his goggles, and synchronized the engines. They ran as smoothly as sewing machines. Rollo stopped grinding his teeth. But now he could see nothing but night: nothing worth filming.

Kate tapped him on the shoulder and led him back to the nav position. They plugged in and she pointed at Woodman's map of northern Germany. 'Worth a few feet of film?' she said. The map was marked with patches of red, and Woodman had plotted a twisting course to avoid them.

'Defended areas,' Woodman said. 'Emden, Oldenburg, Bremen, Osnabruck, and a few Luftwaffe fields here and there. Not a good idea to fly straight to Hanover.'

'Can you say something about that to the pilot?'

'He knows already.'

'Well, tell him anyway.'

Rollo filmed the navigator, full figure, hard at work; then head and shoulders, turning his intercom switch, saying: 'Hullo, skip. We'd better fly a zigzag course, to miss the places where we know Jerry's got a lot of flak batteries and searchlights.'

'What a bloody boring idea,' Silk said. 'I think I'll go down and strafe a few hospitals.'

'Don't worry,' Kate told Woodman. 'We can edit that out.'

'Now point at the map,' Rollo said. 'Follow the zigzag with your finger. Slowly.' He filmed the navigator's hand in close-up.

Another little sequence in the can.

Every few minutes, Woodman gave Silk a change of course. Rollo went to the cockpit a couple of times. He saw searchlights in the far distance and what might have been flak twinkling, but he knew it would be a waste of film. A lot of cloud was building up, white as cauliflower in the moonlight. The flak would look like stars and the searchlights would look like cracks in somebody's blackout. He went back to the bed. His feet were cold and he was afraid to stamp them. The cookie was only inches beneath his boots.

He could feel this opportunity slipping away from him. No chance to film the enemy coast, or the belt of lights and guns behind it. Unable to film the all-important faces of the crew. Not allowed in the gun turrets. What was left? Flak over Hanover: presumably that would be highly filmable, unless Silk desynchronized again. As for the climax, dropping the cookie, he suddenly realized he wouldn't see it leave Dog, wouldn't see it fall, might not see it explode if a wing obscured his view. Then what? A long trudge home, also in blackness. Rollo felt cramp in his left calf. His parachute harness was too tight in the crutch. The awful truth came to him: bomber ops were not necessarily exciting. They were endlessly threatening and frightening and difficult, but the drama was all in the danger and the danger was hidden by the night. You had to fly on ops to know the fear of sudden death, and he couldn't film fear. With everyone wearing oxygen masks, he couldn't even film the *look* of fear. He'd drawn a double blank. That was when Chubb, in the rear turret, said: 'Fighter behind.'

Silk said, 'Which side?'

'Port quarter, a thousand feet below. Five hundred yards away. He's climbing, in and out of cloud, skip.'

'Wireless op to the astrodome,' Silk said. 'Search starboard, Mac.'

'On my way, skip.'

Silence for half a minute. Silk had dropped the left wing a bit to give the rear gunner a better view. 'Lost him, skip,' Chubb said, and immediately shouted, 'Fighter! Turn starboard!' but before Silk could swing the Wellington, Chubb was firing and the harsh chatter of his guns cut through the engine-roar. Then nothing. Rollo stood and cursed. Here was battle, behind closed doors. 'He's buggered off, skip,' Chubb said. 'Dived away. I scared him.'

'Where there's one, there's two,' Silk said. 'Keep searching to starboard, Mac.'

Campbell was standing on a box, with his head in the astrodome, just like the dome on top of the flare-path caravan. *All it needs is a tiny spotlight on his face,* Rollo thought. *Make a hell of a shot. Also a hell of a target.* Another example of Blazer's Law of Bomber Ops. If it's worth filming, you can't see it.

'Some bastard's out there, skip,' Campbell said. 'Maybe one of ours, maybe not. He's following us. Starboard quarter.'

'Don't like it,' Silk said. 'We'll run away and hide.'

He turned towards a sprawling, top-heavy cloudbank. He put the nose down a touch, opened the throttles an inch, and drove into a bleak and gloomy fog. Now he was flying on instruments alone. He sent Campbell back to his radio.

Woodman kept feeding course adjustments. 'Twenty-five minutes to target,' he said. Silk thanked him. Kate, lying on the bed and dreaming of hot soup, was impressed by everybody's calmness. They were as matter-of-fact as if they were delivering coal in Camberwell. Rollo stood and watched the nav draw neat lines and make tidy calculations. There was nothing else to watch. The floor suddenly slanted and he fell to his knees. Kate rolled off the bed. Woodman was grabbing his pencils and maps. In the cockpit, Silk and Mallaby were flung against their straps as the Wimpy plunged into a hole, hit bottom and was kicked sideways. Silk laboured and won back some control but she still kept bouncing and plunging. They knew what was wrong. Cumulo-nimbus cloud was full of tortured air. The Met man had predicted a risk of electrical storms over the North Sea. He'd got the risk right but the place wrong: the storms were still over Germany. Lightning flashes were making the cloud bright. The electrical discharge swamped Dog from end to end and filled her with a pale glow. This was St Elmo's Fire, and the crew had experienced it before, but never so intensely. A blue flame danced from every external point. The propellers were brilliant with multicoloured light; they spun like Catherine wheels. The gunners were looking at flames a yard long sparking between their sights. In the cockpit the instruments were drunk and incapable. That was when lightning struck Dog.

Kate, flat on the floor, was convinced the bang and the flash had broken the Wimpy in half. But when she could see again, Dog was still in one piece, still being bucked and kicked by the cu-nim. Parts of the radio were red-hot and Campbell was beating out a small fire. Just when Rollo's brain told him he should be filming this, the flow of St Elmo's Fire vanished. Silk had flown the bomber out of cloud and into clean air.

He tried to do an intercom check and nobody answered. The intercom was dead. He sent Mallaby to make a tour of Dog. He came back and said everyone was intact. Bruised and scraped, but intact.

Two problems.

The compass was spinning, reversing, chasing its tail. It needed time to recover its wits. And the port engine was surging. Its revs climbed and fell, climbed and fell. The lopsided pull sent Dog wandering about the sky. Silk kept her out of cloud and nursed the engines back to health and harmony. Recovery took many minutes, and Dog lost much height. In the end she was down to six thousand feet, and Silk was lost.

He got unstrapped and slid out of his seat and let Mallaby take the controls. Silk clambered over the spar and had a shouted conference with the navigator. They were off oxygen, so talk was easier. Woodman had tried to keep track of all the twists and turns, but without a compass it was an impossible task. What he needed was a good pinpoint. He went forward. Silk peered at the smoking radio and had a few words with Campbell. Then he spoke to Rollo and Kate.

'Awfully dull, isn't it?' he bawled. 'You should have brought a book.'

Rollo felt useless. He had to do something, so he touched the goggles on Silk's forehead. 'Why wear these?'

'In case we get a brick through the window. Shocking draught.' He went back to his office.

Rollo tried to picture a pilot sitting in the hurricane blast that would rage through a smashed windscreen. His imagination was too good, and he turned it off. The nav hadn't returned. Rollo could see he wasn't in the cockpit. It didn't take long to work out that Woodman must be in the bomb-aimer's position. No flak, no search-lights, so Dog wasn't over the target. Woodman was looking for it. The nav was peering through the window, trying to find Hanover. Silk was stooging around Germany, totally lost, and what's more the gunners couldn't call him if they saw a fighter, because the intercom was kaput. Rollo was about to tell all this to Kate when he saw that she was being sick into her paint tin. He decided that she didn't need to know. He gave her his handkerchief, to wipe her face.

9

The compass settled down and behaved itself. Woodman found a pinpoint. He scrambled up the tunnel from the bomb-aimer's posi-tion and handed Silk a piece of paper with one word on it: Hamelin. Silk shouted, 'Pied Piper?' Woodman lip-read and nodded. Mallaby circled, losing height until they were under the lowest cloud. By then Woodman had scribbled:

> Hamelin Town's in Brunswick,
> By famous Hanover city;
> The river Weser, deep and wide,
> Washes its walls on the southern side.
> Robert Browning, poet.

Silk read it and smiled. They were looking at a town that fitted the description perfectly. A pair of heavy machine guns started pumping tracer, nowhere near Dog, just red stitches on black cloth. Small garrison in Hamelin, probably. Nothing worth defending. All the rats had gone.

After that it was simple. Hamelin was south-west of Hanover. Precise navigation wasn't necessary. Soon the flicker of searchlight beams, gun flashes, bomb bursts and fires guided Dog to the target. Mallaby had coaxed her up to eight thousand. That was her limit. Silk took over the controls and tried to bounce her higher, diving a little and then climbing on full power. It usually worked. Not tonight. Not with this great pig of a cookie in her belly, and the port engine not pulling its weight. High above, Wimpys and Hampdens were unloading bombs. If one incendiary fell out of the night and hit a wing, it might burn a hole so big that even a Wimpy couldn't survive. Best not to think about that. Other trouble was nearer to hand.

Eight thousand was well within the range of light flak. The Hanover searchlights were slicing up the sky. Clouds reflected their beams and turned parts of the night to twilight. Everywhere, tracer criss-crossed in a silent stutter of red and yellow or blue and green. Many shellbursts seemed as harmless as crackerjacks, unless the burst came close enough to create a jagged flash that leaped out of nowhere like an ambush. If you could smell its peppery stink, it was very close. If you could hear the rattle of hot shrapnel on the bomber, it was too close.

Silk's first reaction when they reached Hanover was that he'd never seen flak so thick and nobody could get through it untouched. Rollo's first reaction was sheer glee. He filmed everything. The light was excellent. Tracer left the ground so slowly that he had time to select it, focus on it, follow it all the way to its final rush of brilliance past the Wimpy. He filmed the lights on the ground: the blink of flak batteries, the splash of bombs exploding, the ragged shape of burning buildings. This was the pay-off. This made the whole trip worthwhile. It was only when he stopped to reload that he realized the sound was all wrong. There was no sound. All this mayhem was drowned out by the roar of the engines. Every bang was mute. That was no good. He told himself: *Dub in bangs*.

Woodman was a good bomb-aimer, but without intercom he was helpless, he couldn't tell his pilot to go left or right or hold steady. He had thrown the switches that gave control of the bombload to the pilot, and now he stood in the cockpit, leaning over Silk's shoulder, and together they tried to find the railway station. There was some cloud, and a lot of smoke. Maybe the AP was under the smoke. Maybe it didn't exist any more. He heard an old familiar sound, a *bok-bok*, something like two halves of a coconut knocking together: heavy flak, not far off. Silk weaved, changed direction, couldn't go up so he went down, anything to baffle the gunners. But lower was not safer. Soon there were more *bok-boks*. A searchlight flicked their wingtip and kept going. A poor sodding Hampden was not so lucky. It was pinned in a cone, and kept twisting and writhing but the lights tracked every dive, every turn, while the heavy flak blew holes in the cone and, eventually, in the Hampden.

In the end, Silk dumped the bloody bomb. Smoke was getting worse, some from fires, some perhaps from German smoke generators. He looked at Woodman, and Woodman shrugged. Silk opened the bomb doors. The slipstream hit them and Dog vibrated. Rollo stopped filming. Silk leaned forward and pressed the bomb-release button, and the bomber gave a little leap of relief. Forget the flash, forget the photograph. Shut the bomb doors, open the throttles and piss off out of this madhouse.

The cookie didn't whistle, Rollo thought. *That won't do. Bombs always whistle in the movies. Dub it in later.*

The bomb doors haven't shut, Silk thought. Dog was still vibrating in the old familiar way. This was turning into a dodgy op. He turned the bomb-door handle again. And again. No joy.

It knocked a good twenty miles an hour off the airspeed. And of course Dog wouldn't climb an inch with those doors dragging against the slipstream.

Silk cruised slowly over Hanover, while the flak never slackened. At times like this he took encouragement from the bluebottle in the rainstorm. Logically, it should get knocked to the ground. Yet it flew on. How? Because there was always more space between the raindrops. The trick was to find the space. A silly thought. But it took his mind off the storm of high explosive.

He flew straight. If he weaved, it would only take longer to escape. Maybe the German gunners couldn't believe that any RAF pilot would be so stupid as to fly so low, so slow, so straight; maybe it spoiled their aim. Or maybe the gods of war were tired of D-Dog. Maybe they'd gone off to pull the wings from some other butterfly.

Because, amazingly, things got better. Silk left the flak and the search-lights behind him; and Campbell, with nothing to do since his radio went up in flames, found the fault in the intercom. The headphones came alive. Woodman went back to his nav table and worked on a zigzag route to the coast. 'New course, skipper,' he said. 'Two eight five. That puts us west of the Luftwaffe base at Sulingen.'

'Two eight five. Is that based on the predicted winds?'

'Yes. They were pretty accurate over the North Sea. Spot-on, in fact.'

'The electrical storms are in the wrong place, Woody. Moving north, perhaps, but still over Germany. Predicted winds could be up the creek.'

'They could.' Woodman tidied up the numbers in his latest calculation, lengthening the vertical line of a 4, improving the tail of a 3. 'Any suggestions?'

'A pinpoint would be nice. Chubby, Badge: find a nice pinpoint for the nav and he'll buy you a drink.'

Rollo sat on the bed, beside Kate. Now that the cookie had been dropped and the flak had failed to kill them, he felt a huge sense of anticlimax. The raid had been successful, or at least he supposed so, but what visible difference had it made? For the purposes of his film, none. Maybe the cookie hadn't exploded. Plenty of dud bombs fell on London. And the job wasn't finished, there was still the long grind home over the North Sea. He felt useless, physically drained yet mentally dissatisfied. How did these men do it? Hanover wasn't even a very long trip. Imagine when Berlin was the target. Berlin was almost in Poland, for God's sake. Thirty ops made a tour, so they said. Nobody should be made to do this thirty times. Yet they were all volunteers. Even so, thirty ops ... Thirty chances to get the chop. Why didn't it drive them mad? Maybe it did, some of them. Maybe anyone who went crackers got shunted off the base before he could infect the rest. Rollo shuddered, partly at the idea, partly from the aching cold, partly because the entire bloody Wimpy was shuddering.

10

Nothing much happened for half an hour. Kate dozed. Rollo couldn't rest, he was too cold to feel his feet, his brain was swamped by engine roar, he had no sense of time and not enough energy to look at his watch, and anxiety nagged him. The shots of Hanover were good but they didn't add up to a film, and he couldn't see where the rest was coming from.

Silk was not unhappy. He never allowed himself to be happy; that would have interfered with his cockpit routine. But Dog's fuel tanks were lighter and she was moving faster. Not enough to escape a night fighter, and that was still a risk. He might have a chance to dodge into some clouds, but they were ugly monsters and if one turned out to be cu-nim, Dog with her bomb doors hanging down might not come out the other side.

Then flak began to break out like a skin disease. No searchlights, just flak. Someone down there was good at his job. 'Wireless op, fire off flares,' Silk ordered. 'Red and yellow.' Campbell moved fast. Within seconds he had the pistol in the flare chute. Red and yellow signals arced into the night.

The flak stopped. Silk counted to twenty. Still no flak. 'And for my next trick,' he said.

Rollo pressed his intercom switch. 'What was all that about?'

'Trick of the trade. Red and yellow flares used to be the Luftwaffe distress signal. Mind you, it doesn't always work.'

It didn't work ten minutes later. Woodman estimated they were near the German coast, and the sudden stabs of searchlights and ripples of flak and coloured feelers of tracer suggested he was right. When the distress signal had no effect, Silk told the gunners to fire at the searchlights, and Rollo got some good shots of tracer streaking down from the front guns. Badger claimed to hit a searchlight. It certainly went out. He said, 'Bull's-eye!' Silk said something, but nobody heard him. A shell exploded underneath Dog and the blast hurled the Wellington up and over, until she was standing on a wingtip. Not for long. She was still flying but as she fell, her nose was too high. She stalled and, rather wearily, began to spin.

Silk did what his instructors had told him, years ago: close the throttles, centralize the stick, apply full rudder opposite to the spin, pause, then push the stick forward. The kite will dive and the spin will stop. Total failure. Maybe the controls had been hit. Maybe Wimpys were different. Meanwhile Dog kept rotating, rather ponderously, as if looking for a place to lie down. And kept falling. Several searchlights found her. Now the inside of the fuselage was painted a fierce silver-white. The camera team, the nav, the op, all covered their eyes. Silk and Mallaby were dazzled. Badger and Chubb were still firing. German bullets were punching holes in the fabric. It was a toss-up whether Dog crashed before the flak got her. Silk remembered Langham and the stabilized yaw.

He reached blindly for the throttles, shut the outer engine and opened the inner engine to maximum revs, combat limit, full boost, and commended his soul to Almighty God. The inner engine took command. The outer wing, its engine dragging instead of driving, dropped. The spin was killed. Dog lifted her tail and dived.

That was what Silk believed happened. But what did Silk know? He couldn't see, he was flying by memory, by instinct, by feel. Maybe another shellburst had kicked the Wimpy out of its spin. Who can tell? Who cares? He harmonized the engines and eased the control column back until long experience told him the aircraft should be more or less level.

One advantage of being dazzled was that he couldn't see how bad the flak was. By the time he'd got his sight back, the searchlights were losing him. Soon the flak was behind Dog, too.

'New course, skip,' the nav said. 'Steer three three zero.'

Silk was surprised to hear from him. He had taken it for granted that half the crew were dead. He made an intercom check and everyone answered except Campbell, the wireless op. 'He's got a bit of steel in the backside,' Woodman reported. 'Shell splinter, I expect. He's on the bed.'

Mallaby left the cockpit to check how badly Campbell was hurt, and found him face-down. Rollo was holding a flashlight. Kate had the first-aid kit and she was scissoring through Campbell's clothing. Already her hands were slippery with blood. 'You've done this before,' Mallaby said.

'In the Blitz,' Rollo said. 'We helped out, sometimes.'

Campbell's right buttock had a long, deep cut. Blood was pulsing out of it. She ripped open a dressing and plugged the wound. 'Press the edges together,' she told Mallaby. She cut strips of adhesive tape, wiped most of the blood off the buttock, and taped the wound shut.

She covered it with a bigger dressing and taped that too. 'Does it hurt much?' she asked Campbell.

He nodded once, slowly. His face had no colour and his eyes were almost closed. She found the morphine and whacked it into his thigh. 'Done,' she said. They covered him with blankets, put his oxygen mask in place, made sure he was breathing steadily.

Mallaby went back to the cockpit. 'He'll live,' he said.

'Any serious damage to the kite?'

'None that I could see, but I couldn't see much. This torch is on its last legs. It's black as your hat down the fuselage.'

'Tough old bird, the Wimpy.'

The second crossing of the North Sea was far worse than the first. Flak damage let the slipstream penetrate the fuselage and it bumped its icy blast into every corner. Campbell shivered, even though he seemed asleep. Kate lay alongside him, a barrier against the wind. Rollo sat on the floor. All his joints ached, except his feet. He had no sensation below the ankles. This must be what hell's waiting room is like, he thought. Nothing to do and total freezing blackness to do it in. His brain was so dull that he altogether forgot the flasks of coffee, until the flashlight roused him and Woodman gave him a steaming mug. The coffee trickled down his gullet and promised better times ahead. Five minutes later his stomach felt as cold as stone again. He remembered the Benzedrine. He swallowed one tablet. It did nothing for his stomach. His feet were still numb.

Silk reckoned they were about halfway across the sea, when the compass developed a nervous tic. 'Look,' he said to Mallaby. 'I think it's trying to tell us something.'

The tic became a wild flutter. 'Looks like an earthquake, skip,' Mallaby said. 'Either that or it's desperate for a pee.'

The navigator's master compass was just as bad. 'Forget it,' Silk said. 'The cloud's not bad. I can see the North Star now and then. We can't miss England.' Vibration from the bomb doors put a tremor in his voice that made him sound frail and elderly. But he was right. Silk steered by the North Star and forty minutes later, Badger saw the coast ahead. 'Looks like Harwich, skip,' he said. 'Bloody great estuary. Yes, Harwich. And there's Felixstowe.'

'Defended area. Lots of balloons and bad-tempered sailors.' Silk swung the Wimpy to the right and flew parallel to the coast, losing height all the time.

'Orfordness coming up, skip.' Badger's voice still shook with the vibration, but now it had the confidence of homecoming. 'Lighthouse two miles ahead.'

'You should see this, Rollo,' Silk said. 'Get it on film. 409 returns in glory. How we navigate to beat the band.'

Rollo got his camera and went forward. His brain was working briskly. All his senses were alert and alive. Benzedrine was doing its stuff.

'We turn left at the lighthouse,' Silk said. 'Clever, eh?'

'Too dark for me, I'm afraid.'

'What a shame.' Silk wheeled Dog around the lighthouse and headed inland. 'Now, then. In a moment you'll see the big chimney of the cement factory.' Dog was down to six hundred feet and Rollo felt warmer. 'There it is. Smell the smoke? I'd know it anywhere. Here we go ... Over the chimney and dead ahead is the sugar beet factory in Bury St Edmunds. One of my favourite landmarks. Or pin-points, to be correct. Another delicious smell.' He chatted easily, pointing out church towers and windmills, scarcely visible in the dark, as Suffolk raced beneath. 'At the sugar beet factory we find the railway, which forks left for Newmarket.' Silk flew alongside the line. 'Nice shiny rails,' he said. 'Who needs maps? Now, watch out for the lamps on the railway signals. At the third set of lamps we turn sharp left, and Coney Garth is just beyond a pub called the Lamb and Flag. You can't miss it.'

'Brilliant,' Rollo said. 'Superb.'

'Thanks. You'd better go to your landing position now.'

Rollo sat with his back to the main spar. Kate and Woodman sat beside him. Campbell was strapped to the bed, mask off, face down. The note of the engines changed subtly as Silk entered the landing circuit. That was when Rollo realized that he was not going to die tonight. He had begun to suspect it when he drank the coffee. Benzedrine confirmed it. Now he could relax and enjoy survival.

The nearer Dog got to landing, the less Rollo saw himself as a passenger, mere civilian baggage, and the more he became his true self: a cameraman, a guy who shot movies. This movie was approaching its happy ending. Campbell was wounded, nothing serious, enough to remind the audience that war had its price, just as Rollo had scripted it. Soon this Wimpy would taxi to a halt, the crew would climb down from the nose, weary but triumphant in the usual understated RAF way, and Campbell would be stretchered to a waiting ambulance. He might give a thumbs-up. At the very least he would smile bravely. It would be a hell of a scene. An absolutely crucial, rewarding, clinching moment. Rollo knew he had to have it. Otherwise, everything else was so much preparation without conclusion.

He would have to work fast. No chance of rehearsal. Right first time, or never. But Rollo was good at this, he'd grabbed moments of drama just like it, all through the Blitz. The kind of thing that made other cameramen ask, 'Jesus, Rollo, how the hell did you do *that*?' The kind of shot that got your name in books on the history of the cinema. The big problem was how to leave the aeroplane before the others did. That was the trick.

There would be lights out there, the headlights of the crew truck, and an ambulance, maybe more. They would have to be aimed at the nose hatch. What about sound? He abandoned sound. Dub in any dialogue later. Maybe cover everything with music. He didn't need Kate for this, he could move faster alone.

But how to get out before the others? The cockpit area would be blocked by crew members. Rollo stared at the blackness of the fuselage and saw the answer: the rear gunner's turret. It had a quick exit. When it was swung to the right, it exposed a door on the left. That was how the gunner baled out. Rollo had seen it in daylight when the rear turret was being tested. He wasn't sure of the details but he knew the idea was right. Tell Chubby to rotate his turret. When Dog stopped, Rollo would dive out through that hole.

As soon as he felt the double bump of Dog's wheels hitting the flare-path, he took the torch from Woodman's hands and stood up. Kate shouted. He set off down the fuselage, onto the catwalk that led to the rear turret. The batteries were weak, the beam was dim, and the bulb had worked itself loose. He had to keep shaking the torch to revive it, but even with a healthy torch he was so eager that he probably wouldn't have seen the hole that flak had blown in the floor. One leg plunged into it and dragged down the rest of his body. The last image his eyes saw was the blurred gleam of flare-path lamps, before his head struck the grass at seventy miles an hour. The impact broke his neck. The tail wheel smashed into his body. Silk felt the small jolt and thought he'd hit a badger, or maybe a big fox. They had been known to wander across the airfield at night.

When he taxied to his place at dispersal, and he completed the after-landing routine, and he led the others down the short wooden ladder from the nose hatch, he asked Kate where Rollo was. She said she assumed he was in the rear turret, filming Chubb by the light of the torch; or something. Already, Dog's groundcrew had found the hole in the fuselage floor. Soon, they saw strips of flying clothing wrapped around the tail-wheel unit, and that started the search.

11

The crew followed their familiar routine. Climbed into the truck, drove to interrogation. Clumped into the room and blinked at the light. Drank the coffee with the shot of rum in it. Nobody said anything about Rollo. They were very tired, very glad to be home and alive, and besides, what was there to say? It had been such a freak way to die, you couldn't really blame the war, it was more like a road accident. Getting the chop in the air over Germany was something everyone was prepared for, even if they never talked about it. Poor old Mac Campbell's wound wasn't glorious, but at least his rear end did battle with a chunk of Jerry flak, and now he was in Sick Quarters getting stitched up. Tomorrow they'd all go and visit him and make a lot of bad jokes. But Rollo was in the station mortuary. Nobody would visit him. By all reports, he looked a mess.

Bins asked the usual questions, and Silk let the rest of the crew answer them. Bins wrote fast: good pinpoint at Borkum, night fighter attack, evasion, cu-nim, electrical storm, compass trouble, intercom failed, pinpoint Hamelin, found Hanover. Dog wouldn't climb, thick smoke over target, estimated the AP, bombed it, bomb doors failed to retract. Campbell mended the intercom, compass mended itself. Reached the coastal belt, got blown arse over tea-kettle by a near-miss, flew home somehow, God knew how.

'The Wimpy knows how,' Mallaby said. 'Tough old kite.'

'And you definitely bombed the target,' Bins said.

'Cookie *and* incendiaries,' Woodman said. 'Definitely.'

'We hit it right on the nose,' Chubb said. 'Lovely grub.'

'Well done. Off to your bacon and eggs, chaps.'

'Damned good show,' the group captain said.

They left. Silk remained. He felt grimy, and the rum had not killed the rubbery taste of his oxygen mask. There was a high buzzing in his ears that changed pitch without warning, and then went back to the old note. It was caused by hours of the howl of the propeller tips. None of this was new; it happened after every op. He stayed because the Wingco was there, straddling a chair, chewing on a cold pipe; and Silk felt that someone should say something about Rollo Blazer. He couldn't think of anything that wasn't stupidly obvious.

'Hanover took a pasting,' Rafferty said. 'Group are very pleased.'

'I don't suppose Crown Films will be,' Silk said.

'Sod 'em,' Duff said. 'What did they expect?'

'Not our fault,' Bins said. 'Bound to be an inquiry, though.'

'Let 'em piss in their hats,' Duff said. 'They knew ops were dangerous. That's why they came here. Inquiry be buggered.'

'You sound as if you enjoyed your trip,' Silk said. 'Sir.'

'Compass trouble, like you. All that bloody electricity. Nav got lost, never found Hanover, went to Hamburg instead. Gunners swore it was Bremen, but I knew better. Come on. If we don't get to the grub soon, some bastard will steal our eggs.'

They walked from the Ops Block. In the east the sky was a soft grey. Birds were waking up and being noisy about it.

'Why can't they wait for daylight?' Silk said. 'What's so special about flying at night?'

'You didn't have much to say in there,' Duff said.

'You want to know if our cookie hit the railway station, don't you? Well, the answer is, God alone knows. God and the station-master. Make a bomb like a dustbin and it's liable to land anywhere. Same with incendiaries. They fall like confetti.'

'I don't care. Nobody cares any more. If we keep on bombing the city, then sooner or later we're bound to hit something valuable.'

'I said that months ago, Pug. It's nice to know you've been paying attention. Langham always reckoned you were my greatest fan.'

'Load of balls.'

'Smallest fan, then. That was his joke. I miss Langham. I don't miss any other stupid bastard who got the chop. I probably wouldn't miss you, if you bought it tomorrow. But Langham ... what a waste.'

'You're drivelling,' Duff said. 'Step it out. I'm hungry.'

A CERTAIN
HOOLIGAN THRILL

1

Professor Lindemann knew all about Long Delay Pistols and their fickle behaviour. When he presented the Butt Report to the Prime Minister and the War Cabinet, he privately awarded the bombshell a Long Delay Pistol of twelve hours before it exploded at Bomber Command HQ.

In fact a full day passed. Even then, the bang was muted: more like the detonation of an underground mine than a bomb-burst on the surface. But the shock-waves travelled all the further. Within a week, most station and squadron commanders had heard of the Butt Report and decided that it was all tosh.

Pug Duff was determined to stamp on it before it leaked to the crews. He called a meeting of the flight commanders and Intelligence Officers, and invited Rafferty too. He asked the adjutant to take notes. Total security was paramount.

'We'll start with the facts,' Duff said. 'This so-called report seems to have been cobbled together by a junior civil servant who's never flown over Chipping Sodbury in his life, let alone over Wilhelmshaven, and he did it with the doubtful help of a gaggle of Waafs who claim magical powers when shown target photographs. Have I forgotten anything?'

'No, sir,' Bins said. 'One thing puzzles me. Nobody disputes the colossal amount of flak that the Hun keeps chucking at our chaps. Would he go to all that trouble and expense if they were nowhere near the target? As has been alleged?'

'He might,' Skull said. 'We did, in the Blitz. There were ack-ack batteries all along the South Coast.'

'Stick to the point, man,' Duff said. 'What our ack-ack did is neither here nor there.'

'Jerry flak is both here *and* there,' Hazard said. 'My Flight's got the scars to prove it. So we must be doing something right.'

'Looking at the big picture,' Rafferty said, 'I see the Admiralty constantly turning to Bomber Command and asking us to knock out Hitler's U-boat bases, *and* the docks at Bremen and so on where they build the U-boats, *and* the factories that make the diesels. Surely a vote of confidence.'

'Damn right, sir,' Pratten said. '"B" Flight has been to Bremen so often we can do the trip blindfold.'

'Given the lousy weather over Germany, that's usually the best way,' Hazard said. He got a few sympathetic chuckles.

'The group captain mentioned the big picture,' Bins said. 'That's a very valid point. This chap Butt is only one vote. Other experts disagree, and they have hard evidence of damage to targets, reported by other Intelligence sources. Secret agents, neutral businessmen. Photographs never tell the whole story. When the dust has settled, I think we'll find that Mr Butt is out-voted.'

Everyone nodded agreement, except Skull.

'You look like a dog that's about to throw up on the carpet,' Duff said. 'Spit it out, for Christ's sake.'

'I suspect my views are unacceptable, sir,' Skull said. 'Rather like some of our target bombing photographs.'

'It's a free country,' Duff said. 'I'm free to ignore your claptrap. Get on.'

'I have three points, sir,' Skull said.

Duff groaned. 'Another bloody lecture. Typical university don. Bite him in the arse and he always has three points.'

'Point one: accuracy. One reason the Admiralty makes repeated demands on Bomber Command is our failure to hit the target the first time, or the second, or the third. Point two: target photographs taken over German towns may be obscured by smoke, but when the photograph shows open countryside, we deceive ourselves if we reject such evidence. And thirdly, since you all feel so confident that Butt is utterly wrong, why not let the crews read his report? They know more than we do. Let them judge for themselves.'

'Not bloody likely,' Duff said. 'Cross all that out, Uncle.'

'I didn't record it, sir.'

'Good. For a man with a brain the size of a pumpkin, you don't think much, do you, Skull? The RAF isn't a democracy, for God's sake. Frankly, I don't give a toss what the crews think, as long as they cart the maximum load of high explosive into Germany.'

'For which, morale matters,' Bins said. Almost an aside.

'Of course! Morale on 409 is damn good! And I'm not about to let anyone bugger it about on the excuse of democracy. If you start talking to the crews about bloody Butt, Skull, I'll have you in the guardroom lickety-split. Understand?'

For a moment there was no sound but Pug Duff's breathing and the scratching of the adjutant's pen.

'I have a question,' Rafferty said, and aimed his pipe at Skull. 'If you really believe that our bombing campaign is as faulty as you seem to be suggesting, what is your proposal? How else can this country attack Nazi Germany?'

Skull was silent. Bins screwed the top on the ink bottle.

'Or perhaps we should all just give in,' Rafferty said.

The meeting was over. Everyone except Skull stood and began moving to the door, talking, putting on their caps. 'I know one thing,' Skull said. 'The truth does not cease to be the truth because men prefer to think otherwise.' If they heard him, they gave no indication of it.

2

Tim Delahaye was, after all, Minister of Information. He had no difficulty in concealing the truth without actually telling any lies. Rollo Blazer, cameraman, died in a tragic accident. He was killed when struck by an aircraft that was taxiing at night. What with newsprint being rationed and Rollo not being a famous figure, most newspapers didn't reckon the story was worth more than an inch at the bottom of page four. Some didn't think he was worth any space at all. At Crown Films, Harry Frobisher knew the people Rollo had worked with, and he made half a dozen phone calls. 'Here's a man who went all through the Blitz,' he said, 'came out of it without a scratch, and would you believe it, a freak accident does what Jerry couldn't do. Sad loss, very sad. Pass the word, would you?'

The Minister's limousine took Blake Gunnery, Harry Frobisher and Kate Kelly to the funeral. Delahaye himself sent a wreath, with his apologies: he was speaking in a debate in the Commons that afternoon. Bad timing. The limousine was more than a gesture: Rollo was to be buried in Suffolk, in the village churchyard at Coney Garth. It was Miriam's idea. She was next of kin. Rollo had no close relatives, and since he was already in the station mortuary, it seemed pointless to bring him back to London.

Rafferty took no chances when he heard that Air Commodore Russell, the big white chief of Press and PR at Air Ministry, would be there. All off-duty aircrew were at the service, with the crew of D-Dog in the front pew. Any other officer who could be spared from his duties was there. Service police provided the pall-bearers. The Officers' Mess paid the fees for the organist, the choir and the minister. Kate sat next to Rafferty and watched the unhurried, unsentimental ceremony and thought what a pity it was Rollo couldn't be there to film it. He was a far greater centre of attention dead than he had ever been alive.

Afterwards, there were drinks in the Mess. Air Commodore Russell took Group Captain Rafferty aside. 'Congratulations on your turn-out, Tiny. This filming has put you to a lot of trouble, hasn't it? Sometimes I wonder why we're bombing Germany. Is it to make the civilians feel better?'

'Morale is a big part of the war effort, Charlie.'

'Yes. Blazer wasn't the only casualty that night, though, was he? You lost a Wimpy over Hanover, didn't you?'

'P-Peter. Sprog crew. Only their second op. It's often that way.'

'Six dead. I bet they didn't get half as good a funeral.'

It was a sunny afternoon. Silk and Kate took their drinks onto the lawn in front of the Mess. Servants brought deckchairs.

'Well, he's definitely dead now,' she said. 'I don't think I believed it until the vicar said so. A bit like getting married, isn't it? Only in reverse.'

'Don't know, I'm afraid,' Silk said. 'Never been married. And the chop doesn't get discussed much on the squadron.'

'Death is all part of life. You can't have one without the other.'

'I suppose not.' Silk took a long swig of gin and tonic. He wasn't on the ops board; he was free to get blotto if he wanted. 'I must say, you're taking it awfully well.'

'We weren't married, Silko. That was just a fiddle to keep us together. I was threatened with staying at the Waafery.'

'Oh.' He took in more gin and tonic to help digest this news. 'In that case ... Can I ask you what possessed old Rollo to go wandering off down the fuselage? I know he was a bit eccentric, but ...' Silk took a quick glance at her. Not married, eh? Rollo must have been a bloody hard man to please. Which brought a mental echo: *You're a hard man to please. Zoë had been ready and willing. You cocked it up.*

'I don't know what he was doing,' Kate said. 'We have a word for it in the film business. It's called a BFI. A director or a cameraman suddenly stops and says, "Wait a minute. I've got a better fucking idea." Maybe Rollo had a BFI.'

Frobisher made sure he had collected every last can of film. They were all clearly labelled: *Groundcrew servicing Wimpys; Flare-path officer at take-off; Aircrew briefing; Armourers bombing up; D-Dog over North Sea; D-Dog over target.* And more. Two days later he sat in Crown Films' viewing theatre and watched the lot. Kate sat next to him. 'It wasn't as easy as we thought it would be,' she said.

3

Twin three-oh-three machine guns made the most gratifying racket. Skull sat on a seat rather like a bicycle saddle and merely touched the triggers, and felt all his senses jump as two streams of bullets streaked from the muzzles and lashed a corner of the canvas target fifty yards away. He stopped firing, squinted through the smoke, nudged the guns a trifle to the right, squeezed again and blasted the target to tatters. 'Goodness gracious,' he said.

'Not bad for a beginner,' Silk said.

'It makes one feel like Al Capone.'

That made the armaments sergeant laugh. 'I'd like to see him take on these Brownings, sir. He'd be corned-beef hash in ten seconds.'

Silk had landed after an NFT and noticed a pair of knees poking up in the long grass near the perimeter fence, where the gang-mower never cut. Even from that distance he could see that the legs wore officers' barathea and not airmen's serge.

It was Skull, hatless, tunic unbuttoned, tie loosened. 'Sorry,' Silk said. 'I was hoping you were Sergeant Felicity Parks.'

'Many people hope that. It distresses them when I deny any similarity, which is odd, because Coney Garth is very keen on denial. Have you noticed? There must be something in the water supply. This station runs on denial.'

Silk squatted on his haunches. 'Explain.'

'Well, for a start, the Wingco stoutly denies that 409 ever bombs anything except specific military targets. If that friendly Yank were to ask, the group captain would confidently deny that 409 bombs residential areas. Bins always denies that the bombing photographs contradict the crew reports, and the crews usually deny that they got lost and ended up bombing that long-suffering German target, Randomburg. Mention any of this to Uncle and he denies that any denial has taken place. And of course there was poor Rollo Blazer, sincerely denying that his film about 409 was bogus and contrived, after all those noises he made, denying it would be anything but the plain, unvarnished truth.'

'How about me?' Silk said. 'Didn't I deny anything?'

'Your denials were true.'

'You're pathetic.' Silk's knees were starting to ache, so he straightened up. 'You don't know the first thing about war. Come with me.' He helped Skull to his feet. 'I'll teach you lesson one.'

They went to the station firing range. A sergeant armourer gave Skull ear-plugs and explained how twin Brownings worked. When Skull had destroyed the target he didn't get up from the seat. 'May I have another go?' he asked. The sergeant telephoned the men working the butts. 'You'll see the outline of an aircraft for three seconds,' he told Skull. 'Fire short bursts.'

Five minutes later, Silk took him away. 'What did I score?' Skull asked.

'You missed two Junkers 88s and an Me 110, but you shot down three Spitfires. Exciting, isn't it?'

'I can't deny a certain hooligan thrill. It's a very primitive pleasure.'

'Well, we're a primitive lot. Last week we were swinging from the trees in the jungle. This week we were dropping cookies on Hanover.

Same difference. If you can't understand that, you don't deserve to be in Intelligence.'

That night's op required five Wimpys to bomb Gelsenkirchen. Briefing was at four p.m. It followed its familiar pattern, until Bins finished his piece and nodded to Skull to continue. 'I expect you want to know about enemy defences,' Skull said. 'Well, the truth is, light flak will be bloody abominable and heavy flak will be fucking ferocious. And I challenge Scotland Yard to deny this.'

'That'll do, Skull,' the Wingco said, bleakly. 'Wait outside.'

'I've got the chop, haven't I?' Skull said.

Some of the crews glanced at him as he walked out, but most didn't even look. Nobody smiled. They weren't interested in a middle-aged IO who went off the rails and took the piss out of them. He might think Gelsenkirchen was something to joke about, but he wasn't going on the op, was he? Put him in a Wimpy over the Ruhr and he wouldn't find it so fucking funny.

4

Harry Frobisher had a rough cut made of the best bits from the many cans of Rollo's film. He invited Blake Gunnery to see it. Kate Kelly came along, in case anything needed explaining. The film lasted twenty-eight minutes.

'Scrap it,' Gunnery said.

'You don't mean all of it, sir,' Frobisher said. He was more concerned for Kate's feelings than his own.

'Yes, I do. Scrap the lot. It's unusable.'

'There are some good shots in there, sir,' Kate said. 'The flak over Hanover, for instance. Isn't that worth saving?'

'Okay, save it, keep it in the library. Archive footage.'

'You're worried about the sound,' Frobisher said.

'No, I'm not worried about anything. Let's get out of here. I need some coffee.' They walked along the corridor. 'I'd be worried if you had half a film and we were looking for the other half.' He asked his secretary to organize coffee, and they went into his office. He waved towards armchairs, and he perched on his desk. 'You haven't even got half a film. If it makes you feel better, tell me why the flak was silent.'

'Well, flak *is* silent when you're in the bomber,' she said. 'When it's really close the noise is like someone knocking on a door. If it's louder than that, you're probably dead.'

'The engines drown the flak,' Frobisher said.

'It's a wall of noise,' Kate said. 'Nothing gets through.'

'The audience won't buy silent flak,' Gunnery ruled. 'We must have crumps and bangs and wallops.'

'I thought the shaky shots were effective,' Frobisher said. 'Looked as if the plane was getting knocked about.'

'But that wasn't flak,' Kate said. 'They desynchronized the engines and the Wimpy got the shakes.' Gunnery made a face. 'Well, it's true,' she said. 'Rollo got the pilot to explain, but the vibration shook his voice and he sounded scared, so we cut it.'

'Nobody has the shakes,' Gunnery said. 'Under no circumstances is our pilot scared.'

'I liked what the navigator said,' Frobisher remarked. 'When he spoke to the pilot about flying a zigzag. Nice detail.'

'He can recite *Eskimo Nell*, for all I care,' Gunnery said. 'If I can't see his face, the shot's useless.'

'Everyone goes on oxygen at eight thousand,' Kate said. 'The intercom mike is inside the mask. Rollo was simply showing ops the way they are.'

'Tough men doing a tough job,' Frobisher added.

'That's exactly what the film *doesn't* show,' Gunnery said. 'Our audience wants faces, not masks. Emotions, reactions, expressions.' He got off the desk and prowled around the room. 'Which reminds me. In that scene where they all get briefed for the raid – stupefyingly rigid performances, by the way – somebody tells the crews to attack at low level.'

'Rollo put that in the script, so that we could get a good shot of the target,' Kate explained. 'Actually, crews hate low-level raids.'

'Well, it won't wash. You can't have a low-level raid *and* show the crew on oxygen. Can you?' Nobody argued.

Coffee was brought in. Gunnery took a phone call, signed some letters, looked at his watch. 'Right!' he said. 'Let's put this unhappy baby to bed, once and for all. It has three incurable faults: sound, light and people. Take sound. All those creaky voices on the inter-com. No good.'

'It's the only way they can talk,' Kate protested.

'Too thin. Too weak. Next, the light. That bomber was as dark as the tomb.'

'Lights are dangerous. Night fighters are on the look out.'

'No doubt, but we hardly ever see the crew, do we? The best piece of human interest is that close-up of a pair of female hands, very bloody, strapping up a horrible gash in somebody's buttock.'

'Kate,' Frobisher said. 'Deserves a gong.'

'Agreed, but she's not getting one. 409 Squadron never knew she was on the plane and they don't want to know about it now. Crown Films can't show a woman on an op, and of all the brave wounds suf-fered in action, the last thing our audience needs to look at is a bloody bottom.'

'Rollo couldn't film what he couldn't see,' Kate said.

'Forget it,' Gunnery told her. 'You both did your best.'

'Nobody can do more,' Frobisher said.

'Well ...' She made a gesture of despair. 'It was such a good idea. Rollo would have hated to see it scrapped.'

Gunnery sipped his coffee. 'The idea's not scrapped. Good heavens, no. It didn't work with 409 Squadron, but valuable lessons have been learned. We move forward. North-east, to be precise. To RAF Mildenhall, also in Suffolk, and to 149 Squadron, also flying Wellingtons. We try again. We're going to film the actual crew of F-Freddie, on a typical raid.'

'I don't see how,' Kate said.

'The idea's right. We just have to make it work.'

He thanked her, and she left.

'I never had any faith in pure documentary, from the word go,' Gunnery said. 'Shoot and hope: that never works. But Tim Delahaye insisted that we try something different.'

'War and documentary don't mix,' Frobisher agreed. 'Too many cock-ups.'

'Mmm.' Gunnery stood in the middle of the room, his arms folded, his head bent. He was looking at the wandering pattern in the carpet but he was remembering some of the film that Rollo Blazer had shot over Germany. Brilliant, terrifying images, far too real to be shown in a cinema. 'The audience wouldn't believe it,' he said.

'PIECE OF CAKE'

1

A sprog pilot officer arrived to replace Skull. He was fat, balding, nervous. 'Don't worry if you put up a few blacks,' Skull told him. 'Nobody pays any attention to what Intelligence says. What did you do before the RAF?'

'Lecturer. Camborne School of Mines, Cornwall.'

'What a shame. Well, you forget I asked, and I'll forget you told me.'

Skull didn't feel charitable to anyone. Now that Bins didn't need him, the adjutant took the opportunity to make Skull the Duty Officer as often as possible. The worst part of this was having to walk through the Airmen's Mess with the Duty NCO and call out, 'Any complaints?' A complaint might oblige him to taste the meal. One day he took a spoonful of soup and said he felt it would benefit from a hint of Worcester sauce. The Duty NCO rolled his eyes. After that, so many airmen complained about the lack of Worcester sauce in the food that Skull bought a bottle and gave it to the cooks. Now the same airmen complained of too much Worcester sauce. Sometimes they were right.

The adjutant heard about it. 'You do everything the hard way, don't you, Skull?' he said. 'If you continue like this, you're going to have a thoroughly unhappy war.'

'I didn't realize war was supposed to be happy, Uncle.'

They were standing by the flare-path caravan, waiting in the dusk to wave off the Wellingtons. Gardening at Boulogne. Easy op for sprog crews.

'I'll tell you this for nothing.' The adjutant took him by the arm and led him away from the crowd. 'There's no profit in looking for trouble. Your problem is you're personally offended when you discover a cock-up. Believe me, there's *always* a cock-up. It's in the nature of war. Whoever said truth is the first casualty arrived late on the scene. The first casualty of war is the plan, Skull. The first plan always fails. Usually the second plan does, often the third, too. Then, with a bit of luck, the next plan works, and we win. That's my experience.'

'Not a thrilling prospect, is it, Uncle?'

'All the more reason to cheer up. Look optimistic, even if you're not. It's the least you can do for the chaps. Most of these boys are going to get the chop, aren't they? Two out of three, probably. They deserve to believe it's all worthwhile. That's the least we can do for them.'

They strolled back and joined the others. Fifteen minutes later, when the last Wimpy was climbing away, Skull felt a tap on his shoulder. It was Bellamy. 'A word in your ear,' he said.

'Oh dear. More good advice.'

They sat in Bellamy's car, in total darkness. 'I'll get straight to the point,' he said. 'Someone has gone over my head and complained to Group HQ about the procedure of air-testing radios before ops.'

'Not I. I never complain. Nobody listens.'

'Well, somebody's rocked the boat, and I clearly remember you chuntering on to me about the enemy intercepting my radio instructions at take-off. Utter bilge, and I told you so. These VHF transmissions have a very short range. Twenty-five miles at most.'

'Then we're safe. Huzzah.'

'No, we're not bloody safe. I mean, we shall be, but ...' Bellamy depressed the clutch and worked the gear stick up through its changes and back down again. 'Forget the VHF. The wireless op's main transmitter-receiver has a range of hundreds of miles. Up until now, every wireless op has air-tested this set, well before take-off.'

'Ah-ha,' Skull said.

'It is thought the Germans have been listening to our air tests.' Bellamy sounded as if he had been cheated at cards. 'Estimating the size of the raid. Even the timing.'

'Of course they've been listening. They're not stupid. We listen to them, don't we?'

'Air-testing has been discontinued.' Bellamy started the car.

'Well, I got it half-right,' Skull said.

'No, you got it half-wrong,' Bellamy told him firmly. 'If you'd done your homework before you began jumping to conclusions, it might have been a very different story.'

He drove back to the Mess. As they got out, Skull said: 'It seems that, whatever I do, I can't win.'

'That's my impression, too,' Bellamy said. 'Good night.'

2

F-Freddie made a successful low-level raid on the crucial German target of Freihausen, which did not exist. The raid took place in the studio.

Before he joined Crown Films, Blake Gunnery had made some movies that included flying action. He knew that a camera inside an aeroplane could never get all the necessary shots. To film the pilot full-face, looking ahead, the cockpit must be lit and the camera must be outside the windscreen. To film a gunner searching the night sky, the interior of the turret must be lit and the camera must be outside the aircraft. To film the bomb doors opening and the bombs falling, the bomb-bay must be lit, the camera must be below the bomber, and a descending whistle must be added to the soundtrack. The only way to film a Wimpy that was apparently on an op at night was to create a static mock-up in the studio and let the camera move around it and inside it. For the op to look authentic, it had to be faked.

Crown Films were given the carcase of a Wellington that had crashed in a field. Its wings were broken but the fuselage was in good shape. It was shipped to the film studio, propped on trestles, and cut lengthwise so as to expose the interior. Rear projection supplied the propeller disc; sound effects made a quiet roar for the engines, a roar that could be softened during dialogue. With the studio lights dimmed to suggest weak moonlight, the Wimpy was an ideal film-set.

Harry Frobisher found a new director. Together they read dozens of operational reports and wrote a script that was not unlike Rollo Blazer's idea. It began with a photo-reconnaissance aircraft bringing back pictures of Germany. One revealed a juicy new target. Orders went down the chain of command and reached the squadron which included F-Freddie. All this was shot on location. Frobisher was not too proud to steal a good idea, so there was a decision to make a low-level attack. This solved the central problem of showing the target to the audience. It also got those bloody oxygen masks out of the way.

Filming the ops began at the airfield. They shot the crew assembling, climbing into F-Freddie, starting engines, taxying, taking off. They shot the flare-path officer doing his job. The dome on his caravan had to be underlit, to show his features; and he pointed out that the light reflected off the Perspex and made it difficult for him to see the aircraft. 'Only you and I will know that,' the director said. 'It'll be our little secret.'

Once F-Freddie was airborne, the studio stuff was a piece of cake. The director had the crew all day long. He could rehearse, re-write, experiment, shoot the scene again until he was satisfied. With the camera outside the fuselage he got close-ups of the pilot at the controls, shots of the pilot in profile talking to the second pilot, head-on shots of the gunners in their turrets, slowly rotating, searching the night sky. He got wonderful shots of the bomb-aimer kneeling in the front cockpit, eyes on the bombsight and one hand on the tit, saying: 'Left ... left ... steady ... right ... steady ... Bombs gone!' And a lovely close-up of the gloved hand pressing the tit.

Above all, filming in the studio overcame the terrible problem of sound. The director made a gesture towards authenticity: everyone pretended to use the intercom. They held the mask near the mouth as they spoke. But it never obscured the face; and all their voices were as clear as if they were in the Mess.

F-Freddie reached Freihausen – a genuine shot from a cockpit, showing a moonlit river – bombed it, blew it to bits, thanks to some pyrotechnics in a blitzed factory. The script called for flak. Crown Films dressed the British gunners of an anti-aircraft battery in coal-scuttle helmets and filmed them in action, silhouetted against the night, jumping to harsh orders in German. Flak as seen from the cockpit was real. Rollo's shots were too good to waste.

The fuselage was in a cradle that could be rocked to simulate a near-miss. F-Freddie bounced but recovered. That was when the wireless op took some shrapnel in the leg: another legacy from Rollo.

The flight home was tense. There was a problem with an engine, and then the danger of fog over England. All the time, back at base, senior officers were shown waiting, not knowing that F-Freddie's radio had been knocked out by flak.

The Wimpy found its base, but its landing posed a problem for the director. If fog had, in fact, shrouded the airfield, filming would be impossible. Yet the bomber must be seen to land. He compromised. Senior officers in the control room spoke anxiously of worsening fog. Outside, the night was very dark. Airmen ran through the gloom, lighting the flare-path. When F-Freddie swept into view, black against black, her safe landing seemed magical. The sequence ended with a shot of the Wimpy taxying out of the night, straight at the camera, halting with a tired squeal of brakes and a last gruff burst of power. The propellers stopped. F-Freddie was home. The stillness created a sense of quiet accomplishment.

Blake Gunnery invited the Minister to a showing of the rough cut. Tim Delahaye was silent as he watched it. When the lights went up he was smiling, nodding. He brushed away a tear.

'This is what the British people want to see,' he said. 'Real men fighting a real war. Not actors. A genuine bomber crew, on a genuine raid. I think it's superb.'

'It'll be even better when we've added the music.'

'Noel Coward can act his socks off,' Delahaye said, 'but he doesn't stand a chance against an actual raid on Germany by the actual crew of a real Wellington.'

Gunnery thought, very briefly, about qualifying that claim, and then abandoned the idea. No matter how much credit Bomber Command crews got, it would never be enough.

3

It wasn't always easy to get an officer posted. The decision lay with Air Ministry. Naturally, Air Ministry wanted a reason. The fact that he got up the CO's nose might be enough, but the CO stood a better chance if he phrased it differently.

Pug Duff thought about this before he made his report on Skull. 'Flight Lieutenant Skelton has shown an unusual flair for interpreting Intelligence material in an unorthodox and unconventional manner,' he wrote. 'He applies his critical faculties with vigour and persistence. He has never suffered from excessive caution when reaching conclusions that challenge existing operational procedures. He has made a distinctive impact on this squadron.' Skull, he said, 'would benefit from wider experience in Bomber Command.'

Rafferty saw a copy. 'Not sure about this,' he said. 'You may have over-egged the pudding.' But he initialled it. The report got shuttled through Group HQ and Command HQ without comment, and landed on a desk at Air Ministry. A veteran wing commander read it with one eye and decoded it with the other. He showed it to a colleague. 'This is a classic,' he said. 'We should have it framed.'

'*Unorthodox and unconventional ... vigour and persistence ... never suffered from excessive caution ... distinctive impact ...* In other words, he gets on everybody's tits.' He read on. 'Ah ... This last line is a gem.'

'I thought you'd like it. *Would benefit from wider experience.*'

'They want to dump him.'

'It's a classic,' the wing commander said. 'It's made my day.' He sent for Skull's file.

A week later, Skull got a signal from Command: *Proceed to Hogshead Court, Essex, for conference 1300 hours today. Authority: R.G.T. Champion, Group Captain.* A map reference was given. Skull got the Lagonda out.

Hogshead Court was Georgian, and comfortably big enough to hold a hunt ball. It stood in its own grounds. Cattle kept a respectful distance. Ralph Champion was waiting on the terrace. He was in a dark suit.

'Isn't this an official matter?' Skull asked. 'I could have worn my tweeds.'

'Semi-official. I've got a couple of days' leave. We've found a new home for the Sheldrake Club. Isn't that grand news?'

'It makes no difference to me.'

'I'll put you up for membership when the war's over. The club's acquired the former Hungarian embassy, in Holland Park. Serve them right for joining Hitler. Unfortunately, there's no wine in the place. Well, there's a bit of Hungarian red, but I wouldn't give that to the servants. Come on, I'll show you the house.'

'I'd rather you showed me lunch.'

'All in good time.'

He had keys. The furniture was covered in sheets, and paintings were stacked against the walls. Champion strolled from room to room, telling the history of the Court. The same family had built it and lived here until the owner, a major in the Guards, got killed at Dunkirk a year ago. Next of kin was in California, and staying there. Now the War Office had requisitioned it, but the solicitors acting for the estate saw no reason to give the wine to the army. The Sheldrake had bought the lot, sight unseen.

'I don't care,' Skull said. 'I don't care a little bit.'

'I'm here to organize the transport. I'm on the wine committee, you see. Come on, we'll pick out a bottle for lunch.'

The cellars were long and well-stocked. When Champion showed signs of lingering, Skull said: 'Fifteen seconds. Or I find the nearest pub.' Champion chose a claret. 'A chirpy little beast,' he said. 'What I call a Cockney sparrow of a wine.'

'What on earth is that supposed to mean?'

Champion looked at him with amused tolerance. 'There you go again, Skull,' he said. 'Everything has to *mean* something, doesn't it? Believe me, you're wrong. Most things have no significance whatever. That includes your getting kicked out of 409 Squadron.'

They went upstairs. He locked the front door and fetched a luncheon basket from his car. The late owner had left some wrought-iron garden furniture on the terrace. They sat and ate quails' eggs, roast duck, potato salad, fruit. Champion reminisced about Cambridge.

'Not that I care,' Skull said at last, 'but do you happen to know where I'll end up when I get kicked out?'

'Of course I do. I've still got some pals at Air Ministry. When it became obvious that Pug Duff was about to strangle you, they phoned me up. Just as well they did. Plan A was to send you back to RAF Feck.'

Skull was eating a pear. Juice ran down his chin. 'I'd sooner be strangled. What's Plan B?'

'Ah, that's the bind. We've got a surfeit of flight-lieutenant Intelligence Officers right now. Nobody wants you.'

'Except Feck.'

'Yes, Feck will take anyone. Since you were there, they've had a riot, a couple of suicides and a murder. Morale is not good.'

'It's a penal colony. If the rain stopped, they'd burn it down. The rain never stops.' Skull took the last of the claret.

'Fortunately, I solved the problem.' Champion concentrated on peeling an apple so that the peel made one continuous strip. 'One of my few undisputed skills.' He displayed the strip on the point of the knife. 'Completely worthless, of course, but it impresses the air marshals. I said to my chum at Air Ministry, if you can't find a decent posting for Flight Lieutenant Skelton, then for God's sake, man, promote him!' He popped a slice of apple into his mouth. 'So that's what he's doing.'

'Squadron leader? Me?'

Champion smiled broadly as he chewed. The effect was slightly satanic. 'You've earned it,' he said. 'All that expert advice you gave me on bombing accuracy.'

'You rejected it.'

'What nonsense. We at Command HQ took it very much to heart. David Butt's report came as no surprise to us, Skull. We knew all along.'

His bland self-assurance completely wrong-footed Skull. He had no answer to it. 'I get the chop,' he said, 'so they promote me ... Since you seem to know everything, where is your friend at Air Ministry posting me?'

'You're a very lucky man. He's found a place for you in the Desert Air Force.'

'Egypt.'

'Probably Egypt to start with. Get you acclimatized. Then Libya, I expect. All depends where the front line is.'

'I'm going to the Western Desert. You're getting rid of me.'

Champion found that quite amusing. 'Please don't overrate your importance, Skull. In fact Air Ministry picked the Desert Air Force because that's where your old fighter squadron is based. I understand the same CO and adjutant are still serving. Your chance to meet old friends again.'

'Hornet Squadron,' Skull said. 'I got kicked out of Hornet Squadron a year ago. Now I'm getting kicked back into it.'

'Don't thank me,' Champion told him. 'It's what I'm here for.'

They packed up the luncheon stuff and walked to the cars.

'How can you go on doing your job?' Skull asked. 'Counting the aircrew killed, night after night, and knowing it's so much waste. Death as the price of triumph is one thing. Death as the cost of failure is obscene.'

'I say!' Champion exclaimed. 'That's good. That really is good. Is it original? Stupid question. Of course it's original. I must get it down before I forget it ...' He took out a pocket notebook and began writing. He was still writing when Skull drove away.

4

Silk wrote several letters. Zoë replied with picture postcards of the Tower of London. Finally he got forty-eight hours' leave and drove to London. He found Zoë at the Albany apartment with a five-month-old baby.

'The older she gets, the more she looks like you,' Zoë said. 'Can you see it?'

'Only in the squint and the buck teeth,' Silk said. 'And perhaps the cauliflower ears.'

'If you're going to be vile about her, you can go to your club. Isn't that what men do?'

'I haven't got a club, and when we last met you hadn't got a baby.' He walked away and sniffed a vase of creamy roses. 'Is she definitely yours? Perhaps you bought her. You live inside Harrods' delivery area, don't you?'

'My God, you're in a foul temper, Silko. Did you drive all this way just to be a brute?' She tickled the baby, who chuckled and produced a fine belch. 'That's what she thinks of you.'

'What about Kentucky? Where are the stretch marks?'

'Guy Chard-Cox found me a very clever masseur who made them go away. Fingers like Rachmaninov's, Guy said. They gave me the most delicious *frisson*. I was sorry when the treatment ended.'

Silk was searching through a stack of gramophone records. Anything to avoid looking at her. If he looked, he was lost. 'You can't stop cheating, can you?'

'Can't I? Well, half the fun of playing the game is cheating a bit.'

309

She was brushing her hair, briskly, cheerfully. 'I never *denied* I had stretch marks. Kentucky was a slight fib. The baby was in Kensington, with my cousin. I mean ... Kentucky, Kensington: what difference does it make?'

'Not much. I bombed Koblenz the other night. It might just as well have been Cologne.'

'There you are, then.'

'Come to think of it, it *was* Cologne.'

'Stop babbling, and put your hat on. You're driving us to Kensington, to leave the baby, and then we're going to Richmond for lunch.'

He held a record. ' "Embraceable You",' he said. 'I bet Tony gave you this.'

She put his hat on his head, backwards. 'Do buck up. Men are so *slow*.'

The hotel at Richmond was on the river. They had lunch in the garden. The air was pleasantly mild: autumn was late that year. Silk looked at the clear blue sky and thought: *Mist tonight*, and immediately put the thought aside. Not his problem.

He asked the waitress, 'What do you recommend?'

'Well,' she said. 'Nobody's complained about the rabbit casserole.' They ordered rabbit and bottled Bass.

'This place has gone downhill,' Zoë said. 'I remember when ...' Her glance flickered towards Silk and away from him. She picked up her knife and polished it with her napkin.

'Oh, Christ,' Silk said. 'You used to come here with Langham, didn't you?' She hunched her shoulders, and kept polishing. 'Well, he's dead,' he said. 'Langham bought it over Mannheim.'

'Osnabruck.'

'No. Are you sure? I could have sworn it was Mannheim.' He took her knife away, and gave her his in exchange. 'Don't stop,' he said. 'I expect the hotel's got a few dozen more you can work on.'

'We shouldn't have come here, Silko.'

'Why not? Keep up the good work and we'll get ten per cent off the bill.'

She threw the knife at him. It bounced off his chest. 'I hate you when you're like this. Like ... like a third-rate comedian.'

'Well, I don't hate you.' He moved the knife out of her reach. 'And your jokes are much worse than mine. Mind you, I'm not in love with you, either. But then, you weren't in love with Langham, half the time, were you? Ah, grub.' The rabbit casserole arrived.

After lunch they strolled down to the water's edge and watched the swans. 'That film they were making at Coney Garth,' Zoë said. 'It's on everywhere. *Target for Tonight*. Huge success, the newspapers say. I've seen it three times.'

'I haven't seen it once, and I'm not going to. It's all balls. I bet the kite lands and everyone lives happily ever after. I bet nobody gets the chop over Osnabruck.'

'You're never happy, Silko. What would it take to make you happy?'

He thought about it. 'There's a new bomber called the Lancaster. Twice the size of a Wimpy. It's got four engines and it carries a hell of a bombload a hell of a long way. I saw one the other day. Beautiful beast.'

'Mummy used to say you can tell the men from the boys by the size of their toys.'

They went to the hotel car park. He held open the door of the Frazer Nash. 'Well, are we going to get married, or what?' he asked.

'Not in that tone of voice, no.'

She got in and he closed the door. He went around to the driver's side, got in, shut the door. 'Why do I have to do all the work?' he said. 'You've got the vote and everything. You see if you can do any better.'

'Silko, darling, if I marry you, will you promise to be kind?'

'Shit and corruption!' he roared. 'Of course I bloody will, you bloody silly woman.' He started the engine.

She gave him a bright smile. 'And I shall be kind to you,' she said. 'Now for God's sake try not to die.'

END

AUTHOR'S NOTE

Damned Good Show is fiction based on fact. The reader is entitled to know which is which. In brief: my account of the war, and the way it was fought by Bomber Command in the first two years, is fact, whereas almost all the characters are fiction. 409 Squadron did not exist (409 was the 'last three' of my RAF serial number when I served as a fighter plotter), and although RAF bases dotted Lincolnshire and Suffolk, none was called Kindrick or Coney Garth.

The Phoney War and the Roosevelt Rules, the policy of shipping searches, leaflet raids and mine-laying are all fact; so are the Blitz and Bomber Command's long campaign against German targets. Where specific operations are concerned, I have recorded their success or failure as accurately as possible. For instance, it is true that, on 18 December, 1940, of twenty-two Wellingtons that entered the Wilhelmshaven area in daylight, twelve were shot down by Me 109 and Me 110 fighters and three made forced landings. The tit-for-tat raids on Scapa Flow (by the Luftwaffe) and on Hornum seaplane base (by the RAF) took place as described.

Descriptions of the Hampden and the Wellington are as accurate as I could make them. The same applies to their tactics.

In those days there was no such thing as a bomber stream. Each aircraft made its own, separate way to and from the target. Apart from the pilot, aircrew training was, by later standards, slapdash. In 1939-40, gunners and wireless operators were groundcrew doing an extra job. Some were AC1; a few were AC2 – the lowest rank in the Service. Navigating was done by an Observer, a title left over from the First World War. Often the task was given to the second pilot, who might have had a few weeks' instruction in navigation – during daylight. Before the war, flying by night was not seen to be the function of the RAF. In 1937, when Bomber Command attempted a rare night-time exercise, two-thirds of the force could not find

Birmingham, although the city was brightly lit. The RAF cannot escape all blame for this inadequacy, but by far the greater responsibility lay with successive governments which underfunded the Service. Flying training, especially by night, cost money, and the RAF never had enough. The wonder is that, when war broke out, Bomber Command aircraft found as many blacked-out German cities as they did. What is not surprising is that the RAF lost more bombers to accidents over Britain than to enemy action over Europe. Too many pilots flew into stuffed clouds.

To give an idea of the persistent difficulty of hitting a distant target in a totally blacked-out Europe, let me quote an experienced RAF night-fighter pilot, Air Commodore Roderick Chisholm, DSO, DFC. On 22/23 September, 1943, he was at sixteen thousand feet over Hanover, watching a raid by seven hundred and eleven bombers, nearly all four-engined. (Chisholm's job was to intercept German night fighters.) 'Here, so I thought as we circled high above, was a whole town on fire. The extent of the fires was scarcely credible ... I was to discover some months later ... that the city had hardly been hit in this raid and that most bombs had fallen in woods outside.' (*Cover of Darkness*, Chatto & Windus, 1953.) Sixteen bombers were lost that night.

The cause of the failure was familiar: the forecast winds were wrong. A week later (27/28 September) six hundred and seventy-eight aircraft went back to Hanover. Inaccurate forecast winds misled the Pathfinders. Again, most bombs fell in open country. Thirty-eight bombers were lost. Another week passed. On 8/9 October, five hundred and four aircraft attacked Hanover. Twenty-seven were lost – but this time Bomber Command got it right and much of Hanover was destroyed, with huge fires and heavy damage to war industries.

At first glance, a score of one out of three seems depressingly low. But in this same brief period, Bomber Command attacked *seven other* German cities in force. Five raids were successful, some highly so. This nightly pounding horrified Goebbels, Hitler's Minister of Propaganda. His forecast for the coming year was that 'the British, if they know their business, will be able to blast and burn a major part of the Reich.' The lessons learned by Bomber Command in 1939-41 eventually paid off.

Filling a thin-skinned aeroplane with fuel and explosives is hazardous. Accidents with bombs or mines were not frequent but they could be devastating. As McHarg revealed, some pre-war bombs had 'sweated' their contents and created a layer of explosive crystals on the outside. A Long Delay Pistol (installed in a delayed-action bomb) could develop a fault which set it working prematurely. If it detonated the bomb inside the aircraft, no evidence would remain. By 1942, some Armaments Officers were aware of these hazards; I took the liberty of bringing McHarg's knowledge forward a few months.

Langham's brush with 'stabilized yaw' is a reminder that even the Hampden (which most pilots found enjoyable to fly) could turn round and bite. The trouble was a combination of human error and a design fault in the tail unit. If a ham-fisted pilot made a clumsy turn, the wings and fuselage might block the airflow. The twin rudders and elevators would be useless and the yaw would get worse. At height, the pilot might recover control. At low level, the Hampden toppled sideways and simply fell out of the sky.

Damned Good Show includes some details of bomber operations that may seem strange, even bizarre. Did Hampdens really carry pigeons? They did. The radio might fail; if the crew had to ditch, the pigeons could take an SOS message back to base. Could a woman be smuggled onto a bomber, as Kate Kelly was? It happened. Usually she was a Waaf, and it was a training flight; but at least one Waaf flew on ops over Germany. Did bomber pilots really find their way home by using factory chimneys and railway signals as signposts? They did. Could Rollo Blazer have fallen to his death through a hole in the floor? The hole is not surprising: bombers landed with all sorts of flak damage; and I know of an instance where the rear gunner left his turret as soon as the aircraft touched down, walked forward and suffered the same fate as Rollo. Is it possible that the millions of leaflets dropped on Germany were classified secret in Britain? They were. When Bomber Harris became C-in-C in 1942, he derided 'all the complicated secret document procedure' which Air Ministry ordered for the handling of leaflets, but he could not change it.

I included an episode in which a retired brigadier complains that practice bombs have disturbed his breeding gulls. His attitude may seem absurd, given Britain's desperate situation, but there were instances of similar behaviour. On a night of foul weather in July 1941, an RAF bomber crashed on Northampton. The chief constable telephoned Bomber Command. 'I can't have this, you know!'

he complained. Clearly, many civilians had little idea of the harsh realities of the bombers' war.

The catalogue of catastrophe told to Rollo and Kate by aircrew was based on fact. In particular, the descriptions of Arctic conditions inside bombers were not exaggerated; quite the contrary. All too often the heating system failed and thick frost or ice formed both outside and inside the aeroplane. Air so cold it hurt, teeth-jarring vibration, endless din, electrical interference from St Elmo's Fire, the lethal ferocity of cumulo-nimbus clouds – all this, and more, formed the regular diet of bomber crews. In addition there was the sheer grind of repeatedly attacking German targets that were more and more heavily defended. The odds were against completing a tour of thirty ops. In these circumstances, RAF Intelligence Officers were understandably reluctant to interrogate crews too closely when they came back from a raid that had been long, demanding, probably frightening, usually exhausting.

Nearly everyone in *Damned Good Show* is a fictional character, including those at Crown Films and the Ministry of Information. (Anyone interested in Skull's posting to the Desert Air Force should read *A Good Clean Fight*, published by The Harvill Press in 1993 and now republished by Cassell.) Three individuals are real (although I had to imagine their conversations). Professor Lindemann was in fact Churchill's Scientific Adviser, and it was for Lindemann that David Bensusan-Butt produced the Butt Report, with the help of Constance Babington Smith's Photographic Reconnaissance Unit. (Others played major parts in setting up that Unit. For the sake of simplicity, I allowed her to represent them all.)

It took some time for the Butt Report to be accepted and acted upon, but its findings proved to be a watershed in the bombing campaign. Before Butt, Bomber Command had done negligible harm to Germany, at great cost in men and machines. After Butt, the need for much better methods of navigation and bomb-aiming was indisputable.

The cinema had a job to do in wartime. Rollo Blazer's efforts were all my invention, but in 1941 Crown Films did make a documentary about a Wellington crew's raid on Germany. *Target for Tonight* used the crew of F-Freddie, from 149 Squadron. There are two ironies. One is that *Target for Tonight* was enormously popular and boosted aircrew recruitment just at the time when Bomber Command was at its lowest ebb. After the Butt Report, influential voices were saying that Bomber Command was a waste of men, money and materials. Some wanted it abolished. What the film claimed to show was, in fact, what Bomber Command was *not* doing to Germany.

The second irony is that *Target for Tonight,* heavily praised for its honesty and realism, in fact gave a very cosmetic view of an operation. For all its documentary status, there was nothing spontaneous about it. All the dialogue was carefully scripted, and most of the supposed operation was shot in the studio. The raid was said to be at a low level against an important target, yet enemy defences were skimpy. F-Freddie scored a direct hit. The general impression was that a single Wellington could easily find and destroy any target deep inside Germany.

That, of course, was the message all Britain wanted to hear: something was going right at last. So *Target for Tonight* was completely justified. Morale is a weapon of war. And the hard fact was that, for all its failings, only Bomber Command was taking the war to the enemy homeland. Rafferty was right when he asked Skull to suggest an alternative. In 1941, there was none. The bombing campaign sent a signal to the British people: *Keep it up – Germany is suffering.* It sent a signal to America: *Britain isn't beaten.* It sent a signal to Russia: *Britain is fighting Hitler too.*

So the crews of Bomber Command had to carry on their nightly battle. It was not so much a battle to help win the war – that came later – as a much grimmer battle to avoid losing it. I hope *Damned Good Show* offers at least a hint of the extraordinary courage and endurance shown by the men who kept the battle going.

In preparing this story, I was very fortunate to have the technical help of a former RAF bomber pilot, Flight Lieutenant Frank Lowe, DFM. During 1941 he completed a tour of ops on Hampdens; then, on 28/29 July, 1942, in a raid on Hamburg, he was shot down (and made prisoner of war) when piloting a Wellington with a trainee crew. His advice has saved me from many slips and pitfalls. Any errors that appear are entirely my fault.